THE
ALCHEMIST CONSPIRACY

Also by Jay Lumbert

The Varicose Vigilantes
The Presidential Pretender
The Varicose Vigilantes II - Hedge Money
Working HR For Private Business
Retirement Planning Simplified By Jay
Retirement Plans Simplified By Jay

THE
ALCHEMIST CONSPIRACY

Jay Lumbert

Shaksper Books
USA

THE ALCHEMIST CONSPIRACY

Shaksper books may be ordered through booksellers everywhere, or by contacting:

Shaksper Books
Hingham, MA 02043
www.shaksperbooks.com   admin@shaksperbooks.com

ISBN -13:978-0-9800501-0-3   (pbk)

ISBN -13:978-0-9800501-1-0   (lg prt pbk)

ISBN -13:978-0-9800501-2-7   (ebk)

ISBN -10:0-9800501-0-3   (pbk)

ISBN -10:0-9800501-1-1   (lg prt pbk)

ISBN -10:0-9800501-2-X   (ebk)

Printed in the United States of America

For Deb.
Still more than what I ever dared to pray that I would find.

Acknowledgments

This book could not have been written without the help of many people. I thank you all from the deepest reaches of my heart.

I want to thank my family and friends for all the encouragement and support you have given me. Bringing a book from a simple idea to finished product requires sacrifice. Much of that sacrifice is made by the family who puts up with the challenging personality of someone who spends much of their time in a dream world. The suggestions, criticisms and patience are the nourishment that brings this kind of work to life.

I must thank my wife, Deb, for her many suggestions, and for the countless hours she spent entering my corrections on draft after draft of this book. Without her help and support, this book would never have been completed.

I thank my children, Christi, Sabrina, Allyssa, Billy and Katrina Lumbert. You are my greatest joy.

I must thank Anne Lumbert, Jan Pelzel, Bill Eaton, Marilyn Eaton, Hank and Mo Eaton. No one could ask for a finer family. Special thanks must go to Diane and Donna Eaton. You were like cheerleaders who never lost faith. Mike Ramah and Steve Wilson, you were my first readers. Your words of encouragement helped me believe this endeavor had promise.

I must give special thanks to the Breitfuss family in Austria. You helped me experience your extraordinary culture as few Americans will ever see.

Thanks to Jenni Wheeler for her work on this book's revised cover.

I must also thank a select few of my writing professors: Anne Greene, Judith Tarr, Charlotte Currier and Bill Bevis. I hope you all are well. You taught me much.

Finally, I thank all of the waiters, waitresses and cashiers at restaurants from Maine to California—you kept my coffee cups primed and the words flowing.

"Alchemy may be compared to the man who told his sons he had left the gold buried somewhere in his vineyard; where they by digging found no gold, but by turning up the mould, about the roots of their vines, procured a plentiful vintage. So the search and endeavors to make gold have brought many useful inventions and instructive experiments to light."

"It is true, that a little philosophy inclineth man's mind to atheism, but depth in philosophy bringeth men's minds about to religion; for while the mind of man looketh upon second causes scattered, it may sometimes rest in them, and go no further; but when it beholdeth the chain of them confederate, and linked together, it must needs fly to Providence and Deity."

Sir Francis Bacon

"You are an alchemist; make gold of that."

William Shakespeare

"Amid the vastness of the things among which we live, the existence of nothingness holds the first place; its function extends over all things that have no existence, and its essence, as regards time, lies precisely between the past and the future, and has nothing in the present. This nothingness has the part equal to the whole, and the whole to the part, the divisible to the indivisible; and the product of the sum is the same whether we divide or multiply, and in addition as in subtraction; as is proved by arithmeticians by their tenth figure which represents zero; and its power has not extension among the things of Nature."

Leonardo da Vinci

PROLOGUE

▼
———————

December, 1924

The train chugged eastward, rocking gently as it carved its way through endless rows of snow-capped mountain peaks. A thick plume of smoke snaked from its engines and clung to the valley floor like heavy fog. The first of a hundred railcars sliced through the smoke, all of them laden with chemicals, coal, oil, iron, and finished steel.

At the rear of the train rolled two private railcars. Inside the first, twenty men sat playing cards and smoking cigars. They wore identical uniforms of navy blue, each trimmed with delicate layers of spun gold thread. Their boots were black and expensive, all polished to a gleaming spit shine. A leather holster rested on each man's hip, its flap held shut by a golden eagle snap. Rifles hung along the walls in racks, forty of them, loaded and ready to fire.

The train's last car, coupled in the final moments before departure, was a custom Pullman. Like those used by Vanderbilt and Morgan, it was elegant beyond all reason and function. Inside the car, a man lay sprawled across a blue velour couch, snoring loudly as he slept for the first time in days. His belly full, his body warm, he was content.

The rails squealed as the train approached the outskirts of Salzburg, Austria. The car shuddered and the man awoke. He opened his eyes and blinked, until he remembered where he was and how he'd gotten there. His eyes narrowed and he shivered, as he remembered his years in prison, the empty echo of his stomach, the hollow meaning of the words he'd written in those tortured days. Now this.

The man stood and poked his nose through the red velour curtains that covered the broad side window. His eyes were stung by bright sunlight, and he pulled away. He walked across the cabin and stood before a metal-framed mirror. He ran his fingers across the smooth edges, then leaned forward and bit into the frame. The metal yielded to his teeth and he smiled. Gold. He tried to lift the mirror from its perch upon the wall, and found it too heavy to move.

He took three steps backward and tried to gauge the weight of the frame, but found himself looking at his image in the glass instead.

The man was short and sickly thin. His face looked like a rotting pear, abandoned in the hot summer sun, its juice sucked away to leave skin as patchy and frail as old parchment. Hollow gray circles surrounded his eyes, which sparked out like shiny black marbles. His eyes were embedded underneath a pair of bushy, overgrown brows. Below, his mustache was thick and trimmed tightly at the sides. Long black hair hung unevenly along his forehead. It was flattened and matted across the right side from sleep, and he scratched at it to bring it back to life. The man frowned, as he felt the dirty oil in his scalp. Once again, he vowed to escape his poverty.

The man adjusted his baggy, threadbare pants, and pulled down the sleeves of his faded shirt. He took another step, lifting his head high as he looked into the mirror.

"Someday they'll pay," he said defiantly in German. "Men will quake at the mere mention of my name."

The train jerked to a halt. Within moments, the private car was slowly moving again. Only this time, it traveled in the opposite direction, as it was removed from the train. The car finally stopped and the door swung open.

Outside, a tall man loomed on the platform. He wore a long crimson robe with a wide fur collar. His face was weathered, with a charcoal beard that reached down to the middle of his chest. In his hand he held a smooth black cane, with a thick gold knob nestled in thin, bony fingers.

"Hello, Adolph," he said quietly.

"Who are you?" said the man.

"I have been following you."

"Who are you?"

"I have read your writing."

"Who are you?"

"You are a man with great vision."

"Who are you?"

"I will publish your work."

Adolph looked upon this new, unexpected mentor with curiosity and innate hatred. "Who are you?" he said once more.

"I am known as von Hoffenburg. I am answering your prayers. I will make you great and you will call me father. Together, we shall rule the world."

Sunday, December 17, 1940

General Thaddeus Swanson stared grimly at the thick, well-worn manila folders that sat on his desk. He glanced at the charts and the figures circled in red grease stick pencil. He shook his head, gave a long sigh and said, "Major Miller, this may be the biggest load of cow pie I have ever seen."

"I'm sorry, sir. I know that you have important—"

"You bet your butt I've got important things to do. Hitler is blitzing his way across Europe and I'm sitting here getting hemorrhoids working on ways to get us into the war before the Limey's hand him London with morning tea. 'Good morning, Herr Chancellor...how do you like your new city? Isn't London beautiful this time of year?' I can hear the goddamn Limeys now." He drew a heavy breath and shook his head. "Gutless politicians—"

"If these reports are true, it could very well mean the difference between winning and losing the war."

"Major Miller, doesn't the British SIS have anything better to do than concoct stories about some German Prince—"

"Austrian Baron, sir," interrupted Miller. Swanson gave him a sharp look.

"Penwell *is* head of the British secret service, sir."

"But this project is not sanctioned by his government?"

"Correct."

"Let me get this straight. We are supposed to stop what we are doing, switch our focus, marshal our resources and risk our men for something the British government refuses to do?"

"Yes, sir."

Miller tapped his fingers on the general's desk in contemplation of his next words. After several moments he said, "Whether he has his government's support or not, what he says makes sense."

"That there is some Austrian Prince holed up in a castle sending gold to Hitler from his dungeons? C'mon, Major, give us a break here."

Thaddeus "Bulldog" Swanson, the Army Chief of Staff shoved a wide cigar into his mouth and jutted his chin toward the man he called Creampuff. Miller was one of FDR's Ivy League bureaucrats, chosen for his brain, not his brawn, the kind of man that made the general imagine himself a surgeon, doing facial reconstruction with his bare knuckles.

Michael Miller was tall and thin, and he wore a delicate pair of rounded tortoise shell glasses. He spoke with a clipped Boston accent and reeked of education, money and breeding—the very type of man the general despised. It was men like Miller that were born with names like Thaddeus, not Bulldog Swanson.

"Baron...Austrian Baron, sir." Miller sighed. Why did he have to deal with such Neanderthals? He would much rather be sailing or playing squash. He continued. "I have given the matter a great deal of consideration, General. Whatever you may feel, the British secret service is actually quite competent. They are not a group to raise whimsical notions without a well-researched premise supported by documented facts. I have taken the liberty of speaking with the other members of *The Room*, as well as a number of my contacts in the banks and on Wall Street. Although I, too, consider Penwell's theory to be no more than a jumble of unsubstantiated myth, folklore, and innuendo, there is little doubt that Hitler is being financed from Austria."

Miller paused to make sure that Swanson had heard him. He watched as the general shuffled through the folders in an exasperated manner. He waited until Swanson finally looked him in the eye. "The British and French did a marvelous job at ensuring German economic impotence at Versailles—sentencing them to an enduring financial purgatory, if you will. But in less than twenty years they rebuilt their army and their economy to the extent that they can now lay waste to the entire continent." He paused to make his point. "I expect they intend to do so, now. Who among us could have conceived that this was physically and financially possible? No one, General. I submit that the Germans could not have done it alone. It is my opinion, that when we finally do engage in war with the Germans, we will be fighting only half the enemy. If we don't address their financing soon, it could be the end of us all. Now, I have been conducting an in-depth study—"

"You are a pain in the butt. You know that, Miller?" Swanson spit a small piece of tobacco onto the floor.

"Yes, thank you, General. Now, may I continue?"

Swanson shrugged. "Suit yourself. You've got two more minutes before I throw you out on your tail."

The general looked at him vaguely, doing his best to feign interest. He watched as Miller reached into his attaché case and withdrew another sheath of papers.

"As I was saying, General...With a little help from my friends I have been able to trace the movement of money through Austria and Germany for the past several years."

Miller took several wide sheets of paper and placed them before Swanson. "Before determining the actual war reparations that Germany was to pay to the Allies, we made a detailed study of their economy. We made careful projections as to their industrial capacity and their ability to repay the debts of the nations that fought against them. This page shows you the estimated, and documented, output levels of various industries in Germany. Coal...steel...lumber...manufacturing...You can see here what the estimated production was to be, and the surplus that would remain to repay the Allies. The Allies wanted it all, as you can see."

Miller waited until Swanson nodded his head. "This page shows what the actual figures have been. Far different, wouldn't you say? Notice how the funds correspond to Hitler's rise to power? I have other documentation that shows how much of these funds have been funneled directly through Hitler's organization. This kind of money could buy a lot of guns and planes to use against you, couldn't it, General?"

Swanson sat forward. "Where the hell did all of that goddamn money come from, Major? And what's your source for this information?" The general's eyes were now alert. His breathing began to quicken. Instinctively, the general was preparing for battle.

"My sources are private, General. But I assure you that they are reliable."

Swanson glanced at Miller, and his eyes narrowed into malicious slits. *You pompous little shit,* he thought. But he shrugged his shoulders, deciding Miller had reason to protect his sources.

Miller removed another set of papers from his case and laid them before the general. Swanson's cheeks reddened and his eyes were suddenly clear. *He looks almost intelligent,* thought Miller, ruefully. *We should only be so lucky.*

"These are the estimated production figures for the entire nation of Austria...the Gross National Product...financial reserves. Bear in mind that until only recently the Austrians have ruled much of the world. They have had little need to develop basic industries, as their vassal states were providing much of what they needed—"

"I am well aware of the territories that the Austrians have controlled over the centuries. I am a soldier, Major, unlike you. Soldiers deal in power and control. The Habsburg's...Austria, once had extraordinary power and control. Nearly ruled the world..." The general pressed his thick, pudgy hands together and brought them against his lips. His mind wandered as Miller droned on, his eyes searching some deep corner of his memories.

"Ah...yes...General...now compare these figures to the amount of money that we think has been leaving the country."

Miller removed two documents and set them in front of Swanson. He had taken great care to present them in a way the general's mind could understand. *Even this financial baboon will be able to see that more money has been leaving the country each year than is conceivably possible,* he thought to himself.

"Very interesting, Miller." Bulldog ran his right hand over his balding head as he scowled at the papers.

He can't follow it, thought Miller. "I'll make it simple, General. Each year, more money has been leaving Austria, all of it bound for Germany, than the entire nation could have earned. Of course, these figures have been extrapolated from many pieces of data and are subject to error. But there is one painful fact, and it is quite clear."

"The Fifth Column?"

Miller gave a thin smile. "Someone or something in Austria is financing Hitler."

Realization seemed to sweep through the general. What began as an instinctual reaction made its way into his conscious thoughts. Miller saw the mounting intensity in the general's stare, and the unconscious movement of his ears. He understood now. He believed now. Soon he would begin to sweat.

Swanson began to slowly nod his head. "And do you also believe the British theory that this Ger...ah...Austrian Prince...er...Baron...has been trying to control the world for the past thousand years? What kind of bull hockey do you expect me to believe?"

"I believe that I can go so far as to state, categorically, that without this money, Hitler would not be where he is today. In fact, I don't think that we would even know his name. I'm not sure, yet, of the exact source of the money, or in what manner it has been made. I know nothing about this von Hoffenburg. But I do know one thing, General. If we don't get to the bottom of this, it may very well cost us the war, and our way of life."

Perhaps this guy isn't such a shit after all, thought the general. *This is crazy, but...*"Send in Penwell."

The president's man nodded and moved slowly toward the door. "Wise choice, sir." He pulled open the door.

"Wise choice," mimicked Swanson with a scowl.

Miller reentered the room two minutes later. A willowy man followed closely behind him. The man had a long, sloping forehead and a receding hairline, with silver hair combed straight back over his head. In his right hand he held a walking cane topped by a golden eagle holding the world in its talons. As he reached Swanson, he stooped to greet him. He reached out his left hand, palm down, as if waiting for Swanson to kiss his ring.

"General."

Bulldog Swanson felt an immediate hatred for this man. "Penwell."

"Thank you for seeing me."

"Get to the point."

Penwell tapped his left palm with the end of his cane. He pursed his lips, as if wondering just how to begin. "Are you are aware of the myths surrounding the study of Alchemy?"

"Turning lead into gold?"

"Ah...something like that. Men have been writing about the subject for thousands of years. Carl Jung, the famous psychologist, has spent years giving it study. Isaac Newton, Roger Bacon, Leonardo DaVinci. Hundreds have claimed that they perfected the process, writing their formulas in code so that no one could decipher their secrets. The Bible talks about men living hundreds of years in the days before Christ. Perhaps this, too, is a reference to Alchemy?

"The key in Alchemy is to isolate the *Philosophers Stone*, the *Elixir of Life*, which, theoretically, exists in nature as the purest of things. The Elixir is said to cure any disease, and if taken internally, it can bring about virtual immortality...."

The general began to pace the room. He walked with his right hand against his head, absentmindedly massaging his shiny scalp, his head slung forward, a *Thinker* in motion.

"The Fountain of Youth, General...Shangri-la in modern times," continued Penwell.

"You must have bad water over there, Penwell. You've got shit for brains."

"Has anyone ever told you that your language is rather vulgar?"

"Sit on it, Penwell."

"Right, sir." Penwell took a deep breath and continued. "As crazy as it seems, we think that someone may actually have perfected the alchemical process."

Swanson frowned.

"Turning base metals into gold," continued Penwell. "Is it that far fetched? I mean, it involves only a basic transformation of matter...we do it every day...synthetic diamonds...rubber...steel. There are many theories on how it can be done, theories proposed by learned men, General."

Swanson closed his eyes. He didn't need this.

Penwell continued. "Legend says that this happened more than a thousand years ago, somewhere near Salzburg. The story has been floating around for centuries..."

"Legend or rumor?" interrupted the general.

"Both, sir. Legend holds that sometime before the year 1000 an Austrian nobleman, perhaps even an early Habsburg, employed his own court alchemist, a Merlin, if you will, who perfected the alchemical process. He turned lead into gold, sir. Infinite wealth."

Penwell grew animated. "The alchemist kept the discovery from his lord, but was betrayed by his own daughter, who was being held as a concubine by the nobleman. Greed swept the lord. It is said that he forced the alchemist to translate his formula, tested it, and then brutally strangled the alchemist with his own bare hands.

"With the alchemist dead, the lord controlled the formula and was free to make gold at will. It has been with gold that he has been seeking to rule the world ever since. Given virtual eternal life by the Elixir, it was he that was behind the Habsburg dynasty from beginning to end...Maximillian I, the Holy Roman Emperor...He financed Genghis Khan and Napoleon. He even married Napoleon off to a Habsburg...And now he is behind Hitler."

"Right," said Swanson. *Something is really unbalanced about this man.*

Miller, standing slightly behind Penwell, began to shake his head.

"Legend says that the alchemist's daughter escaped with her own supply of Elixir, and that she has been waiting for the day when she can take her revenge."

Miller walked to a delicate table against the wall and poured a glass of water from a squat, crystal pitcher. He took a sip, and then rested the glass on the corner of Swanson's desk.

Penwell continued, "I received the same response from my superiors in England, General. That's why I came to you."

"You expect me to believe what you say?"

"No, sir."

"Then what do you want?"

"I know that you and your kind are itching to get into this war." He paused. "This would give you a way to begin fighting."

Bulldog Swanson sat back in his chair and began to rock back and forth. With a blank, inner-directed stare he placed the worn manila folders into a haphazard stack. "The whole damn thing is nuts...all this Elixir crap, eternal life. But this other stuff..." Swanson taped his finger on top of the pile of folders. "...all the money passing from Austria to Germany... No doubt in your mind?"

"No, sir."

"Balls! We are in deep shit." He exhaled forcefully. "It is bad enough that I have to deal with that waffler, Roosevelt. Now this." He looked at Penwell. "What the hell do you suggest?"

"I need you to infiltrate the Baron's castle."

"You want me to attack an Austrian baron on foreign soil?"

Penwell shook his head. "What we need is the book."

"What book?"

"The Baron keeps a notebook on him at all times. It's written in code."

"I'll need to run this by the president—"

Penwell shook his head. "No go, General. I already tried this one on that fool, and he won't touch it. Not a very popular political maneuver. You know how he is. Don't even think about it. There is no changing his mind. More influential men than you have tried."

"Roosevelt spends too much time pussyfooting with the isolationists. He knows what's right, but he wants to build a consensus. "I can't conduct this operation behind his back, can I? Why that's...that's—"

"Treason, General?" Miller spoke from behind Penwell, wearing a wan smile.

Swanson's reply came as a whisper. "Don't use that goddamn word around me, Miller. I'm protecting my president." Veins bulged along the side of the general's thick neck. A large, twisted purple line worked its way under the skin from the top of his head along his forehead to his left eye. He bit down upon his cigar, sending bitter raw juices into his throat. He swallowed hard as he pondered Miller's words. Treason? Could doing the best thing for your country be treason? He may be a little rough about the edges, maybe even a little trigger-happy. But treason? No man in America loved his nation more than Bulldog Swanson. He would die for it in a minute, nearly had, several times. Swanson rose from his chair, fingered the two purple hearts he kept in his pocket, and began to pace the room.

"They'd hang us if we got caught."

"I believe they would, sir," said Miller. "But FDR would always have plausible deniability."

"We've got to do it, though, don't we?" A good soldier learns to listen to his inner voice, his gut, and right now his insides left him no doubt. A thousand years in the pursuit of world domination? Lead into gold? Unbelievable. But the numbers...the money...the seemingly unstoppable rise of Hitler...Hitler had to be stopped. He'd have to fall on his sword.

"I am afraid so, sir."

Swanson nodded to Penwell and then looked at Miller. "Then get your ass on it. God help us."

There was a soft knock against the carved oak door that led ominously into the dimly lit office. It was barely a tap, made by a set of gentle knuckles against the thick hard wood. But it sounded like thunder to the six men huddled in the corner. They were talking in hushed tones, looking warily about the room—at the silent walls and the cold, highly polished floor, as if someone might suddenly appear out of nowhere and catch them at their great world game. Although their eyes and ears were alert for any sights or sounds that signaled an intrusion into their thoughts, nothing could have prepared them for the rush of fear and excitement caused by the knock against the door. It had begun.

The general looked at the men around him, one by one, staring contemplatively into their worried faces. He noticed the beads of sweat forming along their foreheads, every one of them afraid, but anxious to begin. He felt his own fingers tremble as he made his way toward the door. His hands were hot and slippery, like the rest of his body. His shirt made a soggy mold of his back.

"Anyone want out?" said Swanson, turning back from the door. Resolute stares were his answer. "All right, here we go." The general opened the door, smiled, and in a cheerful voice said, "Lieutenant Trance. So nice of you to drop by." He gave a short salute and held out his hand.

The younger man gripped Swanson's fingers and replied, "It is not often that someone gets a late-night call and is ordered to the office of the Army Chief of Staff, General." Trance noticed the sweat on the general's palm.

"Yes...well...I want you to know from the outset that what we are about to ask you to do is without the authorization of Congress and against direct orders of the president."

"I see. What happens if I agree with the president?"

"You won't leave this room alive."

"Ah." Trance paused. "Could I have some tea?" There was nervous laughter about the room. Trance continued, "Lao Tzu said that a sound leader's aim is to open people's hearts, and that good government comes of itself."

"And what the hell is that supposed to mean?"

"Perhaps you do what is right," said Trance quietly.

"Of course we are doing what is right!" shouted the general. Then, as if startled by his outburst, he quietly continued, "At least I hope it is."

Swanson's eyes wandered across Trance's face, and then down along his body to his toes. What was it that made this man so special? He had never heard of him before. But Penwell and Miller had insisted there was no other man as qualified to do the job. Trance wasn't tall, perhaps five foot nine. He wasn't big, although Swanson could see that the man was muscular. Yet, when they shook hands, Swanson had felt that Trance could have crushed his fingers with the slightest squeeze. It was like he was shaking hands with the head of a sledgehammer, the hand so hard and cool. But there was a kindness to his eyes, and something else—they were ever-so-slightly Oriental. When he moved he was unassuming, and mildly deferential in his manner. He showed respect, not just to his superiors but to everyone.

"The truth is that some creatures go before and others follow behind," Trance continued.

Swanson began thumbing through Trance's file, which was stacked inside another manila folder. He ignored Trance's comment and said, "It says that you are the army's best in hand-to-hand combat. Is that so?"

"I do not know, General."

"They said you were strange. Your file says that you knocked out the army boxing champion in twelve seconds. Is that true?"

"I did not hurt him, sir. I only wanted to keep him from hitting me. They made us fight. It is not my nature to fight."

"You were born in America, but your mother is Japanese?"

"My father was a chemical engineer, working overseas."

"You spent much of your childhood in Japan?"

"Yes. My mother was an only child. It was necessary that I learn the ways to carry on the heritage of my family."

"Then you later lived in Germany?"

"My father had business there."

"You speak German?"

"Yes, sir."

*Yet you have no accents...not even an Oriental one. You look far more Caucasian than Oriental. I may not have even suspected that you weren't entirely white, unless I knew...I can see it now. It's in the eyes...subtle...*He continued speaking. "You studied religion at Boston University, then engineering at MIT." The general read on, occasionally raising his eyebrows. He continued. "It also says that you were trained in secret Oriental ways of fighting. What the hell is that?" Swanson looked over at Miller, who shrugged his shoulders. He continued, "It says that you come from a family of mountain climbers?"

Trance answered quietly. "I was taught many things. I was schooled in the *I CHING*. I studied Zen and the art of mountain climbing." Swanson waited for him to continue. "I studied Bujutsu, and methods of self defense and mind control that are little known, even in Japan. Buddhist monks developed many of these ways, as protection during their travels. Others come from the darker sides—"

"You were trained to kill."

"I was trained to protect. In Japan we are people of tradition and honor. My mother's village is in Japan's Iga province. For centuries my family has had the honor of serving our lords in a special way. That tradition continues."

"You are assassins. Mercenaries."

"Not my family, General. It is true that others from our village might be what you call assassins. But you cannot understand our culture, General. In my family we follow the divine way of the Spirit. We practice the art of harmonizing with the Universal Force. We are the bearers of the Universal Light in a world that can often grow dim."

"But you were trained as a ninja, and the primary purpose of a ninja is being a spy? Trained to be invisible? Trained in the use of weapons?"

"And where did you learn of ninja, General?" Trance smiled in his gentle manner. "Yes, I have learned the ninja ways, but I am not ninja. Ninja come from the lower classes of Japanese society. I am Samurai. We are those of the highest class. There is a world of difference between the two. We follow a code of Bushido, a chivalry that the ninja do not follow. It was the Samurai who brought the ninja to prominence during feudal times. They hired them to do the deeds that their own honor forbade them to do. Please do not insult me, General. What I have learned is more art and honor. Just as you serve your president and your people—so too, have the people of my village. But I am a scientist. I—"

"You are now a spy."

"But America has no spies. We—" Trance tried to protest. But the general cut him off.

"We do now. Do you recognize any of the men in this room?" Trance looked slowly from man to man, and then shook his head.

"America has no official secret service, but with the war going on it won't be long. You are our first recruit. Sorry, you have no choice, son. This man here is Bill Donovan, a lawyer on Wall Street. To his right is Artemus Penwell."

The general pointed at two stern-faced men by his side. "Penwell is the head of the British secret service, the SIS. With any luck, these men will be able to convince FDR to join the war." The general walked to a wooden cabinet against the wall and removed a fresh bottle of brandy. "Anyone for a drink?" Five men murmured, all of them shaking and bobbing their heads in various directions.

Trance looked perplexed. "I was hoping for some tea?" he said quietly.

The general ignored his plea. He poured seven glasses of brandy, handed one to each of the men, and said, "To the war effort," raising his glass into the air. There was a quiet moment, as six men let the hot liquid melt the icy fear. Trance stared off into space.

The general swept his arms toward the remaining men and said, "These four are from a group called the *Room*. The Room was founded in 1917 by men such as Astor, Roosevelt, Doubleday and Aldrich, all men with a passion for the safety of America. They have been our unofficial intelligence service for over twenty years now. They meet every month at 34 East 62nd Street, in New York City."

"Excuse me, General. But I don't see what any of this has to do with me?"

"Ah...yes...well...er..." The general felt bile force its way into his throat. He was about to countermand the president, and commit what could be deemed an act of treason, even an act of war. The U.S. was loath to enter another war. But there was something else, some other feeling he could not yet quite understand. He continued nervously. "The Room is tied into the international banking system." The general angled his eyes toward one of the men, and continued. "Jacob, here, is a director of Western Union and has been intercepting cables in the U.S. and abroad. We have found some very disturbing patterns. As you know, Hitler is pounding the shit out of Europe with his Blitzkriegs. Penwell and Donovan are convinced that there is a hidden Fifth Column of spies, financed to the tune of hundreds of millions, maybe billions per year and run by elements of the Gestapo. Hitler will attempt to control the world, of that we are sure. But what about this other force? Penwell thinks that if Hitler wins the world, he will only lose his throne to another dictator, someone more ruthless and powerful than that madman."

Trance remained expressionless. He looked serene, relaxed, as the general paced about the room. Trance had surrendered himself to the Cosmic Will.

What an interesting twist of fate, he thought. *I must consult the Sage to see what it is I must do.*

"We are sending you to Europe, Trance."

"I see."

"You will be leaving in three days."

"And what will I be doing, sir?"

"Hitler is being financed out of Austria. Someone has been sending him huge sums of money, funneled through a labyrinth of international financial networks. We believe that we have been able to pinpoint the source to a certain Baron von Hoffenburg. He lives somewhere near Salzburg. We want you to infiltrate his castle. We need evidence that the man is involved with the Nazis. He keeps a book on him at all times. It is written in code. We want the book, along with any other financial proof you can muster."

The details of Trance's mission were outlined carefully in those final hours before dawn. By four thirty in the morning Trance was fully briefed, and an initial timetable constructed for the mission was in place.

The general rose from his seat, motioned to Trance, and said, "That will be all for this evening, Lieutenant. I will see you again at O Nine Hundred."

"I'm sorry, General, but I am not sure whether or not I am to accept this mission."

Swanson looked puzzled. "What?" He paused. "I told you that if you don't accept this mission we would kill you on the spot." The general stared incredulously at the young soldier before him.

"You did, sir."

"Well?"

"I do not know yet what I am supposed to do."

"And how the hell do you intend to make that decision in the next few minutes?" Swanson brought a set of angry eyes to within inches of Trance's face. "I give the orders and you say, 'Yes, sir!'"

"Oh, I can't make that decision, General."

"What?" Bulldog Swanson was at a loss for words. He paced back and forth in front of Trance, his arms held out from his side in exasperation. He bit halfway through his cigar and spit a large wad of tobacco into a dented, brass spittoon on the floor.

"This is a decision that must be made by the Sage," said Trance. There was no challenge in his eyes.

"The Sage?" *This guy has screws loose*, thought Swanson. *If he wasn't so goddamn qualified for this job, I think I just might boot his ass out of the army.* He reached his arms toward the ceiling in a cry for divine help.

A thin smile crossed Trance's lips. "Yes. The Sage. May I have a few minutes alone?"

"Alone? I thought that you had to meet with some Sage?" *This guy is Section Eight.*

"As I said before, General. There is no way that you could learn to understand my culture, the culture of my family. We think differently than you. In my family we do not make important decisions. They are made for us, as they have been for over five thousand years. I must consult the Sage of the *I Ching*. The *I* came to Japan from China. It is the basis of the Chinese culture. Some of us in Japan have learned to use its wisdom. It will allow me to consult with the Sage. Then I will know what I must do."

"And how-the-hell-long do you expect this to take?" *Should I shoot him now?*

"I do not know," said Trance.

"Well, could you possibly guess?" said Swanson. *What the hell am I doing?*

"Perhaps ten minutes, General."

"And where in the goddamn hell do we find this Sage of yours?"

"He is here with us now, General."

"Oh, shit." Swanson looked toward the other men in the room. No man could speak. "This is a life and death matter, Trance. I want you to cut with this crap."

"I'm sorry, General. But I will need a few minutes alone. This decision is too great for me to make."

Swanson stared at the soldier before him. He tried to read the expression in his eyes. He searched for guile or guilt, some kind of clue as to what was going on in Trance's mind. But he could see nothing. The eyes had no expression; they said nothing. *Who the hell is this man?*

"All right," he said. He walked to the edge of his office. "This door leads to a small room that I use for sleeping when I work through the night. In it you'll find a bed and a desk. There are no windows and no other doors. I don't know what the hell you are up to, but in fifteen minutes I am going to open this door with a gun in my hand. You are going to agree to this mission or I am going to blow your goddamn brains out. Have you got that?"

"Yes. Thank you, General." Trance gave a small bow and began to walk through the door.

"Wait," said the general. "I'll bite. Tell me about this Sage."

Trance turned and bowed deferentially toward Swanson. "As a boy, part of my life training was to memorize the *I Ching*, the Book of Changes. My mother was a direct descendent of Confucius. You see, twenty-five hundred years ago Confucius edited and annotated the *I*, which is also known as the *easy* the *changing* and the *constant*. Through the *I* one can touch the fundamental forces of the Yin and the Yang. It provides the gateway to understanding the highest of truths, and gives perspective to the meaning of life. In much of China, and parts of Japan, no major decision is made without it."

"Sorry I asked."

"It is difficult for Americans to understand."

Trance smiled and left the room. He removed a penny from his pocket and began to flip the coin. He thought of how Americans use a coin toss to decide the most trivial of matters, like who kicks off in a football game. His own family used it only for the most important of choices. He always used a penny—the underlying common denominator of all numbers and values, the primal one. He recorded each flip until he had formed the six lines of one of the sixty-four Hexagrams. The Hexagram he formed was called Splitting Apart— with the first, fifth, and sixth lines as changing lines. He let out a long sigh when he saw that the reversal of his changing lines formed the Hexagram *Deliverance*. The first line described the doubt in his mind. The fourth line told of the splitting apart caused by the doubt that had already reached its peak. The top line told him that the splitting apart had reached its end, and that the seeds of goodness were waiting to grow anew.

"Your time is up, Trance." The door eased open and Swanson ambled through. "What'll it be?" he continued, pointing a gun at Trance.

"The Sage has instructed that it is in the highest good that I accept this mission," came the soft-spoken reply.

"Figured you would come to your senses, Lieutenant."

"Of course, General." There was no use in trying to make the general understand.

Swanson patted Trance on the back. "That's it for tonight, Lieutenant. Now get the hell out of here and get some sleep. You're going to need it."

After Trance left the room the general sank into a worn leather chair behind his desk. Desperately seeking to rid the tension from his body, he gave a long sigh, closed his eyes and tried to imagine himself sitting on a warm sunny beach—Miami—with a girl on each arm...But this wasn't Miami, this was Washington and there was snow on the ground. The air wasn't warm and the sun wasn't shining. It was dark and the air outside was cold. Inside, the air felt stifling and it took painful effort for the general to breathe, let alone relax. As he swallowed, he could feel his spit waging war against the lump in his throat.

The room was silent. All the men stood with their eyes focused on the general. This was his show now; it would have to be done his way. They had placed their lives, perhaps the future of the nation, in his hands.

Finally Swanson spoke. "Well, boys, it's done. God knows how you got my butt into this sling, but there is no backing out now." He grew animated, like a weight had been lifted from his mind. "Miller, I want you to work out the final details with Donovan and Penwell. This is strictly a non-military operation. Everything is to be run on a need-to-know basis. Trance may already know too much, and I am not going to bother his mind with any of this mythical hocus pocus about gold and eternal life. All he need ever know is that he is to steal financial records for his country, and that's it."

Swanson was exhausted from the day's events and it was beginning to show in subtle ways. It was in the way that he carried himself. He had begun to stoop. There was a faint slur to his words. He was pushing sixty now, and although his mind had him convinced that he could still handle the long, tedious hours of preparation, his body was giving him a good argument. He gave a long sigh and continued, "Penwell, this was your idea. Do I have your assurance that the SIS is committed to its success?"

"I am the SIS, General." *And even if I were including them in this matter, they would support me,* he thought. *But this is far too important to involve those worthless idiots. I wouldn't be using you, you crude, effete dinosaur if I didn't have to.*

The general regarded Penwell with a wary stare. "Tell me something. Why the hell did you come to me? Except for Trance, this is really your show."

"Perhaps, General. But now you are in." *And I can blame you if we fail.*

"And what is that supposed to mean?"

"It means that, while on the outside, we British are keeping a stiff upper lip, on the inside we are shaking in our boots. Did you know that we have transferred all of our gold to Canada?"

"But Churchill says—"

"A facade, General. Without America in the war, Europe is…how would you say it…going down for the count. You know that I have been meeting with FDR. God knows I've tried to convince him of the sheer folly of your neutrality. I've given him the same information, but he's got his bloody head stuck in the sand. Our only chance was to get you involved, only then will any *proof* have meaning. You wouldn't fabricate it. Your president doesn't believe what we are saying. But he trusts you, General. You can convince him of the strength of our enemy. You can get him into the war."

"You are risking my life," said Swanson. He spread his arm around the room. "Mine and those of all these other patriotic Americans."

"You are a soldier, General. You are an ally. I knew you would understand."

"The hell I understand," said Swanson. "All I know is that you come to me with some trumped up story about some secret Fifth Column of spies, and money, and gold, and some German Prince financing Hitler—"

"Austrian Baron," interrupted Penwell.

"All I know..." Swanson felt his blood pressure rising fast. His face grew crimson, the muscles twitching around his eyes "...is that I do have the sense to realize that if there is any truth to what you say we could all be in deep shit. I can't ignore that."

Swanson shrugged his tired shoulders and slumped into his chair. After a long moment he continued softly. "So I put my whole career, my life on the line. I put one of our best in harm's way."

"You did the right thing, General."

"And Trance?" His voice was little more like a croak. "What becomes of him?"

"We searched your files for months, General, long before we contacted you. Trance is the one we need. There is no one else like him. No one else could get those records. It's almost too bad that he will have to die."

Swanson stared at Penwell in silence. He felt his stomach tighten, twisting against all sense of honor. There was something vulgar about spying. They called it the world's second oldest profession. Sometimes he wondered if the second and the first weren't one in the same. Finally he said, "No loose ends, Penwell?"

"No loose ends, General."

"May God help us all."

The wind blasted through the airplane door as it flew open. Icy shards of frozen needles whipped against the faces of the men inside. Down below, the snow-capped peaks of the Austrian Alps glowed in the moonlight. The jagged shafts of stone were smothered with pillow-soft mounds of snow, dripping along their sides like smooth vanilla ice cream.

Trance stared out into the void, letting his eyes and mind wander through the darkness. He thought of himself sitting in sunlight, warmed by summer breezes, and he felt relaxed. His breathing came in a slow rhythm, his pulse calm and regular, his hands warm and dry.

Trance looked down the dark tube of the plane. It was bare, except for a long strip of rope webbing hanging from the sides. He made one last slow and deliberate check of his pack, his climbing gear and his weapons. He looked across the narrow chamber to the man chosen to support him in the mission. They had met for the first time that morning. He knew little about the man. He had simply been introduced as Netherby, a British officer, a communications and alpine specialist. That was all he needed to know, all he wanted to know.

William Netherby was half a head taller than Trance, but he was thinner. His face was gaunt and tinged the color of aging newsprint. A sickly child, his life had been one unending attempt to prove himself. He had played rugby. He was a boxer. He was a member of the British biathlon team, where he starred in this demanding combination of cross-country skiing and shooting. Few sports required this unique blend of endurance, patience and skill. Netherby had taken a gold medal in the 1936 Olympics demonstration of the sport.

Netherby had drawn the interest of the British Secret Service, and for ten years he'd accepted every assignment willingly, until now. This one had been hell to accept; it seemed so senseless.

William did his best to appear calm as he thought through the plan one last time. His job was really quite simple—a nighttime jump into the Austrian wilderness and a long march through deep snow to the mountain peak that bore the Baron's castle. They would climb with skis and snowshoes until the snows yielded to rock and ice. At eight thousand feet they would switch to picks, spikes and ropes until they reached the base of the massive natural wall—the wall that had shielded the castle from outside intruders for centuries. It seemed easy enough for a man with his skills. Unfortunately, this may not be his ultimate mission. He might have to kill Trance.

Trance was to scale the final two thousand feet alone. In its easy stretches the wall was vertical. Close to the top, it pitched outwards at an angle exceeding fifteen degrees. For his final five hundred feet of climb, Trance would dangle with nothing below him but air, and a long fall to death. But he may never get that far…

One other man sat in the rear cabin of the plane. He was thick and broad in the shoulders. His features were dark—black hair, brown skin, and a three-day stubble of angry whiskers that obscured the contours of his weathered face. He seemed like a grizzled sailor. The plane was his ship and he rocked easily in the wind. He stood in the doorway peering out at the mountains below, listening intently to the set of earphones strapped against his head. Any moment now he would motion the soldiers forward, and then shove the men and their gear into the empty space. Any moment now…

Trance watched him through hooded lids, as he sat quietly in his inner sunshine. The bone-chilling air whipped around him, but he felt warm, balanced comfortably by meditation.

"Thirty seconds!" shouted the man. The time had come.

Both men rose slowly, William with trepidation, Trance with great calm. The air sailor pulled at their gear, making sure the lines were secure and their packs were fastened tightly. He began counting backwards from ten...nine...eight...

They jumped, and fell into the arctic blast of high altitude flight. The noise was deafening as they left the plane. The air spill tore at their white-masked faces. Then, as quickly as it began, everything seemed calm...quiet...as they drifted, tightly bundled toward the ground.

William giggled as his fear melted into the darkness. He could just make out Trance smiling serenely, and felt a sudden rush of emotion toward his partner, although he couldn't name what emotion it was. Was it comfort, companionship, maybe trust? There was something about Trance that made William feel safe.

"You poor bastard," he muttered beneath his smile.

The calmness ended when the ground rushed toward them. The men angled their parachutes toward a large patch of white, an open meadow surrounded on all sides by towering mountain peaks.

"That's the spot," said William to himself, remembering the films he had been shown by Penwell at the SIS. *Perfect.*

The men fell with a quiet whoosh into ten feet of freshly fallen powder. When William's feet hit the snow he gave a thankful sigh and started to relax his knees and roll to one side. His comfort was shattered as he plunged deep into the snow. William gasped for breath and began to blindly claw at the dark, amorphous prison growing around him. His breath came in choking gasps as he struggled to lift his head toward the winter sky. Snow was everywhere. It filled his eyes and mouth with its cold wetness, and it sucked the oxygen from his lungs, until there was nothing left. William waved his arms wildly and twisted himself, slowly wrapping into his parachute cord. The more he struggled, the deeper he sank into the snow. He tried to yell, but it came out as a whimper. His strength gave way. He was dying. They had barely started and he was about to die. He began to let himself drift. "I failed," he mouthed silently.

William felt a sudden shudder as a strong hand gripped his shoulder and pulled his head into the cool night air.

"Are you all right?" asked Trance.

William's face emerged into the moonlight, his mouth wide as it sucked air back into his lungs. "Yeah...yeah...thanks..."

"Sorry I didn't find you sooner," said Trance. "I should have looked for you, but I was putting these on." Trance looked down to his snowshoes. "You've never been in this kind of snow before, have you?"

"This isn't snow, Trance. This is…this—"

The two men laughed.

"I've spent a few winters skiing this stuff. The Austrians call it *tief schnee,* deep snow," said Trance.

"You bet your bloody bum it's deep. It's like quicksand. I've seen plenty of deep snow, but not like this, and only with my skis on. I've never been buried, with no ground to touch or purchase for my feet…. I nearly drowned."

"It is like many things in life, William. You can't fight it. The harder you struggle, the more difficult it becomes. The best way to deal with this snow is to relax. Allow yourself to emerge from it, become one with it."

"I'd like to become one with a bottle of scotch right about now," said William. "By the way, call me Bill."

"And you should call me John. Now sink back into the snow, Bill."

"Are you daft?"

"Do it, then allow yourself to *emerge* from it…be in harmony with the snow."

"No thanks, John. I'll just harmonize with those snowshoes."

Bill reached for the snowshoes in Trance's hand. But as Bill stretched his arm forward, Trance kept them just out of his reach.

"This is what my master would have done, Bill. You have an unusual opportunity to learn, and we cannot let it pass." Trance's eyes willed Bill back into the snow. His voice was calm, almost hypnotic.

"Pass? A learning opportunity? They warned me that you were a strange duck. Now give me those bloody shoes."

"Relax, Bill. Allow yourself to be in harmony with your surroundings. Relax."

Bill found himself drifting back into the snow. He began to panic, but in the background he could hear Trance murmuring, "Relax, Bill. Relax."

Bill realized he was safe. He let his body melt into the snow and felt the softness. He heard Trance repeat the melodic words, *relax,* and he stopped struggling against the world. He felt almost giddy when he realized that he could emerge from the snow with just a little movement, a little support from surrounding objects, a little leverage. It was all so simple.

"Hey, you were right. A piece of cake. Well, what d'ya know."

"We cannot struggle against the limitless and the unknown. We must become one with ourselves and with nature."

"Yeah, right. While you're being one with nature, I'm going to get these snowshoes on and then get our gear. We've got less than eight hours of darkness left and over fifty kilometers to cover before sunrise. Think you can handle it?"

Trance stood silently, then said, "We shall see." Trance took his bearings and continued, "At two hundred miles per hour our plane was traveling close to three hundred feet per second. I estimate fifteen seconds for our crewman to maneuver the supply crate to the doorway and drop it safely. That's nearly a mile." Trance sniffed the air. "These mountain winds are tricky and unpredictable when they snake through the peaks."

Trance pointed toward the far end of the valley. "The wind is funneling this way. I'm guessing our gear was blown a mile or two in this direction."

"Oh, bloody hell," said Bill. "That means we've got to walk through this shit in snowshoes?"

Trance nodded, turned and began moving again.

The powder was deep, but light. Walking was more awkward than difficult, but the lifting and thrusting motion needed for snowshoes used muscles Bill didn't know he had. In a few short minutes he was dripping sweat in the cold mountain air. Steam wafted from his body, like mist from a heated pool in a Minnesota winter. Trance hardly breathed.

Bill stopped to shed his facemask. "Hey, stop for a moment, will you?" He stripped down to his white Icelandic sweater. Trance did the same.

"Can you believe that people do this for sport?" asked Bill, still struggling for breath.

"Actually, I rather enjoy this," replied Trance. "It's not often these days that I get the chance to be in the mountains. The air is so clean and refreshing. The purity of nature is unspoiled by the intrusion of man. I remember when I was a boy—"

"I didn't ask for a speech, Trance." Bill paused. "Hey, how come you're not tired?"

"Why should I be tired, Bill?"

"You're carrying ten kilos of gear on your back and breaking tracks through the snow. That's why."

I'm carrying a lot more than that. Trance thought about the special items he had added, some of them handed down in his family for dozens of generations…shuriken throwing blades, a hanbo cane and a Samurai short-sword that had been in his family for nearly 500 years. He also carried a 32-caliber Colt Automatic pistol. He hoped that he wouldn't have to use any weapons at all.

"Tiredness is more of a state of mind, Bill. Accept what you are doing. Don't fight it, and it will be easier for you. Just like getting out of the snow. Besides, we will be carrying far more weight shortly." Trance moved on at a heavy pace.

It took half an hour for the men to reach the white wooden crate holding their supplies. Trance pried open the box and laid out their packs, cross-country skis, ropes, boots for climbing, pick axes, spikes, crampons, and ice pitons. He checked the radio, and secured their dried food.

Satisfied, he began to fill his pack. "I was told that you climbed the north wall of the Eiger," he said. "Quite a climb, isn't it?"

"North wall, hell," said Bill. "Only fools attempt the north wall, Trance. I did scale the east flank with Hans Lauper." *Of course, we paid him well. He carried the gear...and did the real work.*

"That, too, is a difficult climb. Well done."

"Thanks. Why do you ask?"

"No reason." Trance had hoped that they would have something in common. He was one of the few who *had* climbed the Eiger's north wall, and also the north face of the Matterhorn in that same busy year.

"You must have had a bloody reason."

"We'll be climbing together. I'm glad that you have the experience we will need. This looks like a difficult climb."

"They said you're a climber, too. Any majors?"

"Nothing to talk about. But I do know my way around a mountain."

"If you need any advice, don't be afraid to ask."

"Thank you, Bill. I'll remember that."

Trance consulted his compass, lowered his head and began to ski. Because of the deep snow his legs had to work hard to break their trail. He charged forward, with his ski tips raised high to break and push down the snow. Bill struggled to follow, despite skiing a far smoother trail. Trance pushed on, half madman, half packhorse, rarely taking a break. He felt a bone-tired weariness dragging each step as he fought against the snow, and the sixty pounds on his back. But he wrapped the pain in a soft blanket and put it in a closet. Out of sight, out of mind.

Bill labored behind Trance, watching for some sign of fatigue or weakness. His lungs were on fire. His legs grew so heavy he was sure that each step would be his last. He knew what effort it took him to heft the weight and keep up the pace. But he was a top Olympic-class competitor and he weighed twenty kilos more than Trance. He was following behind, a far less demanding task than breaking the trail. He could only watch Trance in wonder, as his own time passed in agony.

They were getting close. Just two more ravines to traverse before they could put up for rest. Trance began to attack the snow with what seemed like joy. He pounded forward leaving behind an easier trail for his companion to follow. Even so, Bill began to fall back. He could not maintain Trance's manic pace.

"Stop!" yelled Bill. He doubled over and gasped for breath. "Don't you get tired, Trance? I'm a member of the goddamn bloody British National Biathlon Team, and I've never seen anyone ski like you. You're a bloody animal. Almost inhuman, I'd say."

Trance stopped at once. He turned around and smiled. "Of course I'm tired, Bill." His breath was already returning to normal. "But if we move slowly, we must suffer for that much longer. I don't care to suffer, so I get it over quickly."

"Well, slow down."

"So sorry, Bill. I will be more considerate."

It was nearly dawn when the outlines of Baron von Hoffenburg's immense fortress emerged against the opaque sky. Swirling clouds smothered the castle. They seemed to form out of nowhere, and dodged in and about the cold-gray stone turrets with an angry fury. Even from a distance the castle called out a warning to the curious, and issued unveiled threats to those who might wish to venture forward.

Trance pushed the final feet to a mountain crest and stopped. Suddenly it was there. Trance felt a rush through his body as his eyes fell upon the weathered stone. Bill gasped and stood motionless, as if under the influence of a witch's hypnotic stare, slowly swaying from side to side in the wind. There was an ineffable energy, a surrealistic evil force that seemed to take hold of their thoughts. Their eyes were drawn upward, higher and higher, to the massive walls of ice that Trance must climb, and then to the sheer stone face that guarded the castle walls. This was a vicious mountain, and it bid them fair warning. The two men stood silently, feeling the power before them, neither of them wishing to acknowledge its presence.

"We can't climb that," mumbled Bill. He raised his voice, "not without more preparation, John, maybe not even then. If you've never made a major climb, you don't know what you are up against." He wiped his lips with his glove and continued, "That face makes the Eiger look like a picnic. You can't climb it. Not in one night. Not alone. Not in the dead of winter...not without preparations...not without...maybe not ever. I'm sorry, but there's got to be some other way..." *Maybe if we turn back now we both can live.*

"It does look like a bit of a challenge, doesn't it, Bill?" replied Trance. He smiled. "If there was another way, don't you think they would have tried it? There is more going on than they are telling us...I *feel* it. Besides, I'm afraid that we have no choice but to try, Bill. What good is failing without trying?"

"But this is suicide." *Doesn't he know?*

"Is it? We will both die sometime, Bill. I expect death will come at a time we wouldn't choose." Trance reached into his pocket and fingered his penny. "We are part of a large Cosmic Order, something we cannot change or fight, at least for long. All I know is that we are here, Bill, and we have a job to do. So I suggest that we go do it."

The men found a shelter among the rocks, near the base of the mountain. It was a hollow, glacial carving that dug far into the stone, not quite a cave, but calmly protected from the wind and the biting cold. They set up a makeshift camp and ate from food tins that they kept close to their bodies so they wouldn't freeze. They camouflaged themselves with white and prepared to sleep through the daylight hours. As the sun began to peek over the mountains, the two men dug themselves into the snow. Trance fell into an easy sleep, somewhere along a warm beach in his mind, while Bill struggled against his clothing and the wetness in his face.

After struggling for hours, Bill drifted into a fitful, tossing sleep. Throughout the day he dreamt of falling into an abyss, clutching vainly for a rope that remained only inches outside of his grasp. He was falling when the gentle shaking of Trance awakened him. It took him a moment to remember where he was. When he finally did, he had the urge to return to the comparative pleasantness of his dream.

"Time to go," said Trance. "I've got us packed."

"Bloody hell. What time is it?"

"Just after four. We've got to move quickly. Here's your lunch." Trance handed him a piece of jellied bread.

Trance fingered the animal skins he had put on their skis for the upward trek. The animal fur let the skis slide easily forward, but provided solid resistance when pushing against the grain.

"You brought skins," said Bill. "How did you know to bring those along?"

"A good climber never travels without skins. Let's go. I'll lead."

"But I'm supposed to lead..." Bill began to protest. He was the one with all the climbing experience. Then he remembered the previous day and he knew it was Trance that should lead them up the mountain. They stored much of their gear in their small canvas tent, choosing to carry only the bare essentials— ropes, crampons, picks and pitons. Bill took the radio. There was one extra bag that Trance placed carefully, almost religiously into his pack. These were the tools he hoped he wouldn't need.

"Why are you bringing the radio?" asked Trance. "Wouldn't it be better off at the base?" He waited, but Bill stayed silent. "I see no sense in carrying it all that way, unless it's for safety. But they'd never come in to pick us off the mountain."

"They didn't tell you?" said Bill.

"Tell me what?" asked Trance.

"Before you go in, you are to survey the entire grounds and describe what you see. You are to relay your message with this." Bill produced a smaller radio from his bag.

"But they might hear us, Bill," said Trance quietly.

"Yes, I know. But those are the orders, Trance. You know that I am in charge—"

"But the risks of being caught—"

"Don't complain to me about the risks, Trance. You know there isn't a snow-ball's chance in hell you'll come out of this alive. They say this place is overrun with soldiers, Gestapo. If that is true, we need to know. Your first priority is to find proof that the Baron is tied to Hitler. We also need his book, the one he carries at all times."

Bill's eyes held a look of compassion. Trance stood silently, so he spoke on.

"Once I have a rough body count of the castle grounds, you're to find the Baron, secure some documents and get the book." Trance nodded and Bill continued. "By the way, how will you do it?" He looked up. "How will you climb that thing?"

"Haven't been told, yet," replied Trance.

Bill noticed a strange look upon Trance's face...pain...confusion.

"They don't expect us to survive, do they?" said Trance.

"Of course not, John. Didn't you know?"

"Never thought about it."

Bill searched his soul for compassion, but it fought against his sense of duty and honor toward his country. He, and he alone, was to return with the book. Then he was to be killed. He sighed and said, "I've made arrangements with the authorities to look after my family. They'll be well taken care of."

"I see," said Trance softly. "You are afraid of death, aren't you, Bill?"

"Of course I am." There was a look of puzzlement on Bill's face. "Aren't you?"

"No, I suppose I am not. Why fear the inevitable?"

"But you can control when it is you die, Trance."

"Can we?" Trance turned and began striding up the mountain.

Something had triggered an unfamiliar feeling in Trance, anger. He thought back to his first painful years of training. His teachers had told him, "Anger can only spring from within. One cannot be truly angry at someone or something else, but only at oneself." Why was he angry with himself? It was time to consult his *I*. Consciously there was no reason to feel this way. He began to ski with a vengeance, driving himself up the mountain toward exhaustion. Perhaps there was no message. Perhaps it was just tension. He could hear Bill straining behind him, doing his best to maintain the pace. Trance pushed harder, then harder until Bill yelled for help.

"For God sakes, Trance, slow down! You'll have no energy left for the climb."

Trance stopped abruptly and gazed at his companion. There was a strange fire in his eyes. All peacefulness was gone.

"What's the matter, John?" said Bill, between gasps.

"I'm not sure," replied Trance. "Could we stop for a few minutes?"

"If you must." Bill fought to regain his breath. "What the devil is wrong with you?"

"I hope to know in a few minutes. Relax. I'll be back shortly." Trance pushed off into the snow to find a secluded place to flip his penny. He found a rock ledge that acted as a natural barrier against the wind, and sat down upon the rocks. Slowly he withdrew his special coin and began to flip. He made a mental note of each, and tossed his coin eighteen times before he finished. Then he leaned back against the rock and pondered his message. He was being used. There was treachery all around, and he was moving headlong into it. Was he acting against the higher good? He wondered. He flipped his coin again, eighteen times, until his new Hexagram was formed. He was following the highest good. That was plain. So what could it be? He flipped again—then again. After he had formed a total of six hexagrams he was convinced there was much more behind his mission than he had been told. The force he was about to confront was far more than just a money source to Hitler. It was the seat of power...control. There was something that he must search for, something he must obtain. But he could not understand yet what it was. It was something old, and something powerful, something that men would kill for. He could trust no one, especially those who had sent him.

Trance flipped his coin for one final set to determine how much he should tell Bill. Was he one of them? Was he trustworthy? His answer came in the form that said a *little knowledge shared with others could be of great help*. He should tell Bill about his fears, at least some of them. Trance returned to Bill's resting place, smiling again, his inner and outer selves once again in balance. Bill was stretched out in a patch of packed snow, his eyes closed as if he were asleep. He looked almost peaceful, for a change.

"Wasn't sure you were coming back," said Bill as Trance approached. "I got in a good little nap." His eyes searched Trance's peaceful face. "Well, it's nice to see you back to your old self. What got into you back there?"

"There is a lot more to this than they are telling us, Bill."

"No shit, Sherlock," replied Bill. *You poor fool.*

"There are things that our leaders are not sharing among themselves. There is treachery going on, Bill, of the greatest magnitude. I don't know what it is, yet, but it is there. Beware...my friend." Bill looked for a sign of humor in Trance's face, but there was none. Of course there were things that they were not being told. They were spies.

"Can you elaborate, ol' boy?"

"So sorry, I cannot." Trance made an almost imperceptible bow toward Bill.
"So what do we do?"

"Continue. It is in order." Trance pushed onward.

Before long the men were forced to remove their skis and continue on foot. The mountain sloped steadily upward. Soon they had to break out their ropes. Bill had been climbing for most of his life. He had been on major climbs, climbed with men considered to be the best in the world. But he had never seen anyone who could scale a rock face as quickly and effortlessly as John Trance.

"Are you sure you've never made a major climb?" he asked.

"Perhaps I have been on a few."

"The way you move, I am sure that you have." Both men fell silent until Bill finally continued. "Which peaks?"

"Does it matter?"

"I'd like to know."

"Climbing is not something I talk about. It is like a religion—best observed in the company of one's own thoughts."

Bill ignored him. "So, where have you climbed?"

"Oh, Asia...Europe...America..." *What difference did it make exactly which peaks he'd climbed? Why should it matter to others that he had conquered the most challenging mountains?*

Bill fell silent.

The men climbed through the night. Just before dawn they approached the base of the final mountain wall. It towered above, a menacing face of ice and rock rising vertically before curving outward to form the final jagged lip. A treacherous wall to climb.

"Holy mother of God..." said Bill as he took in its grandeur. Most of the wall was flat and vertical. There were a few scattered ledges protruding outward, all covered with light snow that the wind whipped into the air to form a constant blizzard. Now that they were close they could see thousands of chip marks on the wall. Bill and Trance looked at each other. "This wall has been *made* impossible to climb," said Bill. "Who the hell—"

"This is where we camp," said Trance. "It feels like snow in the air. If it comes I'll be able to start the climb before dusk, without risking discovery."

"You're not going to climb in the bloody snow, are you? If the winds pick up—"

"Of course." Trance smiled. "Once I get the proof, we'll need a five hour lead time to clear out of here. You can bet your bloody bloomers they'll be all over this mountain if they discover anything missing, so be ready to fly."

Bill watched Trance closely as he spoke. *He doesn't know...He doesn't know. The goddamn fool is making jokes.* Bill's pursed his lips as he prepared to speak. He had grown to like and respect this unique man.

"You really don't know, do you?"

"I'm sorry. I don't know what you mean?"

"You expect to live."

"I suppose I do. But, that is out of my hands. Whatever will be...will be."

"You're not supposed to live...*We're* not supposed to live, Trance. That's not part of the plan. I thought you knew."

"I don't understand?"

"They expect us to die." Bill pulled a Browning P-35 Hi-Power automatic from his coat pocket. It was a killing machine, 9 millimeters of powerful sting with no grip safety. "I'm going to have to kill you."

Trance replied calmly, "What do you mean, Bill? We haven't even begun."

"This whole operation is a ruse designed to draw America into the war, John. I have the option of whether or not to let you climb. I let you climb only if I think you have a chance of returning with the documents and the book. If you return with the documents, I am to kill you. If I feel you have no chance of returning, I am to kill you before you begin. Once you are dead I am to radio that what we suspected is true, that the castle compound is loaded with Nazi's. I am to turn on a homing beacon, and then kill myself..."

"That doesn't make sense."

"Oh? Do you expect Penwell to tip his hand by sending just one man into that castle? After I send the message, Penwell will launch a team to find our dead bodies. He will produce his own set of documents. He will draw America into the war. Then he will come in here with an assault force flown in out of the sky. They'll storm the castle and kill the Baron. They have no need for you and me, except as cover. We are just pawns in the game they play."

"I see."

"I'm sorry, John. I rather grew to like you—" Bill began to squeeze the trigger of the automatic. He looked directly into the eyes of his friend. "Goodbye," he said and fired his gun. A booming crack split the hollow silence of the night, sending echoes through the mountains. It sounded like thunder, pounding through the valley on the wings of a storm. Bill saw the muzzle flash. Then he was flat on his back, with Trance above him holding his weapon. Trance pointed the pistol at his face, moving it to within inches of Bill's right eye.

"Do you really want to die?" asked Trance.

"We have no choice," replied Bill with a whisper. "Kill me," he said. "I've got to die."

"But I don't want to kill you," said Trance.

"Then they will."

"I don't think so."

Trance took hold of the gun with his left hand and offered it, handle first, to his prone companion. "I don't need this," he said.

Bill stared back at Trance, with no move for the gun.

"Take it. You may need it. I'm going to make that climb, and you're going to help me. But don't think of killing me. I have been trained against far more dangerous men than you, and more dangerous weapons than this."

"How did you do that?"

"You would never understand."

Trance turned and walked toward his pack. His senses were on edge as he listened for Bill's reaction. Had he judged him correctly?

"Who are you?" came the words.

"I'm going to sleep for six hours."

When Trance awoke, the afternoon sky was dark with clouds. It was snowing but the winds were calm. Trance emerged from a restful sleep to find Bill sitting across from him, pistol in his gloved hand, staring intently at his face, wondering if he should kill him as he slept. If Bill didn't, and somehow they both survived, what would they do to them? *Perhaps I should just kill myself and give up on the whole thing*, thought Bill.

Trance arose slowly, gave a wink and said, "You're not going to try to use that on me again, are you?"

"I...What in the bloody hell do you plan to do?"

"I must do what I am destined to do. I will climb this wall and obtain documentation to prove that von Hoffenburg is financing Hitler..." *And I will find whatever it is I am supposed to take from within those walls.*

"Then what?"

"Deliver them to Bulldog Swanson..." *And keep what I must.*

"They'll kill you, John."

"They sent me here to do a job. I will do it. It is the right thing to do." Trance looked up at the sky. "I learned many years ago that if you are right, you are right. That is the only way to be."

"Then I suppose I should wish you luck." *Perhaps, if we're lucky, you'll fall and smash your head against the rocks—*

"With the vision so poor, I am starting now. If I'm not back by O Three Hundred, please leave without me."

"But—"

There were so many things to say, but Trance wasn't listening. He attached his twelve point high angle crampons securely to a well-worn pair of stiff-soled climbing shoes and began to scale the ice. These were his own custom-built spikes, with the outside front point slightly longer, so he could splay his feet farther outward for better balance and still keep two spikes securely driven into the ice.

Soon the wall grew vertical. Trance climbed with an ice axe in each hand using the *piolet poignard* technique. The ice was somewhat soft, so he drove the axes securely into it by using them like daggers. When the ice hardened he would need to switch to the *piolet ancre* technique and wield his axes by the shafts for more head speed. He climbed with the longest axes he could swing accurately. They were fitted with 10-millimeter webbing for wrist loops. The webbing was run through the top hole of each axe and sewn into loops that extended just to the end of the spikes at the base of the handles. They were whipped securely onto the shafts just above the balance points of the axes, leaving just enough room to accept a gloved hand. For much of his climb he would have to hang suspended from these wrist loops, with nothing else holding him above the empty space below.

Climbing alone, Trance opted to use no rope for his upward ascent until he reached the overhang. Any mistake would be his last, so he climbed with care. Trance drove his axes one after the other into the ice, alternately digging secure footholds into the vertical wall with his spikes. Fatigue began setting in after he had climbed less than half way up the face. Under normal circumstances he would have trained for months for such a climb. With only three days notice, there had been no time for that. His arms grew heavy with the continual pounding of the axes into the ice and he felt like a punch-drunk boxer. The snow fell harder and wind began to spin around him. The snow came in small, hard crystals that stung his face as they pelted through the air.

Bill watched from below as Trance climbed out of sight. He stood, staring upwards in amazement from his camp down below. *This is truly a madman*, he thought.

Trance was alone now. He liked it that way. He felt at peace. His arms ached painfully. His legs began to quiver. With each thrust of an ice axe he felt a searing heat shoot through his arm. His arms felt dead, and he began to wonder just how he could scale the overhang with no support from his feet.

Trance carried too much weight. Under normal circumstances he would make this climb with nothing but a light pack on his back. This was anything but normal. This was uncharted territory. Five hundred feet of thin rope was slung across his shoulders. Its dead weight torched his arms each time he muscled his way upward. He needed this rope for a rapid decent. But would it be enough? A string of pitons weighed heavily upon a strap hitched around his hips. Tucked inside his pack was a pair of soft rubber-soled shoes. He would need these to move silently through the castle. Beside the shoes rested a black wool uniform and mask. With these he could remain unseen when he dropped within the castle walls, provided everything went according to plan. Then, of course, he carried weapons.

Trance reached the outward sloping overhang of solid rock and stopped to rest. Less than two hundred yards of climbing and he would reach the top. He grasped one of his custom-designed 28-centimeter tube screw pitons and pounded it into the rock. The piton's teeth were filed to razor sharpness and it cut through the ice like a canoe paddle on a peaceful lake. He followed this with two more, then slung his rope through them and drew it up through the center piton. He let himself hang, gradually removing his weight from his axes until nothing was supporting him but the rope. He rested. Then he set about to scale the rest of the peak.

Trance climbed methodically. Each foot upward was fought for with the same laborious routine. He would make a hole with his pick, and then hammer the piton into the ice until the threads would catch. Then he would take another piton, or his axe head, and screw it into the ice. He would unhitch the rope from the piton below so that the rope would remain free except for the one supporting piton. Later he would need the rope to swing freely, if he lived that long.

After two more hours Trance let himself rest upon the rope and waited until the strength came back to his arms. It was an eerie feeling, to have his body hanging above two thousand feet of empty space in a driving snowstorm, but he felt his calmness return. He was close.

Trance reached the lip of the cliff before midnight. He set several pitons into the ice and made a small dangling cot out of the rope. He lay there, suspended upon the cliff, with the snow piling upon him, and soon fell into a deep meditation. He collected his "Chi," the energy, the vital life force that he would need for his mission. Tranquility flowed through him. Soon he felt refreshed, his psychic energy replenished, his muscles renewed.

Trance's black-gloved hand emerged from outside the castle walls. It was followed by his darkened figure, moving quietly and quickly through the night. The fluid shape seemed to mold into the wall, passing like a shadow from stone to stone. Within minutes the shadow filtered its way around a dozen uniformed soldiers, often crossing silently within inches of their backs. The soldiers stood in small groups, huddled against the cold, smoking cigarettes and talking quietly about women and beer. The shadow listened to the night for direction, feeling its way forward, until it had darkened the entire perimeter of the castle wall.

They had been right, thought Trance. The castle was a fortress, a heavily manned garrison, replete with stores of weapons, and enough grain and animals to withstand a ten-year siege. It smelled like a country barnyard. Trance worked his way inside the perimeter guards and located the military command post. It lay within a cluster of small buildings and stood halfway between the wall and the center of the grounds. He moved in and about the buildings,   surveying each one, making mental notes until he could visualize the entire compound as a whole. This knowledge could be vital to his survival.

An unconscious fear swept through the castle guards, as the shadow shifted from observer to predator. There was a new danger lurking, one that the soldiers would not acknowledge to each other, yet could not quite ignore. Their voices grew perceptibly louder, and their laughter more boisterous as they fought to appear calm to one another.

Underneath his blackened hood, Trance's watchful eyes glinted with unwavering determination. Nothing would stop him as he made his way toward the central castle, this ageless core of power. Trance's heritage held centuries of commitment to a purpose, and he had years of training for this moment. He was part of the Cosmic Order.

He gazed upward. The castle rose skyward, reaching toward the heavens in a vain attempt to dominate his will. It had been built to impose fear, with oppressive size, massive iron doors, hundreds of gargoyles and dragons glowering from above...and now, with soldiers patrolling its walls. But Trance felt no fear, only a peaceful sense of oneness with his surroundings. He was having fun.

Trance searched the dark recesses along the outside of the castle until he found a corner where the walls obscured all light. He began to climb. As he rose toward the sky he could hear the voice of his master. "Always keep three points of your body against the wall at all times...There is no need to hurry." He smiled as he remembered the little man with the long gray beard.

The stone was cold and slippery with the snow, but Trance climbed like a squirrel on a tree. He reached the top and angled his legs over a balcony wall. The wall surrounded a small patio that lead into a large chamber that looked like a library. It was lit by torchlight. Through a window he could make out tall shelves of leather-bound books, stacked to the ceiling throughout the cavernous hall. He picked the lock on the balcony door and slowly stepped inside. He felt the thickness of deep Persian carpets through his rubber shoes. His eyes wandered to the faded tapestries that were scattered along the walls of the room to ward off the cold drafts of winter.

Trance dissected the room, searching for the proof that Swanson demanded. He knew information would present itself to him, if it were meant for him to have. He worked like a surgeon, picking first through the large desk of inlaid mahogany that ruled the far corner of the office. There were volumes of papers inside. Some related obliquely to the financing of the Nazi war machine. There were summary reports detailing the industrial production of dozens of companies throughout the world, profit and loss statements, budgets and marketing strategies. Somehow, von Hoffenburg was privy to a myriad of financial details concerning some of the world's largest international corporations. These figures seemed interesting, but Trance could not see how they would constitute the "proof" that the general required.

Trance turned to several large filing cabinets built into the panel-covered walls. He worked like a machine, systematically moving from file to file. He had hoped that the information would present itself to him; he had such a short time to find it. But as the minutes dragged on he grew anxious that he would fail. He could not cover the entire castle, so he had made the decision to concentrate upon the two areas most likely to produce results—the Baron's library and his sleeping quarters, whose locations had been disclosed to him by Penwell. If the papers he needed were not in the files or the Baron's desk, perhaps they were hidden somewhere in a safe, or some other secret hiding place.

Trance exhausted the Baron's library and decided to move to the Baron's bedchamber. He had hoped it wouldn't come to this. The risk of detection had just multiplied, and no matter how good he was, it would be difficult to survive being hunted by hundreds of Hitler's best.

Trance was turning to slip back out through the balcony when he heard the muted sound of shuffling footsteps. There was the distinct step-step-stepping of a solitary walker, someone older, perhaps. The gait was slow and steady. He couldn't quite tell where the footsteps were coming from, but he moved as best he could toward the sounds. If the intruder came into the room he would have to be right upon him. A warning cry would be his death knell.

An entire section of books began to slide inward towards the center of the room. It moved in absolute silence on hidden hinges and rollers. Trance pressed his back against the rolling bookshelves, sure that whomever he had heard would be following quickly behind them. Could this be the Baron? He had hoped to avoid confrontation; but now with time perilously short, perhaps this was a stroke of fate. He hugged the wall as a lean, towering figure emerged from behind the shelves. The man was dressed in a thick black robe with gold filigree trim. His face was lined, weathered, but of indeterminate age. A mane of charcoal-colored hair flowed well over his shoulders. It was speckled with patches of white along the sides. A full, thick beard stretched a foot below his lips. In his hand the man held a thin, tattered book. He walked with it held delicately in front of his face. With his eyes resting upon his precious book, he was murmuring a soft chant as he entered the room. The man walked in front of Trance, without noticing his presence. As he passed, Trance slipped behind him, wrapped his mouth with one hand and shoved violently outward against his back with the knuckles of the other. The older man was thrown off balance. An indignant, muffled roar replaced his first cry of shock. "Who dares to attack me!" the Baron screamed in German. He struggled to twist out of his captor's grasp, surprising Trance with his strength. He nearly broke free. Trance reacted by digging his thumb and forefinger into the Baron's neck, until he located a nerve that made the Baron stagger.

"Cry out and you're a dead man," said Trance in German. The Baron spit into Trance's hand and raked him with fingernails that felt like claws.

"Who are you?" cried the Baron.

"I am your assassin, if you wish. Or I am a seeker of information. Which shall it be?"

"You can't kill me," said the Baron in disgust. Trance struck the Baron in the chest with an open palm. The Baron doubled over and fought for breath. Trance pressed up on the Baron's neck with his right hand, just under the chin with his thumb and fingers on either side of the Baron's Adam's apple. The Baron seemed to jump off his feet, then sank to the floor as Trance let him go. He lay choking on the antique carpet. The Baron couldn't move. His eyes bulged as he struggled to regain his breath. His bowels let go and filled the room with the stench of death.

"Your next threat is your last," whispered Trance. "I don't like this any more than you do. But like you, I have no choice."

"What do you want?" stammered the Baron.

"You are financing Hitler. I want evidence. Give it to me and I will let you live. You have my word on it."

"Is that all you have come for?" said the Baron.

What a strange question, thought Trance. "No. There is something else." Trance watched as the old man shuddered and grew pale in the dim light. The Baron's knuckles flashed white, as his hands clutched the small book. Trance watched as the Baron buried the book in the folds of his robe, while staring into Trance's masked face.

"No! I will give you nothing else. I will die first!"

Trance was surprised by the strength of the outburst. The man should be like wet spaghetti at his feet, but somehow the Baron had summoned strength and rage from somewhere deep inside. Trance searched the man's eyes and he knew that he had spoken the truth. He *would* die first. But it didn't matter now. He had found what he was sent for. He stood for a moment, staring intently at the Baron's defiant face. He said, "I don't wish to kill you. Just give me the proof of your support of Hitler and I will leave. You will never see me again."

The Baron's face twisted into a contorted grin, the grin of a madman. He became strangely jubilant and began to bounce up and down like a small child at an amusement park.

"Of course, of course!" he cried. "Right this way!"

The Baron shuffled to another part of his library. As he turned, Trance caught a glimpse of the Baron's eyes. He shuddered. This man was dangerous, with the hollow, carved-out eyes of a deranged killer.

The Baron opened a hidden cabinet and removed a pile of papers.

"Here. Here you are. Now leave!"

Trance reached for the documents. With a glance he could see that they were the ones he needed. On top was a list of companies, hundreds of them. Beside each name it showed the percentage owned. Trance shuddered again. Many of the company names were household words in America. He wondered what sort of power, what sort of spell could possess a man to part with these documents so easily. What could it be that took such hold of the man that he would give anything and sacrifice everything to keep it? Soon he would know...

There was a blur of movement. Before the Baron could react, Trance stood above him with the ancient book in his hands. The Baron cowered like a child, his precious rattle suddenly gone. A scream began to leave his throat, but it was cut off by another blur as Trance thrust forward with a fist against the base of his skull. The Baron fell in a lump on the floor. He wouldn't die, thought Trance. Not today. It wasn't Trance's place to kill him. The Baron would lie unconscious for hours, though, long after he had made his escape. What happened to him next was out of his hands.

Trance looked at the Baron lying at his feet and paused. Perhaps he should end his life? No, he thought. His training had been to kill only when he must. Life is sacred. Better to let live than to fight the Cosmic Good. He lifted the Baron, carried him to a far closet and stuffed him inside. The Baron would emerge long after Trance had made his escape.

"You won't feel very well tomorrow I'm afraid," said Trance. "Sorry."

Trance turned his attention to the still-opened doorway behind the library wall. What could be so important? He walked softly down the stairs, deep into the bowels of the castle, to an old dungeon, which was being used as a laboratory of some sort. He could smell the acrid scent of sulfur, and he felt the heat of fire. Slowly he moved his head beyond the staircase, and saw an immense cavern. At one end of the room stood a large work area filled with smoke and fire. Through the hot haze he could see a row of great stone containers. They were filled with various substances—powders, liquids and metals. At the other end of the room stretched a long, tall pile of mottled canvas. It towered over the room. He walked carefully along the floor until he reached the pile. He lifted one end of the canvas. Suddenly all of the questions fell into place. Underneath the protective covering he found a thick bar of gold...and hundreds more...

Trance spent just a moment more in the dungeon. He had found what he had come for. There was no sense in overstaying his welcome. He took one last look at the room and smiled. What would he do with such a fortune? He took the stairs three at a time until he reached the top. He walked to the Baron's desk and grabbed another stack of files. He placed the two sets of papers into water-proof pouches and stuffed them into separate pockets of his knapsack. He did the same with the Baron's book. This he placed carefully into a special com-partment sewn into the bottom of his bag.

Trance slung the knapsack over his shoulder and poked his head out the doorway leading to the Baron's snow-covered patio. Seeing no one, he found his rope and climbed over the side. Removing himself undetected from the castle grounds proved far easier than getting inside. He quickly rappelled through his 500 feet of rope, but it ended abruptly, thirty feet above a small ledge. He was another thirty feet out from the rock wall.

Trance stared into the darkness, trying to sense where he was. He could see nothing in the driving snow. He laughed. How easy this could have been.

After a moment's reflection Trance began to swing on the rope. He pushed out with his feet, then back. Out, then back. Soon he was swinging in a wide arc, with the snow pelting into his face. How long would the rope withstand rubbing against the rocks? Would someone discover him from above and cut the rope? Or let fly with a shower of bullets?

Trance's feet struck the ice-covered rock wall. He let himself swing back-ward, then pushed as hard as he could with his feet. At the last moment he leaned forward and grasped for the wall. His hand slipped on the ice, and he swung back into the void.

This wasn't going to work. Trance slithered down to the end of the rope and tied a quick bowline knot at the base. He took a carabiner, clipped it to his climbing harness and then around the rope. He checked the knot to make sure it was secure, then let himself hang by the end like a spider. He reached around to the back of his pack and removed two climbing axes, slinging a loop around each wrist. He began to swing again. Soon his boots hit the wall. He pushed out with all his strength and swung himself backward into the night. He counted off the seconds and leaned forward. Just as he saw the wall before him, he dug the axes deep into the ice and braced himself for a fall. The fall didn't come. The axes held. Trance took a deep breath, reached down with one hand and unclipped the carabiner. He was now at the mercy of the fates, again.

Trance struggled down the rock face. By the time he reached solid footing his arms hung lifeless by his side. He sat quietly to give thanks for his safety. With effort, he stood and slowly began crawling backwards down the mountain.

When Trance approached the camp, Bill Netherby was sitting opposite the base of the wall. He was absentmindedly throwing snowballs toward a distant crevice to his left when Trance eased down from above. Netherby nearly wet his pants. He stared up at Trance, wide-eyed in fright, then began to laugh. He wasn't sure whether he should rejoice or cry; he had no clue how they would extricate themselves from Austria. There would be no rescue plane unless he called in dead. If he made it back to England, his fate was dubious, at best. Even so, as the shock waned he felt the thrill of accomplishment and the warmest of joy at Trance's safe return.

"Well, I'll be bloody damned," he said.

"Good to see you, too," said Trance. "We got what we needed. Now let's get out of here."

"Where to?" said Bill. "There's no one to help us."

"Not a problem," said Trance. "Get your gear. I have a friend that lives close to here. We should be there for lunch."

"No shit?"

"No shit."

After an hour of intense skiing Bill called for a break. Trance, with little energy of his own, gladly stopped. He dusted snow off an old log and sat down for a breather.

After a few minutes Bill caught his breath enough to ask, "How does one get to know someone in the middle of nowhere?"

"It's a long story," said Trance.

"I'm not going anywhere."

Trance pondered Bill for nearly a minute. How far could he be trusted? Would he be putting his family friend in danger?

"Wait a moment," said Trance. He took out his penny and began to flip it to form the hexagrams that would tell him how to act. Should he tell Bill that Alfred Breitfuss lived barely one hundred kilometers from the Baron's castle? That he owned and operated a small inn called the Pinzgau Hutte, halfway down the Schmittenhohe Mountain in Zell am See?

"What are you doing?" said his companion.

"I must consult the Sage to see whether or not it is safe to tell you."

Bill Netherby shook his head. "Whatever…" he said under his breath.

Three minutes later Trance faced him and said, "We are going to see a man who lives in a small town here in the Alps. This man, my father, and I have made several climbs together. Our families go back generations. In fact, my father arranged the loan for this man to buy his business. I will not burden you with his name or the town where he lives." Trance paused. "Let's go."

Four hours later they came to a village, whose post office had a working phone. Trance placed a call, hung up the receiver and smiled.

"He will be here soon," he said. "Let's go eat."

"I thought we were going to eat with your friend?" said Bill.

"Change of plan."

Bill shrugged and followed Trance to an inn along the main street of the small town. It was nestled between a bakery and a butcher shop. Two pairs of wooden cross-country skis were nailed to each side of the front door, and three dead ducks hung from a ceiling overhanging the porch.

Inside, there was a small entryway. Stairs lead to the left and a narrow corridor angled off to the right. Trance followed the passage until it ended at a squat wooden desk. Behind it stood a square, matronly woman dressed in Lederhosen, with peppered hair tied up in a bun. She had an unfiltered cigarette hanging from her lips, which moved up and down as she said, "Grus Gott."

"A room and a meal would be nice," said Trance in the same Austrian dialect.

The woman offered Trance a guest book to sign and rang a bell for someone to lead them to a room.

"The kitchen is down there," she said, pointing to her left. "It looks out onto the street."

Three hours later a Volvo swung to a stop outside the inn. Trance saw the driver and waved. "Time to go," he said. He picked up his gear and walked out the door.

Alfred Breitfuss opened his car door and walked around the front to embrace John Trance. "It is good to see you, my friend." He was wearing a pair of loose blue ski pants and furry après ski boots. Black hair wandered across his forehead and over his ears. A thick mustache sat neatly on his upper lip.

Trance smiled and nodded. He turned to Bill Netherby, "Mr. A, this is B."

Breitfuss nodded toward Bill, then looked back to Trance with a questioning glance.

"Where are we going?" he said.

"Can you head toward Zurs? I'll direct you from there."

"Ya."

That night the two men made a clandestine crossing into Switzerland. The next morning they caught a train to Berne where Trance contacted his mother's cousin, a Japanese diplomat posted there. The diplomat brought them by limousine to the British embassy. Along the way, Trance and his uncle carried on a long conversation in Japanese, occasionally nodding somberly, as if agreeing to some secret pact. That evening the men were on their way to England.

Penwell was sitting in a deep, red leather chair, smoking a pipe and reading the *Times* when the phone rang.

"Mr. Penwell? It's Bill Netherby."

Netherby could hear Penwell inhale deeply. He waited through the silence, until Penwell replied quietly. "Well?"

"We have the proof you wanted."

"You have the book?"

"The book?"

"Yes, the book. Have you got the book?"

A muffled silence hung over the loud static on the receiver, as Netherby asked Trance about the book.

"Trance is opening his pack to see if the book is in there. He says he took a pile of documents, the only ones that seemed to be about business."

Penwell muttered to himself as he waited impatiently for the results of the search.

"No. Nothing I can see," said Netherby. "What's so important—"

"Goddamn son-of-a-bitch!" Penwell dropped the receiver back into its place. He turned on his short wave radio, which was connected to a large tower structure that rose high above his residence.

Five minutes later Bulldog Swanson was crackling faintly on the airwaves.

"Any word?" said Swanson

"No, not yet. You hear anything?"

"No, sir."

"Let me know when you do."

Penwell picked up the phone, dialed a series of numbers and arranged a greeting party for the two men entering the country.

At the same time, Trance placed a call back to his uncle at the Japanese legation in Berne. He thanked him again, in Japanese, for his help, then informed him that he and Netherby would soon be on their way to England, via Lisbon. "Would you be so kind as to do the favor we discussed?" asked Trance.

"Of course, my son. Do not worry. You will be safe." After all, they were family. They were also Samurai—honor bound forever. "Be careful," continued his uncle. "It will not be long before Japan engages America in the war. Your loyalties may be questioned. You must distance yourself from your family—however hard it may be. We will always be here for you if you need us—but you must protect yourself."

When Lieutenant John Trance and special agent William Netherby emerged from the military transport there was no welcoming celebration. There were no marching bands to hail heroes of the war, no welcoming smiles of faithful women they had left behind. There were no colorful signs to ease the fear and fatigue they had felt throughout their silent trip. Six uniformed men met them at the plane. Each soldier carried a rifle, and a holstered sidearm. Trance and Netherby were escorted separately to waiting Mercedes limousines, and whisked to Penwell's home. Penwell lived in a 17th century castle along the Thames. It was surrounded by a full moat, harboring a scattering of contented ducks chuckling as they fed. Ivy-covered walls rose high into the air, and stretched several hundred feet to each side. The men crossed a drawbridge and were led along a drafty corridor that was dimly lit by electric torches, until they came to a cozy, book-lined study. Penwell rose from his soft leather chair to greet them.

Penwell reached out his hand for Netherby to shake. Then he drew Netherby close to him and whispered, "You are a dead man."

"I know," said Netherby.

Penwell motioned for the men to sit. Penwell was accompanied by another man, who wore a white lab coat and carried a black leather case. They all waited in silence, until a dozen soldiers entered the room and escorted them away at gunpoint. Within minutes they were locked into separate cells for an SIS debriefing by Penwell.

"How in the holy hell could you have let this happen, Netherby?" The words came from the shadows behind a glaring light. It shined like a laser into the agent's tired eyes. Netherby's story hadn't changed in twenty-four hours of interrogation. Penwell was beginning to lose an already splayed temper. He'd had the same difficulty with Trance.

Penwell pulled his medical assistant to the side and said, "Deprive them of sleep for another twenty-four hours."

"Wouldn't it be better just to give them a couple of injections?" said the man. "I could—"

"Not yet, doctor. I want their minds clear for a while longer," said Penwell. He paused. "Besides, we still have to have our fun."

Interrogation was one of Penwell's favorite activities. There were so many ways to bend the mind—ways that were far more entertaining than the drugs, and more predictable, too. Pain had its way of producing results. One just had to have patience.

Penwell forced Trance and Netherby to remain awake. He allowed each man to come within a blink of sleep, before shocking him with bright lights and a full-fisted slap on the face. Soon they would begin to lose the energy, thought Penwell. He'd let them cling to their sense of self for a little while longer. Then he would destroy their will with crushing ferocity. Yes, soon they would be willing to tell him anything, confess to any crime he told them they had committed.

Penwell was interrogating Bill Netherby when he was interrupted by a knock on the thick steel door.

"Yeah," said Penwell.

The door opened and his male secretary came scurrying over to him. The aid was in his late forties, willowy, with just a few dozen hairs remaining in a small tuft in the middle of his otherwise bald head.

"Sir. I hate to disturb you but—"

"What is it?" shouted Penwell.

"Sir. We've had two telephone calls for Mr. Trance from someone claiming to be a Japanese diplomat."

"How in the bloody hell did someone find this number? Another goddamn security breech. Tell them he's not here...Tell them he's never been here...Tell them we don't know who the hell Trance is."

"Yes, sir." The aide clicked his heels, preened himself like a bird and scurried away.

Penwell was running out of time. He walked to the edge of the room. Along the wall there was a series of pegs built into the wood. From them hung various "instruments of delight," as Penwell called them. He selected a small, leather riding whip and carried it casually back to Bill Netherby.

"You mean to tell me that you took a shot at Trance from ten feet away and missed? You? A member of the bloody National Biathlon Team? Then, after you shot at him he handed your weapon back to you and you let him live?"

"I couldn't shoot him. We had a mission. Besides, he had some kind of...power...or...something over me—"

Penwell slashed the whip across Netherby's face. "Do you mean to tell me that you never asked to see the information that Trance took off of that mountain?"

"It wasn't my place to ask. Besides, you don't know him—"

"Enough!" Penwell slapped the whip against his palm. "Do you realize that the information he supplied is absolutely useless to us? It is junk, things we already know. We sent you there to get information!" Penwell lowered his voice. "I sent you there for a book."

"I thought you sent us there to die?" Bill struggled against the lights, trying to see into Penwell's eyes. Bloodied spit dripped from his chin.

"You are going to die. But not until you tell me what really went on between you and Trance. Now, whom are you working for? What did they pay you?"

Penwell cracked the whip in a wide arc, slashing Netherby across the face. "Once again, from the top," he said.

Trance endured the same torture. But where Bill had told the truth, Trance hid everything. He never told Penwell that he had left documents with Breitfuss. That the most incriminating papers, as well as the Baron's formula, were now buried safely under four feet of dirt and ten feet of snow, somewhere halfway up a mountainside in the Austrian Alps.

Penwell could sense the lies. The stories were not identical, and the slightest variations loomed large under the magnifying glass of anger. He was hell-bent to tear out the truth. He had been easy on them so far—a few bruises, a little blood. Soon he would open the floodgates to pain. If that didn't work, he would lay on the drugs. The drugs would be the last, for there was always the risk that the mind would never return. He may need them coherent before he killed them.

What should he use next? He loved this feeling of anticipation. Perhaps a little burning? A little flame...hot irons...glowing embers...maybe a little acid in the eyes? Electricity? Maybe a cattle prod? That was always stimulating. Castration? That had a way of making a man talk. Or perhaps the gradual crushing of the fingers...or toes? Maybe a little intrusion into the body orifices...Penwell was having fun anticipating his next delicious action, despite his billowing anger.

He's got my goddamn formula. I know he does. That formula was for me. Not that madman Hitler. He's only got one ball for Christ's sake! He's half the man I am...

Penwell made his choice. He selected a thin canvas tube filled with small ball bearings. It was perfect for crushing bone and cartilage without marring the outer surface of skin. He worked on Netherby until, mercifully, he drifted into unconsciousness.

"Doctor. Wake this sonofabitch," said Penwell. The doctor injected Bill with a powerful mixture of stimulants, followed by a wave of smelling salts under his nose. Within moments Bill was coughing and choking into a dazed wakefulness.

"All right, you bloody shit. Tell me where you and Trance hid the book."

"I...I...We didn't hide any book. We..." Blood streamed down Bill's forehead and mixed with the sweat to form a dripping river of agony under the broil of the lamp and heat of the room. Bill's vision blurred into blindness. All he had the energy to say was..."Why....sir?"

"Doctor. Make this man talk!"

"Yes, sir. Thank you, sir."

The doctor withdrew a needle from his bag and slowly filled the syringe with a clear liquid. It had a slight greenish tint in the naked light. He pulled back Netherby's shirtsleeve and swabbed his arm with cotton and alcohol in a highly meticulous in his manner. Then with a compassionate motion he injected it all into the semi-conscious life form.

Two minutes later Bill Netherby was dead.

"You killed him, you bloody shit. What in-the-goddamn-name-of-hell did you give him?"

"It's the same—"

"Get out of here! Get me Trance."

It was nearly six o'clock in the morning. Penwell was beginning to ready himself for one final session with Trance. The son-of-a-bitch kept mumbling about everything being in Cosmic Order and Penwell could take it no more. He was going to break Trance's teeth. *Maybe this will keep him from escaping into that sick world he keeps falling into...*

Trance was tethered into a chair before him. Penwell grabbed hold of his hair and strained his head back. Trance's eyes remained closed, and Penwell shook him violently to keep him from drifting away. His hot breath felt like dragon smoke against Trance's face, and it seeped through his eyelids to burn against his weary eyes.

"I am going to break your teeth now. If that won't make you talk, I am going to shove this little glass tube up your privates and crush it—"

As Penwell spoke, the door behind him opened and a hooded figure crept into the room. The man moved like a shadow, dressed entirely in black.

"I wouldn't do that if I were you," came a quiet voice. "You have already killed one too many."

"What the—" Penwell reached for his pistol. But before he could move, the gun lay on the floor, and his hand was stinging from the blow of the shadow's wooden tube.

"You will let him go."

"The hell I will. You'll never get out of this place alive. I'll have you strung up by—"

"Pick up the phone." The voice spoke cultured English, with a soft Oriental lilt to the accent.

"What?"

"Pick up the phone. Or I will break your leg."

Penwell reached for the phone. The shadow continued, "At this moment there are three other men with visitors such as myself. Swanson, who you have so neatly manipulated...your Prime Minister...and the American President."

"You're full of shit."

"Call your Prime Minister at his home. Here is the number." The voice was nearly a whisper. Penwell called the operator. A minute later he had Churchill on the line.

"Penwell. What the hell is going on?" said the agitated Prime Minister.

"Sir, is someone with you there, right now?"

"You bet your bloody bum there is. Some guy dressed in a costume holding a knife at my throat. He says that only you can call him off. I suggest you do that."

"Ah...Wait a minute." Penwell looked up and said, "You don't expect me to believe that you have men holding knives to the throats of Swanson and Roosevelt, do you?"

The shadow nodded. "You will use the short wave radio to check overseas with Swanson. You and he will explain to your leaders that you felt they were not being adequately protected. So you arranged a test of security, which failed. My men will leave as soon as they hear, from me, that Trance is safe. You will now tell Churchill he must contact the American President in exactly...." The shadow looked at his watch."...six minutes. He is to explain to Roosevelt that this was a joint mission with the British SIS, and that his security was similarly breeched.

"Then you will tell Swanson that Trance will be arriving in Washington, from London, and that he will be treated as a hero, which he is. My man there will give him more specific instructions."

Churchill received Penwell's explanation with a mixture of gratitude, awe, and outrage. As Penwell set down the phone he looked into the eyes of the shadow and said, "I'll see that you are dead for this. All of you."

The shadow drew close to Penwell and touched a razor-sharp knife blade against his throat. He slowly pressed it into the flesh until there was a steady dropping of blood onto the glistening steel.

"For what you have done I should kill you now. But for the sake of my...this man...I will let you live. But I warn you, if any harm ever comes to this man, I will come looking for you and I will kill you. Don't think that you can stop me, because you can't. And don't think that you can kill me and live. Because there will always be others behind me—always."

With that the shadow unstrapped his brother from the chair, and they were gone.

CHAPTER 1

▼

Many years later

Retired general John Trance was sitting comfortably in the waning summer twilight. He was ensconced in his favorite chair, with his evening constitutional martini by his left side—a ritual he had acquired rather late in life. His wife of many years sat by his side. They were relaxing in a whitewashed gazebo off their back porch, gazing at the sun setting over the purple mountains of Williamstown, Massachusetts. Upon his retirement from active duty, Trance had accepted a one-year visitor's chair at the Williams College Graduate School of Developmental Economics. He and his wife Patricia had lived there ever since. They had found life peaceful in the secluded valley, far from the everyday hustle of the urban sprawl.

Each summer Trance made a ritual of skiing the Austrian glacier of Kaprun, where he would secretly meet with Breitfuss. Trance and his wife would then tour Europe, starting with the Mozart Fest in Salzburg at the end of July, and finishing with the Oktober Fest in Munich. They would visit the mineral baths of Badgastein and Badhofgastein, swimming in the thick hot waters, which always seemed to take years from John's bones.

Although John Trance had reached an advanced age, he could still outpace men thirty years younger. His wife, Patricia, criticized him for his excessive activities, often wondering aloud how he managed to stay so young.

As the last faint rays of the orange sun dipped below the mountains, the phone rang.

Patricia watched out of the corner of her eye as Trance slowly lifted himself out of his chair. She knew of the pain he must feel. Wounds from the Second World War had left him with shattered knees and multiple contusions pressing mercilessly against his spine. It was a miracle he could walk at all.

"Good evening," he said quietly. "Trance residence."

"General John!"

Trance pressed the phone against his thigh and said to his wife "It's your brother." Then he said warmly, "Good evening, Senator. Patty and I were just talking about you. How are things in Washington? And to what do we owe the pleasure of your call?"

Winthrop Hopewell was the senior senator from Massachusetts, with over thirty years in Washington on his résumé. His closest friends called him *Winner*, as did the voting public he did not know at all. After his wife and children had perished in a tragic, summer boating accident, Hopewell had thrown his hat into the ring for the presidency. His traditional popularity combined with the sympathy vote made him a lock for the White House.

"Aw, you know Washington, John. A veritable steam bath, with more hot air coming from the mouths of politicians than even I can stand."

"The more things change the more they remain the same," said Trance. "How's the campaign?"

"Looking good, John. Real good. Now if I can just keep my ass out of trouble..." The two men laughed. Their friendship was not intimate, but it was amiable and based upon a deep mutual respect.

"You will make a fine president, Winner." Trance spoke quietly and with ingratiating politeness.

"Thanks...Hey, did you get the tickets I sent?" Knowing Trance's passion for the annual music festival in Salzburg, he had pulled his weight to secure the best seats, along with engraved invitations to all the right parties.

"Yes, this morning. Patricia was very pleased."

"Ah, they were offered to me by the Austrian Ambassador last week. My wife used to love the symphony, but I'll get no use from them...Look, I don't mean to cut the conversation short, John. But I am worried about Jack."

"Oh? So is his mother," replied Trance. "But I am confident he will work things out. He's had a rough go of it these past few years."

"I feel responsible," said the Senator.

"For appointing him to Annapolis? For treating him like your own son? For steering him to the CIA like his father? Or for aiming him toward law after Janice..." Trance's words trailed away.

"Was murdered," finished Hopewell coldly.

"The CIA didn't kill her, Winner. She was sworn to the Company, and she tried to support her husband in the best way she could. She knew what she was doing."

"Did she?" said Hopewell. "I call it murder, John. The girl was three months pregnant. Her resignation had been tendered, and she was supposed to be shuffling paperwork, not meeting with terrorists. That ass Miller had her killed....You should have let me set up a Congressional committee to—"

"What was done was done, my friend." *How could they have let that happen to her? Her own people! She had no business in the line of fire.*

"By the way, General, your son just pulled off another miracle. Ambassador Abrams was returned unharmed after his kidnapping in Italy. Never made the papers. The President's wants to pin another medal on Jack's chest, privately of course. No publicity for his kind of work." Hopewell paused. "But Jack's disappeared," he said slowly. "Any idea where he might be this time?" His deep concern showed in his voice.

"He was in Nepal," said Trance. "He returned yesterday. The Italy affair disturbed his inner harmony, Senator. The missions always do." *He only takes them as punishment*, he thought ruefully. "He had to kill six men."

"It was a messy business. But he was the only one we could count on. God knows we didn't need another hostage crisis."

"Use someone else for these missions. It takes so much—"

The Senator interrupted. "You think we haven't tried? We sent the 121. They were decimated. Jack went in alone and returned Abrams unharmed. In fifteen years your son hasn't failed once. Sometimes there's just no one else we can send. You must know that, John. When it's a matter of national security, national stature..." The Senator let the words trail off. This was always their excuse.

John Trance knew it well, what it was like to be the only person they would send. Yes, he knew it only too well. He knew the bastards would never step forward to defend his son if he were caught. Jack wasn't military now, not officially. He was a civilian, ever since the death of his wife. He worked privately, ostensibly for the money, paid to him in numbered Swiss bank accounts. But John Trance knew better.

It was true that his son made more money in two weeks than he had made in a lifetime. But John knew the real reason his son couldn't quit. It was his destiny. His son was following The Creator's will. John's *I Ching* had told him so.

"When you see him, have him call me?"

"But of course, Senator. Good luck on the campaign."

"Thanks, my friend."

John Trance sat back to reflect. He thought of how he had escaped death at the hands of Penwell. How his younger brother, Tony, had rescued him from the interrogation compound with the help of three cousins. Of the years they had trained together in Japan.

He thought of his long recuperation and his surprising, immediate promotion to captain. He thought of those days long ago, when he had become the first Army liaison to the newly formed Office of the Coordinator of Information, later rechristened the Office of Strategic Services, the OSS. In 1946 he was assigned to the Central Intelligence Group, which soon became known as the Central Intelligence Agency, the CIA. In the ensuing years Trance was a leader behind the scenes, helping shape and control the nation's entire spy network. Spies that were needed to ensure the continuing freedom of America. John Trance had done his part.

Then there was Patricia. She had started as his secretary in 1957, a bright dedicated girl of eighteen, barely half his age. She was an heiress; but he didn't know that then. They had fallen in love and were married the following year. They had one child, John, Jr., and they called him Jack.

Trance and his wife had grown apart over the years. It saddened him, but there seemed to be no tangible thing he could fix. Outwardly, there was nothing wrong with their marriage. Neither complained. But Patricia had grown distant, not only with her husband, but with her son as well. Neither man could bridge the chasm.

Jack had spent his childhood living in a dozen countries. He was raised as an American, but also as an Oriental child—trained in the Oriental languages, religion, the marshal and mystic arts. For three of his teenage years he had lived among his people in the Iga Province of Japan, and he had learned to follow the honorable traditions of his family.

Jack had inherited his father's mental and physical prowess, and he had been able to excel in both cultures. It came as no surprise when his uncle, Senator Winthrop Hopewell, had appointed him to Annapolis.

Trance was graduated Summa Cum Laude. He lettered in football and track. More importantly, he was the school's top theoretical and practical war strategist. He worked with the top brass in designing game scenarios, and he had helped construct and moderate the annual Navy Global War Games.

Trance went on to Top Gun, then the Seals, where he helped execute covert campaigns against terrorists in more than a dozen countries. From there he was recruited to build and run an elite team of soldiers known as *T Force*, chosen from the country's four major military branches and trained in the most effective methods of fighting and espionage. Trance vanished into the joint operation between the military and the CIA.

This was where Jack met his wife. She was a new CIA recruit, training under Trance at the covert training facility known as The Farm. She had made him happy and they had married. When she became pregnant they decided that she would retire from public service, only to have her gunned down on the Washington Mall by the terrorists Jack had worked so hard to stop. Now Jack was driven by his own guilt, never shedding the pain, lost somewhere between life and death.

John Trance closed his eyes and wept. He thought of the book, the formula. His son was the only person he could trust with this burden. He was the only person who could carry the great secret he had been hiding for more than fifty years. Someday his son would hoist the world on his shoulders. This was the Way, his *I Ching* had told him so. John Trance relaxed and fell into uncluttered sleep. It was almost time.

CHAPTER 2

▼

Present Day

There was a slight chill to the mountain air, with the morning sun beginning to peek over the hills in the distance. The ground was still wet with dew, and it had begun to sparkle with the first light of day. Water gurgled in the small man-shaped stream that ran through the neatly manicured garden stretching out from the back of Trance's Vermont home. The sound was relaxing, hypnotic, carefully created over a period of many years. The air smelled faintly of flowers.

Trance had finished his daily ten-mile run. It had taken him fifty-five minutes, not bad for a man in his middle thirties. He'd lifted weights and run through twenty katas, shaved and showered, and was now dressed in a pair of running shorts and a workout shirt that said, *Takuro Spirit* on the back. His feet were bare.

Trance carried a plate of bacon and eggs and a pot of coffee outside the house to a small round table that sat at the far end of the garden. Surrounding the table on three sides was a large alcove of polished marble. Two ponderous bronze doors stood at the entrance. They opened to the outside, revealing a small altar of hand-chiseled stone and wood within. Above the altar sat a vase of delicate porcelain, and beside it, a smaller one. Trance removed a single red rose from the small vase and replaced it.

"Good morning," he said. "I miss you today."

Trance sat back by the table and began to eat. He spoke to an empty place setting across the table.

"You know, when I was a boy, I used to have breakfast like this with my father. Mom never joined us...I don't know why." Trance laughed. "I asked dad about it once, and he said that `every flower must grow in its own place.' Just like him to speak like that." Trance paused to reflect. "You know, the only time I ever really felt like I belonged anywhere was with you."

Trance dabbed at the egg yolks with the corner of a piece of toast.

"Today it's going to be bright and sunny...a great day for painting. I'll set up an easel by your window."

Trance's eyes began to mist and he wiped them absentmindedly with his napkin.

"I'm still mad at you, you know...You should have known better than to listen to Miller...Leaving me here alone like this...I hope it's sunny where you are so you can paint."

Trance heard the low hum of an alarm sensor coming from the receiver on his belt.

"Crazy to have to live this way..." He put his mind on alert.

Trance walked to his study, where he twisted a round light switch on the wall. The study's wooden paneling slid back to reveal a bank of wide screen monitors. Trance caught a glimpse of white cloth in the woods behind his house. He smiled, then returned to his eating, keeping his senses stretched out behind him.

Trance faced away from his house, toward Janice's shrine. He made no motion as a man emerged from the bushes and approached him quietly.

"Get out of here," said Trance.

The man stopped. Trance turned and peered into the eyes of his intruder.

Jacob Miller smiled and held out his hands palms up, as if to say 'I'm unarmed.' His gaze turned from Trance to the shrine behind him.

"You're not welcome here." Trance followed Miller's eyes as he studied the altar.

When Miller's eyes stopped on the porcelain vase, Trance said, "That's what's left of my wife...after you sent her to die."

"Jack, I—"

"I said get out of here."

"If you would—"

"If I would what? What can you say that I would want to hear? Tell me that it wasn't your fault? Or that the country needs me for some other bullshit mission?"

Trance slowly stood, walked to the great bronze doors, and gently closed them. "I'm sorry, honey. I'll make him leave."

"You've got to let go of her, Jack...Let go of the past. It's been six years—"

"Six years?" asked Trance softly. Then he laughed. "No, Miller. It's been a lifetime."

"I'm sorry."

"Just leave."

"I can't...I had to come here myself...Jack, it's your parents."

Trance felt his heart stop. His lungs fought for air, then he began to pace. Miller watched the muscles ripple along Trance's body as he moved. Not a spare ounce of fat anywhere. Each sculptured part had been formed through years of painstaking work on free weights and specialized machines, countless hours of exercise and training. Drill and re-drill, tune and retune, until Trance's entire being could function as a unit with perfection. *What a waste*, thought Miller, *to have him so dead.*

Miller waited in silence. He was glad that Trance had not greeted him with a handshake. Whenever they shook, Miller felt like his hand was in a nutcracker. The many years of martial arts training had turned Trance's hands into weapons, his fingers so strong and hard they could crumble bricks. Like a full-grown Saint Bernard who still acted like a puppy, when Trance shook hands, he crunched fingers.

Miller studied Trance's face, focusing on the prominent cheekbones that gave it a distinctively angular look when he set his jaw. He knew that Trance could neutralize this feature at will, suddenly looking like the boy next door. It was the kind of face you could never forget, and never remember when you had to. Trance's eyes shifted color depending upon the light. They could be intense and alert, a laser that never blinked, so powerful that they could back off any man who dared to stare into them. But they could also be compassionate, vulnerable, and filled with pain.

Like his father, there was a slight Oriental hint to his eyes. They were almond shaped, and surrounded by a smooth baby-face. Now in his middle thirties, Trance's face had taken on maturity, still young looking, but weathered.

Trance was less than six feet tall. But when he took a step toward Miller, Miller felt himself cower involuntarily. What was it about Trance that gave him such power? Perhaps it was that Trance could kill him in seconds, with no effort at all. Miller hated himself for that.

"Your parents were kidnapped and killed while in Salzburg," said Miller. "Their bodies washed up on the banks of the Salzach River yesterday. We have no suspects."

Trance closed his eyes. When would this end? He felt his chest tighten and burn. His father had been his anchor, his tether to the world of the living. There were so many questions, yet nothing to say. He felt only emptiness. He shrugged his shoulders, and said, "I see."

"We thought you might want to prepare the funeral. The President has offered Arlington."

"He liked it in Williamstown," said Trance. Then, as if with an afterthought, he said, "Were they tortured?"

Miller nodded his head solemnly. "Your father was."

"I see."

"There are no leads, Jack."

"They'll pay..." Trance stared ahead blankly. "Whoever did this...This time I won't stand by...Heads are going to roll."

After Jacob Miller left, Jack Trance walked to his bedroom, dropped to the floor and curled himself into a ball. He began to cry with loud, powerful sobs. Rage and sadness rode through his mind, like dark wraiths, spinning in confused circles. Around and around with no place to fly. Eventually the tears went dry, leaving bitter thoughts of revenge etched forever on his heart.

Early the next day, Trance drove south towards Williamstown. As the world passed by Trance thought about his father.

Trance's father had been an anomaly among the army elite. His fellow officers had never understood him, or trusted him with their personal lives. They had kept him at a distance, treating him with a mixture of awe and contempt, like they might a famous movie star with a drinking problem.

There were few who would call him a friend, but none who would call him an enemy. He had been quiet and unassuming, yet his toughness was legendary. No one had stood in the way of his success, yet no one had actively worked to help him succeed. He had done everything on his own; though very few knew what that true job had been. Few knew exactly how, or why, but whenever his name had been mentioned, it was in hushed tones. It was the same with his son.

When Trance entered his father's home he found it ripped apart, room-by-room. The furniture was slit and overturned. The covers had been torn out of every book, and his father's personal files lay strewn along the floors.

His father's desk was cleared of debris, with a solitary piece of paper resting on the polished wood.

Your father would not return what was mine. Now he is dead. I will have less patience with you.

"And I with you," said Trance.

Trance stood alone along the secluded bike path. Beside him stretched a well-manicured garden sporting roses, marigolds, dahlias, petunias, hydrangeas and an assortment of other perennial flowers. There were no walkers or bikers to break his morning solitude, and Trance let his mind drift back to when he and his father used to walk this same path. His father had often commented on how lovely it would be to put a Japanese garden off the path, just far enough away to allow quietude and a natural place to meditate. There were a hundred and forty unspoiled acres here, a bucolic setting where one could ponder the emotional and artistic attributes of man. Today he would get his wish.

The air was crisp and clean, as a high-pressure system swept in from Canada, drying the morning dew and buffing the air to a shine. *A great day to be buried,* thought Trance. He looked at his watch and sighed. It was time. He headed back along the path until he came to the rear entrance to the white marble building that housed the Sterling Clark Art Museum. He could see a crowd of people milling about—far more than he had expected. He approached the throng and positioned himself at the entrance to the museum. The crowd began to organize into a jagged line that stretched well toward South Street.

The first to greet him was Marshall Abrams, vice president of the United States. Beside him stood his wife, Miriam.

"Hello, Marsh," said Trance. "Thank you so much for coming." They embraced briefly.

"The country will miss both your parents," said the Vice President.

"Thank you. They would be proud to have you here."

Trance gave an air kiss and a hug to Miriam Abrams, the vice president's wife. "We will both miss her," he said to his mother's younger sister.

"She was a true patron of the arts," said Miriam. "She would be proud of what you are doing."

"Thank you," said Trance. "She did love her art, and she loved this place."

Behind the vice president followed Senator Winner Hopewell.

"Hello, Jack," he said. He embraced his nephew, pulling Trance toward him like a big bear.

"I'm sorry for your loss," said Trance. "This must be terribly difficult for you, after…" Trance lowered his head.

Hopewell kept his arm around his nephew. "I've come to grips with that, son. How are you?" He paused. "What can I do? Just name it."

"How about if you do the talking today?" said Trance. "I'm a little—" The words trailed off.

"Sure, Jack. No problem."

The Secretary of Defense and the Secretary of State, two Cardinals and an emissary from Rome, twelve former cabinet members, four U.S. senators, sixteen congressmen, business leaders and several heads of state followed Senator Hopewell.

As the procession thinned, an unfamiliar man approached Trance. The man appeared to be in his middle fifties, and carried himself with elegance. His hair was silver, and combed straight back on his head. His skin was tanned and smooth. His eyes were slate blue and lifeless. He wore an immaculately tailored dark blue suit, and sported a woman half his age on one arm.

"Hello, Mr. Trance. My name is Guillermo Vasquez. I manage my family's interests in Buenos Aires. Your father and I conducted business on a number of occasions. We shared a passion for gold."

"Gold?" said Trance.

"Yes, alchemy, in particular. I lent him an old book of mine." Vasquez handed Trance a card. "Please call me if you come across any old alchemist's note-books. Mine has a red leather cover. It is an old family heirloom."

Trance took the card. *How odd*, he thought. "I'll call you if I find anything."

Moments later Trance was approached again. "Mr. Trance. My name is Henri Villiers. I am the chairman of Villiers Industries in France. We had many deal-ings with your parents over the years. Did they ever speak of me?"

"We didn't talk much about others," said Trance. "But I am glad you came. Thank you."

Trance turned to greet the next person in line, but Villiers grasped his shoul-der and whispered, "Did your father ever mention his interest in gold?"

Trance shook his head. "I'm sorry. He did not." *What is going on here?*

Other men and women made this same request during the next half hour, and Trance became keenly aware that many of the people attending the memorial service had a far different agenda than paying last respects.

Near the end of the line Trance saw a slim, dark-haired woman dressed in a simple black dress. Her hair was tinged with gray, which she seemed to wear with pride. Beside her walked a man in his early sixties, with white hair and mirth lines creasing his eyes. The man walked with an easy grace, but wore the solemn countenance of a man in grief. These were the parents of Trance's closest friend, Lauren Haverford.

The woman reached her arms around Trance and held him. "We are so sorry for your loss, Jack." Trance embraced the woman and gave her a soft kiss on the cheek. "Thanks Angie."

"Lauren's in China and we can't reach her."

"I know," said Trance.

"We'll call her every hour. She'll want to be here."

"When you reach her tell her I'm okay. Tell her to finish what she's doing. There's nothing she can do, but I do want to see her. I'll go to Boston after I've settled things here—"

"But—"

The man patted Angie on the shoulder. "It's okay, sweetheart. Jack can handle this. You know that."

"It's just so sad…"

The man extended his hand to shake, and then pulled Trance against his chest and whispered, "We're here for you, son. Just let us know what we can do."

Trance sniffed and broke away. "Thanks, Max. Guess I better get this done."

Trance gazed toward South Street and saw a small bus from Enterprise Rent-A-Car turn in the drive. It stopped behind a line of cars. Twelve men with shaved heads wearing black silk robes emerged and floated toward the art institute. Trance's jaw dropped and he began to smile. He ran toward the men and embraced them like a football team.

"I am so glad to see you," he said in Japanese. "My father would be so honored."

The leader took Trance by the shoulders and gazed at him for more than a minute. His eyes twinkled, but there was a solemn look on his face. "It has been a long time, Red Dragon," he said. "You appear wiser, but the years wear heavy on your frame."

"The burdens of the few are many," said Trance.

"The wise man carries only one burden, my son—to be spiritually pure and serve others honorably."

Trance bowed. "Thank you, Sensei. I am learning still."

"As are we all, Red Dragon. As are we all."

The other men embraced Trance one-by-one, each murmuring words in his ear. Each time Trance nodded and bowed.

After all the men had passed Trance made his way through the reception area toward the amphitheater. He gazed at the hundreds of people packed side-by-side in the confines of the room, all waiting to pay their last respects. How many of these people had his parents really known? How many were here for some other reason?

Trance passed along a well-lit hallway that led to a set of wide alcoves that had been hastily converted to show a portion of the Trance art collection, one part fine European impressionist paintings, the other part an enormously rare assortment of Japanese feudal art and weaponry. He threaded among the pieces, acutely aware that he had never laid eyes on most of it.

Until two days before, he had paid no attention to the family wealth or his parents' collections. It had been the call from Boston that had forced him to accept his family legacy.

"Hello. Mr. Trance, my name is Jason Ricard. I am an attorney with Hale and Dorr in Boston. I represent your parents' estate. As you probably know, you are the sole heir—"

Trance interrupted him. "Did they make any provisions for charities?"

"No. They wanted to leave you with flexibility…and the burden."

Trance closed his eyes. He wasn't ready for this; he wasn't ready to have them gone. "I think I want to give it all to charity," said Trance. "Any suggestions?"

"Perhaps you don't know what we are dealing with here," countered Ricard. "Your mother's investment portfolio exceeds eight hundred million dollars. Then there is her stock in Hopewell Industries. As you know, this is privately held, but exceedingly valuable. It's probably worth another three to ten billion, but we'll need to do a full valuation." He paused. "Then there is her art collection, which is priceless.

"Your father also left you many rare, one-of-a-kind articles from Japan. He wanted you to know that some of them have been handed down in your family for centuries. Sotheby's estimates the worth of this collection to be in excess two hundred million."

"That should go to my uncle, Tony. My father's brother."

"It was all left to you—"

"Mr. Ricard, I know this might sound funny to you, but my father and I were simple people. Because of her name, my mother was sometimes thrust into the spotlight, but even she shied away from the glitz that can come with wealth. We were comfortable, but we used our money as a credit card to bring good to others. Please humor me, leave my father's heirlooms to my uncle."

"Yes, Mr. Trance. I will contact him. You will need to pay the tax on that…a hundred million, give or take."

"Please do it."

"All told, Mr. Trance, the estate you have inherited easily exceeds five billion dollars…probably closer to ten."

"I don't need that kind of responsibility," said Trance. "Let this money help others." Then he hesitated, thinking better of his decision. "No, that's not right. I will retain the real estate. That, I want. Set aside enough to pay the estate taxes and maintain the properties. Then put everything else into a charitable lead trust, say, for thirty years—enough time to zero out the tax."

"Then what do we do with the trust?"

"Leave it to my cousins, on my father's side, I guess."

"You…ah…don't plan to have a family?" asked Ricard. "You're not that old…I could have the trust default to your children if you ever—"

I have no family. Trance had lost his chance for a family, years before. But, he decided, the world was unpredictable. "All right. Let's do it that way, then."

Trance entered the amphitheater and walked to the podium. He attached a portable microphone to his lapel. Beside him rested the closed coffins of his parents. He waited for each seat to be filled, and for the remaining mourners to pack into the auditorium. All three hundred and fifteen seats were filled, and the aisles were packed like a rock concert.

"Thank you all for coming," he said softly. "You must be wondering why we have gathered here." There was a murmur through the crowd. "Most of you know that my mother's family traces back to the early American settlers. Over the years her family has been able to collect a little art—"

Another loud murmur spread through the crowd, accompanied by a spattering of laughter. The Hopewell family was considered an American dynasty. They were well known around the country—for their triumphs, their tragedies, and their devotion to charities.

"My mother was a passionate, unbridled patron of the arts. She devoted her time toward bringing fine art to all levels of society.

"Many of you do not know that my father was a collector as well." Trance paused. "He could trace his family back more than fifty generations. Over the centuries, his family, too, was able to accumulate a collection of rare artifacts.

He paused. "My father's life was spent in the service of this country. Those of you outside our government will never know how much he served us. Perhaps his true legacy rests inside me…if I am worthy.

"My mother was an extraordinary woman. She will be fondly remembered for the exemplary life she lived and those whose lives she has touched."

Trance could feel his fingers tremble, and he fought to keep his emotions under control.

"How do you sum a life in a few short minutes? How do you ensure that the legacy of two great people is not wasted or forgotten?

"My father helped ensure the safety of our nation. My mother helped shape our culture."

Trance looked out over the crowd. What were they expecting? He smiled. "I have asked you here today because I was given the burden of deciding what to do with what they left behind. Their shadow is long, and I can only hope to be worthy of their legacy.

"The trustees of this fine art institution have graciously accepted my outright gift of two hundred million dollars to build and maintain a new wing that will house the Trance art collection for at least the next thirty years. This money will also be used to provide community outreach programs designed to bring our finest art to those who might otherwise never have the chance to see and appreciate it.

"I have also established the John and Patricia Trance Foundation. The foundation will sponsor college scholarships for high school graduates with great ambitions but modest means. It will also provide educational funds for patriots leaving our military, particularly those who have helped pay for our freedom with pieces of mind and body. I am pleased to announce that the first scholarships have been offered to five outstanding men and women who have been accepted here at Williams. The foundation will also sponsor young individuals from developing nations who have overcome the enormous obstacles placed in their way.

"I have chosen this path as a lasting tribute to my parents and their way of life. They were outstanding people in very different ways. I only hope that I can follow their example."

Trance cleared his throat and took a sip from a bottle of Poland Spring water. He fought to remain composed, but felt like a flag whipping in a strong wind. "My uncle, Senator Winthrop Hopewell, has agreed to speak on behalf of the family." Trance backed away from the podium, turned off his microphone and took a seat between Angie and Max Haverford as Hopewell took his place.

"My friends, colleagues, guests and countrymen. We mourn here together. Our nation mourns with us. Rarely have the lives of others touched us so much." He looked to Trance and motioned with his hand. "Rarely have two parents left a legacy like the son who sits before me...."

By the time Senator Hopewell finished speaking the auditorium was filled with sniffling noses and looked like it had been dusted white with tissues.

After the service, John Trance's brother, Tony, drew Jack aside and said, "Are you all right, Jackie?"

"Sure, uncle Tony. I'm just going to miss them." Trance paused. "Why didn't you take it?"

"What would an old man do with a bunch of old art and obsolete weapons?"

"It is from your family, Tony. There is nothing more important than family."

"Oh?" said Tony. "I have something for you. Perhaps you will change your mind."

"What's that?"

"Your father asked me to give you this when he died." Tony withdrew an envelope from his jacket pocket and pressed it into his nephew's hand. There were tears in his eyes. Jack wondered if they were tears for the father or for the son.

"When did he give this to you?"

"Ten years ago. But this letter results from an event that happened before we entered the big war. Your father was recruited for a mission in Europe, one he nearly didn't survive." Tony's lips spread into a grim smile, remembering the night he had snatched his brother out of Penwell's grasp. "There are things you don't know."

Trance chuckled. *That's for sure.* He took a long look at his uncle. Tony was so much like his father, and yet so different. Both had risen to high positions in government service—dedicated, loyal and generous to others. Trance's father seemed driven toward achievement, more taciturn, while Tony was far more apt to laugh and make friends. John Trance seemed consumed with destiny, convinced that greater powers controlled his life. Perhaps this was why he never seemed to age; he never worried. His life was controlled by the flip of a coin. Tony was more American. He believed that men could change the outcome, that individuals had a choice in their actions.

Tony was two inches shorter than Trance, but still lean and straight. He had aged, but gracefully. He bowed politely as he spoke, glancing over a set of half-rimmed glasses that rested upon the end of his nose.

"I know," said Trance. "My father was different. There was always this under-current—the way people treated him, something I could never quite grasp. I used to think it was because he was part Japanese, and fought for our side during the big war. But it wasn't that. They treated him with respect, but also like a pariah."

"I am afraid that what was once his burden will now become yours."

Trance glanced sideways at his uncle. His uncle's hair was still onyx black, the years wearing lightly upon him. Trance opened the letter from his father and laughed.

"He did this in that silly code we developed when I was a kid."

"No one has ever broken that 'silly code'," said Tony.

Trance laughed again. "I'm sorry to disappoint you, Tony. But the NSA could break this code within an hour."

"Or so you think."

Trance shrugged his shoulders. "It's really not that complicated. It has a single roving key—a simple function of dates, combined with specified books from our library. That is what provides the challenge. The books are from our own *unpublished* books, books in nobody's database. A referenced event in the text triggers a new date that alters the code. Events are used for the key. A birthday, graduation, anniversary, vacation…It could never be used in the field between strangers, but within the family it worked well. We had a lot of fun with it."

"I'll leave you alone now. I'm tired...and my kids are flying me back to a new home—a transition community in Miami." He shook his head. "It's called the Final Rest." He smiled at Trance. "A fitting name don't you think? They are sending me off to die." He sighed. "I've got to go. I am afraid an old man like me can't be of any help to you."

"Tony, you're not old and you know it. Your children just have their own lives now. Come stay with me. You are always welcome here. Remember that."

"Oh, Jackie. You know that your cousins will deny me visits with my grand-children unless I am *safely taken care of* in Miami." He patted Trance on the shoulder. "You're a good kid, Jackie." He paused. "You've shouldered more than your share of responsibility, far more than you know. Your father placed it upon you and you accepted it without question. He guided you into areas that you would not have chosen on your own. I…I know of the pain you have felt. I know of the conflicts that you, your family, and your occupation have created inside you. All that you have done...become...was for a purpose, Jackie. Believe me. Soon you will know."

"What's up, Tony?"

"I'm so sorry. I cannot say. I must go now. I've got to go back to Miami. You are right, Jackie. I am not so old. Just don't tell my kids. Goodbye, Jack Trance. May good fortune and God's will follow you."

Trance watched as his father's brother walked slowly away. He thought of how much more philosophical he had grown with age, and the patience Tony had always shown with him and his American compulsiveness.

Later that night, he unfurled the coded letter from his father and retired to the remnants of his father's library. He located several of the defamed books and began decoding his father's final words. As the letter unfolded, Trance found himself smiling, realizing that his father had undertaken to impart one final lesson to him—and to play one final game.

My dearest son,

There is so much you do not know. But your road to knowledge will be long and dangerous.

Since you are reading this letter I must assume that two things have happened. The first is that I am now dead. Do not grieve for me. I have led a full and useful life. But whether I have died from natural causes or not, there will be people you must stop, perhaps even kill. It was not my fate to stop them, or kill them. That much was made clear to me. But I suspect it will be yours.

The second gives me grave cause for concern. For, if you are reading this letter, I considered this information too dangerous to give to you while I was alive. As of the time of this writing, it has been decades since I unraveled the secrets. Perhaps you were not ready and able to receive them—not that you were a source of disappointment to me. On the contrary, Jack, I have never been disappointed in you. Only once in your life did you incite my anger. You have done much during your short life. But you have not found perspective. Perhaps I allowed you to become too American, too self-focused. You must understand that in our Universe, as individuals, we are not important. Each of us makes a small difference, like one grain of sand will make upon a beach. The difference is there, but quite hard to measure. You have never been able to accept your own insignificance in this world, and allow yourself to surrender to the Cosmic Will.

Although each of us is insignificant in the greatness of the Universe, we can, and do play a major role in the small part we inhabit. Our mistake, my son, is that we believe we are in control of the moves we make, and the actions we take. That, my son, is up to the Creator.

I was tempted to feel concern at the pain this has caused you. But I also understand that this is all part of the Divine Order. So too, I believe, is this letter.

I will give you the information in stages. I cannot take the risk of the whole falling into the wrong hands. If it did, life as we know it will be forever altered. It was not my place to let that happen. Perhaps it will be yours. Each stage will lead you to the next. You must surrender yourself to the Divine Will. Use your "I", and you will know what to do. Fight it, and I am afraid you will fail, and millions will die.

Remember our Friendship. Keep it as your anchor in the storm that will surround you.

Love, Dad.

Trance let the letter fall through his fingers, pondering its possible meanings. They had played the game before, back when he had constructed the code while in grade school. It had been his father's idea, designed to give his son the experience he would need with ciphers. He had been good at the game, always decoding each message, leading on to the next like a scavenger hunt.

Now he drew a blank. He let his pen wander, repeating the key words of the letter, writing combinations of words.

Knowledge… long… dangerous… grave… information… disappointment… anger… perspective… self-centered… insignificance… Cosmic Will… Divine Order… information… stages … Friendship… anchor… storm...

Was there another code within the letter? Where should he look next? He must look for what is out of place. Match the words and events.

Trance read the letter for the fifth time and still found no direction.

"If this was so goddamn important to him, then why the hell didn't he make it clear?" Trance threw the letter down in disgust. Anger was a familiar feeling with him these days, and he could feel it welling inside. He thought of the irony, of how his father had never expressed anger, while Trance seemed to live it constantly. Why did he fight himself?

"Anger," he said. Trance cocked his head and took the letter back into his hands. He began to read a passage of the letter aloud, so he could hear the words from the outside.

"Only once in your life did you incite my anger." Where had it been? Maine. It had been in Maine, their home on the coast. In Friendship. Friendship, Maine. Friendship...anchor. *That's it!* He had been helping his father set a new mooring for their boat in Friendship harbor. They were working together, underneath the boat in scuba gear. Jack had stalked off to snag two lobsters along the ocean bottom. He hadn't been gone for more than a minute when his father had emerged from behind him and torn the mask off of his face.

That had been the only time that he had seen anger in the eyes of his father. That must be his clue. The boat mooring in Friendship harbor.

Trance spent two days closing his parent's home off River Street in Williamstown. He wondered whether he should sell the place. It was a rambling old mansion, and it did have a certain comfort. But he felt no comfort now. In fact, there was something unsettling on the fringe of his senses. It nagged at him incessantly, although he could not pinpoint the stress. Perhaps he would figure it out later.

Trance made arrangements for the caretaker to look after the home. He convinced Professor Robert Lelander, a retired economics professor at Williams, and a long-time friend of his father's, to move into the house, rent-free, for as long as he wished. His father would have liked that. Lelander enthusiastically embraced the idea of using the home to host the disadvantaged students who were being sponsored by the Trance foundation to study at Williams.

It was an unusually hot August day and the sun had been glowering upon the Trance home all morning. There was no wind to stir up the oppressive humidity, and it clung to Trance's body until it began to wear into his patience. He could not yet leave for Maine, so he decided that a trip to the Dorset Quarry in Vermont was well in order. His father had never believed in air conditioning, and a swim in the cold spring water would do him good.

Trance grabbed his car keys from the kitchen counter and jumped into his classic Porsche 959. It was a white convertible with wire wheels, twin turbo charging, and custom black trim. His initials had been etched ever so subtly into the design, so that only he knew they were there. As he sat behind the wheel he felt a brief tinge of guilt for spending a quarter of a million dollars on a used car. But when he sat in the solid leather cockpit, turned the key and heard the throaty rumble of the engine, he remembered why he owned the car. He felt life spring into his muscles and a tinge of excitement flow through his blood. He was alive again. He headed north along Route 7, letting his mind drift back to his wife. Would there ever be another Janice? He felt tears struggling to break through his control. Why did he always want to cry? Why couldn't he let go? He gripped the wheel tightly and pressed on the accelerator. He rode along the country roads at a comfortable 85 miles per hour, pushing the car faster as he hit the corners, loving how the wheels clung to the road. In moments like these he could almost understand what his father had told him about feeling one with the universe. In this brief space in time he and his car became one. His hands became part of the wheel, and the car became part of the road. He pushed the car faster, and felt the familiar sense of danger, the thrill, the thought that any moment could be his last.

He glanced into his rear view mirror and saw another car a couple hundred yards behind him. Was he being followed? He'd soon find out.

After turning west on Route 30, Trance swerved his car into the parking lot of a souvenir store. He spun the car, curving it back out toward the road to watch as two men sped by him. It was a BMW 7 Series. Silver. Both men wore Bausch and Lomb Ray Ban *shooter* sunglasses, like the ones he wore himself. Perfect for driving, cutting the glare without reducing too much light. But Trance used them because of their purpose. The nose pads pushed the glasses higher than the standard aviator frames, so the frames didn't get in the way of a rifle. Were these men shooters, too?

The men kept their eyes stiffly forward as they passed, but Trance could feel their attention upon him. He had a sixth sense for that sort of thing, when he took the time to listen to it. He wondered if there were others, and why they were following him.

Trance set the alarm on his watch for ten minutes. He reached under his seat, unlocked a hidden compartment, and removed his father's old 32 caliber Colt automatic. It had been his graduation gift from college, his prized possession. He had carried it into danger dozens of times. He wrapped his hand around the grip, pulled back the safety and snapped it ready. Automatically he replaced the manual safety, even though there was a second one on the grip.

He thought of how this gun had always felt so natural in his hands. Others may carry Colt 38s or 45s, Rugers, Walther PPKs, or Berretta 9 millimeters for their power, but Trance had always felt more comfortable with his father's old Colt. He had modified the twist inside the barrel for extra bullet spin. It now took a higher-powered shell. But there was also a little magic to it, his father had said. Trance had seen that magic in action. The gun wasted no space. It fit perfectly in his hand, and comfortably into the small of his back, almost like a part of his body. He fingered the safety again, leaving the gun ready to fire.

Trance stopped to fill his tank with gas. When the regular tank was filled, he checked the spare he had built into the car. It was full. As he finished, his watch began to beep. He handed a wad of cash to the gas attendant, saying, "Keep the change," and hopped into his Porsche. He swung it back into the traffic, moving along at a leisurely pace, just under 40 miles per hour. He knew that any moment he would see the Ray Ban twins waiting for him along the side of the road. His eyes darted from side to side searching for the silver car. Finally he saw it, sitting at an angle in the parking lot of another gift shop. The men were hunkered down into the seats with the mirrors of the car angled to detect Trance's approach. Jack saw the movement of their glasses; they had seen him and reacted.

"Amateurs," he whispered.

Trance drove his car past the BMW at a slow speed. As he passed by, he hit his brakes, then gunned the car forward, turning the wheel sharply as the wheels spun him around. In an instant he was staring directly back at his pursuers, their cars nose to nose. He smiled broadly, and saw panic spread across their faces. The driver jammed the car into reverse. Trance laughed. They'd never lose him. Their cars were a mismatch, and he could drive with the best. His mind flickered back to the one time that Janice had watched him take a third at Le Mans. He gritted his teeth and blinked.

He waited impatiently for the driver to stop the BMW and shift it back into forward.

"Hey, buddy," he yelled. "My mother drove better than you—"

Then he heard a muted crack from behind him and felt a jolt as a bullet hit his left rear tire. The tire spit in response, deflating in a blast of air. Trance knew that he was done for the day, despite his run-flat tires. He looked back and saw a second BMW spin away after the first.

"Damn" he said. There was a second car. "How the hell could I miss it?" These men were not amateurs. They were pros, and he'd been careless.

Trance slapped his hands on the wheel and chuckled. "At least they're not trying to kill me," he said. "But why are they after me?" The answer had to be in Maine.

CHAPTER 3

▼

The phone buzzed in the executive offices of Global Credit Bank in Boston.

"Lauren Haverford's office. May I help you?"

"Ms. Haverford, please."

"May I tell her who's calling?"

"This is Jack Trance."

"Oh, hello, Jack. Just a moment, please."

Jack and Lauren had been high school sweethearts. In those young and simple days they had romantically thought of marriage, a house in the suburbs with a white picket fence, a two-car garage, and children playing in the yard. But it never happened. Lauren had gone on to Princeton and the University of Chicago while Trance pursued Annapolis, the Navy, then Harvard. Twenty years later they were still the best of friends. Lauren had chosen a career above marriage, and she had risen quickly in the banking world. She was now just one step away from the presidency of one of the country's largest financial institutions. She also looked the part. She was slender and impeccably dressed. She could be ruthless in the boardroom when the game was on, but selfless and down to earth when someone needed a friend.

"Jackie. I've been trying to reach you. I just got back from China this morning. I am so sorry—"

"I'm okay, Lauren. Really. But I need you."

"Really? I need you, too. Your place or mine?" Lauren could sense that Trance needed levity more than sympathy. This was a long-standing joke between them. Neither would chance ruining their friendship by trying to recapture the sexual innocence of their youth. Trance had not slept with another woman since his wife's death. Lauren's celibacy had endured twenty years. Yet both had a hunger for closeness, a need for intimacy and physical release. It was a hunger that had nearly drawn them into each other's arms. Now they told jokes to remove the tension and make light of the needs that went unfulfilled. Perhaps he really needed her now, she hoped.

"I'd love to, Lauren. I'll take a rain check on sex. I need you for something else."

"Only if you'll promise to turn my lights out later."

Trance laughed for the first time in days, as he envisioned her using such language in the boardroom.

"Are they going to make you president of that financial colossus with a mouth like that? What in the name of God is this world coming to?"

"They never see me like this, Jackie. You know that. To them I'm Virgin Lauren. I can't tell you how many of them have made it a quest to climb my little mountains, and failed. I've heard they call me the Terminator. Only you see me like this, Jackie. Only you..." The last two words trailed softly over the phone.

"You know what kind of work I do."

"Adult toys, right?"

Trance laughed again. "I'm going to give you the chance to play with some new toys."

"Shoot."

Trance chuckled again. Only Lauren could make him laugh like this. He told her what he needed her to do. They didn't talk about the death of his parents. They would do that in person.

Trance hopped into his car carrying a small blue gym bag. He set it on the passenger seat and fired up the Porsche. He drove leisurely, heading northeast toward Brattleboro, Vermont. He knew that somewhere, someone with a wireless device had alerted his pursuers. Soon he'd pick up a tail or two. How many ticks would there be? He wondered.

It was two o'clock on Wednesday afternoon, two days after his call to Lauren Haverford. When Trance reached Brattleboro, he glanced at his watch and then headed south on Route I 91 until he hit Route 2, the Mohawk Trail. He took it east toward Boston. He watched as two cars pretended not to follow him. They took turns in the lead, always keeping at least one or two cars between themselves and Trance.

Trance took the Copley Square exit off the Mass Pike and began to meander about the city. He drove with no apparent direction, keeping his eye on the mirror, memorizing license plates and the types of cars behind him each time he looked. At 4:40 he climbed along Beacon Hill. When he reached the top of the hill he swung past the Statehouse and then made his way toward the financial district. He continued to drive at his leisurely pace, circling around Post Office Square until he saw a red Mercedes and a blue van slip in behind him. Ten minutes later he pulled into the Aquarium garage off Atlantic Avenue. As he took a ticket and began climbing the ramp he couldn't help but laugh, as he saw the woman in the Mercedes pull awkwardly to the ticket dispenser and clumsily reach in vain for the ticket just out of her reach. The van blocked the other entrance, leaving no way for Trance's pursuers to follow. They leaned on their horns, but to no avail. The woman got out of the car and began shaking her fist at the men in the car.

Trance swung around the corner to the second floor where he saw Lauren's blue Lincoln Continental parked exactly where he had requested. The trunk was raised and the car was running, with its driver leaning forward out of sight. He stopped his car where it was, leaving his motor running, grabbed his gym bag and climbed into the trunk of the Lincoln.

The Lincoln swung forward, headed down the ramp and became the third car in line for the exit. Meanwhile, an old friend jumped into the Porsche and began to spin it toward the top of the garage.

Fifteen minutes later Trance emerged from the trunk of the Lincoln, kissed Lauren gently, and left her standing in tears on the tree-lined Commonwealth Avenue.

Trance was now free from surveillance, for the moment at least. But he would have to move quickly. They would find him soon enough.

Trance drove the Lincoln north on Route I 93 to I 95, then followed the highway toward Maine. He took the Brunswick exit, passed by Bowdoin College, and followed Route 1 North through Wiscasset and into Waldoboro. From Waldoboro he headed east toward the coast. The drive brought back the comforting feeling of his childhood, when everything was light-hearted fun. He felt almost young again. He drove his car quickly over the sweeping bumps in the road that made his stomach reach for his throat.

When he reached the small village of Friendship, Trance parked the car half a mile from the family compound. He would enter the grounds on foot. He cut through the woods and approached the family home from the rear. In the darkness he could see the distinct outline of the old wood and stone farmhouse in the moonlight. He threaded his way through the thick pine forest, feeling glad that there were no rattlesnakes in Maine. So much safer than the jungles of Southeast Asia, where pit vipers, cobras and coral snakes grew like locusts. He carried a black rubber flashlight with a red lens placed over the face. This gave it a luminescent glow that could not be detected easily from a distance. He could see well enough, and would pass though the woods with less risk of detection.

Jack and his father had spent their lives in espionage, a business that inspired retribution. So the home was well protected. They had built an elaborate fence and alarm system around the outer perimeter of the grounds, and then twice more in concentric circles as one drew closer to the house. Once inside the ten-foot fences, there were weight and heat sensors, as well as a crisscross of infrared beams aimed across the grounds.

The outside alarm system was kept off unless someone was in the house. Friendship had no formal police department, so there would be no response to a burglar. Trance had taken his own precautions to ward off intruders. Only an advanced professional could penetrate this home unharmed or undetected.

Trance satisfied himself that there was no outside surveillance of the immediate area. He moved closer toward the rear of the home and walked to the edge of the woods that surrounded the house. The closest trees stood at a distance of fifty yards on all sides, except in the back, which opened out to the broad expanse of the coast. As he approached he could discern the outline of the impressive home, and he could also hear the water of the harbor lapping gently behind him. He thought of how nice it would be in the morning to eat breakfast in the dining room, with its 270-degree view overlooking the ocean. Trance removed a large, flat stone. Underneath it was an airtight seal over a hidden switching system that lead underground to the home. He shoved a sensing device, shaped like a fat pen, into a membrane covering the hole to detect the trace gas he had injected inside the casing. It read positive. No one had tampered with the system, at least from the outside.

From his vantage point, Trance could now monitor various other sensing devices within the home. Through a series of steps he could discern the intrusion of any but the most highly skilled intruders. Even someone who knew his system would have a difficult time evading his elaborate series of fail-safe mechanisms. He tested them one after another. He tapped onto a notebook computer that was wired into the central computer inside the home and reviewed the data recorded during the past few weeks. When he had finished, he was satisfied that no one had attempted to invade his home. He couldn't be sure they weren't waiting just down the road for him to appear, but he had other precautions that would take care of that contingency.

Trance entered his home through one of the side doors and grabbed a Sam Adams beer from the refrigerator. He dropped his iPhone into a sound docking system, selected a set of Jimmy Buffet tunes, then went through the house room-by-room until he was satisfied that he was alone. It was half past eleven, and he felt a comfortable weariness spread through his body. The alcohol hit and he began to relax. The tension began to dissipate slowly, now that he no longer needed it to keep on edge.

He walked over to a computer terminal and gave verbal commands to turn on the furnace, water pump, and the air compressor. Then he slid down the smooth wooden stairs that wound into the basement, feeling comforted by the thought that in thirty minutes he could immerse himself in his Jacuzzi. Perhaps he would follow that with a hot shower rinse, and hopefully, a couple hours of sleep in his old feather bed.

Trance's pleasant reverie faded as the reality of the situation came back into focus. He pulled open the top to a long wooden case of roughly hewn oak. Inside he found his diving gear. A brief wave of sadness flowed through him as he fingered his father's diving pack. For a short moment he closed his eyes. Then he turned his head toward the heavens and let out a silent roar.

"I'm going to find the suckers," he whispered. Trance closed the top of the case, sat down upon it and wiped stray tears off his cheeks. He thought of how many times he had fired point-blank into the eyes of his enemy, feeling no remorse, no more pain than if they had been annoying mosquitoes, probably less. They had been *enemy*, and an enemy was something less than human, something worse than animal. It had also been his duty.

He thought of how he had been trained to mask his emotions, cloaking them in a prison of mental walls. Yet how many times did he now feel his emotions trying to brim over his eyelids? Too often. He wasn't very good at the game, was he?

Trance reopened the diving box and withdrew an air pack, a wet suit and a dry suit, and all of the paraphernalia he would need. He glanced briefly at his oxygen closed-circuit rebreather, but decided it wasn't needed. He checked the pressure in his traditional tanks and carried his pack to the air compressor that was already coughing and chugging in the corner of the basement. When he was finished, he began hauling the gear up the stairs and out the front door of the estate to the garage. The garage was a freestanding building. It would have made a good size home on its own. It had three wide doors in the front, with each port nearly wide enough to allow two cars through. Trance opened the middle door. Inside was a white Chevy Blazer. He drove it forward slightly and piled his scuba gear into the back. Moments later he was winding along the narrow gravel driveway that took him back to the main road. He followed it for a quarter mile, driving slowly with his lights off, hoping not to arouse any of his neighbors. The fewer the people that knew of his arrival, the better. When he reached the road, he took a sharp left, turned on his lights and followed the road down toward the docks.

Friendship was a small village, in a two-industry town of a few hardy souls. Some residents still headed out at four each morning to their lobster boats. Others began at dawn building Friendship sloops, the solid, elegant wooden sailboats that had served the fishermen so well before the coming of the Chevy inboard engine.

Trance drove cautiously down the steep hill that led to the harbor and looked out at the dozens of lobster boats floating gently in the calm of the night. He thought of how hard, yet how easy, the lives of these robust fishermen must be. It was hard physical labor but easy on the mind, when the money was there. Unfortunately, these men were a dying breed, and were gradually being priced out of their homes and their lives.

Trance drove the Blazer out onto the public dock, clear to the end where there was a square wooden float measuring about ten yards to a side. Attached to the float was a clutter of small floating craft, the skiffs used by the fishermen to row their way out to larger boats moored in the harbor. Trance dumped his gear into his ten-foot skiff and began to row in relaxed strokes out to the family mooring. Each resident of the town was assigned their own special spot for their mooring, in a unique small-town caste system. The best spots were reserved for the oldest and most prominent families of the village. These spots were handed down from generation to generation, hoarded like football season tickets to the University of Michigan, Denver, or the Washington Redskins. The Trance's were newcomers to the town, only fifty years of residence. So, Trance had to row well away from the dock.

As he approached, he could see the outline of his classic J-36 sailboat rocking slightly, its bow pointed into the wind. A J-36 was large enough to be built for comfort. But any comfort comes as a sacrifice to speed. So, the inside of Trance's boat contained only the bare necessities for overnight sailing—two austere web bunks, GPS, a depth-finder, a small portable gas stove, and a tiny titanium sink. Where others may have added to the boat's weight with pillows or a bed, Trance had an on-board notebook computer with custom software that could give him up to a tenth of a knot edge in a stiff wind. The one small luxury that Trance had availed to himself was a narrow removable diving platform off the stern of the craft. It was upon this that he began to unload his gear.

Trance immersed himself in the darkness of the cold, bone-chilling waters. As he plunged back first into the night, he could feel the wetness seep through his wet suit, and his body shuddered against the cold.

In his right hand he held a black rubber flashlight that spread a milky whiteness in front of him. He could see mackerel darting in and about the beam of his light, and he thought of the sand sharks that dwelt along the harbor floor. He followed the thick, rusted chain down from the bow of his boat as it stretched into the murkiness of the mud-covered bottom of the harbor. As he drifted down to the thirty-foot depth he felt his heart beat with anticipation. What would he find? Would there be anything at all? What could there be that would have caused his father to be treated with such deference by his peers? What kind of information would cause someone to desecrate his father's home in its search? What could be so important that it could alter the course of world events?

When Trance reached the two hundred pound concrete block used to secure their boats over the years, he felt his heart sink. He could see nothing attached to its base. There was nothing there. But there had to be. He felt the seeds of panic sprout as his fins began to stir up the ocean bottom, reducing the already murky visibility to only two or three feet. He forced himself to relax. What had his father said? Friendship in the storm? He tried to think. What had they gone there for ten years before? He remembered. Their mooring had shifted, from the boat pulling against the winds of a storm. That's why they had made the dive. They had chained another cement block to their mooring. It had to be underneath.

Trance clipped himself to the chain to give himself leverage. He began to tunnel into the mud to the second mooring buried deeper below. *Ah...there it is.* He began to feel around, searching for anything irregular through the thin rubber mitts covering his hands. Trance found a square metal box, with a chain attaching it to the mooring. He would need cutters to remove it.

Trance followed the chain back up to the boat. He pulled his mask off for a brief moment to look around, searching for anything out of the ordinary. Something seemed out of place. What was it? He had looked out into the harbor from this vantage point a hundred times, and he could feel that something was out of place. What was it? He moved his eyes from boat to boat, looking for one that wasn't where it was supposed to be, perhaps one that was new...no...each boat was familiar...but something was out of place...Then he knew what it was. Peter Murphy's 20-foot Sea Ray was never moored this close to his boat. How many times had he glanced toward it thinking how it might be fun to buy a pleasure powerboat like that? The goddamn thing was moving. The Sea Ray also towed a motorized skiff with a 20 horse Johnson, a boat that didn't belong to Peter Murphy. It must have been stolen from one of the docks. Both boats were drifting outward with the tide, directly toward his boat. They would make contact in no more than three minutes at the speed they were traveling.

"Shit," he said. "Just what I need." *Should I ignore them and get the hell out? Christ, I'd have to leave the box on the bottom. Should I challenge them directly? Good way to get shot. When will these observers become killers? Didn't dad say they'd have to be stopped? I should have taken the rebreather; now they will see my bubbles.*

There was only one thing he could do. He reached into the dinghy, opened his blue gym bag and removed several metal articles. He put them into a net strapped to his side. He then checked his compass, submerged himself again, and began heading toward the drifting boat.

He judged the distance to Murphy's boat to be no more than two hundred yards. He was now faced with the decision of whether to wait for them to come to him, or to catch them out where they were. He'd prefer to swim toward them, surprising them if he could, but there was no vision under the water without his light. He was swimming blind. He cursed himself for not bringing his wristband GPS, and opting against the closed circuit rebreather. A compass and telltale air bubbles would have to do.

Trance found his way to the bottom, letting out air in his dive vest so that he rested comfortably on the floor of the harbor. He began a half-swim, half-crawl forward, counting the steps of his hands to give him some bearing on his distance.

He had to emerge behind them. Otherwise he'd be dead before the night was through. Every few moments he glanced upward, hoping he'd be able to make out the shape of the boat against the faintly luminescent sky. After he had traveled what he figured was close to a hundred and fifty yards, he could make out the shape of the two boats drifting above him. He swam upward to a depth of around ten feet, exhaled slowly and began swimming forward so when he emerged from below he would be hidden by the smaller, trailing boat.

When Trance's hooded head broke the plane of the water he was just two feet from the stern of the skiff. Pulling on the shaft of the motor, he lifted an eye above the side of the boat. He saw one man with an oar in the water, paddling quietly at the back of the Sea Ray. They were guiding it gradually forward toward his boat. There was one other man peering out from the bow.

Do they know I'm diving? They must. They think I'm still down below. I don't have much time.

Trance removed his gloves, then his pack, and fastened them to the propeller of the skiff's motor with a shock cord from the bag on his hip. He lifted the cowling on the Johnson and yanked the spark plug wire free. Then he pulled his way along the boat until he was within a few feet of the stern of the Sea Ray. He took several breaths and then dove forward, feeling his way along the side of the boat in front, until he had made his way close to its center. He reached his left arm upward along the curved side until he had it by the gunwale, leaving his right arm free to reach inside the netting at his side. He withdrew a weighted throwing knife, balanced perfectly to his own style of toss. As he brought it close to his face, he felt a brief pang of nausea, as he contemplated his next action. He would have to immobilize one of them; he couldn't risk them teaming against him. Another death? Would they ever stop? He remembered his father's assassination and his hesitation ceased. In one quick motion he pulled himself upward with his left arm and swung his right hand forward. The knife left his hand like a missile. The butt struck the base of the skull of the rowing man with a distinct *thunk*. The man crumpled unconsciously to the floor of the boat. With the same upward thrust Trance pulled himself over the side until he stood in the center of the boat, all before the bowman knew what was happening. He launched himself forward, catching the startled man with a swift kick to the face. The man staggered. That was all the advantage Trance needed. Before the man could react, Trance stripped him of his gun and pressed its barrel hard against his throat.

"I want to know what the hell is going on," said Trance, spitting the words through gritted teeth. The man choked, shaking his head violently against Trance's grip, clawing at him with his hands.

Trance let him go. The man turned, and this time Trance kicked him in the groin. The man buckled over and spewed vomit on the seats of the bow.

"My friend, Murph, won't appreciate having that in his boat," said Trance quietly. "You've got ten seconds to tell me who the hell you are."

"CIA."

"What?" said Trance. Not his own people?

"Miller sent us here to protect you."

"Oh, shit...What are you guys, trainees or something? Is he only sending out the puppy squad?" *How many questions should I ask him?* he thought. *What can I believe?* He followed his gut. "What are your op orders?"

"Our orders were to keep you under surveillance and to come to your aid if needed."

"Needed against whom?"

"I don't know, sir."

"How many more of you are there?"

"I...I don't know."

Trance's hand shot forward, ripping the man's arm and twisting it behind him. "I said how many more of you are there?"

"I said I don't know. For God's sake, I really don't know!"

Trance knew this was a judgment call. One slight pull of the arm and it would snap. Was the man telling the truth?

"Guess," he said.

"We're to radio in at any sign of trouble."

"How long have you been here?"

"Two days."

"If I leave?"

"We're to call in and follow you."

"What's your name, soldier?"

"Jeffrey Beaman, sir."

"Welcome to war, Jeffrey Beaman. I'm going to release your arm now. I believe you, so I won't break it. If you are a good boy I'm going to let you live.

Your first screw-up will be your last. Understood?"

"Yes...sir."

Jesus H. Christ. The goddamn CIA. They have me attacking our own men. Oh, God. When will this stop? He let go of Beaman's arm and said, "Okay, Jeff. Keep those arms above your head, will you?" Jeff raised his arms while Trance pulled his knife from the floor of the boat. He used it to cut a piece of rope from the tie line of Murphy's boat. He nodded toward the unconscious man.

"Gag him and tie him up. Damn lucky I didn't choose to kill him. He'll wake by morning." Trance nodded again toward the unconscious man. "I'm sorry about this. Didn't Miller tell you that my standing orders are to kill at the first sign of danger?"

Beaman looked at him blankly.

"That sonofabitch." Trance looked to the nearly dead man. "What's this soldier's name?"

"Atkins, sir."

"When this is over, you tell him he owes me one, ya hear?"

"Sir! Yes, sir!"

Trance looked at Atkins for several moments, saying nothing. Then he turned to Beaman and asked, "Why didn't Miller have you contact me?"

"Don't know, sir."

"You're a barrel of information."

"They didn't tell us much, sir."

"I bet he's got crew all over New England right now...shooting in the dark for where I'll show up. How are you making contact?"

"Telephone."

"Give it to me."

"Public telephone, sir."

"Public telephone?"

"All in all, we felt it would be best. Rather than risk being monitored on an open channel."

"What about a parallel tap?"

Beaman looked at Atkins's inert body. "The man you almost killed is a communications expert. Everything was worked out in advance."

"How long ago did you tell them that I had arrived?"

"We didn't, sir. By the time we detected you, you were on your way out here. Our primary directive was surveillance...and protection."

"When is your next scheduled contact?"

"O seven hundred, unless you move first."

"Do you know who I am, Jeff?"

"Of course...You're sort of a legend...sir."

"Remember this, Jeff. Legends don't die easily. I'm going to see to that. Give me your hands." Trance tied Beaman's arms behind him with the rope—in a way that if he pulled at them, the knots would grow tighter. "Sorry about having to do this, but I'm sure you understand."

"What's next, sir? Are you going to kill me?"

Trance flashed a brief grin and pointed toward the small dinghy. "Into the skiff. We're going back to my boat. I haven't finished."

"If I may ask, sir, what is it you're doing?" asked Beaman. Trance answered by staring into his face. The less this man knew the better off he was.

Trance tossed Murphy's anchor overboard, then guided Beaman into the motored skiff. He rowed it the short distance to his own sailboat. He stretched a handkerchief across Beaman's mouth, blindfolded him, and tethered his arms to his boat. Satisfied that he would be no problem, he retrieved the metal box from the ocean floor.

Trance took Beaman and Atkins back to the entrance of his driveway in the Blazer. He carried Atkins and guided Beaman on foot through the woods. Trance repeated his elaborate security procedures. Satisfied again that no one had invaded the house, he led Beaman inside, sat him in the kitchen, then dropped Atkins to the floor.

"I'm going to remove your gag now. But I warn you, the first warning cry you make is the last time your tongue will work. Understand?" Beaman nodded calmly, but his eyes darted around bulging sockets underneath the blindfold.

As Trance removed the cloth he said, "Are you hungry, Jeff?"

Beaman said nothing.

"I'm going to heat up some rice, shrimp and tea. Want some?" Trance spoke like he were entertaining—his conversation light.

Beaman nodded.

Trance continued like he was speaking to a friend. "There were ways that my father and I were different. But there were a number in which we were the same. One of them was food. Americans eat too much fat, too much red meat. Don't get me wrong. I mean, I like a good steak, and I love cheeseburgers...hot dogs at the ballpark. But all the fried food...the Atkins thing...can't be all that healthy, can it?"

Trance walked toward the dining area of the spacious kitchen.

"You just make yourself as comfortable as you can for a spell. I have a few things to do before I remove your shades and bring the food. We'll talk then."

Trance turned his attention to the metal box. It looked like an oversized cookie tin and it was strapped with two small chains and welded shut. He cut the chains easily. As he held the box in his hands he could feel something heavy inside, something that seemed to roll from side to side. Trance jimmied at the edges with a hunting knife. As the container split open it took only a second to realize that it had become filled with water in the years it was lying in the mud. He looked more closely at the tin box. There was a small pinhole in the bottom. The weight of the mooring must have pushed something through it.

Inside the box he found several large ordinary Tupperware containers. Inside each container he could see two plastic bags, one inside the other. Trance smiled. There had been ways in which his father was tediously meticulous, and there had been others where he seemed inordinately careless. Perhaps that's what came of letting the dice rule your actions. The contents of two containers appeared undamaged. The other was filled with seawater, as were the two bags inside it.

"Shit," he muttered.

Trance carefully lifted the innermost wet bag, looking through to the wad of paper inside it. Whatever it had been, it was ruined. He opened the bag and briefly considered drying the contents, hoping that some of the words may be legible inside the wad. But the thing was in shreds, except for one small corner. The only letters he could hope to discern were smeared lines that looked like the letters *i* and *l*, followed by the word *tank*.

Inside the next bag he found a stack of what looked to be financial documents. They were written in German, with an elaborate coat of arms imprinted upon the papers, which read *von Hoffenburg* across the top.

The third contained a tattered old book that crackled as he opened it. The book was written in some language he didn't recognize, perhaps some derivative of Latin, English, Greek and German. It was also laced with many strange looking symbols.

It appeared that the sea had destroyed his instructions. All he had were documents and a book. Had his father's plan been ruined by a pinprick?

Why were these documents too hot for his father to share? Could these old papers really shake the world? He wondered how. He shook his head ruefully and said, "Fate...Of all the things to have to fight, I have to fight fate."

Trance could hear the voice of his father saying, "I don't know whether it is good or bad that the instructions were lost. All I know is that they were lost...except for one word and two letters..."

Could it possibly be that this isn't bad news? thought Trance. At least he knew where to start looking, Austria, where his father had been murdered. Perhaps von Hoffenburg held the answers.

"Jeff," he said. "What words would you use before the word tank?"

"I'm sorry. What'd you say?"

"What single words would you use before the word tank?"

"You mean like gas tank?"

"Yeah."

"Gas tank...scuba tank...fish tank...German tank...water tank...storage tank...oil tank—"

"Thanks. That's enough for now." Oil tank. It was worth a try.

The first yawn of dawn was stretching over the eastern sky when the front door to the estate clicked open. A pair of watchful eyes was followed by Trance's weary frame. He had spent the past ninety minutes dismantling the twin two hundred gallon oil tanks in the basement. He had poked and prodded inside them and found nothing. Frustrated, he had siphoned the oil from one to the other. After a thorough search had revealed nothing more in the first tank, he had repeated the process with the second. Nothing again.

There was another set of oil tanks buried beneath the front of the home. These had been used in the first years after the estate had been built. But their use had been discontinued in later years when several neighbors had found their artesian wells fouled by leakage from their underground tanks. Many of the town's water wells were drilled deep in the ground, with the base of the water pipes set into underground rock foundations. No one had thought that oil tanks so close to the surface would ultimately rust and leak, and that oil could seep downwards and settle upon the rock ledges at the base of a well.

The Trance's well had never soiled. But after his retirement from the Army, John Trance had made many changes on the estate. He had built the pool and the tennis court. He had replaced the underground tanks, retiring them with an elaborate ceremony—passing from the old to the new. The ceremony had seemed odd at the time, but then Trance had never fully understood his father.

Had his father's odd ceremony been designed as an event to be remembered by him? The mooring...they had put the new mooring in during that same week, he was sure. The anger. Was his anger contrived as well?

Trance took a shovel and dug through the two feet of rocky soil above the rusted metal frame that sheltered the old oil tanks. The steel crumbled as he ground the shovel in with his boot. Within minutes he was able to clear a space above the trap door that opened to the tanks.

Trance retrieved a crusted twelve-foot measuring stick from the basement, a long piece of tar-blackened pine that had been marked for measuring the oil level in their tanks. He carried it over his shoulder to the twin pipes sticking up through the casing, pipes used to fill each tank. He opened the cover clasp to one of the pipes and thrust the pole to the bottom. The pole sank nine feet, and when Trance removed it, he could see that there were still ten gallons of oil inside. Why would they have left oil in the tank? he wondered. He did the same with the second tank. This time the pole would dip no more than five feet in. Something was blocking the way.

Trance took a flashlight and tried to peer through the small hole of the pipe. He saw nothing but blackness. He sat back on his haunches, rocking backwards and forwards as he pondered his next move. Should he take the time? He had already found what he had come for, or had he?

Trance gave a tentative tap with his shovel to the top of the tank. The tank had rusted heavily, and he figured that with a little effort he would be able to split it open. He stood up and walked to the garage, grabbing a fire extinguisher and a long-handled axe, sharpened to an edge thin enough for shaving. After clearing enough space to swing, he began to chop into the tank, ripping long tears in the softened steel until he had opened a hole a foot and a half wide. He shined his light again, and this time he could see that there was a thick sheet of oil-stained canvas covering something underneath. He reached down to remove the cloth. As he pulled it toward him, there was a brief, sharp reflection from the flashlight as the beam bounced off of something. Something with a rich golden color.

Trance pushed off the canvas with his pole and aimed the light back into the tank. He peered forward, not knowing what to make of what he saw. He glanced around him, checking for anyone who may be watching. Then he looked back into the hole, and stared. Passing from the old to the new, his father had said...*I wonder*...he thought. The tank was stacked with metal bars.

Trance took the axe and used it to peel back enough of the tank to allow his body to snake through. He tied his feet with a rope and attached it to a nearby water faucet, then lowered himself headfirst into the hole. He grabbed at one of the metal bars. It was far heavier than he had imagined, and it took considerable effort, in his awkward position, to pull himself and the bar back out of the hole. When he had done so, he sat back into the grass, staring at the twenty-pound bar of golden metal in his hand. He wiped it clean and bit into it. It gave against his teeth. Gold. Pure gold.

There were thirty-six bars in the tank. Seven hundred and twenty pounds, eleven thousand five hundred ounces, give or take a few. It was all worth millions. Just how many would depend upon the purity and the London gold fixings at the time of sale. He could smuggle it into India and get twice the price. But why take the risk? As he removed the final bar, he found a note inside a plastic bag attached to the bottom. It read, *Did you ever wonder why I didn't seem to age in my later years? It works, Jackie. I never used it for personal gain, as I was chosen only as the keeper. It is now your turn, as I always knew it would be. I left you this to help you stop them. Do not forget that he who lives by the sword, dies by the sword. Perhaps this challenge will help you under-*

stand that there is so much we cannot know or control. We are like ants cross-ing the floor, not aware that we are part of a world far greater than what we perceive. Give yourself up to the Cosmic Will and you will know what it is you must do. Please give my regards to the Black Madonna, and to our friend in Austria.

Remember that I am with you, always.

Dad

Trance glanced at his watch. 6:20. Forty minutes until Jeff must make his call to Miller. He'd have to move fast. He ran up the road, taking the chance that he was not being watched. He got into Lauren's Lincoln, which hadn't been moved. He drove it back down the driveway and through the gates to the estate, to where millions in gold lay openly on his front lawn. He loaded it into the trunk of the car and covered it with a blanket. He then went into the house, checked both prisoners, and then untied Beaman.

"C'mon. We're going to town to make your morning call." Beaman still wore the blindfold, and walked awkwardly with his hands tied behind his back.

"I'll untie you and let you see some light as soon as we're off the estate."

"What was all that noise before?"

"Beaman, the less you know the better off you are. I'm going to give you and your friend the chance to live. God knows, you don't deserve to die. You keep your questions to yourself and do what you are told. In another day you'll be just fine. Got that? Your partner should be okay. I'm sorry about him. Miller's a stupid shit—sending you out like that after me. He should know better."

"What should I say to Miller?"

"Tell him you haven't seen me." What Trance wanted to say was, "Tell him to lay off… Tell him I haven't trusted him since he sent my wife to die..."

Trance's thoughts caught in his throat. How could Miller have done that to his wife? His hands squeezed the wheel and his knuckles grew white.

As they drove, Trance's father's note twisted over and over in his head. The Black Madonna? What the hell was a Black Madonna? Our friend in Austria? Was von Hoffenburg a friend? Or was he the enemy? Who should he trust, and what should he do next? They made the call.

Later, Trance gave Beaman and Atkins a full meal. He let them use the bath-room. Then he left them sitting, tied to chairs in his living room in front of an impressive voice controlled home theater, with glasses of water with straws nearby. He wrote a short note and folded it into an envelope. Then he took a wireless phone and placed it before the men.

"I'll call Miller in six hours, so they'll come for you soon. In the event that something happens to me, I've also programmed this phone to activate in seven hours. Just say *dial* and then the number and you'll get through. Say *end call* when you're done, so you don't ring up my phone bill. The home theater activates with the words, system on."

Behind Trance, the wide digital screen sprang to life, showing ESPN.

"There's a Red Sox game this afternoon on NESN," whispered Trance, so the TV wouldn't change. "Just say the channel name and it will change." Trance paused. "Sorry for the indignity of all of this, guys. If I had more time I would make this easier for you. If something happens to me and I can't call, and if the phone doesn't work, they will come when Miller gets this letter. I'll post it on my way out of town. So, rest easy. Make yourself at home once you're released. There's beer in the fridge and food in the cupboard. Just clean up after yourselves and lock the door when you leave."

Trance closed the door behind him, got into Lauren's Lincoln, and headed back toward Boston.

"Good morning. Lauren Haverford's office. May I help you?"

"Hi, Shirley. It's Jack. Is Lauren there?"

"Oh, hi, Jack. She had to go to Washington for a few days. May I leave her a message?"

"A message...no...no, thank you." Trance hung up the phone. Who could he call? He needed someone to go over the financial reports he had found, someone who could tell him what the hell they meant, someone he could trust. He also needed someone to explain the obscure little book. He needed more information, and he needed it fast. He needed it now. He dialed another number.

"Harris Investment Group. May I help you?"

"Bill Harris, Jr., please." Bill Harris would know. Trance had studied with Bill at Harvard Law. Bill was the scion to the sprawling Harris family fortune. The family had begun manufacturing cannons and muskets during the Revolutionary War, and had parlayed that business into an empire that stretched into banking, real estate, insurance, and investments. Trance and Harris had become close friends during their three years studying law, and he was the next logical choice for Trance to call for guidance on the von Hoffenburg papers.

"Hey, Jack. How goes the indecent exploitation of innocents in the adult toy business?" Harris was savvy enough to beware of others listening to their conversation.

Bill Harris was short and solid like a wrestler. When he moved it was with a gentle demeanor, but when he spoke it was in the same booming voice of his iconic father.

"Outstanding. How goes the pillaging of helpless victims in the world of finance?"

"Good...good. Still making a fortune. Just can't help it, Jack. It's in the genes."

"Bill, I need a favor."

"Sure. Anything for one of America's finest."

"I need to see you. As soon as possible. Like now."

"You in town?"

"I'm a block away."

"Using a disposable, encrypted burner phone no doubt. Or are you over with that cute little vixen at Global Credit?" He chuckled. "C'mon by, ol' buddy. I can juggle my schedule."

Five minutes later the two men were meeting over coffee in the confines of Harris's plush corner office, in the Harris Towers, overlooking Boston harbor.

"I need you to tell me what these figures mean, Bill."

Trance passed the von Hoffenburg papers to his friend. Bill took them and ran his eyes down the first page. Trance watched him closely, noticing the slight raise of the eyebrows, then a frown as Harris turned to the second page. For ten minutes neither man spoke. Bill's eyes never left the papers in front of him. Finally he said, "Holy shit, Jack. Where did you get these?"

"Does it matter?"

"Sure as hell does. I know that these documents must be over fifty years old...companies change...ownerships changes...but do you realize what we are looking at here?"

"Haven't really looked at them, Bill. They just sort of fell into my possession."

"Papers like these just don't *fall* into someone's possession, Jack. These documents link von Hoffenburg to the financing of Hitler during World War II. But, even more than that, do you have any idea what these companies are doing today?"

"Well, I thought that since you have been running your daddy's investment firm, you might be able to give me a little help there, Billy."

"You stole this stuff, didn't you, Jack? This is some kind of CIA shit. Papers like these don't exist. Do you understand that? Not if these are real. These documents link some of the world's largest corporations, and a dozen of the world's wealthiest families together in a crime so heinous...But Jesus, Jack...Do you *know* what some of these companies are doing today?

"Look at this. This company reprocesses half of the spent nuclear fuel in Europe. This one makes missiles...this one, fighter jets. These three produce half the gold in the Southern Hemisphere, for Christ's sake. Then there's banking...finance...media...computers...software."

"So, what does it all mean?"

"Can I make some copies of these? I'm going to have to do some checking before I answer that question. These papers could probably blow the whole frigging financial world apart. That's what I think they mean…the anti-trust issues, the national security threat—"

"No copies, Bill. For your own sake. Take a few notes, but no copies."

Bill began scribbling information. Thirty minutes later he was escorting Trance to the door.

"You sure you can't stay for lunch? You look like hell. A good meal—"

"No, Bill. Thanks. I've got someone else to see. When should I call you?"

"Call me first thing in the morning. I'll have something for you then." Bill grabbed at Trance's shoulder as he turned to leave, and said, "Is everything okay, Jack? I get the feeling that you're into something over your head, and that's deep, way deep. Take it from a lawyer who's been trained to—"

"No, Henny Penny, the sky isn't falling. I'll talk to you in the morning."

"Later, Jack."

Trance drove a few blocks and checked into the Langham Hotel, leaving Lauren's car parked safely in the garage under Post Office Square. He was on his second day without sleep and he had no stomach for traffic congestion. He also didn't want to take the chance of an accident that might reveal seven hundred pounds of unexplained gold resting comfortably in the car's trunk. He made one phone call before heading to the hotel lobby.

He walked out onto Congress Street and hailed a taxi, then settled tiredly into the back seat, saying, "Harvard Square, please." Then he closed his eyes to collect his thoughts. With fatigue he had grown careless. He didn't see the car pull out behind them, the car that followed them across the lazy Charles River and into Cambridge.

Trance had one more stop to make before he could slow down long enough to rest. Sir Godfrey Hind, professor of history at Harvard College. Formerly of Oxford, Hind's specialties were medieval European and Oriental history. Trance had met Hind by accident while studying at Harvard. It had been at one of the cocktail parties designed to mingle the students and normally reclusive faculty. Left alone, many of the big name professors would go for months immersed in research, without student contact whatsoever. This was one of Harvard's answers to the criticisms that its true faculty consisted of graduate students.

Hind had been fascinated to learn of Trance's education in Japan, what little of it Trance had been willing and able to share with him. Trance had given Hind a glimpse into a world that few Westerners would ever see, one that many would never believe could exist.

The taxi left Trance at The Square. He glanced up to read the Dewey, Cheetham & Howe lettering in a second-story office window, and wondered what arcane and flippant topics they might be discussing now on Car Talk radio. There was still a half hour to kill and Trance felt that a nostalgic walk through the quads might do him good. He walked past the John Harvard statue and then the library on his roundabout way to Quincy Street and Robinson Hall. He didn't notice the two men following him at a discreet distance. As he opened the door to Hind's building, he missed the distant pairs of eyes that made notice of his entrance.

Hind was a stout, portly man in his middle seventies. His head was bald except for a few wisps of hair along the edges just above his ears. His eyebrows were his most prominent feature—huge, white bushes. They dominated his face, and they moved with animation as he spoke with his laconic British accent.

"Trance ol' boy. So nice of you to drop by. May I offer you some tea, or perhaps some cognac?"

"Tea would be fine, Professor."

"Ah...well...I'll have to make some up. Though I think I might have a touch of brandy within reach." Hind looked toward Trance expectantly.

"Tell you what, Professor. Pour us a couple of stiff ones, will you?"

"Gladly, my boy!" Hind's face spread into a wide grin, happy for the implied acceptance of his nipping before evening. "Nothing like a little lubrication for the mind. Now, what's this you tell me about some old book?" said Hind as he handed Trance a large snifter well primed with V.S.O.P. cognac.

"Here." Trance withdrew the thin, red leather-covered book from the blue gym bag and handed it to the curious professor. He then sat quietly as Hind opened it and began reading its contents.

"This looks like an alchemist's notebook, Jack. See all these symbols? This one stands for the moon, this one for the Sun...Mercury...Venus. From the looks of the Latin and the symbols, I'd say that this is from the eleventh, twelfth century. Although I'd guess that the binding wasn't done 'till the seventeenth, eighteenth century. See these marks here..."

"Excuse me for interrupting, Professor. Could this notebook represent the notes of someone turning something into gold?"

"I wouldn't say that at all, Jack. I said that this is an alchemist's notebook. They always wrote in code, although this one seems to be a bit more straightforward than most, if one understands the ancient languages, of course. Did you know that this is a hobby of mine?"

"I was hoping—"

"Oh, yes. I've studied all of the great alchemists," He took a sip of his drink. "Ripley, Philalethes, Aquinas, Bacon, Pope John XXII, DaVinci. I've read much of their writings, most of it gibberish. In fact, the word gibberish comes from the great alchemist Geber. His writings were so difficult to follow that the word gibberish was created— "

"I'm sorry, professor, excuse me for asking again, but would you say that this book could possibly contain a method for the transformation of certain substances into gold?"

"Let me take a look." Hind began thumbing through the pages. Now and then he scribbled a word or two on the note pad on his desk. He would alternately shake his head and say "Hmmn" or "I see..." As he continued through the notebook he began turning the pages faster. Neither man spoke for over an hour, until Hind said, "Yes, Jack. It implies here that the process described does indeed result in gold. Of course, most of them do. But this one appears to be an approach that is far different than other ones I have read...I'm sorry to say this, though, but the last few pages seem to be missing."

Trance was lost in thought and did not hear the professor's words.

"I said the last few pages are missing," repeated Hind.

"Oh, how wonderful." Trance hesitated. "But what I need to know is...could this thing be valid? I mean—"

"Jack. Come on now. You and I are intelligent men, educated men. There has never been any proof that this has been done. Rumors...legends, but no proof."

"But you say it's been a hobby of yours."

"Yes, but the hobby of studying alchemy encompasses far more than the manufacture of gold, Jack. It's a religion of sorts, a way of life, a way of thinking. The study of alchemy has influenced today's life far more than you can imagine."

"Oh, I know, professor. Remember, I am my father's son. I know a bit about the theology of alchemy. But you do believe it may have been done, don't you?" said Trance. *You've got to humor him, Jack.*

Hind sat back in his chair, causing his rather ample stomach to protrude outward. He then let it fall comfortably upon his tightened belt.

"Did I ever tell you that Carl Jung and I were good friends?"

"No, you didn't. He shared your interest in alchemy?" said Trance.

"Carl believed that modern man has become too technologically oriented, too intellectual, and that many of the psychological problems his patient's developed resulted from the western culture's preoccupation with intellectual thought at the expense of emotional growth."

"In Japan I was taught that the higher self is the emotional self, not the intellectual self. I was taught that the emotional self is much more in tune with the creative, universal force, and that the intellect tries to dominate the emotional side, thereby putting us in direct conflict with our true direction."

"Exactly! Has this worked for you?"

"I'm afraid that I haven't been very good at following what I was taught. I find it hard to subjugate my sense of self, what Jung might have called my ego, to something that to me resembles chance as much as some kind of *Cosmic Will*. I'm afraid that I have never been able to give up control. My father did. But I can't."

"Are you happy?"

"It has nothing to do with happiness."

"I said, are you happy?"

"I...don't...know."

"Was your father happy?"

"That's not a fair question. His life was different."

"I said, was he happy?"

"Yes."

"So, there you are. That's all I can tell you today." Hind drained his glass with one large gulp. "But if you wouldn't mind, I'd like to study this for a few months."

"What? No. I can't let you do that."

Hind fingered the book longingly. "There *are* a few things I'd like to check. I'll copy some pages, and run a few calculations on the computer. Why don't you call me in the morning?"

Trance nodded, and allowed the professor to copy several pages from the odd little book. As Hind turned to one of the book's pages he frowned. "That's strange." He walked to his computer and started his Internet browser. After a few minutes he clapped his hands. "Aha!" He bellowed. "I knew it!"

Hind rotated the flat screen monitor so that Trance to view it.

"See that symbol?"

Trance nodded.

"That is a registered genome symbol."

"What does that mean?" asked Trance.

"Let's say that that I'm working on genetic research, working on stem cells, for example. If I start a new stem cell chain I would register it—with a symbol—a symbol like this." Hind pointed to the notebook. He clapped his hands again. "This is interesting...very interesting."

Hind stood up abruptly and reached out to shake Trance's hand, smiling broadly. "This is extraordinary, son. This may be—" He looked to the copied pages. "Call me tomorrow. I have much to do."

Trance took the notebook and put it back inside his gym bag. "Thank you, Professor. I'll call you in the morning."

Trance took a taxi back into the heart of Boston's financial district. He got out on High Street near International Place. He needed to walk for a while as he tried to comprehend the power of the information he now controlled. A formula, or at least most of a formula that would allow him to make gold? His father said that it worked. That must have been why he had spent so much time in Maine when he first retired from the service. Where were the missing pages? Or did they matter? Jesus, with a formula to make gold, he could debase the world's financial structure. He could easily wreak havoc with the money markets, and society, too. Entire cultures were based upon gold, and with an unlimited source of money, he could do almost anything.

Then there were the financial documents. What was it Bill had said? They could *rip the whole frigging financial world apart...*

If only it were that simple.

Trance meandered through Boston Common and into the Back Bay. He walked for hours. He always liked Boston, the blend between the old and the new. Skyscrapers of glinting glass casting shadows upon monuments to the past. The cobblestone streets, the narrow brick buildings standing side by side, the churches, and shops dating back to the Revolutionary War. As he bought a hot pretzel from one of the street vendors, Trance caught a sideways glance from a face that looked familiar. Where had he seen that face before? Friend or foe? It was the sunglasses that tipped him off. The Bosch and Lomb frames. It was one of the men from the BMW. Now where was the other, and how many other men were there? Were they just following? Or was he now a marked man? He had found the gold, the formula, and the financial documents. Is that what they were waiting for? Trance pondered what to do. Out of the blue he laughed, as he thought of what his father would have done. His father would have started flipping his coin. But Trance had no time to flip a coin. He had to think fast, and he had to act fast. Because each moment he waited could bring him that much closer to death.

CHAPTER 4

▼

A thick, white mist was spinning in and about the mountains as the final faint rays of sunlight stretched over the rippled horizon. The fog brought a sudden chill to the Austrian night. As the air and the mountains turned black, the Baron prepared to begin his meeting inside the castle.

Outside, the broad courtyard buzzed with the arriving helicopters—carrying many of the world's most powerful men and women to rendezvous with their leader. Each of them bore the crest of von Hoffenburg on its side, a screaming Bald Eagle carrying the world in its talons. One by one they emerged, influential politicians, industrialists, revolutionaries, and soldiers from dozens of nations around the globe. They had nothing in common except blood, and one common purpose. These were all von Hoffenburgs by birth and spirit, though they were known by many other names. Together they planned to rule the world.

von Hoffenburg stood on his balcony, watching the scene below. This was truly the beginning of the end he had planned, so many centuries before. He closed his eyes and turned his weathered face toward the skies. How many hundreds of years had he sent his children out into the world to colonize and dominate nations? He had sent them to India, China, and Japan during the twelfth century. He had helped seed the Mongol Empire in the years it had swept through Persia. In the fourteen hundreds he had controlled the Holy Roman Empire through Maximilian I. His children had been early settlers of North and South America, taking new names that fit the land, but bringing riches with them from the Baron's gold. They had helped shape these continents. Now, the Baron was preparing his most ambitious attempt at bringing it all under one rule, his own.

The world had grown smaller with the advent of global communications. Satellites could bounce his orders in seconds, where it had once taken him months, even years, to issue them by ship and caravan. He could bring about more destruction in minutes than the world had endured in its entire history.

Where it had taken him hundreds of years to create his first empire, his last would take only hours.

More than a millennium in the making, fifty years in the final planning, and over a trillion dollars invested, the time was drawing near. Now only two things remained to be done. First, he must recover his formula. It was his prize possession, and the world meant nothing to him without it. Now that John Trance was dead, it would be only a matter of days before he would possess it again. Without the Elixir he would die, and the Baron's quest would die with him.

There was no second copy of the formula. It was a possession too precious to duplicate. He'd kept it too heavily guarded to be stolen. Yet, stolen it was; but he would soon have it again.

With the formula back in his hands, only one more piece of the puzzle must fall into place. Then all could proceed. Just one more piece.

"Everyone has arrived, my Lord."

"The Chosen One?"

"He, too, is here."

"Good...good." The Baron moved to his library and warmed his leathery hands by a brightly burning fire set back against the far wall. Above the polished marble mantel hung portraits of the Khan, Maximilian, Napoleon, and Hitler. Soon a new face would be placed among them.

"Send him in," continued the Baron. He pressed his hands closer to the fire. There was nothing worse than a cold handshake, he mused.

As the sleek, finely dressed man entered the chamber, the Baron looked upon him with pride. How handsome he is, how confident his walk, how sincere his smile. The face, so much like his own, aristocratic, with the signs of breeding written all over its tanned features.

"My son," he said as the Chosen One approached him, smiling. "So nice of you to honor an old man with your presence..."

The visitor chuckled, "Of course, Father. So nice of you to invite me. May I ask the purpose of the invitation?"

"To announce your appointment."

"So, the decision has been made?" asked the visitor quietly.

"You have done well."

"But so have the others."

"Ah, but you are the best."

"Was Hitler better than Penwell? You chose an unstable unknown over a man with influence, and a political future."

"They were both of my loins, but Adolph had fire, my son, raw driving ambition. Much like yourself. The Germans were ready and able to do our work. Just like the leaders of your country are today."

"Will I become another Hitler?"

"No. Hitler was a failure. You will not fail. You cannot fail." The Baron threw a thick log onto the fire. "You will direct the world's policy. You will have the cooperation of your brothers. I already control the United Nations."

The Baron pressed his hands one final time against the fire, turned, and led his visitor out of the room. They walked in silence through the drafty hallways. Along the walls stared dozens of faces, men who had altered the course of the world through the ages, all von Hoffenburgs. It was a gallery, a tribute to the endless quest of the Baron, a quest that, until now, had remained unfulfilled. But soon he would complete his dream. With this man by his side, and with the dozens of others, they would make it possible.

As the two men entered the great central chamber of the castle, a hush fell over the room. It was apparent. The decision had been made. The words spread in quiet whispers from man to woman to man. A wise choice...

"My children," the Baron began. He addressed all of the family members as his children. Many present were indeed his own, but others were grandchildren, great grandchildren. Some traced their roots back more than forty generations.

"Every one of you here has passed severe tests of loyalty to reach this, the inner core of our family power. I congratulate you all. You will not be disappointed. Soon we will be standing upon the threshold of a new world government. A government run by you in the name of von Hoffenburg. The world's three major powers will soon be destroyed through mutual nuclear annihilation. As you know, we have been planning this event for decades, and every small detail has been studied and put into place. All except for the triggering events, which shall commence in just a few short months. With the devastation of America, Russia and China, we will be left with the world's greatest military arsenal. Combined with the political and economic influence that you represent, it will be but a small step to coalesce the few parts of the world we do not already control into our firm command. No one will challenge our solution for avoiding total global annihilation."

Each of the people standing below the Baron felt his power pumping through them as he spoke. Each felt the tingle of excitement as he outlined the details of his plan. Their emotions rose and fell with the volume of his voice, and he played them like a concert musician, his talent honed through centuries of practice. He was Bach, Beethoven, and Mozart combined. His creative genius was not flawed by any clinging to convention. He was a man of vision, and his words reached out and moved them like no others had done before. He teased them with softness, and then swept their emotions upward with a flurry of words and hypnotic movements. He was Orpheus come to life.

"In the campaigns of Bonaparte and Hitler we were forced to stretch beyond the capacity of our resources. This time it will not happen. The world is different now, smaller. There will be no Waterloo, no Russian front. There will be no Russians fighting us at all!

"The road to power hasn't changed. Our weapons may be different now, but the mind is not. Economic destruction, emotional disenchantment, religious differences...greed, hate, power, love...All still play their part.

"Each of you knows what it is that you must do. You have all been trained since birth, and the world will no longer deny you your true position in life! Each of you shall rule, with more power than you ever dreamed possible. I bid you now to go forth and await my call. Our time is near!"

CHAPTER 5

▼

"Hello," whispered Trance as he walked along Commonwealth Avenue. He was being followed, and one pursuer was making no attempt at concealment. He followed Trance from a distance of thirty yards, never taking his eyes off his quarry.

Why in hell would a tail allow himself to be so conspicuous? wondered Trance. They must want him to know he was being followed. Was he being team tailed? How many more were in his wake?

These people were professionals. They were forcing his hand. He would need a team. That much was plain. Unless, unless there was only one of them. If there was just one, he could isolate and interrogate. If so, he would have to do it soon. He could *feel* the eyes of his tail upon him. Any moment those eyes could become the barrel of a rifle.

Trance looked for a public phone, stopping periodically to glance at the faces around him in the hope of spotting other pursuers. He couldn't run the risk of using a wireless, even one that was encrypted and routed through his own network. The chances were too great that they could listen in. He crossed over to Newbury Street and walked by the shop windows, glancing at the reflections to see who was around him. Too many people stood at the phones at the corner of Newbury and Dartmouth Streets. He crossed up Exeter Street and took a right onto Boylston. He'd use one in the mall.

Trance entered the Prudential Center Mall on Boylston Street and took the escalator up toward the shops. He checked the directory and located a phone bank. Moments later he lifted a receiver and dialed the number of an old friend, and former CIA operative. His friend was a financial advisor, offering insurance and investment services to the wealthy throughout the Boston area.

"Good afternoon, Capital Resources Group."

"Roger Angleton, please." Trance kept his eyes moving through the crowd.

"I'm sorry. But Mr. Angleton is out on an appointment at the—"

"I've got to talk to him. It's urgent. Can you contact him?"

"I could call him—"

"Please do so. Tell him Jack Trance needs him to call 617-555-0879 immediately. I'm at a pay phone. I'll wait." Trance hung up the phone. Two minutes later the phone rang.

"Jack?"

"Roger. I need your help."

"Aw, shit, Jack. I'm in the middle of an appointment with an important client." So much for friendship.

"Fee or commission?"

"What?"

"I said `Is it a fee case or a commission case'?"

"The latter."

"So what's the commission?"

"Oh, I don't know. Five grand, maybe—"

"I'll pay you twenty for two hours of your time. Then I'll throw in a private dinner at the Algonquin Club for you and your client. Hell, include your spouses. I need you to reschedule your meeting…Please?"

Roger was the best person for the job. He was experienced, and they looked almost alike.

"Jack, you don't need to pay—"

"Look, Roger. I don't give a shit about the money. I need your help and I need it now. God knows I've saved your ass a number of times."

Roger grew more attentive.

"Yes, Jack. You have. What d'ya need me to do?"

"Where are you?"

"Downtown."

"Good. I want you to take a taxi to the front of the Hancock Building in exactly one hour. Only I want you to be hidden. Down in the seat, Roger."

"Shit, Jack. Not—"

"Pay the driver a hundred. I'll reimburse you. Tell him to look for a man wearing tan khaki pants and a blue shirt, carrying a newspaper in each hand. Have him stop, and I'll get in." Trance set the timer on his watch. He knew that Angleton was now doing the same, because he had trained him. "Mark the time."

"Go," said Roger. "Who's following you?" he continued tentatively, wishing that he had said he couldn't make the pickup. He was out of the spy business. He no longer got his jollies risking his life against phantom enemies.

"One man. Not dangerous, I think. But I need to make sure. Not to worry, Roger. You're safe. Questions?"

"No."

"Good...and Roger?"

"Yeah?"

"Thanks."

Roger laughed and replied, "You're a shithead, Trance."

With that problem out of the way, Trance could concentrate upon cornering the man on his trail. He'd have to hope that others didn't rush to the man's aid or put a bullet through his head. Trance drew a mental map of the city, thinking of the most likely place to confront his pursuer. Indoors? Outdoors? The street? The mall? The park? A deserted alley off of the street? Perhaps a bar...Then he knew.

There was a church less than two blocks away in Copley Square, right by the Hancock Tower. It was an old church, and big, with dark hallways. Trinity was a major tourist attraction. He knew. He had used it before. There were several potential exits on opposite sides of the church. A solo tail would run a greater risk of losing him by remaining outside, than by following him in. There was also a basement that stretched under the building, just above the hundreds of wooden pilings that provided support to the church in the soft sand and silt of Boston's Back Bay. The cellar and its tunnels were often kept unlighted and were rarely used.

Trance climbed the steps to the church at a measured pace. He glanced at his watch; there were forty-nine minutes to go. He peered out peripherally at the people on the street. He knelt down to tie his shoe, finally locating Mr. Ray Ban attempting to look confused by the fountain, a tourist deciding which way he should turn.

Over this way, thought Trance as he turned toward the church. When Trance opened the door he stopped to allow his eyes to adjust to the dimness inside. A filtered light came through the impressive stained-glass windows along the walls. His eyes adjusted quickly. He paid to enter, then walked down the aisle toward the altar, which was adorned with several burning candles. There were a few sinners doing penance, and two small groups of tourists, but the church echoed in silence.

Trance planned to use his silhouette to draw the tail forward toward the cellar stairway. He would lead the man into the tunnels and take him there.

Trance waited. Three full minutes passed. Had they covered all his exits? Were they simply waiting for him to emerge? Or... the figure of Mr. Ray Ban emerged, now removing his glasses. Trance knelt at the far end of the church on one side of the altar. He watched through the corner of his eyes as his pursuer took a seat at the back of the church. It was time for move two. Much like chess. Perhaps more like the Japanese game of Go, which required art as well as skill. There was an art to what he was doing, an art to staying alive.

Trance made a sign of the cross and stood as if to leave. He stopped momentarily, knowing this would draw the eyes of his follower to him. Trance glanced toward the man, and he could see the round, wide eyes of fear etch the man's face in the hollow outline of the dim lights. Trance took the stairs down into the cellar, groping his way in the darkness. Would they be waiting for him in the tunnel? Was his trap now theirs?

Like his father, Trance had been born with a photographic memory. It had been five years since Trance had last used this tunnel, but even in the darkness he could recall it as if he were in daylight. Eight steps forward, two steps to the left, fourteen steps forward and he came to the stairs. He descended the nineteen stairs, scuffling slightly in his rubber-soled running shoes so Ray Ban could follow his sounds. He reached the bottom of the stairway and took three steps forward. Then he retraced his path and waited underneath the stairway for his pursuer.

The minutes passed like the slow drip of cold honey as Trance waited in silence. Were his pursuers in wireless contact? Was he trapped? Was the man getting his orders? Or was this a *rough tail*, designed to keep him under surveillance without worrying about the risk of exposure. The man would soon answer his questions. If he came. *Perhaps I should have taken him in the church?* he wondered. *No. Too much risk.* This was right. He could *feel* it.

There he is. Trance heard the man's feet coming cautiously down the stairs. This guy was an amateur, or he was very, very good. Trance counted the steps, fifteen, sixteen, nineteen...*Now!* Trance raced forward and shoved the man's face into the wall, feeling his teeth crack against the stone and his body go slack. Trance twisted the man's right arm behind his back, to the point where one light tug would break it.

"Who the hell are you?" he whispered. "Tell me why I shouldn't rip your frigging heart out." Anger was his best chance to elicit fear, thought Trance. An angry man was unpredictable. Angry men killed. He was more curious than angry.

The man grunted against the wall but gave no answer. Trance pressed his face within an inch of the man's eyes.

"Listen, asshole. You're going to start giving me answers or I'm going to begin breaking your bones, one at a time. I said who are you, and who do you work for?" No answer. *Oh shit, I hate doing this...*He pulled up on the arm. The man whimpered as it snapped at the elbow. The man bit into his free arm to stifle the pain, making several rows of teeth marks in his skin. He kept biting.

"Look," said Trance. "I don't like this any more than you. I know how this hurts. But I've got to have answers. Tell me who you are. Please." The man turned his face toward him and smiled. There was a look of raw hatred in his eyes. A moment later he lay limp in Trance's arms.

Trance pressed him once more against the wall, fearing some sort of trick, knowing the man could respond with a swift blow that could cripple him in one brief moment. The man showed no sign of resistance. Trance felt his head sag and he felt for a pulse, fearing the worst. He was right. The man was dead. He sniffed Ray Ban's mouth and smelled the almond scent of cyanide. The pill had been sewn under the skin of the man's left forearm, and in the darkness Trance had not seen the man biting it out of his flesh.

"Of all the..." The man had been no amateur. He had been a fanatic, dedicated to some obscene cause. Why else would he have chosen death so quickly? The man couldn't have been CIA. What was he after? The formula? The financial papers? Perhaps both.

"He's dead, ain't he?" came a voice from several yards down the hall. Trance fell to the floor, rolling forward as he hit the ground. A second later he pressed the speaker's face against the wall.

"Who are you?" he asked. The smell answered his question.

"I...live...sleep here," he said. The man's breath confirmed his words. The air around his face had the odor of rotten fish. He was wrapped in a torn, heavy, hooded blue jacket with the words BOSTON GLOBE written on the chest.

Trance kept his hold of the man, thinking painfully of what he should do. Had the man seen him? Could he recognize him? Could he let him live? What should he do? He knew what he would have done years before. He wouldn't have thought twice, couldn't have. But things were different now. He was different now. Wasn't he?

"That man killed himself," he said. "He took a cyanide pill."

"Uh, huh. Anything you say," spoke the rotten mouth. "I didn't see nothin'."

"I should kill you," said Trance. The old man wheezed. "But I won't. You did nothing wrong. I suggest you get out of here. After I leave, of course."

"Y...yes."

Trance released him and quickly searched the dead man's body. He found what he expected to find, nothing. Except for one thing, a thin gold chain. On the end of it swung an old pendant—of a hammer and sickle.

Trance peeled a wad of cash from his wallet and gave it to the homeless man.

A moment later Trance was gone.

He still had eighteen minutes. He walked across Copley Square and crossed the street. He bought two papers from a street vendor, and then walked back toward the church. His eyes roved along the sidewalks and the streets, looking for anything out of the ordinary, anything that might help him spot his tails. They had to be there. He knew they were. It had been years since he had taught the art of surveillance. But he could still spot them a mile away, when he wasn't preoccupied with other issues. *I'm acting like the amateur here,* he thought ruefully.

As Trance neared the church, he caught the glint of the sun on another pair of gold-framed sunglasses. He considered cornering the man in the park, but thought better of it. There would be too much disturbance, and the very real possibility of another death, this one in clear daylight. Better just to get away.

Trance walked leisurely along Boylston Street, and then meandered across the park toward the Hancock Tower. Soon a taxi swerved to his side and its door flew open. Trance jumped inside and gave a quick salute to Mr. Ray Ban as they sped away. Trance smiled as the man waved frantically for a taxi that didn't come. Trance directed the driver to the Massachusetts Turnpike, where they made several entrances and exits after they got beyond the Allston tolls. Trance memorized the types of cars and the license plate numbers around them at each stop. Finally, Trance was satisfied that they were not being followed, unless there were a dozen cars involved in the chase. At this point he would take that chance. He said to the driver, "The Langham," then turned to Roger and said, "Thanks. I'm glad I could count on you."

Roger whispered. "Shit, Sherlock. What are you going to ask me for now?"

Trance smiled and patted his friend on the shoulder. "It's good to see you, too. Just like old times, eh? Am I that easy to read?"

"Like a book. Don't forget, I know you. Christ, you trained me."

Trance winced, as he thought of the driver listening to their conversation. The less he knew the safer he would be.

"Just one more thing, Watson." Trance leaned over and whispered into Roger's ear.

When the cab reached Post Office Square, Trance had the driver pull down into the parking garage off Congress Street. He let Roger out at the bottom. Then he had the driver meander around the garage for over five minutes.

By now Roger would have found Lauren's car and be waiting for him. Trance told the driver to stop. He handed him three one hundred dollar bills and said, "Get this thing out of here, buddy. You were great. One of the best. You may not have guessed this, but you were just part of an anti-terrorism exercise. The less you say about it the better off we'll all be. Understand?" The man nodded. "Now I want you to take a leisurely drive along the Turnpike. For at least thirty minutes, out past Natick. Got that?"

The man nodded, smiling.

"Good."

As Trance closed the door the driver said, "Talley ho, Sherlock." Then began to drive away.

"I've got your cab number!" shouted Trance. Then he laughed.

Trance walked through the garage to the Lincoln, which was already running, with Roger at the wheel. He opened the driver's door, reached in and popped the trunk. He withdrew one of the gold bars and wrapped it with a towel from inside the trunk.

"Let's go," he said, as he slid in the back of the car. He lay down.

"What's that in the towel?" asked Roger, knowing that Trance may or may not choose to tell him.

"Your money," said Trance. "I'm afraid that it is a bit more than I promised. I can't make change, but I suppose you've earned it. Such short notice and all."

"What the hell are you doing? Carrying wads of bills in the trunk of this car? I want no part of this, Trance—"

"Not quite, Rog. It's gold. Twenty pound bars." Trance grew silent for a moment, watching Roger run the figures in his head. Twenty pounds was three hundred and twenty ounces. At current prices the bar was worth hundreds of thousand of dollars.

"That's a lot of money, Jack."

"Sorry. I don't have my checkbook. I'm going to be rather busy for the next few weeks. So let's not worry about it, huh?"

"You steal it?"

"Actually, Rog, that gold is legally and rightfully mine. I'm involved in something that is rather...complicated at the moment. The less you know about it, the better off you are. I suggest that you take a little vacation or something. I'll pay for it."

"What do you expect me to do with this?" He pointed toward the gold.

"Hell, Roger. I'd paint it green and use it as a doorstop."

"How about giving me another and I can use them as bookends?" Roger chuckled. "May I ask how many of these little babies you're carrying?"

"Enough," said Trance softly. *What the hell am I going to do with them? I've got to get them out of the country.*

Roger drove south on I 93 to Route 3, and headed toward Cape Cod. *Ah,* thought Trance, *what I'd give right now for a few quiet days on Nantucket.* Then he thought of Janice. She had liked the island. He had a home there now, thanks to his dead parents. *Sometimes life really sucks,* he thought.

As a teenager, Trance had learned to fly single engine planes. While at Annapolis he had become certified for twin engines, and finally for jets. In the Navy he had learned to fly helos. Flying always seemed to clear his mind. He supposed it was the freedom, or perhaps the relaxed concentration one needed in order to fly.

Trance knew most of the small airports along the southern New England coast, and he knew many of the men that ran them. Now he needed to get to Washington D C. He knew just where to go.

"Take the next right," he said to Roger as they edged toward Plymouth. Over the next few minutes Roger drove along several back streets until he stopped by a fence and a small building. Trance bounded out of the car and walked inside. If he could, he would fly from this small airport with the gold, while Roger returned to Boston with Lauren's car.

"Hey, gorgeous," he said to a plump middle-aged woman wearing thick, black feline glasses. She had a hefty double chin and it wobbled as she looked up from her desk. Peering through her myopia she made a double-take at Trance and screamed, "Jackie!"

"Hi, baby. Is Cubie around?"

"Sure. Up in the tower. But give us a kiss first." The woman looked up at Trance with a coquettish grin and offered her cheek for him to kiss. Instead, Trance wrapped his arms around her and planted one squarely upon her lips.

"Martha. When I'm around you I just lose control," he said laughing.

"I'll tell you, Jackie. If I weren't a happily married woman, I might be tempted to teach you a thing or two."

To this Jack leaned close to her ear and whispered, "I'll talk to Cubie about it. Perhaps I can get his permission."

Martha roared and shook her head. "Men. All you think about is sex. Now, get out of here. I've got an airport to run."

Cubie Drake had gone to Annapolis with Trance. They had spent hundreds of hours in the air together as Navy pilots. Drake got the Cubie handle because he was completely bald. His head looked like a cue ball, perfectly round, white and shiny. His face was also round. It looked like a moon with craters for eyes and a nose. His eyes had thin, blond eyebrows, and they emanated warmth and friendship to even the newest of strangers. When he saw Trance walk into the small control tower, he gave a shout and held up his arms.

"Well, it's about time you showed your ugly mug around here. How the hell have you been, JT?"

"Fine, Cubie. You're looking great. Martha is as sexy as ever."

"You didn't kiss her again, did you? Last time you did that it was all she could talk about for days…" Cubie suddenly grew serious. "What's the deal?"

"You still have that souped up Apache of yours?"

"Runs like a tiger."

"Mind if I borrow it for a few days?"

"No problem, JT...Sorry about the old man. Read about it in the paper. I tried calling."

"Thanks, man. I've been a little busy."

"Martha will quit talkin' to me if you don't stay for dinner."

"I'm sorry, ol' buddy. But I can't stay tonight. Maybe in a couple of weeks."

"Are you okay, Jack?" Drake knew that Trance had planes of his own. He also knew that Trance would never turn down Martha's cooking unless something important was happening. But this was all he would ask.

"Fine, Cubie. Just a little tired. That's all. You got that baby fueled and ready?"

"Give me fifteen minutes. I'll have one of the boys pre-flight it for you."

"You're a sport. Thanks. I'll go file a plan." Trance started down the stairs.

"It'll cost you a ride in your Sopwith, Trance."

Trance turned to face his friend and smiled. "Tell you what...If I live through this, I'll give you the damn thing."

CHAPTER 6

▼

When Trance approached Virginia in the Apache it was dark. Flying IFR, with his instruments rather than by sight, Trance floated along the coast, enjoying the lights as they sparkled upon the water. As he neared Washington, he radioed ahead to the military attachment empowered to protect the city from acts of terrorism. He spoke with an old friend who reconfirmed his authorization to fly nearer the city.

Trance took several high passes of Washington, staying just outside the no fly zone, marveling at how Congress had been able to do one thing right. There were no skyscrapers dwarfing the reminders of our heritage. Our symbols were not diminutive in stature, hunkered below a series of towering structures, each taller than the next. Instead, they spread majestically against the sky, illuminated in all their glory, surrounded by a park. God, he loved this country.

Trance flew past the Washington Monument, spiking regally into the air. He always felt a surge of pride whenever he gazed upon that simple, monolithic structure. He saluted as he flew by the World War II Memorial toward the Lincoln Memorial, then gazed at the reflecting pool as it shimmered from above.

These sights always sobered Trance. He wondered how so many so-called leaders of this great nation could speak with conviction about freedom and equality while they did their best to undermine its greatness. To him they seemed like *holier than thou* politicians, flying in their Lear jets and G5s to tax-sheltered hideaways where they would screw their secretaries on Sunday afternoons and fleece the taxpayers on Monday.

They had made him part of it all. They had convinced him with their rhetoric, that the cause always justified the means. He had needed a cause. He had wanted to follow. He had craved for something to believe in, and they had provided it for him. Do this and you will promote freedom. Kill this man and you will save thousands. Politicians measured life on a scale, weighing everything. Nothing was sacred, not even life, only numbers and the polls... How did he measure life?

Trance had a problem, a big problem. He held information so explosive that it could alter the course of world events. He hadn't asked for it. He didn't want it, and he didn't know what the hell he should do with it. Should he give it to the politicians? Some would seek ways to use it for their own benefit. They had done that too many times, and he had lost faith in their words. He couldn't trust many of them. But that wasn't the real problem, was it? There was something more dangerous going on. Handing over such information to the politicians would set them fighting against each other for media coverage, the next scandal, the next glorious *cause* to keep their names in the press, while whatever he was trying to stop would continue, unmolested. By then his hands would be tied. Should he give it to the CIA? To Miller? To the men who had killed his wife? There was no telling what they would do with the information. Perhaps they would take his formula and use it to make gold to fund covert operations throughout the world. No more begging Congress for money. No more diverting profits from arms sales. No more funneling opium from the golden triangle and cocaine out of South America. They'd have their own printing press. Then, what would they do with the financial secrets? Auction them off to the highest bidder? For what? Trance loved the CIA. It truly was America's frontline against foreign threats. God knows they need more funding, he thought. But, at what cost? And, ultimately, the Company answered to Washington.

Trance tugged at his hair with both hands, trying vainly to release the tension. He wondered if his views had been jaded by his own overly idealistic expectations. There were honest men in government. Hell, most of them were honest. The CIA? The CIA was built upon a foundation of honor—men and women routinely placing duty and country above all else. Life couldn't be nobler. But who could he trust? Power corrupts. Absolute power destroys.

Where could he turn? Killers were following him. It wouldn't be long before they found him again. Could he live his life on the run? He could destroy the information. But would they believe him? Impossible. He could already reproduce what part he had of the formula with his eyes closed. What then? Was he marked for death? Would they bargain? No. They wouldn't bargain. They had already proven they would die before revealing who they were. Who were they? Did they share the same ultimate goal? Did they want to see that the best thing came from the information? And what the hell *was* the best thing? Even he didn't know. He didn't know enough, and he would have to find out. He would have to go to Europe.

Trance circled the small Virginia airport, waiting for clearance.

"You're clear for landing..." he heard through his headphones. He banked the plane and guided her to a soft touchdown on a newly paved sheet of tarmac. He paid cash for hangar space and called a taxi. He took it to the Presidential Limousine Service Company.

Trance had many identities, and many passports—with different names, faces, and countries of origin. The CIA had prepared two passports. They were the ones he used on government business. Robert Clark, American businessman, and Aristotle Nikonos, Greek shipping executive. He'd had other identities created for him in Paris. He was Jean Pierre Monseau, a flamboyant but reclusive film producer. He was also Claude D. Perot, a Dutch dealer in rare books. He spoke fluent Parisian and Deutschland French, and it was easy for him to assume an identity on a moment's notice. He was Arthur Applegate, a potato farmer in Maine, with a glitzy Park Avenue Coop. Trance's prized identity had cost him over two hundred thousand dollars to obtain. He was Swiss, and nobody could become Swiss. Trance's passport's numbers matched information contained in the Swiss computer banks. He had birth records housed in a Geneva hospital. Educational records. Fingerprints. Employment records. Bank accounts and credit cards that went back years. Jack Trance was the Swiss citizen Johann Tarrance.

Jean Pierre Monseau rented a Ferrari and left a cash deposit of ten thousand dollars as security. Using a custom credit card, Jean Pierre had booked himself a room at the Ritz-Carlton on Massachusetts Ave. in Washington. He walked into his room and went immediately to the sink. He splashed water on his face and gazed at his reflection in the mirror. There were black crescents under his eyes. Red streaks ran dark from the inside of his eyes, clear across the eyeballs.

Trance had avoided sleep for two full days and his body was crying for rest. He would have to meditate. During most of his childhood, meditation had been taught to him as a religion—something that could never be separated from self, philosophy, love, and hand-to-hand combat. Now, he simply needed rest.

Trance sat upon the bed. He was surprised at how easy it was to return to his quiet place. Back straight, breathing in through the nose and out with the mouth. Twenty minutes later he felt renewed. Then, suddenly, he was hungry. He realized that he had not eaten since breakfast. That could wait. He had a call to make. He picked up the phone and dialed the number of Jesse Tompkin. Tompkin was an old friend he hadn't seen in years, and a man Trance had commanded during missions in a dozen countries around the globe. Tompkin had played halfback for Stanford. He was big, quick and smart. Trance had recruited him into his squad, and for six years they had fought side by side behind friendly and enemy lines. Tompkin had no fear of losing his life. He was living his second anyway, one given to him by Trance. With his new life came the comfort of knowing that each extra day he lived was a bonus. He gave thanks for every one of them, never worrying that he could lose it at any moment.

Tompkin was Trance's first recruit into T Force, and with the years of tutelage he had become nearly as good as the teacher. Tompkin now headed the covert organization.

"Jesse James," said Trance when Tompkin answered the phone. "It's JT."

"Where are you, for Christ sakes? And what the hell have you done? Two minutes ago I was alerted that you're dead meat. Not beyond salvage, but damn close. A million dollar bounty—unofficial, of course."

"And they didn't give you a chance at the money, Jesse?"

"Hell, I wouldn't know what to do with that kind of money." He sobered. "The orders came from the top, JT—"

"Are we sterile?"

"As of ten minutes ago, yes."

"And now?"

"I'm in a quiet room, but hold." Tompkin ran a quick scan of the line and said, "Far as I can tell, JT. But you know as well as I—"

"That's okay, Jesse. Will you help me?"

Without hesitation Tompkin replied, "Of course."

"They'll take your job and your life."

"Maybe."

"Thanks."

Ninety minutes later the two men were seated together in a topless bar on the outskirts of Georgetown, eating greasy hamburgers and drinking draft beer in a dimly lit corner.

Trance told Tompkin all he knew.

When Trance finished speaking, Tompkin said, "Jesus, JT...I don't know what to tell you. I knew they had a loose cover on your ass. But how many times over the years have they done that? You're always drifting off somewhere, and we never know when we might need you. I know nothing about those following you. I'm not on the inside. They'd never let me in on this. They know how far back we go. They even tried to tail me here, but I shook them at the Watergate. I did my best to make it look natural. But you know as well as I that they'll take me in when I surface."

"I need your help before then, old friend."

"Name it."

"I've got to get out of the country, to Zurich...and I've got to smuggle seven hundred pounds of gold with me."

"That's all?"

Trance smiled. "I don't need the money, really. But the gold itself might be significant. I just don't know yet."

"Anything else? Papers? Weapons?"

"I'll need to get a bag through."

"No problem. You'll have to take a puddle jumper to Newark. I can get you out of there on Swiss Air tomorrow evening. They run for us sometimes. We'll pack the gold in a Pentagon crate. I'll be on the inside to remove the labels once it's on the plane. I'll take your bag through myself, and let you go through the grope and hope with nothing to hide. I'll put your bag, with your weapons, in the compartment above your seat. Once on the plane, you're home free."

"They'll have your head for this."

"Perhaps. But then, we never know when our time is up, do we? Anyway, I know what I'm doing."

Trance got an hour of abbreviated sleep. When his watch alarm began beeping he sat up in bed and made a call to his banker in Switzerland, to inform him that the holder of account number JTT211650jldl004 would be arriving from America on Swiss Air with a rather substantial deposit. Would he please be so kind as to arrange for someone to meet him at the airport? Customs could be so tedious, and they might wish to raise questions regarding a perfectly legal transfer of funds, the verification of which would be counter to the wishes of the U.S. government.

There were two more calls to be made before he left for Zurich. Trance needed to speak with Bill Harris and Professor Hind. Their answers might provide him with enough clues to know how he should handle his affairs in Europe.

"Mr. Harris, please."

"I'm sorry. But Mr. Harris won't be in the office today."

"Thanks. I'll call his wireless."

"Mr. Harris won't be answering it, sir."

"Is he all right?"

"I'm...sorry...sir...Mr. Harris is dead."

Trance felt the blood sink in his stomach. His cheeks flushed crimson and he closed his eyes tightly. This couldn't be happening.

"What happened?"

"It was a bombing, sir. His car. We suspect they were terrorists—"

Trance hung up the phone. "This is my fault," he muttered. He shook his head. "Trance, when are you going to learn to keep your friends out of your problems?"

Trance sat upon the edge of the bed, cradling his head in his hands, thinking of the senselessness of it all. Bill Harris dead. The heir to one of America's great fortunes, a close friend, now dead because of him. Then he thought of the professor. He had seen Bill before the professor. If they had followed him to Bill, then the professor…Quickly he dialed another number.

The phone rang for minutes with no one answering. He dialed Hind's home number and the result was the same. Hadn't the professor asked him to call at the office at nine? He tried one final number—the graduate department of history.

"History. May I help you?"

"Yes. My name is Trance. I'm an old friend of Professor Hind's. I was supposed to be calling him at his office this morning. Would you happen to know how I might be able to reach him?"

"I'm sorry. But professor Hind had a heart attack in his office last night."

"Is he alive?"

"No, Mr. Trance. He is dead. But Mr. Stevens will be taking his students."

Hind was dead, too. Was this coincidence? Retribution? How many more would they kill? Angleton? Lauren? *Oh my God, Lauren!* Trance dialed frantically.

"Global Credit Bank. Lauren Haverford's office. May I help you?"

"Has she returned to the office?"

"May I tell her who is calling? Is this Jack?"

"Hi, Doris." Trance waited for no more than five seconds to hear Lauren's voice, but the time seemed to drag like rush hour traffic.

"Hello, sweetheart," she said.

"You're okay. "

"Thanks. So are you."

"No. I mean you're safe."

"I only went to Washington, Jackie. Roger brought me my car this morning. Gee, I love your Porsche. Care to trade?"

"You haven't been driving it, have you?"

"No, Jack," she laughed. "It's not like you to be worried about a car—"

"Don't go near that car, Lauren. Please." He paused. "You won't be hearing from me for a while. You say Roger's all right?"

"Yes. Are you okay, Jack?"

"I don't know. Too many things are happening that I don't understand. Do me a favor. Would you take a vacation?"

"Now?"

"Yes."

"Not even if my life depended on it."

"I'll send you anywhere, just name it."

"I'm working, Jack."

"Never mind. Just a thought. I'll call you when I get back. You're—I'll miss you."

And what the hell should I do now? Two friends dead. How many more were going to die? Lauren was safe. He could feel it. Roger would be all right, too. But what would happen next? When they found him again would he be the next to die? Or would he kill them instead? He had to get to Europe. He called and confirmed his two first class seats for his flight.

At 9:15 PM., Trance was safely on his way to Zurich.

When the wheels of the plane left the ground, Trance exhaled deeply. He closed his eyes and allowed sleep to beckon. In several hours he would be back to full strength. He would need every bit of it for what he would have to do.

Trance was sleeping in the first class cabin when he was jerked awake by the rumbling of a meal cart behind him. He was stretched out in the seat, making it into as much of a bed as possible. There were two rows of three seats each in the first class section of the Airbus A330. There was only one other man in his row—a well-tailored, middle-aged executive with brown hair and a thin mustache.

Trance normally liked the Swiss Air food and today was no different. His scrambled eggs were light and fluffy, the bacon was crisp and the croissants appeared to be just out of the oven. Trance sipped a black coffee and sat back to relax in comfort. He perused several magazines, letting his eyes wander through them, not really reading but allowing his mind to clear before it limped back into the swirl surrounding him. The lights were turned low and Trance started watching an action spy movie, where the hero blows up half of New York City to save the other half. As the movie played, Trance drifted back into a calm, untroubled sleep.

Without warning the aircraft fell into chaos. The lights flashed on—a sudden, harsh change from the quiet darkness. As Trance awakened he could hear several men in the main cabin of the plane. They were shouting in a broken mix of French, English and German. A baby wailed and children began scream-ing for their mothers.

The crack of a pistol came from the cockpit in front of him. A moment later Trance saw his neighbor push the captain's dead body out the cockpit door. The door quickly closed and snapped shut.

A shot went off behind him in the main cabin. Several women screamed and the children cried louder. Trance assessed the situation quickly, but before he could move a man appeared above him, leveling a pistol twelve inches from his face. A second man stood two feet behind with an identical 9 mm Ruger P-85 in his hand. These men held killing pistols. They were no amateurs.

"You're going to be coming with us, Trance," said the man.

"I think you should land the plane first, don't you?"

"Shut up."

The second man frisked Trance for a weapon, while the first kept his pistol trained at Trance's head. Nothing was taken from him. Trance stared back into the man's face, studying it for strengths and weaknesses. It was amazing how much you could tell from a man's eyes and the way he carried himself, which direction he looked, even when he was in a position of dominance. This man wore no fear, only hatred. The same sort of fanatical hatred as he had seen in the eyes of the man in the church. Men without fear were dangerous.

Trance listened to the man's speech. It bore an accent he could not place. Perhaps middle Europe, he thought. He held the gaze of his accuser and listened to the yelling of two other men in the back of the cabin. Their accents were different, too, and each unlike the other. Who the hell were these men?

"May I ask where we're going?" Trance asked quietly. The man beside Trance reached back with his pistol, preparing to answer with a blow to Trance's temple. The man behind him grabbed his gun.

"We have orders not to harm him."

Where was that accent from? Chechnya, perhaps?

"I suggest that you rest now, Mr. Trance. The next few days will be very long ones for you, I suspect." The man with the gun chuckled and took the seat across the aisle from Trance, being sure to maintain enough distance between himself and his prisoner. The other man took a seat directly in front of his partner, grumbling as he sat.

CHAPTER 7

▼

It was late afternoon. A fine, misty rain was falling in the Alps south of Salzburg. The sky was filled with angry, rolling clouds passing briskly toward the east. The floor of the clouds began at seven thousand feet, and obscured the view of the castle from below. At nine thousand feet the clouds broke entirely, so that the castle itself was bathed in the warmth of the late summer sun, now a shimmering orange glow falling toward the horizon.

The Baron was seated at a large, age-worn oak desk. The collar of his purple robe was pulled tightly against his neck. Disheveled stacks of papers rose in front of him, a myriad of financial figures being reviewed methodically. At the Baron's feet lay three Doberman attack dogs, part of a pack that patrolled outside the castle grounds. No one would ever again pass unseen through his guards, or escape alive from within his lair. On his desk sat the most recent reports from his companies throughout the world. The records were separated into thick piles stacked one upon the other. Next to them, on the edge of the desk, sat a flat computer monitor linked to a mainframe, housed in an adjoining refrigerated room. Beside the terminal stood a shiny suit of dented armor, armor the Baron had ridden into battle centuries before. The armor had been the lightest and most durable of its day, high technology of the middle ages, now resting beside the most sophisticated supercomputer of its day.

A voice came over an intercom. "There is a report from Reilly, at the CIA, saying that Trance took a jet out of the country."

"Where to?"

"He is landing in Zurich, my Lord."

"Marvelous...Where from?"

"Washington, via Newark, my Lord."

"Good. We have men stationed there. D'you have a status report?"

"All Washington operatives have checked in, except for Himmel. We think he made the flights. We already have men stationed in Zurich."

"Don't lose him. I want him here by tomorrow."

"Yes, my Lord. Reilly also reports that there is still no identification of the man Trance killed in Boston. He took a potassium cyanide capsule when Trance caught him. Some old drunk claims to have witnessed the death. He said Trance was holding the man against a wall when the man just died."

"And the others?"

"Before we could talk to Harris or the Harvard professor, they were killed."

"I'd say that we are being out-maneuvered, Major," said the Baron, raising his voice. "I do not accept incompetence or failure. You know that. What of the banker lady?"

"Still under surveillance."

"Don't lose her. She is our best link to Trance."

The Baron returned to his reports, occasionally entering figures into his computer. There was still so much to be done, he thought. World tension still had to be elevated. Assassinations must take place. But it was now only a matter of weeks.

The Baron leaned back in his chair, and thought about his many sons. One of them had been special, closer to him than all others he had conceived during the centuries. He had even taken time to know this child, far more than he had spent with the others. He had been a good son, coming to visit him often, like a good boy should his father. His other sons were afraid of him, but not Ferdi. He'd had such love for Ferdi, the Archduke Ferdinand. It was so unfortunate that he had had to sacrifice this son to begin a war. Wilhelm II of Germany was the Chosen One. Ferdi had been a good boy, but too weak a man. Unfortunately, Wilhelm failed in the First World War and Ferdi was dead, for no good reason. He wondered if he would miss any of the children he must soon sacrifice, as much as he still missed Ferdi. He pressed his intercom again.

"Send in Vladimir." Vladimir Verushkin was the Golden Boy of Russia. The Baron had other sons of higher rank and power, but none with his talent and prospects. Vladi had risen to the number two position in the FSB, the Russian secret police. He had benefited, of course, from the help his own family had been able to provide. Money...drugs...blackmail...women...and the closely guarded secrets they had fed to him over the last few years. The Baron's other sons in the Russian government may shake the world, but none of them had the same potential to reach the absolute pinnacle of power. Vladimir could—still in his early thirties, he was destined for greatness.

"Good evening, father."

"Vladi. Come sit down. I want you to know that I considered you seriously as the Chosen One. But your brother is in a better position to help us now."

"Yes, my Lord. I understand."

"However, I wanted to compliment you upon the way in which you have helped foment terrorist attacks around the globe. Brilliant. You have shown the most remarkable skill."

"I am honored."

"Yes. You should be. You will get your chance, Vladi. Very soon."

Vladimir nodded. He knew it was the luck of the draw. Russia had receded into the backwaters of economic power. Only his brothers within the European Union and China could hope to challenge the bully Americans for power.

But father ignores the power of our nuclear arsenal, thought Vladimir. *Our missiles still do our talking. They give us flexibility. We can use them. We can sell them. Will they ignore us when I fly a nuclear warhead into the Lincoln Memorial? Or put one into the hands of radical terrorists in London? Either way, we will make the world stand and take notice…*

"And how go the rest of our plans?" said Vladimir quietly.

"Everything is on schedule here. What about your end? Will the Russian nuclear meltdown occur as planned? And the oil fields and refining facilities—"

"Will be burnt to a crisp." The Russian nodded.

The Baron continued. "The Americans will be blamed. Your counterpart assures me that a similar failure at Duke Power the following day will be tied to Russian retaliation."

"And the Middle East?"

"The war with Israel could begin any day. We have men stationed in Tel Aviv and Cairo. Our Palestinian faction in HAMAS has grown particularly vocal. As soon as I give the word, both sides will begin shooting. No one will be able to determine which side began the war, but the Americans will be forced to intervene, if Israel is to be saved. I've seen to that."

"And will they intervene?"

"They will have to, my son. Because your brother, the Israeli defense minister, will threaten nuclear retaliation if they don't." The Baron gave a deep sigh. "But we can never be sure, with Israel. That's why you must take care of your end."

"All is in place."

"I want you and the Chosen One to supervise all of our day-to-day operations from this point forward. I am going to devote my entire attention to Trance."

"We will be honored, father."

So many details to cover. So many pieces to the puzzle, thought the Baron. *Nearly every piece in place. Now to convince the Americans that the Russians are preparing an all-out nuclear first strike—in one final, desperate grab at world domination by a country quickly sinking into an economic afterthought. Convincing the Russians that the Americans are planning the same will be easy. Their suspicions are always aroused. With my sons working together it won't be long before it all becomes reality.*

CHAPTER 8

▼

Trance leaned back in his seat and reviewed his options. He was in the middle of an international incident. The last thing he needed was publicity. Should he go with the men and take his chances once he was on the ground? He could lose the gold and the formula, but he might get away. Then again, he may be facing hundreds of them when he landed. There were only a few of them now.

"Who are you?" he asked the man to his right.

The man laughed and replied, "That I cannot tell you. But we may be far better friends than you imagine."

"Where are we going?"

"That you will learn when we land."

"Are you part of an organized army?"

"No more questions, my friend. The others, they may hate you. But me, I think I understand you. I think you are innocent, not the man they say you are."

Trance's other guard began to snore. The man beside Trance kicked the seat in front of him, and said, "If you fall asleep again I'll slit your throat."

The man in front grumbled, while the man across from Trance got comfortable in his chair, farted loudly, then folded back the pages of a Playboy magazine.

Trance thought of his weapons in the blue gym bag above his head. He knew that any motion to get his bag would be met with force, so he reached slowly into the left pocket of his jacket and removed his iPhone.

"Do you mind if I read?" he said to the man across the way. He stretched it across the aisle. "You should have taken this from me before," he continued.

The man took the iPhone and nodded grimly. He checked for a wireless signal and returned it to Trance. He looked at his watch. "The plane's wi-fi has been disabled. You have an hour. Consider it your last wish granted." The man laughed heartily, pleased with his gallows humor. "I will need to take it when we get closer to land."

Trance grinned with him. *You, my friend,* he thought, *are far too nice and much too careless.* Turning his body to the left, Trance pulled back a metal flap on the phone's case. Inside was a plastic tube less than four inches long. Beside it were five small pins. They were darts, tipped with a deadly nerve toxin made in his family's village in Japan. Distilled from the roots of a very ordinary plant, once in the bloodstream it could paralyze or kill a man in seconds. Taken orally it was harmless. A perfect poison.

Trance had been a student of weapons since his father had introduced him to them at the age of five. Almost anything could be one. A piece of paper, a comb. He made a hobby of inventing them, much as his father had done with climbing equipment. These were among his favorites. Easily concealed. Silent. Deadly, and reasonably accurate at close range.

Although Trance always traveled with weapons, he hadn't used these darts in years. How had he known to put them into his iPhone, with its custom case? It was the little voice inside him, the one that was always right. It had told him to do it, and he had listened. He inserted one of the darts into the tube, and palmed it. He watched the man across the aisle with his peripheral vision. The man still read his magazine, a bulge rising from his pants.

Trance set the iPhone upon his tray. Then he brought his hand to his lips and turned to his captor. There was a soft spit. The man beside him blinked dumbly and fell sideways. Trance reloaded and glanced toward the sleeping guard across the aisle. He looked behind him to the closed curtain separating them from the rest of the passengers. He brought the tube back to his lips and eliminated his other captor. A single dot of blood gathered below the dart behind his left ear. A few seconds later the man slumped outward into the aisle.

Trance peered cautiously through the curtain. Two men were brandishing pistols in the rear of the plane. There was at least one other man inside the cockpit. After making sure that the curtain was fully closed, Trance reached up and removed his gym bag from the overhead compartment. He thought of the men behind him. He would have to keep one of them alive. That would be the tough part, the dangerous part. It would be easier to kill them, but he needed one alive, to find out what the hell was going on. He also had to make sure that no one put a bullet into the fuselage of the plane. That mistake could kill them all.

Trance reached into his bag and removed a wide leather belt, similar to those worn by weight lifters, but somewhat thinner and softer. He withdrew a cluster of spring-loaded shuriken blades from his bag, snapped them open and placed them one by one into the small pockets created for them in the hand-crafted belt. Certain blades had certain pockets. He removed two throwing knives from a thin, soft leather case and placed them into his belt. He then took his father's old Colt 32 and stuck it into the small of his back. Trance worked calmly. When everything was in place, he took his blow tube and loaded it with another pin-like dart.

Then Trance did something that he hadn't done in years. He sat upon the floor to collect his force, his *Chi*. Several moments later he was ready. He tugged at the curtain hanging between first and second class until he could see the back of one of the gunmen, barely three feet away. Like shooting fish in a barrel. Beyond him, at the rear of the aircraft, he could see the final gunman holding a hostess at gunpoint. He placed the tube between the two curtains and blew a dart into the neck of the gunman. As soon as he blew the dart, he reached back and grasped two throwing knives, one in each hand. As the man staggered in front of the curtain, Trance burst forward into the cabin.

He ran straight toward the man at the rear of the plane, filling the air with a loud yell, *Kiaah*! The hijacker froze briefly, then threw the hostess to the ground. He raised his gun to fire at Trance, but before the gun reached his waist, Trance's arms moved forward with a blur. One of the blades caught the man by the shoulder, snapping him backwards with the impact. The other tore into his gun hand, and the weapon fell to the floor. Trance advanced and drove his right fist into the man's chest. There was a loud crack and the man slumped to the floor, his sternum split in two. His breathing was labored under the fractured bones, and his face contorted with a sickly combination of pain and anger. Blood was pumping in rapid spurts from his hand, and a dark, sticky wetness spread across his shirt at the shoulder.

"Who are you?" said Trance into the man's ear, as he pulled him from the floor. The man's eyes were dazed. His mouth tried to move underneath his matted black beard, but no words would emerge.

Trance felt movement to his left. Without thinking, he swung his prisoner toward the movement to use him as a shield. A loud pop split through the cabin. Trance felt the man beside him shudder, and a mass of bloody fluid squirted from one of the man's eyes. The hollow point bullet had carved a wide and jagged path into his skull. He wouldn't talk now.

Trance looked up to see two passengers leering at him from across the aisle. Their guns were pointed squarely at his chest. Trance screamed to himself. How could he have been so stupid? He ducked to the left. A shot went off and he felt a searing pain in his right triceps. The bullet passed through the fleshy part of his arm, leaving an exit wound the size of a quarter.

"Oh, shit," said Trance. He dove to his right. As he moved through the air, he caught another shot in the left shoulder.

Trance listened for the crack of broken bone, but strangely, there was none, just the hot pain of burning flesh. In mid-air, he twisted and reached for the gun in his belt. He landed painfully on his injured right arm, while doing a somersault forward. Somehow he escaped the next bullets. The two men were on their feet now, walking toward him. That was their mistake. Trance launched into a back handspring. While in the air he let off two quick shots, hitting both men in the face as they watched in surprise.

The men wavered for a few brief seconds. In unison, their ceramic guns dropped to the floor and they sank together into a pile in the aisle. Small caliber guns, probably 25s, so an errant shot might not rupture the plane fuselage. That explained why Trance's shoulder wasn't a mass of bone chips. Trance briefly flashed to a time when he had watched a man take a 25-caliber bullet straight against the forehead. The bullet had traveled between the man's skin and his skull, up over his head, finally resting at the base of the man's neck. He was just as lucky today—if you could call this luck.

Trance spun around to search for other attackers. All he saw were frightened faces. "Where's the marshal?" he said. He was met by silence. "I'm with the government," he said. "Is there an air marshal? I need help."

"Dead," said the airhostess. "There were two. They're both dead now."

Trance closed his eyes and took a long, slow breath. Then he ran forward toward the first class cabin, gaining speed with each step. When he reached the cockpit door he knocked. There was no answer so he knocked again.

"Open up," he said.

"Screw you."

Trance shook his head and exhaled deeply. "You want to play hard to get? You don't want this, I assure you."

"Blow it out your ass."

Trance pulled off the heel of his right shoe and withdrew a thin plastic tube from inside. He broke open the tube by cracking it against the side of his hand. He removed a strip of brown putty and molded it against the cockpit door. He reached back into his shoe and removed a thin filament and attached it to a glass bulb the size of a marble that he pulled off his keychain. Trance pressed this into the putty. He then knocked on the door again. "Stand back," he said. "I'm going to blow the door." He reached into his blue bag and removed what looked like a car alarm clicker, then walked toward the rear of the cabin. He looked to the frightened faces in the plane and said, "Please cover your ears. This is almost over."

Trance pressed the clicker and an explosion shook the air. The cockpit door came off its hinges and bent inward toward the pilot. For a brief moment the plane tilted to the left, and then stabilized. Trance walked to within fifteen feet of the door, drew his pistol and pointed it forward.

"You can come out now," he said. Trance waited for a face to appear in the door. After five long minutes he inched slowly forward. Then he broke into a run and launched himself through the air, feet first into the loosened opening. Trance felt a man crumble beneath the door as he crunched inside.

The hijacker lay trapped and groaning beneath the door. The co-pilot took over the controls.

"You okay?" said Trance.

"Glad you could finally make it," said the pilot in heavily accented English.

"Sorry. I was detained."

Underneath Trance, the attacker was still pinned awkwardly against the floor. His gun lay a foot beyond his reach and he flailed fruitlessly with one hand to reach it. Trance broke the hijacker's knee with the butt of his pistol. "Don't move," he said. The man hissed in anger but stopped moving. Trance reached for the man's gun

A blast rocked the small cabin, a thundering echo that sent Trance's ears ringing, combined with a flash of heat that seemed to suck the air from the cockpit. Trance mentally searched his body for the new wound. But there was none. Trance realized that the highjacker couldn't free his other weapon to shoot at Trance, so he had done the next best thing. He had shot himself. Trance put his ear next to the dying man's lips and said, "Why?" The man spit in his face.

Trance sat down on the floor and sighed. His left side was in spasms, and his right arm throbbed. He fought off anger and looked back at the hijacker. "Why are you doing this?"

The man spit again, and choked. Then he said to Trance, "You will not succeed. There will always be one of us to stop you."

Then the man smiled, grimaced and died.

"Where were they taking us?" he asked the co-pilot.

"Israel," came the answer.

Israel? thought Trance. What the hell? Mossad? He searched under the man's shirt until he felt the thin gold chain in his fingers. Dangling from the end he found a Star of David. What would the Mossad want with him? This couldn't be the Israeli secret service. They would never sanction an action like this, and they'd been far too careless. These men had to be part of some splinter group, terrorists. They had to be. Some group of renegades who believed that they could actually make a difference. Trance looked down at the man and felt sorry for him; he felt sorry for all of them. They were dying for a cause they believed in, just as he had been willing to die, for so many years. The causes never stopped, and they always outlived the men that littered their wake.

Trance was in trouble. He was being hunted by men who would stop at nothing. But his most pressing problem was that the passengers on this plane would be quarantined, and then questioned until the Swiss authorities were assured that the matter was under control. He would be cross-examined for hours, perhaps days for the part he had played. The Swiss don't appreciate strangers who dispose of seven terrorists on one of their planes, no matter how righteous the cause. They would detain him until he died from the loss of blood, or the CIA took him into custody. Either choice wasn't acceptable.

"I'm with INTERPOL," he said to the co-pilot in German. He knew that he could have spoken any of several languages—French, German or English, and be equally understood. But he could gain this man's confidence more quickly if he spoke to him in his own tongue. He had heard the accent. The man was Germanic. "We've been tracking these terrorists for months. I commend you for responding so well under pressure." Trance walked back to his seat and removed half a dozen documents. He returned and showed them to the co-pilot.

"You'll get a medal for this," said the pilot.

Trance ignored the compliment. "No. *You* will. But we're going to need your assistance."

"Of course."

"I need to use your radio."

"I'm sorry, but that is highly irregular. Only we are allowed to communicate." The Swiss were so pragmatic.

Trance stared at the pilot for thirty seconds. When he replied he let his voice rise until it was close to a controlled scream.

"Irregular? You've just survived a hijacking attempt and you've got ten dead bodies in the cabin of this plane."

The co-pilot's eyes grew wide as Trance grabbed him by the collar. His eyes showed his shock. "Ten?"

"Ten! Seven terrorists…" Trance's voice grew quiet. "…two unfortunate air marshals, and your captain. We are lucky that is all we lost. Does ground control know what has happened?"

"Our last transmission was slightly irregular. But the man…the man with the gun...he knew what he was doing."

"What about the air phones?"

"Turned off. There is no wireless signal in this part of the ocean."

"Satellite phones?"

"Possible, but unlikely through the ship's hull."

"So, as far as Zurich is concerned, this flight is proceeding normally?"

"Yes."

"We're going to keep it that way. For the good of Switzerland, and for the good of Swiss Air." Trance took several shallow breaths. The pain was getting severe, now that his adrenaline was gone. Blood had soaked the entire right side of his shirt, and he fought off successive waves of nausea.

"Will your superiors appreciate your informing them over the open airwaves that there are ten dead bodies on this plane? Do you expect they will welcome the photographers and the television news crews with open arms? You know damn well that they wouldn't. My job is to see that doesn't happen. Look...I'm an employee just like you. We both want to keep our jobs, right?" The co-pilot dipped his head. "If I do my job correctly, your superiors will be issuing statements in two or three days that won't even make the front pages of the paper. It will be just ho-hum news to the public, a non-event. Old news is stale news. If you open your trap now, media from around the world will hype this thing so far out of proportion that you will never have another job flying again." Trance paused to let the image sink into the pilot's brain. "You do want to keep your job?"

"Ya." The pilot nodded.

"You won't, if you don't allow me to diffuse this incident before it occurs. I guarantee that you will never fly again if you fight me. Ask this dead man on the floor if you should fight me." Trance released his grip on the co-pilot and let him fall back into his seat. The man looked into Trance's eyes and nodded again.

"I'll do what you say."

"Good. Can you reach Zurich?"

"Of course."

"Call ahead and tell them that you have an important passenger on board. I am to meet with a man who works for Nicolas Klug and Company." The co-pilot's eyes narrowed at the mention of one of Switzerland's largest and most influential banks.

"The man is also INTERPOL. His name is Franz Koenig. He should have already made arrangements with the authorities to meet me at the airport. Tell them that, on behalf of the United States, I have requested that I be allowed to deplane alone, five minutes before the other passengers. There is a crate by the baggage door of this plane. Someone will be waiting to remove it as soon as we land. If they ask you if anything is out of the ordinary, you are to tell them that everything is fine. Understand?" The pilot nodded.

"Now repeat what you are to do." The pilot repeated the directions verbatim. Then he did the same over the radio. When he had finished Trance said, "Good. Now I need your shirt."

The pilot raised his arms and began to protest, until he looked at Trance. In the split second that their eyes met, the pilot felt a foreboding shiver run through him. He felt death. So he made it all into one motion—raising his arms, and then taking off his shirt. He handed the shirt to Trance in silence.

Trance walked unsteadily back to his seat and pulled the pillowcase off a pillow. He tore it apart and wrapped a makeshift tourniquet around his arm. He looked at his wounds dispassionately. The hole in his right triceps was only a flesh wound, but it was still bleeding. The puncture in his shoulder showed little blood at all; it was still plugged by the bullet.

Trance took the pilot's clean shirt into the lavatory. The moment he closed the door behind him, Trance looked in the mirror, wiped the beads of sweat off his brow and retched. Wave after wave of turbulent spasms began deep in his abdomen, and flowed upward through his throat and into the toilet. He stood with his head against the bowl. *It's over. The killing is over.*

It often happened this way, after death. He could watch people die impassively, reacting only by instinct and training. He was a soldier, a warrior. He was a finely tuned machine that could move faster, farther, and with more control than any other. Sometimes his mind gave up control of his body when he was fighting. Sometimes he had no mind at all. Everything was instinct, an instinct melded into a man so well trained, and so well conditioned, that no physical act seemed impossible.

But there was always the aftermath, the time when thoughts returned to his head. Consequences. The moment of realization of what he had done, the moment when he tried to understand the world. He knelt with his head in the bowl, hating himself for the ten men who were dead. How had he become what he was? A killer. They called him a patriot. He was a decorated hero, with two purple hearts, a Congressional Medal of Honor *and* a Medal of Freedom. He'd earned the highest honors his country could give. What had it all meant? The clandestine trips into foreign countries to slit someone's throat, the months crawling through deserts and jungles to overthrow would-be dictators and topple governments…He was trapped. It had hold of him. They had hold of him. They told him it had to be done, and he would do it. They were right. Someone had to win and protect the peace. But, why him? Janice…she had been his one chance out.

But what was happening now? Was this his punishment? In the past two days thirteen people had died. Thirteen! Two of them had been close friends. So, what was it for? He didn't know. He only knew that it was something he couldn't let go of. He couldn't walk away. What was it his father had said? This was his destiny. What was his destiny? He had to find von Hoffenburg, and the Black Madonna. Then he would know. He emerged from the toilet and walked calmly down the aisle of the plane collecting cell phones, PDAs and computers. Then he went to the cockpit to wait.

Life in Switzerland often follows procedure like clockwork. There are few breaks in precise routines, and business is conducted according to time-honored methods that are rarely altered. Except when it comes to money. Only money makes the Swiss alter their pragmatic demeanor. The Swiss cater to wealth like royalty.

The methods used to transfer money are often irregular. For centuries the Swiss economy, and much of their financial existence, has revolved around their position as the world's bankers. Depositors often receive no interest on their accounts. Why would a man deposit millions into a numbered account that paid no interest? It was because the bankers did things like meet clients at the airport, and whisk them away…it was because the Swiss ask as few questions about the sources of money as the laws will allow. They have no interest in who you are, where you live or what the laws of your country might be. They will take your gold in a limousine and ask only for a handwritten sequence of numbers, then deposit your gold for you and credit your account. Then, when you call upon them to withdraw ten million dollars in cash they won't blink, even when you present your numbers or a laser-etched key and code at 2 AM on Christmas Eve.

Trance walked off of the plane into the friendly embrace of Herr Koenig. They walked past customs with a wave of the hand. Less than three minutes later they were leaving the airport in a Klug limousine.

"It is good to see you again," said Koenig in a quiet and understated voice. He was dressed in a fine, blue pinstriped suit, with gold and diamond cufflinks. His shirt was made of finely woven silk. He wore a red power tie with a subtle pattern of small gray hearts. The skin on his face was smooth and tanned. There were just a few thin wrinkles along the sides of his eyes, well hidden by his gold-rimmed glasses. His eyes were liquid blue and penetrating. His hair was Aryan blond.

Koenig angled his head toward a bucket of iced champagne and a well-stocked mini-bar. Beside it rested an assortment of exotic looking finger foods. "Would you care for some refreshment, sir? A late breakfast?" His eyes flicked to Trance's wounded arm and shoulder, but he said nothing.

Trance began to say, "No thanks," but changed his mind. "A nip of scotch might be helpful," he said quietly. "No ice, please."

Koenig broke open the seal on a bottle of Johnny Walker Blue and poured three fingers into a crystal glass. He handed it to Trance, watching silently as Trance's shaking hand took the glass from his outstretched arm.

Trance raised the glass and emptied it with three quick gulps. "Thanks. I had a hard flight," he said.

Koenig waited through ten minutes of silence as the limousine traveled southwest for twenty kilometers and then weaved its way toward the Klug bank offices. Trance sat across from him with his eyes closed. Koenig pondered whether or not he should offer help in any way. Finally, Trance opened his eyes and smiled. "Have you got the paperwork?"

Koenig nodded. He pressed a small button on the seat beneath his legs and a drawer opened beside Trance. On it lay two of the bank's forms, ready for signature. Trance signed both papers, then punched a series of numbers on the keypad resting beside them.

"You will fill in the amounts later?" he said.

'Of course," said Koenig.

Trance smiled and waved his bleeding arm in a sweeping gesture toward the bustling streets. "How about a morning tour of the city?"

Koenig arched an eyebrow but said nothing. He pressed the intercom button and instructed the chauffeur to drive around the city.

Trance looked out the window at Zurich—so clean, so precise, so businesslike, so orderly. Orderly traffic, orderly shops, orderly pedestrians. Even the tourists seemed orderly. Trance spotted at least one car tailing them, perhaps more. He instructed the limo driver to crisscross the city and began to fit the streets into the map burned onto his mind. He formed a plan and reviewed what moves he could make. He devised a flexible template that could be changed as each situation dictated. These plans provided him with a sorely needed emotional support, an edge. Only he would know where he was heading. The others would have to react to *him*, not him to them. That was his only chance.

"Let me off here," he said suddenly. Koenig began to protest but stifled his words. Men like this knew what they wanted. There was no sense explaining that he had made exquisite lunch plans, and that he had arranged for a companion, if his guest so desired.

"Certainly," he said, waving the driver to the side of the busy street. "I hope to see you again soon, sir."

Koenig did not know his client's name. He hoped that he never would. Knowing a man's name could be dangerous in his business, and he wanted to stay alive.

CHAPTER 9

▼

Trance watched wearily as the Klug limousine glided from the crowded street corner and disappeared into the traffic. He leaned against a black lamp post, closed his eyes and reviewed his options. None was appealing. He decided to make his way to the Dolder Grand Hotel. The Dolder was on Kurhausstrasse, in the southwest section of the city, a good drive from the central business district. The old castle rested high on a steep hill, and was accessible only by a funicular train. What he wanted was a hot mineral bath, a mud wrapping, a full eight hours of sleep, and a nine-hole round on the hotel golf course. What he hoped for was three hours of time to regroup.

They would be searching for him in the finer hotels. It was no secret—the way he traveled. Whoever was following him appeared to know his every move. They knew his friends. They seemed to know everything about him. How? He wondered.

Trance watched a black Mercedes sedan pull to the side of the curb. Behind it stopped a green Citroen. There were four men in each car. He waited to see what moves they would make. Would they open fire? Would they keep their distance? Or would they...They walked rapidly toward him. Six men had emerged from the vehicles, leaving only their drivers. They fanned out like spiders as they quarried their prey.

"Hi, guys," said Trance. He smiled, waved to the men, and bolted.

Trance knew that, under normal circumstances, none of the men could outrun him. He could still run a four-minute mile. But how fast would he be with two bullet wounds?

Several of the men carried phones, so they'd be in contact with the cars. Hopefully, there were no others. If he could outrun these men and lose them, he might have a chance. Perhaps he could hail a taxi out of the city and lose them in the countryside. He had friends he could call and favors to collect. But did he want them dead, too? He also knew many European mercenaries, men who were loyal only to money. He had plenty of that.

Trance ducked into a narrow alleyway. His conscious mind was gone. It was replaced by a second mind, one that made decisions instantly, one that didn't hesitate to pull the trigger of a gun, or put a knife into someone's neck or back. He was controlled by the patriot he had trained to be. The patriot heard the footsteps of his attackers close behind. The alley was over a hundred yards long, and the moment he turned into it he thought he had made a mistake. What was he thinking? A hundred yards. Ten seconds. His pursuers were five seconds behind. There was nowhere he could turn. He put his head down and sprinted. His left arm hung by his side and the pain shot through his shoulder like fire. He counted off the seconds, four...five...one second to set up and fire, and dive to the right. Then dive to the left. They would fire at him...But there were no shots. The men just kept on running toward him. The cars! He knew they were coming. The patriot knew. He reached to the small of his back and withdrew his Colt. Had he taken the time to reload? He couldn't remember. It was so natural...but had he? He had lost more blood than he cared to admit. His entire left side was stiff and swollen. His right arm ached. His mind was dizzy. His mouth was filled with the taste of bile. As he emerged from the alley, he could see the Mercedes coming around the corner. Its tires screeched as the driver used every inch of speed the car could take. What about the Citroen? Where was the Citroen? Trance leveled his gun and fired as he ran. The bullet bounced off the windshield.

"Shit," he muttered. Bulletproof glass. He ran past the car as it skidded to a stop. The driver inside smiled and flipped him his middle finger. This is a game, thought Trance. Some kind of game. This can't be real! Then the first shot came. He heard the muted spit of a silenced automatic pistol. He felt the ping of shattered concrete beside him, just as he turned the corner and ran into the street on his right. As he continued sprinting, he looked above him to the sky. No helicopters. The buildings were a combination of low rise residential and office buildings. No snipers, yet. Fewer people were left in the streets now. If he could only widen the distance, he could lose them.

Then, abruptly, the patriot turned from prey to predator. How it happened, Trance never knew. There were parts of him outside of his consciousness, parts that were tuned to other forces.

Trance could hear his father's words. *Just because we cannot feel a magnetic pull, slight electrical charges in the air, ultraviolet radiation, or neutrinos with our consciousness, it does not mean they don't exist. They can be measured. We have machines that can do such things. There are other things that exist, like fear, love, hatred that we cannot measure accurately with machines. But does that mean that they're not there? They exist outside the measurement capabilities of machines. The mind can feel hatred, love, and fear. It can sense danger.*

It can sense advantage. Sometimes this 'sense' is nothing more than a vague feeling. A 'hunch'. While at other times it screams inside our heads. Every person has the ability to sense the immeasurable, some of us more than others. You have the ability, my son, to measure the immeasurable. To feel the unquantifiable is a gift. You can sense advantage. You can taste fear in others. These things you can feel, as others can't. You were born with an internal radar that can detect the energy fields that emanate from living beings, as if they are on radio. But you must keep your radio on. You must surrender to the Cosmic Will.

Trance had turned his senses off on the plane. Now he could feel them hard at work. It made him stop, draw his gun, and turn around.

Trance waited for six seconds. He heard the footsteps draw closer. He heard the labored breathing. Then he felt his attackers coming toward the corner of the street. He stood erect, with his gun drawn level to his chest. As two of the men came around the corner at full speed, he cut them down with two quick shots. The odds had shifted.

Trance turned and ran into the adjoining street, listening behind him for more footsteps. There were none. He stopped and allowed his inner eye to search for the cars. They were gone, too. How odd, he thought.

Trance walked cautiously for an hour, spiraling his steps in the direction of the Dolder Grand. As he drew close he felt enormously tired. The lack of sleep, the tension, and the bullet still lodged in his shoulder didn't help. A hot bath, clean sheets and a full night's sleep beckoned him...He stopped in mid-step, then sat upon the curb. He'd have to think this through. His arm had to be worked on fast. It was still oozing blood. He couldn't function without sleep. He had false identities that no one could trace. If he could slip in unnoticed he might be safe for the night. Perhaps. The proper tip to the concierge would ensure that anyone acting suspiciously would be brought to his attention. He wondered if Carl had been retained through the hotel's extensive renovations, and if he was on the desk today.

Still, something nagged at him. He couldn't determine what it was. Perhaps he'd know by morning. He would be rested by then. Yes, he'd think better after some rest. He stood up and headed toward the funicular. They wouldn't look for him there, not now. He prayed he was right.

Carl Sauerbrunn was indeed working the day shift at the desk. When he saw Trance, he gave a smile of recognition.

"Monsieur! So good to see you again!" he said in French. Trance had been using this hotel for nearly ten of the thirty years that Carl had worked the desk. They had become good friends, and had spent several nights together on the town. But this was Trance's first visit back since the hotel had reopened.

"But I have received no reservation from your company, Monsieur." Trance's reservations were always made at the Dolder Grand under the corporate accounts of dummy corporations—Transcontinental Consulting Group, and more recently, International Capital Resources. This policy had been instituted while he was with the CIA, and he had changed the company name when he had left.

"I'm sorry, Carl," replied Trance in German, knowing that Carl preferred speaking in his native tongue. "I was called late in the evening and there was no time to make a reservation. Can you find me a room?" Trance extended his hand and the two men shook. Carl looked down at Trance's hand, as he always did. He had shaken hundreds, thousands of hands, and Trance's was the only one that felt like a brick. The edges were like steer horn, and his grip, even though Trance tried to soften it, was like a vice. Carl had always wondered what this man did for a living. A couple of times, when they had been out drinking together, he had nearly had the poor taste to ask him.

"For anyone else, no. But for you? The best room in the house. At regular prices."

"I could live for a year on your regular prices," said Trance with a smile.

"Not the way you spend money, mein Herr."

"You know, old friend," said Trance with a shrug of the shoulders and a wink. "Expense accounts..." They both laughed at their running joke. In the years Trance had been on an expense account he had taken full advantage of it, much to the chagrin of his superiors in Fairfax, Virginia.

"I need a favor, Carl."

"Of course, my friend. This *is* Zurich. Anything for a price."

"I'm going to go upstairs to take a bath. In an hour I will need a set of tweezers, a needle, and some thread." He grimaced. "I'll also need some rubbing alcohol and enough antibiotics to last me two weeks."

"Of course. Anything else?"

"Yes, I want a pair of dungarees, Levis if you can find them, within the next half hour. I'll also need a long-sleeved cotton shirt. I believe you have my sizes. I'll also need two liters of mineral water." Carl stood quietly waiting for Trance to catch his breath. He could see the lines of pain creasing his face. He glanced discreetly at the blood seeping through Trance's sport coat, but said nothing. After nearly a minute Trance continued, "Oh, could you find me a bottle of Pinch? Have that brought up right away, please."

Carl smiled and spoke in a hushed voice. "Please remember that this is not America, mein freund. So, if I cannot get you a pair of Levis within the hour, it will not be because I haven't tried. Will Wranglers do?"

This was Zurich, and this was a hotel that catered to the strange whims of eccentrics, the wealthy, the famous, and sometimes, the infamous. Carl could get anything, anytime. He didn't discuss what the cost to Trance would be. These kinds of requests didn't have set prices, and it would be in very poor taste to discuss a subject so gauche as money with a patron of the Dolder. It was up to Carl to make the negotiations, then add a little for himself in the process. The total would be added to the bill and it would be paid by Trance without question.

"I understand. Thank you, old friend." He'd have his Levis. He wondered if his last act in this world would be to buy a pair of pants.

"And I will not forget your scotch, sir," said Carl as Trance reached his hand into his pocket.

"Of course."

Trance palmed Carl five hundred Euros, turned, and allowed the porter to take his gym bag to his room. He shuffled behind, still dressed in his blue sport coat, with the pilot's ill-fitting shirt fully stained with blood.

When he got to his room he gave the porter a hundred Euro bill. He closed the door and walked into the bathroom. He sat heavily on the side of the tub, turned on the water and adjusted it to a point just hotter than he could stand. As the water ran, he carefully peeled off his clothes. He glanced into the full-length mirror to judge his appearance. Appearance could mean everything in this business—so much was bluff and fake.

At thirty-five, Trance was on the backside of his physical prime. He worked hard to keep his body toned. There was no fat on his frame and it cut a sharp V as it tapered from his chest to his waist. He had seen so many of his athletic friends grow lazy and fat when their playing days were over. Unfortunately for Trance, his playing days might never be over. He stood naked in the mirror, and looked at himself—first from the front, then from the side to see what parts needed attention. He smiled ruefully when he saw the red dragon tattoo that stretched across his shoulder blades. Forced upon him by a Yakuza gang he would not join, it served as a constant reminder that the world was filled with evil people, people who had to be stopped, people who took pleasure in inflicting pain upon others, simply because they could. Suddenly, he felt very alone.

Trance thought of his wife. Perhaps it was the sharp ache in his body. He was used to aching, the pain of a man alone. For six years he had slept alone. Sometimes, he wondered, if it wasn't fear that kept intimacy from happening, the fear that he would fall in love again—and then lose another.

Janice would want him happy, that much he knew. He tried to leave himself open, for one special woman. He was hoping to find her, someone who could erase the pain of his life without Janice. But he had built a shelter against the pain. No one could touch those tender nerves. No one had reached inside his soul to draw him out, or made him feel that everything would be all right.

Perhaps she was out there, somewhere. He would wait for her, alone. He would not desecrate the memory of his wife with someone less

The bath water brimmed close to the top of the tub and Trance forced himself to slip in. Sweat broke out across his forehead as his body reacted to the intense heat around his legs. This was what he needed. The sweat would help draw the lactic acid from his muscles. It would help him relax, so that his next act would be less painful. He immersed himself fully, to the point where he couldn't move a muscle without feeling the scalding heat of the water. When the knock came upon the door, he shouted for the porter to come in. A plump, obsequious man brought a bottle of Pinch to the bathroom. His eyes didn't leave the floor.

"Pour me half a glass, will you?" said Trance in French. The porter showed no reaction, except to pour the scotch.

"Would you like ice, sir?" The man stole one quick glance at Trance and the bloodied tub of water, then focused on the bottle and glass.

"No. Straight will be fine. Thank you. That will be all." He pointed to a one hundred Euro bill on the bathroom sink. "That is for you," he said. "Please make sure the door locks on your way out."

Trance took a hard sip of his drink. He sat back as the liquor burned a path along his throat. Burning like General Sherman on his way to Atlanta. He took a second gulp, downing half of the contents in the glass, hoping it would help.

After thirty minutes in the bath Trance stood to shower and let the water fall gently upon his wounds. He dried himself, patting his towel lightly against his arm and shoulder. He took the robe, which was laid neatly on the bed, and walked to the phone. These calls couldn't wait. He took off his watch and set it by the receiver. The first number he dialed was to the home of an old friend, and nemesis, Richard Swartz in Tel Aviv. Trance routed the call through his own switching network to avoid tracing.

"Dicky. Trance here." Swartz hated that name. Only Trance was allowed to call him that, a small concession given to Trance for saving half a dozen of his men one night.

"Hello, Batman." The voice was sleepy and without emotion. Swartz ran field operations in the Israeli secret service, the Mossad. Trance had earned the name Batman by the way he flew jets in combat, and by the way he could move in the darkness.

"Why are your men after me?"

"You don't know?"

"You know damn well that I don't know. What the hell is going on?"

"If you don't know what is happening, Jack, then come see me. There is more to this than even you might imagine." Swartz paused to give his men time to trace the call. "By the way, that was a nifty piece of work on the plane...Still as good as ever, I see."

"Don't stall me, Dicky. I've routed this call through six countries."

"Don't worry, Jack. I'm not tracing this. Believe me, ol' boy; we've got plenty of men on your six. For us, this is as big as the Six Day War. We'll find you within hours, I assure you. Or at least someone will. We want you alive. The others may not."

"Who's after me?" asked Trance.

Swartz laughed. "Who? A more appropriate question might be 'Who isn't?'"

"You're lying."

"Oh? You've got friends at the SIS, INTERPOL, and the Russian FSB. I suggest you call them. You already know that the CIA is all over your ass. Call them, Jack. Then call me back. I'll be waiting. We want you alive. Come for a visit. The oranges are great this year—" Trance hung up the phone. He dialed a second number, this one at INTERPOL, London.

"Charlie? Trance."

"Batman? Where in the bloody hell are you? Do you realize that we've got orders to shoot you on sight?"

"Why, Charlie?"

"Hell, I don't know. I just take orders...To keep you from the Russians, I suppose."

"And what do the Russians want with me?"

"Ya got me. All I know is that they're burning up the airwaves, more than at any time since Iraq started. Shit, Jack. What the hell have you done?"

"I'm not sure, Charlie." Trance let the receiver fall back onto the phone.

There was a knock on the door. It was Carl. Trance unlocked the door.

"You are in luck," Carl said. "I don't know how I did it, but I was able to get you the pants."

"And the rest of what I asked for?"

"Of course, my friend." Carl noticed the deep furrows of stress lining Trance's face. He discreetly looked to the side and saw Trance's matted shirt lying on the floor next to the bathroom door and two bloodstained towels.

"Are you sure there is nothing I can help you with?" His voice had a soothing, melodious tone. It was as if he were saying 'It's all right. I'll give you all the help you need.'

Trance considered allowing this man to give him the help he desperately needed. Then he thought of Harris and professor Hind and said, "No, Carl. That will be all. But, do let me know if anyone comes looking for me, will you?"

"Of course."

"How long are you working?" asked Trance.

"As long as you need me to."

"Thanks, old friend."

Trance took the linen bag from the concierge's hand and waved for him to leave. He walked to the far end of his suite to a sprawling anteroom, perhaps twenty-five feet long, that was set up as an office/reception room. Against one of the walls sat a dark cherry desk. The desk was highly polished, and was complimented by a blue leather Queen Anne chair with a back nearly five feet high. Across from the desk, at the opposite corner of the room, was a delicate Louis XIV table facing the wall. Behind it hung a gold-framed mirror, giving Trance a complete view of himself and the room behind him. He sat himself at the table and placed the bag in front of him.

Trance pulled out one of the two pairs of Levis he found in the bag. They fit perfectly, as expected. He walked over to the slacks he had thrown upon the floor. They were hardened with blood and resembled Swiss cheese more than clothing. He pulled out his custom black leather belt. It looked like a Neiman Marcus, the hide of the highest quality, the buckle unique. But this belt had been designed for a specialized purpose, defense. As he threaded it through the loops of his new pants, he took a quick inventory, making sure that everything was in place.

Carl had brought him two shirts, not one, the ever-efficient Swiss. Trance checked them and was satisfied that neither would press against his wounds. They were loose fitting but stylish. Each would allow him to give the appearance of a wealthy tourist on vacation, or a starving student, whichever he may need to be.

Inside the new bag he found a plastic bottle of Tetracycline, perhaps fifty pills. It was weak stuff, but it would have to do. There was a small bottle of rubbing alcohol, and a plastic bag filled with cotton balls. He chuckled when he saw the self-contained, sterilized packets of stitches, with a thin needle and dissolving thread. Carl was observant. Yet, Carl was diplomatic. Trance also found the requested needle and a spool of thin, black nylon thread.

He took another swallow of scotch and began to swab at the black and purple puncture in his shoulder. The wound was puckered and swollen shut, and the dried blood had coagulated around the opening. Trance pondered the shooter's choice of weapon. A twenty-five-caliber bullet is larger than a twenty-two, but it travels with less velocity. Twenty-five caliber pistols were made more for ladies to carry in their purses, than they were for killers. Was this choice of weapon deliberate? Perhaps the shots had been meant just to slow him down, not kill. Who wanted him so badly?

The scotch had dulled the his senses, but the moment he touched his shoulder it felt like a blowtorch searing at his flesh, perhaps more like a branding iron. He had never been branded. But he could imagine it now.

Trance realized he could not do this without help. So he leaned back in his chair and drew on the training of his youth.

Trance's parents had moved every two years when he was a child, and every two years he had been immersed into a new culture, a new language and a new set of friends. There was the clash between the Eastern and Western cultures. The intellectual, ego-driven society where he was born and raised, fighting against his father's Eastern training in the mythical forces that he could not see or understand. Throughout his life these two worlds had waged war, his mind the battleground where each fought for the domination of his thoughts. Trance struggled to stay in control, to preserve his sense of self, and succeed on his own in the culture of his choice.

In Japan, Trance had felt like an outsider, forced to become someone other than who he perceived he was. He could never completely allow his world to unfold around him, as his masters had tried to teach. He felt like a failure, yet his masters were secretly astounded that he had been able to grasp so much of the true essence of life in just three short years.

Trance was taken to his first dojo at the age of three, where he studied Bujutsu. By the time he was six he had earned his first black belt. At the age of ten he entered into the care of his masters in Japan. Trance was a child prodigy, a Mozart of the martial arts.

Only in the art of combat could Trance surrender to his inner self. It happened naturally, without thought or control. After so many years of practice, so many hours of work, awkward movements became natural. In this, he was truly Japanese.

Trance's training told him there was something more, a higher self. His father had tried to tell him too, but he couldn't listen. In Western culture they had a similar notion. They called it God. Trance wasn't sure what or who God was.

It was into the world of Japan that he retreated. He allowed himself to descend into meditation, gave away his control of the moment, let all sense of ego flow from his body. He was left with peace. There was no conflict. There was no pain. He simply *was* of the moment. As he floated calmly upon his inner ocean, he opened his eyes and took hold of his Victorinox Swiss Army knife. In his calm, he thought of how the knife had been named after the inventor's mother. He had never been close to his own mother. Why was that?

His knife was sharpened to a razor's edge. He snapped opened the smaller blade and put it under the flame of a butane lighter. He wiped the blade with a cotton ball swabbed with alcohol and did the same with his hands. Calmly he took the knife, watching himself as if he were a spectator, and cut away the surface skin where the bullet had entered. He allowed the wound to bleed, noticing with detachment that the blood flow was still surprisingly small. When he had made enough space to probe for the slug, he opened the nail file of his knife. He heated and cleaned it as he had done the blade. He then pressed it into the hole made by the bullet. He probed dispassionately until he found the exact location of the bullet. He felt a deep, gut-wrenching twinge in his muscles when metal hit metal. The bullet didn't move, and he knew it was flattened against the bone of his shoulder.

Trance closed the thin nail file and wielded the knife like a scalpel. He made a clean incision, cutting deeply lengthwise along the muscle. He pulled the skin apart and the wound started to pour blood. But, in the mirror, Trance could see the back end of the twenty-five-caliber bullet. *Goddamn lucky those things don't pack any punch,* thought Trance. If it had been a twenty-two, he'd be a mess, a forty-five and…He didn't want to think about it. He moved placidly and put down the knife. He sterilized the tweezers, then washed his fingers once more. With the fingertips of his left hand, he pulled back on the flap of skin. He swabbed it with cotton to remove the puddle of blood that had formed in the wound, but the moment the cotton was gone it was filled again with blood. That was okay. Bleeding was good, as long as he didn't bleed out.

With the tweezers in his right hand he pulled at the bullet. It wouldn't move. He tried to wiggle it back and forth. At first it wouldn't budge, but finally, he pried the bullet from its nest. He looked dispassionately at the slug, noticing how it had been deformed into a mushroom during the entry into his body. No wonder it had been so hard to remove.

"Stronger than steel. But slower than a speeding bullet," muttered Trance. He was no Superman.

Trance applied liberal doses of alcohol to the wound. He noticed with child-like wonder how cool it felt against his skin, not the burning sting he had expected. His endorphins were raging in full force. He ignored the free flow of blood that dripped onto the expensive Persian carpet. He lit the lighter and held the broad edge of the knife against the flame. When the knife bristled with heat he laid it flat against the wound until it sizzled and stopped much of the blood. Then he proceeded to sew the opening, stitch by stitch.

Trance sutured a fine line along the edges of the flap he had made in his skin. He pulled it tight, noticing how pliable his skin could be. With each pull the skin stretched from his shoulder. When he had sewn the edges, he went to work on the middle, where the bullet had been. He stitched it underneath, making as clean a row as he could. Then he made a series of surface stitches, pulling each one tighter than the next.

When he finished, he glanced dispassionately at his watch. It had taken him just over two hours to complete the procedure. He swabbed outside of the wound again with alcohol, and then let himself float upward out of his inner calm.

Within minutes Trance found himself swearing at the pain.

"Damn, that hurts!" he cried. He took a large swallow of scotch. He swore again when he realized that he had not asked Carl to provide bandages, or painkillers. He took another swig of his drink and reached for the phone.

"Carl. I need another favor."

"Of course."

"I need some bandages...and something for pain..."

"I just happen to have some Percocet, bandages and tape—all of it right here, my friend. Shall I bring it to you?"

"Please, Carl."

Had Carl known that he would be calling? Had he known that in his pained and tired state he had forgotten to ask him for all he would need? Trance smiled. The Swiss were so efficient, and Carl was as good as they came.

CHAPTER 10

▼

"We've lost him, sir."

"You've lost him? You've lost him? You stupid shit. You're supposed to stick to his ass like flypaper. How many men do you need, Garner?"

"He's rather elusive, sir."

"How many goddamn men do you need? You want another frigging dozen? A hundred? Five hundred? You've got them. I want Trance's ass back here at Langley by tomorrow!"

Jacob Miller threw the phone down in disgust. "First, it's those lamebrains in Maine, and now this. How the hell am I supposed to run this department when they keep sending me shit-for-brains idiots?" There was no one in Miller's office. He had cleared them out so he could have his tantrum. It was not often that he got like this, and he didn't want any of his men to see him fly off the handle...*but for Christ's sake. You'd think they'd be able to follow one man. They had dozens of agents in Zurich. They were waiting at the goddamn airport for him when he arrived. They should have taken him there. Now they say they've lost him? What kind of morons are we hiring?* "Imbeciles. I'm running a department of frigging imbeciles."

Miller's phone rang briefly and stopped. A moment later a voice came over the intercom. "There's a call for you, sir."

"I'm not taking any more calls," he said. But then he reconsidered. "Unless it's from those lame brains in Zurich."

"It's Senator Hopewell, sir."

"Well, why the hell didn't you say so?" Miller grabbed his phone. "Hello, Senator. I suppose you've heard?" Hopewell was the chairman of the Senate Intelligence Committee. For two decades he had been exerting more influence on the CIA than anyone, including its various directors. Hopewell had helped create T Force, the covert operations group headed by Trance and run by Miller. Similar to the better-known Task Force 121, but more secretive. Now the son-of-a-bitch was going to be president. Miller had to handle Hopewell with kid gloves.

"I'm worried about my boy, Miller. I heard you lost him."

"For the moment. But we'll be finding him soon."

"How did your men screw up?"

Miller sighed into the phone. "Trance pulled some kind of shit at the airport. He left three Israeli agents, four terrorists, two air marshals, and one pilot dead on a Swiss Air flight. Then he managed to avoid customs. Before we knew it, he was gone. The next thing we know, we're picking up the freakin' Russians on the radio as they chase him through the streets of Zurich. Before we could intervene, Trance killed two of them. We were able to neutralize the rest. But at the same time we lost Trance. Strange thing though, our men were followed, and it wasn't by Russians. There are a lot of people interested in our boy—a lot more than there should be."

"The banker that helped Trance escape has been cleared. He was an innocent pawn. But now, the Swiss authorities are breathing down our necks. They want answers. They want justice," said Hopewell.

"You're lucky they're only *breathing* down your neck. They're shitting down mine."

"They should be." Hopewell paused, and his voice grew somber. "I've been able to get the Swiss authorities to back off, for now. But, I want you to find him, Miller. You bring him to me. I'm leaving tonight for Europe to mend some fences. I'll e-mail my itinerary. If Trance moves, I'll move along with him. I want him and I want him alive."

"I still can't believe that Trance would snap like he did," said Miller. "He was the best we had."

"He didn't snap, Miller."

"Oh, but I think he has."

"He's under pressure. He needs help."

"But to kill two friends? The professor and that investment banker were his friends. It doesn't make sense. He must have snapped."

"I'm sure there's an explanation, Jacob. You find him. Then leave it to me. I don't want any of your trigger-happy boys putting holes into *my* boy's body. You got that? The kid has been through enough, and I feel responsible."

"Yes, sir. We'll find him." *But will we find him before the Russians? Will we find him before the Israelis? The SIS? And now all of frigging Europe will be after him. With twelve men dead in his wake they are going to shoot first and ask questions later.*

"O'Malley! Get in here," yelled Miller.

"Yes, sir?"

"Get me another pot of coffee...and order a pizza, the works...and another bottle of Pepto Bismol. My ulcer is killing me."

Miller sat back into his chair and pressed the tips of his fingers into a steeple against his chin. "Where are you, you son of a bitch? If I were you, where would I go? You always stay at the Dolder, but you know I know that. So where would you go? For all we know you're half way around the world by now. Spending money you've stolen from the taxpayers. Now you're murdering your friends. You finally snapped, didn't you? Or did you? What are you doing, Jack Trance? Did you finally give in? Did you join the other side? Or have you gone into business for yourself?"

Miller pounded on the intercom. "O'Malley! Get me Garner on the line." Miller reached for his stomach. *Damn this stomach. Damn this job...damn you, Trance.*

Miller heard a beep on his phone. "Garner?"

"Yes, sir."

"Garner, I want you to check the Dolder Grand. Check every alias he's got. Show pictures. It would be like Trance to choose the obvious."

"Exactly how do you want me to proceed, sir?"

"He'd register under a corporate name. Never his own. We used to use Transcontinental Consulting Group. Then he switched to International Capital Resources. I doubt he'd use one of those. But check the obvious first. It'd be like him to play with us like that—"

"But how can we be sure, sir? We can't go knocking down doors at a four star hotel, can we?"

"You screwed this one up, Garner. You figure out what to do. If you wait 'till he shows, you wait 'till he shows. But don't let him get away." Miller rang off. "I'll let that bastard stew in his own mess. I'll teach Garner to screw up. He's following one man, one goddamn man, and he's got a whole goddamn army to do it…"

Miller walked to his door and snapped the dead bolt shut. Then he reached inside his briefcase and removed a mobile phone. He set it into a small scrambler and punched in a code. Seconds later he heard three beeps, then dialed.

"Yes?"

"It's me."

"You're clear."

Miller spoke quietly, "We still don't have a lock on him. We lost track of him after we picked up the Russians. I just sent Garner to check out the Dolder Grand. I suggest you do the same."

"Anything else?"

"No, but keep me up on any developments."

CHAPTER 11

▼

Trance toweled himself dry and sat heavily upon the king sized bed, with his belongings laid in a neat row beside him. He slipped new bullets into the magazine of his Colt automatic. He wiped down his shuriken blades with alcohol and placed them back into the seams of his belt. He did the same with his throwing knives. Then he packed his toothbrush, toothpaste and razor into a small toiletry bag and zipped it tight. Once everything was in proper order he set the alarm on his watch for eight PM. He couldn't risk more time. They would find him here by morning, hopefully not before then.

They would search the city methodically—every hotel, every rooming house and hostel. The most likely places would be watched with vigilance, the Dolder too. He must leave before then. Carl would protect him with anything but his life, perhaps even with that. Would his pursuers put Carl in that position? Would they come waltzing into the hotel and threaten the life of a thirty-year employee? He wouldn't—not if this were his operation. But this was a game of odds, a constant gamble. One didn't raise the stakes unless the odds shifted into one's favor. They would wait outside for him, for a while.

As in any gambling, there was an ebb and flow in the odds, with the advantage shifting from time to time. Momentum was on his side, but it could shift any moment. By daybreak, his advantage would be lost.

Yes, they would wait a while, even if they knew he was there. They would take him when he left, and he had to leave. But there were dozens of hotels in Zurich. He could be in any one, or any European country by now. The chances were remote that they would choose this exact hotel and overpower Carl within three hours. They were odds he must accept, so he drifted off to sleep.

The press of cold steel against Trance's cheek awakened him from his druglike slumber. The moment he raised his head, another pistol slammed into his temple. His head snapped back into the pillow, and a small circle of blood spread into the fabric from under his ear. He fell into unconsciousness. He would remain that way for a long while, and when he awoke, his head would beat like a snare drum at a rock concert.

Trance's first thought, when he fought to regain his consciousness, was that he had fallen asleep while flying one of his planes. Somewhere in the back of his mind he could hear the incessant drone of an airplane engine. The engine worked too hard; he could hear it straining in the vague space between dream and reality. He opened his eyes and saw nothing, complete blackness. Was he blind? No, he was blindfolded, with a thick, black cloth wound tightly around his skull. His head felt like it was lying at the base of a waterfall, with a constant rushing of noise, and a continual thrumming inside it. Wet drool had accumulated on his chin and he wiped it away with the fabric of his shirt.

Trance's hands were in front of him, bound by a nylon tie. A rip of pain coursed through his shoulder as he tried to reach up to pull off the blindfold.

"Where are we?" he said in English. There was no answer, only a faint whispering several feet away.

"Where are we?" he said in French. More whispering.

"Where are we?" he repeated in German.

There was a laugh and a booming voice replied in German. "He awakens! We thought that you might sleep forever." The man laughed again.

"What's going on?" said Trance.

"I am no prophet. Although, I suspect that you are going to your death. It would surprise me none if it were a slow, painful death at that." This time, several others joined the man in laughter.

"How did you find me?"

"My, aren't we inquisitive?" The man laughed again, obviously impressed with his facility for words.

"The man at the Dolder desk. What happened to him?"

"Ah—most unfortunate. He did his best to protect you, mein Herr. He had rather remarkable stamina…I am afraid he may never be the same—"

"Bastards."

"And who is this talking? The man who leaves death behind him like discarded gum wrappers."

"What did you do with my bag?"

"I am afraid that it is no longer 'your bag'," said the loud voice, once again laughing. "It is here next to me where it will be safe. Perhaps it contains something important? Alas, I am afraid I will never know what it contains. Because I wish to keep my balls intact!" More laughter. How many voices were there?

"Where are you taking me?" Trance had to know what his next move should be.

"We will be there soon enough. It is of no real concern to you. Enjoy the flight while you can. I suspect that you are about to enter hell." He paused. "Yes, hell is where you are going."

"We're flying at high altitude," said Trance. "The pilot is pushing this bird well beyond its limits." Trance sniffed the air. "This cabin is pressurized, heated, too. Are we traveling far?"

"You are very observant. Now keep your mouth shut. We are not supposed to be talking."

"What else is there to do—" A deftly placed kick bit into Trance's crotch. He had not seen it coming although he had somehow felt the motion—just enough to move so that the kick missed hurting him by an inch. He feigned discomfort, coughed and bent forward over his knees. As he bent forward, he dipped his hands to his belt and pulled out a thin, flexible blade that was resting in a narrow space within the leather folds. In one smooth motion he severed the cord binding his hands. At the same time he yelled, "You bastards!"

Trance knew that another kick would come, so he braced for the blow. The moment his captor's foot stretched out he grabbed it by the ankle, snapped it to the side and twisted it forward. There was a loud crack as the man's bone tore from its socket. When he heard the scream, Trance reached up and pulled at his blindfold. Then he sprang forward toward the direction of the voices. As he jumped, a fist met him squarely on the nose and knocked him to the floor. His nose broke cleanly and crumpled to one side, spurting blood. Trance pressed his elbows to the floor and responded with a donkey kick to the body of his attacker. His left arm gave way, and his kick fell short of lethal force. The man fell back, then reached down for his gun. Trance knew he had only moments to live.

The world seemed to slow down for Trance; his mind saw things as if they were a slow-motion movie. For the first time, he saw the entire cabin, noticing that there were not three, but twelve men inside. Most of them were sitting back watching the action, some with smiles on their faces, while others had grim looking rifles pointed at him. They could kill him at whim. Beside him was the cabin door, with a row of parachutes hanging beside it.

In that brief instant, everything around him seemed to move with vivid exaggeration. Trance had just one hope. He reached below with his useless left hand and willed it to obey his command. It grabbed the pistol from the opened holster of the loud man whose leg he had broken. He pointed it forward, yelling, "Stop, or I'll shoot!"

He knew that it made no difference what he yelled, only that the sound would startle the men, just long enough to give him the precious seconds he needed A grizzled man pointed his gun at Trance's face. Trance shot him between the eyes. Blood spattered throughout the cabin. Trance used the moment of shock to grab the handle of his gym bag from between the dead man's legs. At that same instant he threw open the cabin door to the outside air.

"Don't anybody move!" he shouted in German. Trance grabbed a parachute, turned and jumped. One shot rang out from the startled army in the plane. A 38-caliber slug whistled through the air and snaked its way through Trance's ribs into the left side of his lower chest. He had no time to react, for he was in free fall, his gym bag in his left hand and the shoulder strap to a parachute in the other. He couldn't worry about a bullet playing footsies with his intestines. Somehow he had to get the parachute on his back. He had to live.

CHAPTER 12

▼

Two imposing stone pillars guarded the driveway to the secluded estate. Between the stanchions hung a gate of heavy, vertical, black wrought iron bars. Each bar was rimmed on top by a large gold cap in the shape of an eagle. There were twelve eagles in all, and they formed a horizontal line exactly twelve feet from the ground. On each pillar stood a golden globe of the earth. Both worlds rotated slowly.

The driveway was smooth, almost like pavement, but it was made of small stones carefully brushed each day by hand. The road wound through a forest of tall pines for nearly a mile. It rose and fell with gentle undulations, hugging the natural contour of the land. It blended with the forest, forming a peaceful co-existence with the unblemished surroundings.

Before reaching the main estate, the driveway passed several large three-story homes made of brick, painted white, and trimmed with black shutters. Each of the homes sported a polished brass weathervane in the finest of New England traditions. The first was of a rooster, the second a retriever, and the third a pelican. The colors of the buildings' stained glass windows could be seen from a distance, giving each house its own special hue. The grounds of these homes were impeccably maintained. There were rose gardens and walkways bounded by trellises covered with ivy, and several white gazebos. Two deep, man-made duck ponds shimmered in a teasing breeze, reflecting an unusually bright sun, while white swans swam effortlessly along the surface. Under the surface, brightly colored carp swam lazily in and about underwater cities created by the hands of a master sculptor.

As one passed toward the estate, there was no mistaking that this was opulence at its finest, befitting one of the richest families in America. As one drew closer, the drive took on an even greater grandeur. A series of Japanese gardens surrounded by clear, slow moving streams of water greeted the eyes. Delicate bridges of ivory, jade, and black lacquer crossed the streams. Connecting the bridges were marble steppingstones set meticulously into the streams, each stone polished to brilliance and reflecting a unique shape and hue.

Through the trees surrounding the gardens, one could make out the tall white pillars of the central estate. It looked like a magnified version of the White House, which indeed, it was. Facing south, as in the original, there was a great rounded portico of white marble columns. Inside, there was a stately reception room, with the dominant colors of gold and white. An oval rug, woven in the Aubusson manner of gold, white, and blue tint, lay upon the floor. But where the White House rug had the emblems of each of the fifty states embroidered along its edges, this one had the emblems of nations of the world.

The west wing of the home opened to an expansive garden, identical in shape to the famous Rose Garden of the White House. But, rather than the mixture of springtime tulips, grape hyacinths, columbine, summer roses, anemones, and other bright warm weather flowers, mixed with autumn chrysanthemums, heliotrope, and salvia for the fall, in this garden the mixture had been altered to correspond to a cooler climate.

French doors, under a white-pillared colonnade opened into an impressive oval office. Upon the ceiling, set in low relief, was a carving much like the one of the Presidential Seal in Washington. Yet this was the seal of a different nation, a nation that was yet to be born.

"The Americans will never stop their imperialistic ways, General. Of that we can be sure. They will never rest until they have removed all chances for equality among the peoples of the world. They will not stop until they have crushed the Socialist Ideal like a cigarette under their mighty boot." The speaker stood over six feet and was muscularly built. His hair was closely cropped and he had the face of a male model. His eyes were slate gray, with no hint of life or compassion. In contrast, the general was advanced in age. He was shorter, with muscles that had grown soft with the years. His tired brown eyes seemed to glisten with weary compassion.

"Yes, Vladimir. I understand the childish selfishness of the American philosophy. The capitalistic propaganda claiming that freedom must be won for all nations, just so they can continue to exploit the downtrodden peoples of the third world. Unlike you, I am not sure that force is the answer. You are young, Vladi. You have not lived through the ravages of war like some of us. We remember what it was like...and we have tried to bring about our purpose in a more—" He paused to search for the proper words, "—peaceful manner."

"And where has it gotten us, General? What has our new capitalism done for us? Our standard of living is *less* than what it was twenty years ago. We spend so much of our national budget on the military, just to use it as a bluffing tool. Our people have to wait in line to buy fresh bread, if they can get it at all. Is this the capitalist ideal? Meanwhile, it is too expensive for us to support puppet states, as we once did so well. We have lost our grip upon the world. Third world countries have begun to embrace the short-term wonders of capitalism. Using oppressively low wage-bases, with western capital and technology, they are building entire industries overnight. They no longer want our money, General. Our technology is inferior. What were once rice paddy nations are now growing at more than twice the rate we grow. Even China, our most feared enemy of all, has sold out to the capitalists. During the past twenty years their growth has been obscene. Since the fall of the Union, while our economy has stagnated, theirs has grown more and more rapidly. Now their GDP is now many times that of Russia. They dwarf us like a giant and they are trying to crush us under their boots.

"But we both know that the ultimate form of world government *must* be socialism. Like every candle, each nation will burn itself out, even America. As each nation falls from the pinnacle of competitive edge, they grow progressively socialistic—like our Western European friends. They find ways to blame their declining standards of living on trading partners, overvalued currencies, or excessive government spending. They have not learned to accept that the natural progression of society will lead them inexorably to socialism, the elimination of class envy, of those feeling superior to all others."

"Do you truly believe those words, Vladi?" asked the general softly.

"Wasn't that the official party line, General? Before our failing experiment with capitalism? Wasn't that the basis for your entire philosophy? How could I believe otherwise?"

"I do not question your loyalty to our movement, Vladi. I simply ask for your true opinion."

"I believe in Russia, Comrade General. I can see that Russia has but one direction it can follow if we are to avoid falling into the list of discarded also-rans in the quest for global power. The list of nations under our control has grown short. The few that remain are becoming increasingly expensive to maintain. They continue to fall farther and farther behind the other nations of the world, and they have become chains around our neck. When do you plan to admit your failure?"

"We have not failed, Vladimir. We have kept the world in peace…" *But he is right,* thought the general. *We are losing our control. We have become an also-ran.*

"Yes. You have kept peace, with the power you once had. But now, now that two dozen nations can launch a nuclear missile, now that we can no longer bully our way around the world with money and weapons, we have but one option," said the young man, his voice growing soft.

"And what is that?" said the old general, with a weary smile creasing his face.

"We are still a great military power. Yes, we can no longer compete in the world economic arena. Yes, our people go hungry. Yes, our women prostitute themselves for spare change. But there is no disputing our military capabilities. Even the Americans tremble at the thought of our might."

"You are delusional. Our might is an illusion, and useful only as a deterrent to war."

"Or as a threat, Comrade General."

"Are you suggesting that we use force, Vladimir?"

"Russia is a tinderbox ready to ignite. It is our last and final chance."

"Many others are beginning to speak like you, Vladimir. It is becoming a source of worry to a tired old general. Soon my generation will no longer be able to guide the Mother Country." The general sighed and massaged his forehead. "We will have to entrust her into the hands of the young, like you. I will discuss this with the others." The general stood up from his chair. "I must be going. So nice of you to invite me to your—" The general looked up at the ceiling and around the walls. "What do you call this place, Vladi? And how is it that a young Russian can own such a home?"

"We are a capitalist country, no? My family controls much of this land, General." Vladimir sighed. "Good bye, Comrade. It was nice to see you again. Remember what I told you. The Americans view us as a terrorist threat. They are preparing for a strike against us. You've seen the evidence."

"What evidence?" said the general. "I've seen no evidence."

"Ours is the only answer." Vladimir waved his arm at the room. "Tell me, General, would I risk losing a place like this? Oh, and General—" Vladimir's eyes showed a brief spark as he leaned to whisper in the general's ear. "You know that my grandfather supplied much of the financing for the great revolution. Without my family there may have been no revolution at all. As thanks, we were allowed to retain a small part of the grand style in which our family lived. Now? Now that capitalism runs rampant over our once-great nation?" He shrugged. "We own far more than you know. Make the right choice, General. Goodbye."

CHAPTER 13

▼

Trance fell from the plane into a whirling vortex. He felt like he was spinning into some great celestial black hole, powerless against the darkened force pulling him to death inside the void. The wind whipped in face-pealing gusts and gave his skin a patina of frosty white crystals. He fought to breathe in the thin air, and because of his wounds, he could not stabilize himself by holding out his arms. His right hand held a tight grip on the parachute, while the other fought against the pain and the brittle cold to clip his gym bag to his belt. He counted off the seconds, knowing that any one of them could be his last. How far was it to the ground? He knew that they were high in the air, but they could have been at high altitude for any number of reasons. They could have been avoiding the cumuli nimbi of a major thunderstorm. They could have been riding a favorable wind at that altitude, or seeking to avoid detection. The worst of his fears was that they were flying high over the mountain ranges of the Alps. As the seconds ticked by, he envisioned himself falling, face first, into the side of a mountain. How many seconds more would he have? He thought of dropping the gym bag, but he couldn't. He had chosen this mission above his life. It was needed. He struggled with the bag for a few extra moments until it was clipped to his side. Next he fought against the sub-zero wind to wrap the parachute around his injured shoulder.

Each movement brought sharp stabs of pain. He felt like he was hanging on a meat hook, helplessly suspended in the air with a sharp iron poker lodged in his ribs. Each labored breath felt as if someone were pulling down on his feet, jamming the hook ever further into his ribs. But he had no choice. How many times had he strapped a parachute to his back with no effort at all? Countless. He felt no consolation knowing that it would be easier next time. There might not be a next time.

A voice from his childhood said *relax*. He saw the face of his master, then that of his father. How many times had his father told him, "You must learn to relax and allow things to happen; you shouldn't try to force every action." Hadn't this always worked for him, no matter how much he had tried to fight it?

Trance stopped his struggle against the parachute. He held it in his right hand and let it fly freely in the wind. Then he simply rolled the left side of his body into the strap of the chute. It happened so easily. Within seconds he had it strapped against his chest. Then he pulled the cord.

He felt the white chute fly out above him, and braced himself for the sudden thump when the chute took hold of the air. He heard the pop and the pack pulled up against his chest and skewered another shish kabob through his left side. Then he listened to his father. He relaxed.

Trance swayed from one side to the other, then back again. Trance's next sensation was that of his knees driving into his chest as the ground raced to meet him. Trance gave a loud "Ugh," as he fell to the ground and rolled to break the fall. But the roll didn't stop. He was falling down a mountainside. He felt the hardness of the stone against his body. Rocks tore into his flesh as he tried to stop, but the ground was too steep, and Trance kept rolling. The parachute cord began to wrap around his body. He fought to keep his arms outstretched to break his slide, to stop the death roll, but the rope wound tighter against his arms until he was helpless. Trance's face cracked into the ground, tearing a wide gash in his right cheek and driving his already broken nose farther off to one side. He looked like he had been shaving with a food processor. There was nothing he could do but allow the fall. He curled his head against his knees to keep it from being crushed by the rocks. That was no use, so he let go. He relaxed and let it happen.

Trance thudded hard against an outcropping of rocks. It nearly brought him to a stop. He teetered in the balance between stopping and going onward, for the briefest of moments, then he was falling through the air. There was nothing underneath him, no rocks tearing at his face and arms, no pain, only the calm feeling of knowing that he was about to die.

"How undignified," he murmured. How many times had he flirted with death and laughed in its face? It had finally come to claim him. They were even now.

But death didn't settle the score. The parachute behind him caught in the rocks. The lines drew taught and Trance unrolled like a yoyo. His body stopped at the bottom, like the sleeper trick. But Trance wasn't sleeping. He was half dead.

Trance hung motionless in the air, swaying from side to side in the darkness. He looked like a spider dangling on thin lines of silk. He gazed around, trying to gauge his position. Now that he had stopped, he was able to make out some of the surrounding shapes. He was suspended over the edge of a cliff, with two or three hundred feet of air between himself and the rocks below. Above him he saw the parachute partially caught between two boulders. The rest of the parachute fluttered casually in an intermittent breeze.

"This isn't my day," he muttered. Trance shook his head and tried to laugh it off. But as he laughed, the metal wedged under his ribs quickly forced him to stop. He turned his mind toward getting himself to the top of the ledge. "Just another Sunday afternoon climb," he said cheerfully. *What day is it, anyway? God, what I would give for a bowl of ice cream.*

This was the kind of situation that Trance trained for. This was his hobby. Other successful men relaxed with golf. Getting a little white ball to do Herculean tasks could be an all-consuming event, and men could forget all other problems in their lives. Forgetting allowed them to relax. Trance liked golf, but this was better. Deep inside he knew it was why he continued to accept the government assignments, why six or seven times a year he would risk his life, bet against the odds, knowing any mistake could be his last. This made him forget. It allowed him to erase the memory of Janice, erase the recurring thoughts of how different his life would be if...always if. In brief moments like this he felt free.

Trance's golf course was above him now, strapped to his chest, and lodged between his ribs. He felt the same tension as trying to decide between a four or five iron into the wind. Should he keep himself strapped to the end of the ropes? Should he unhook himself and free climb to the top? It was a difficult decision, given the condition of his body. If he decided to free-climb and slipped, he was disqualified for life. There was no 'two-stroke penalty and move on to the next hole' in this game. This was Amen Corner, at the Masters, on Sunday, with a one-shot lead. It would be less awkward to climb without the straps and the ropes clinging to him, but if he miscalculated, it *was* over.

Trance reached into his bag and withdrew his Swiss Army knife. He cut one of the ropes extending from his harness, then pulled himself upward and cut again, four feet above the loose end of the rope. He tied two bowline knots six inches apart onto another of the ropes, leaving a foot or so of rope hanging free below the bottom knot. He made these knots tight enough to cling to the rope, but not so tight that he couldn't slide them upwards. He then tied a third bowline at the bottom end of the rope, leaving a loop on the bottom large enough to hold a shoe. He placed his right foot into the loop and used it to stand on the rope. As he placed his weight upon the rope, he felt it tighten with the added strain. But there was no slippage in his knot. He cut another one of the ropes at the base of his parachute pack, just as he had the first. He made the same two knots as before, but this time to another strand of rope. The bottom end of this he tied to his belt with a taut-line hitch.

When his knots were secure, Trance cut away most of the remaining ropes to his parachute. He slung his gym bag into the air, smiling as it thumped safely onto the ledge above. Then he took hold of the cord tied around his waist. He fingered the knot and pushed it upward as far as it would go. He then stood upon the rope around his foot, standing as straight and high as he could. This gave more slack to the cord attached to his waist. He pushed that knot higher again. When he had taken all of the slack out of the cord about his waist, he took the pressure off of the foot loop. This put all of his weight upon the cord about his waist. He then reached down, fighting against the pain in his side, and pulled the knots of his foot loop upward on the other rope until they were eye height. His foot loop now hung next to his belt. He reached his leg up, pulling his knee against his chest. This left all of weight on his belt rope. He maneuvered his foot back into its loop. He pulled against the rope and stood up on it again. He then repeated the pressing upward of his waist rope. When he had taken out the slack, he repeated the process with the foot loops.

When Trance reached his parachute he found it wedged precariously between two man-sized boulders. He heaved himself up and over the rocks and lay exhausted on the ground. Faint splinters of daylight were spreading over the mountaintops to the east. Trance took twenty minutes to meditate, then calmly watched as a hot orange sun climbed into the sky.

Trance reached into his bag and withdrew a small mirror to survey the damage to his body. His face looked like it belonged to the loser of a prize-fight. His nose lay flattened to one side, and flecks of dried blood mottled his pallid skin. Trance set down the mirror, wedged his hands against his nose and snapped it mostly back into place. He spit into a piece of his shirt and used it to wipe away the blood. Then he closed his eyes. He mentally searched for and localized each injury, then removed them from his consciousness. His masters had told him that pain was a choice. They could do this easily, but it was something Trance still had to work at. He wondered how long he would be able to keep the pain at bay.

Trance's wounds were still oozing blood. With psychic detachment he pressed on each one until the bleeding retreated. He might have enough blood left to live, if he could find water soon. Infection was another matter. He took two more of his antibiotic pills, hoping they were strong enough. Using these pills against these wounds was like trying to catch a Great White Shark with a fly rod and twenty-pound line. Possible, but the odds were against him.

Trance looked around. He was in the mountains, of that he was sure. Most likely the Alps. The range extended northward and the air was warming comfortably. He looked down to his watch, noticing that the dawn was corresponding roughly to the time zone for which it had been set. Yes, he thought. They hadn't gone far. These were the Alps. He had climbed them enough with his father to feel the familiarity in the stone, and the shape of the peaks. But he couldn't place the country. Was he still in Switzerland? Or, had they flown west into France, east into Austria, or south to Italy? He'd find out shortly, he was sure. Once he knew that, he would know whom to call.

To Trance's relief, his descent from the mountain was only a moderate challenge. Soon he was back on level ground. He walked unsteadily toward the east and descended gently into a broad valley. After thirty minutes he came to a fast moving stream of icy, mountain water. He sat to rest, and drank as much of the water as he could stand.

Trance felt his dizziness begin to fade. With better focus, he set about to dress his wounds. He put a fresh bandage over his shoulder, noting with a touch of pride that his stitching job had remained almost intact. He then examined the newest addition to his body decorations. He felt gently with his fingers for the slug, tracing the puncture where the bullet had hit against his backside ribs. As he pressed against the bones he felt them begin to separate, and a sharp pain ran through his chest. One of the bullets had passed through the cartilage and now rested somewhere in his chest. There was no way he could get to this one on his own. He would be lucky to avoid a punctured lung—lucky to remain alive.

Trance fanned his bloody shirt in the frigid stream to rinse it clean, then used it to give himself a shivering sponge bath. He put a couple of quick stitches over the puncture above his ribs. This quelled the last bit of external bleeding. The rest would have to be fixed by a specialist. He put bandages over each of his wounds, so that anyone seeing him would not be looking at a bloodstained shirt. Trance's face was hopeless. Trance took the bloody shirt and ran it through the water again. Once he had washed out the blood he slung it around his body to create a makeshift wrap for his ribs. It wasn't much, but it would have to do. He slipped on his remaining clean shirt, silently giving thanks to Carl for caring enough to get him a spare. He wondered if Carl was alive, or if he would ever see him again. Trance vowed that if he did see his friend, he would reward him well for his loyalty.

Trance walked north along the valley until he came upon the rolling fields of a farm. He had traveled no more than two or three miles, but he was calling upon his last vestiges of strength. He saw a small farmhouse of white stucco and brown wooden trim. Outside the home stood a meager, but well-maintained, corral. Inside it, two broad-shouldered workhorses stood calmly munching on tufts of grass. They were the color of brown moss, with their characteristically wide hooves and shaggy hair at the bottom of their legs. They were well groomed and appeared healthy.

"Poor, but proud," said Trance to himself. He tried to gauge what kind of person would own such a farm, and whether he could trust these people. He could be easily betrayed, unwittingly or with purpose. For all he knew there was a substantial reward being offered for his capture. Maybe his picture was all over CNN, a rogue CIA operative, a killer on the loose. Find him and you will be a hero as well as rich…Trance could kill these farmers with impunity. They were remote enough. Did it make sense to allow such a chance? "Yes," he said. "I could kill them. But these people have done nothing wrong. I will ask them for help. If they refuse, I will move on."

CHAPTER 14

▼

"Baron von Hoffenburg, my Lord, we just received a transmission that Trance has jumped from our plane." The Baron's communications officer cringed at the oppressive silence that met his news. As much as he tried, he could not raise his eyes to meet those of the Baron. His Lord was obsessed by Trance, and losing him again would put him in another foul mood. When the Baron was in a foul mood, heads rolled, literally.

"What was that, Lieutenant?"

"Trance jumped from our plane."

The Baron appeared surprisingly calm. "And what is it that our men have chosen to do, Lieutenant?"

"It just happened, my Lord. They are awaiting your instructions."

"Where are they?"

"Less than one hundred kilometers from the castle, Sire."

"Tell them that if they return here without Trance, I will personally torture each of them in a most painful way—until each has died a most unpleasant death. Tell them that if Trance is not delivered to me within the next twenty-four hours they need not return to the castle at all. Tell them they can await my wrath wherever they may choose to hide." The Baron stopped and scratched his bearded chin. "By the way, did Trance use a parachute?"

"He pulled one off the rack, but we don't know if he got it open. He was pretty shot up."

"Resourceful men, Trance and his father. He'll be alive. Get me the exact co-ordinates. Immediately, Lieutenant." The Baron pressed his intercom and said, "Major. Come to my study, now."

The Baron sat tapping his fingers on his desk. He was doing his best to remain calm. The mark of a true leader is to remain calm in the thick of battle, he reminded himself. How many times over the centuries had he said that to his generals? He had trained some of the greatest ever, and he himself, was perhaps the best. Yes, he *was* the best, though he had always avoided the limelight.

By the time the major lifted the knocker on the ponderous doors leading into the Baron's study, he had heard about the Baron's threat. The pit of his stomach warned him that he was about to receive a challenge just as onerous. But this was expected of the Baron, and it didn't bother the major in the least. How many years had he been working for him? More than six. In that time he had been paid enough money to last him several lifetimes. He had lived well, and he would die without regret.

"Yes, my Lord."

"You've heard the news, I'm sure. What would you suggest we do?" *Allow a soldier to suggest an idea, and he will fight that much harder to see that it is successful.*

"I suggest putting a greater force of men into the area to find him, Baron."

"And how many would you suggest?"

"I can transport two hundred and fifty men on a moment's notice, my Lord."

"Will you find him, Major?"

"We will find him."

"Your life may depend upon it."

"Of course."

"Leave immediately."

The Baron reached for his phone and pushed a speed dial button.

"Hello."

"Are we sterile?" asked the Baron.

"Of course."

"Trance has escaped."

"Yes, I know."

"How could you possibly know?" cried the Baron.

"Your men used an open channel."

"My men? They *were* my men. They are now dead men."

"They should be."

"We will find him," spit the Baron coldly.

"One of us will."

"I want him."

"Then you will get him."

"Yes, I will. How is everything else proceeding?"

"Right on schedule, my Lord."

"I will not proceed until I get my formula."

"The formula is secondary. We have more money than we need. It is the power that counts. Soon we will have it all. What is gold when you rule the world?"

"With the nuclear fallout we will need the Elixir to stay alive. I will grow old without it..."

"Growing old is natural, my Lord. Perhaps you should let others—"

"Talk like that to me again and I'll feed your balls to my dogs for dinner!"

"Of course. Is there anything else you need? I have many things to do."

"Get me Trance."

"You will have your man. Dead or alive."

The Baron chuckled at the impudence of his young son. *Why must we all act that way in our youth? I will have to dispose of him, too, when this is all over. Perhaps I will feed his balls to the dogs...*

The Baron pushed another button on his phone. He waited through the series of beeps as the call connected a thousand miles away.

"Yes."

"Trance has escaped."

"I have heard."

"If your men find him before mine do, I want him. Do you hear?"

"Of course, my Lord," said the Russian.

"How is everything else?"

"I have convinced our leaders that war is inevitable. The majority now agree that a first strike may be most advantageous."

"Good. Good. So all is proceeding according to plan?"

"Did you expect anything less?"

"No." The Baron cradled the receiver. Then, almost as an afterthought he picked up the phone again and dialed.

"Hello." This time the answer was female.

"Hello, darling."

"Bubka! How are you?"

"Troubled."

"Poor dear," she cooed. "Do you need to talk?"

"Just the sound of your voice makes me feel better."

"Of course, darling. You know how much I care for you..."

"Good night. Come to me tomorrow."

"I will count the hours. Good night, my love."

The Baron was not as ancient as they thought.

CHAPTER 15

▼

"Grusse Gott," said Trance, hopefully, to the farmer. Trance used the friendly form of greeting used through much of Austria, one that had a way of forming kinship quickly among Austrians when it was spoken.

"Grusse Gott," came the reply. So he was in Austria. The farmer looked to be in his eighties. He wore a pair of tan and green leather shorts, the lederhosen that the tourists so often liked to buy. Unlike many of the European traditions that could be found only among tourists, lederhosen were still used among the country people. They were functional and durable.

The man was in no hurry to make conversation. He stood looking at Trance, letting his eyes move from a face that looked like a bruised plum to the bandage lines underneath his shirt, and finally to his hands. He noticed the calluses along the edges and on the tips of his fingers, and he wondered what it was that could have hardened such hands, even more so than his own. The farmer was not tall, but neither was he short. His most predominant feature was that he was lean. No part of his frame contained anything extra, no extra bone or skin. But there was strength in each sinewy muscle, and he moved with a deliberate, laconic grace that belied his profession.

"You're the one they are looking for," he said.

Trance gave a slight nod of his head.

"And what is it you have done, I wonder?"

"I need your help," said Trance. He spread out his hands in a gesture of submission.

"I believe you are beyond help," the farmer replied. "There must be two hundred men in this valley looking for you. I have received several calls of warning from old friends...They come from the von Hoffenburg castle—these men who are forcing their way into each home along the valley. There are others, too, I am told. I do not think that it would be wise for an old farmer to meddle in the affairs of the von Hoffenburgs. Men who oppose them have a way of disappearing." He paused. "Or turning up dead."

Trance searched the eyes of the farmer, reading the truth in his words. Two hundred searching, all von Hoffenburg men. Perhaps he should let them find him? Could this be the simple solution?

"Who are the von Hoffenburgs?" he asked.

The old man's eyes crinkled in a smile.

"Who are the von Hoffenburgs?" he cried. "How can one describe the von Hoffenburgs...They are money and power, avarice and greed. They are myth and legend, and as real as you and me. Little is known about them. But there is nothing in this country, some say the world, that they haven't touched or controlled."

"Should I let them find me?" *What should I do?* Trance wondered.

"You are not considered a friend by the von Hoffenburgs. I suspect that when they find you, it will be the last time that you are heard from—in this country. Perhaps anywhere. I suggest you leave."

"Yes. You are right. Would you mind telling me where I am?"

The farmer looked at Trance's dazed face. The blood had drained from his cheeks, and his eyes had the far away look of a man who was dying. How many times had he seen that look before? The thousand-yard stare. He'd seen it many times—too many times in war.

"Come with me," he said. "You do not look well."

The farmer took Trance by the shoulder. He recognized the signs of shock, and he knew that soon his visitor would fall into it deeply, then into death, unless he helped him now. There was an innocence about this man that caused him to disregard what he wanted to do, and do what he felt was right.

The man led Trance into the farmhouse. Inside it was clean and surprisingly modern, in most respects. Next to a large, stone, wood burning oven stood a new refrigerator and dishwasher, both made by General Electric. The farmer's younger wife was kneading rolls of dough on a marble kitchen counter when her husband entered, trailed by their unexpected guest.

"Pour this man a schnapps, will you, Juli." Schnapps, the Austrian equivalent of chicken soup. Juli poured Trance a good measure of kirche—a clear, almost tasteless liquor distilled from various fruits. She guided it into Trance's tentative grasp and said, "Here, young man. Drink this. Then come and lie down."

Trance mechanically followed her directions, drinking the kirche as if it were water. Three gulps later he stood with his eyes suddenly wider. He numbly followed Juli into a bedroom just off from the kitchen.

"Here," she said, pointing toward a bed. "Lie down here. Were you hit by a car?" She looked at Trance's broken nose and the lacerations all over his body. She took him gingerly by his right shoulder, seeing how he was favoring the left, and set him gently onto the bed. She propped his feet on three fat feather pillows so that they were well above his head. When she was satisfied that he was as comfortable as she could make him she said, "It would be best that you do not fall asleep. I suspect you know that. I am going to guide your nose all the way back into place now. It will hurt, I know. But it is best that I do it now."

Trance looked at the woman and said, "You know how to do this?"

Juli nodded. Trance relaxed and leaned back against the bed. "Thank you. I'm beginning to feel better already. Go ahead, Juli. It must be done." Trance felt weak, but his mind was already clearing.

Juli placed the edges of her hands along Trance's face, with her little fingers edging toward his ears. She took the middle and index finger of each hand and braced his nose between them, then snapped it roughly back in position. She gently massaged it until it fit smoothly. Her eyebrows raised in surprise when she saw no sign of pain on the stranger's face. Trance's eyes had a far away look, almost as if his mind wasn't there. But she knew that he was aware. He was no longer in shock. The color was returning to his face and his eyes were more alert. But still, he was somewhere else.

"There," she said. "Good as new."

"It feels much better," said Trance in his perfect Austrian dialect, for the first time smiling.

"And you are looking much better. Are you from around here?"

Trance shook his head. "My father was in the Service of the United States. We traveled a lot when I was a child. I just seemed to pick up the languages wherever we went. I'm American."

Juli looked at him shrewdly. "Is there anything else I can help you with?"

"You have done enough already," Trance replied. "I understand that my being here is causing you danger. So I must go soon."

"Where?" said the farmer, standing at the door to the bedroom. "And how? I give you two kilometers, at best, before you fall to the ground. Your brain is returning, but your strength is leaving you by the minute."

Trance watched the farmer speak, saw the conviction in his eyes, and decided to accept his help.

"There is someone I must see. I have never met the man, but my father told me I would need him, someday. He never said more than that—just that someday he would play an important role in my life. I never paid much attention to those words. My father was...different. There were many things he said that I did not understand. This Austrian and my father were close friends, but to my knowledge they never saw each other while I was alive. Strange...I never questioned things my father did. He and I didn't think alike, but somehow my father knew that I would be in this position. He made sure that I would be able to recognize the time when I should call the man he called his closest friend."

Trance's words were barely a whisper.

"And who is this friend?" said the farmer.

"Should I trust you?" said Trance. Confront people unexpectedly and directly and they will reveal their true feelings with a glance or coloring of the skin. He was reacting with instinct refined by years of training.

"I don't know," replied the farmer. "Perhaps, you must."

"I must," said Trance. "His name is Breitfuss. Alfred Breitfuss."

"Freddy? The innkeeper on the Smittenhohe?"

"You know him?"

"But, of course. He was the youngest member of the Austrian ski team when he left unexpectedly for America. That caused quite a stir in our ski-crazed country. Freddie and I used to ski and climb together. Your father was a friend of his? What was his name?"

"Trance."

The farmer's eyes clouded, and he looked as if his mind was very far away. After several moments he said, "So you have come...That was a long time ago...Yes, I knew your father well. I see the resemblance now, even in your condition. John was a very interesting man, and so must you be. You can trust me, Herr Trance. I am one of those that will support you, for I know you mean no harm."

"Where are we? Exactly," asked Trance.

"You're in the Kaisergebirge. Do you know the area?"

"Near St. Johann? There's a small airport in St. Johann, just a few kilometers north of Kitzbuhel. We used to land there to ski."

"Yes."

"So, we are not too far from Zell am See," replied Trance.

"Which lies between here and the Baron's castle in the Dachsteingruppe."

Trance tilted his head, as if to ask "Where?"

"Southeast of Salzburg. There is a ridge of mountains close to three thousand meters. Rugged country. Some of it remote, except for the occasional trains that pass nearby."

"Can you hide me? Get me to Zell am See?"

"Can the Austrians ski?" The old man walked over to the bed and patted Trance on the shoulder. He didn't notice Trance's wince of agony.

"Don't worry," he said. "You will have more help than you ever expected. It appears that there was much your father did not tell you. I am sure that he had his reasons. So, there is much that you must learn—"

"Excuse me," said Trance. "I don't mean to interrupt, but we must move quickly. There are people looking for me, and I am afraid that my strength won't last much longer. You must get me to Zell, and then find me a doctor, a good one. My face is the least of my problems. I've got a low-grade infection in my shoulder, and a slug, probably from a thirty-eight, resting somewhere under my ribs. I have some internal injuries, perhaps some bleeding. I am in pain, sir, and I have much to do—although I still do not know what that is. I won't live without medical attention soon." Trance fell back against the pillow, closed his eyes and began to snore.

For days after that, Trance remained asleep. Occasionally, he drifted toward consciousness, pulled by wrenching nightmares of death. Burning bodies of third world villagers—the agonizing cries from fellow soldiers with gangrene-covered bodies. Boys, who had once been young and optimistic, now reduced to horrible shadows of men, praying for a quick end to their misery—but somehow clinging to some faint hope for survival. He was running through the asphalt jungles of cities—first chasing and killing—then fleeing, his feet struggling to touch the ground as hundreds of men dropped to their knees in slow motion, all taking aim to shoot him in the back as he ran.

He would wake up screaming, with sweat pouring from his body, and saliva frothing at his mouth. Then he'd fall back against the mattress, not yet ready to face a reality that might be even more difficult to survive.

Then, one morning, Trance's eyes came into focus. They rested upon the compassionate eyes of a most beautiful woman. Trance gazed at her, stunned. For a brief moment, as he approached total consciousness, he wondered if this wasn't Janice come back to be with him, or perhaps, this was heaven. He gave a slight shake of his head to remove the final vestige of his dreams, then looked back at the woman.

She had a delicately contoured face, and prominent cheeks that gave her appearance a certain elegance, despite the fact that she wore no makeup. She had shaggy blond hair that fell randomly over her forehead and her shoulders. It was full on the sides, falling as much outward as down. In the front, her hair rose slightly upward before falling in thinned wispy strands. Her eyes were green, and they shimmered like the Mediterranean in the early afternoon, when the sun drops to mid sky. Her eyes became gray when she turned to the side, as if there was only one way to see into the depths inside her. She was thin, yet full-figured. Trance could see the outline of her breasts underneath her flannel shirt. He found himself wondering what she would look like naked, then felt embarrassed and slightly guilty.

"Where am I?" he asked in German.

"You are safe," she replied in English. "They brought you here a week ago, Mr. Trance. At first we thought you might not make it. The bullet inside you had caused some hemorrhaging and your infection was severe and required great care. The doctor who worked on your shoulder did a very messy job. There were bone chips still inside the wound and it had been poorly sterilized. We had to remove the stitches, give it a good cleaning and stitch it back up. I suggest that you find a different physician the next time you get shot. He nearly killed you."

Trance smiled. "I will." *And I thought I had done such a great job on that shoulder.*

"And who are you?"

"My name is Gretel. I come here, to the Inn, every year."

"So, we made it?" The woman looked uncertain of what her response should be.

"Is this the Breitfuss Inn?" said Trance.

"Ah," said Gretel. "Yes, then. You have made it. Excuse me. Herr Breitfuss has asked me to inform him if you awakened." The woman rose from the side of the bed and turned to leave. Trance couldn't help but notice the sensuous curve to her tight-fitting jeans. He felt a flush in his cheeks and began to smile. How many years had it been since he had felt that feeling? Nothing like a brush with death to awaken the soul.

Soon Gretel returned, followed by a swarthy, strongly built man. His face was weathered. His hair was black and was cut neatly around his ears. He wore a full black mustache with a few gray hairs. His sideburns also had a touch of gray, but the rest of his hair looked like tar. He could have passed for a man thirty years younger than Trance knew he must be. His eyes glowed with good-will.

"So," he said loudly. "You have decided to remain among us."

Trance smiled meekly. "It appears that way."

"Welcome to my home, Herr Trance. The man gave a short bow. "Alfred Breitfuss." Breitfuss extended his hand and Trance shook it.

"Your family and mine go back many years, Jackie. May I call you Jackie?" Without waiting for an answer he continued in his husky voice. "Your father always called you Jackie. Oh, I know that as far you knew, your father and I hadn't seen each other in over fifty years. That was for your benefit. But we were able to find ways to meet. Now I finally meet you, John's son." The man reached again for Trance's hand, grasping it firmly. He turned it in his palm, looking at the calluses that made the hand feel like rock.

"Just like your father," he said. "I am sorry that I have to ask you these questions. But John and I agreed that I must be completely sure that it is indeed his son who comes to see me, and not some impostor." Breitfuss withdrew a letter from his pocket and handed it to Trance.

"He said you could decipher this."

Trance looked at the letter and laughed. "Not without a few books I can't."

"These books, perhaps?" Breitfuss left the room, and returned carrying half a dozen volumes in his arms. He placed them on the bed.

"Yes, those. Give me some time alone, please. I'll call you when I've finished."

Breitfuss smiled. "Your father told me you would say that."

"This was written in our code. No one else knows it. I am surprised he gave you these books."

"Your father and I were forced to share confidences," said Breitfuss. He put his arm around Gretel and ushered her out of the room. Turning, he said, "Gretel will be attending to your needs. You can trust her. Call for her when you are ready, Jackie."

Trance began to decode the letter, stopping every few minutes to regain his concentration. He was having difficulty keeping awake.

As the letter unfolded before him, Trance began to understand the importance of the information he possessed, and the unique role that was being played by Breitfuss. At the end of the letter he found several personal questions Breitfuss was to ask, ones that only he could answer. Questions no impostor could know the answers to. Breitfuss obviously had the answers. In addition, there were several questions he was to ask of Breitfuss, along with the answers that the man should give. If he could not answer these questions, then the man posing as Breitfuss was to be killed without question.

"Dear Jackie,

I am leaving this letter with my most trusted friend, Alfred Breitfuss. I am sure that you have many questions by now, and this letter is intended to begin answering them. Breitfuss and the Black Madonna will be able to help you with the rest.

In 1940, before America entered the war, I was ordered to the office of General Thaddeus Swanson. There I met with Bulldog himself. He was a man that I grew to respect, by the way. I also met with Bill Donovan, who later went on to form the OSS, which became the CIA. As it turns out, I was his first recruit. Swanson was working with a man by the name of Penwell, who, at that time, was the head of the British Secret Service. There was also a young major by the name of Miller. I believe you know his son, Jacob, at the Company.

These men suspected that a Baron by the name of von Hoffenburg was secretly financing Hitler. I was to infiltrate his castle, and return with proof. Since I had learned our ways in Japan, much like you, they claimed that I was the only person in the United States Armed Forces that was qualified for the mission—the only one who could enter and come out alive. The Japanese had yet to bomb Pearl Harbor, so I did not feel singled out because of my heritage.

As it turned out, from the beginning, I was never expected to return alive. There were many things I was not told. Swanson admitted this to me later, much later.

But just as Swanson kept information from me, Penwell and the others kept vital information from him.

What I am about to tell you will seem hard to believe. Since I embrace our way, it was easier for me to accept than, I expect, it will be for you. Understand that many myths and legends are based upon true events. I have no doubt that when you have finished reading this letter, and then spoken with Breitfuss and the Black Madonna, you too, will understand.

From the first days of recorded history, man has shown a fondness for gold that is like no other. Man has killed for it, worshiped it, and built entire cultures around it. He has used it as a sign of wealth and power. With it man has made his finest jewelry, his most valuable forms of currency. Collecting it has become a passion of kings, causing entire armies to be formed to obtain it. How many people have died because of fighting over gold, wealth and power?

In ancient days rulers sent explorers to the far ends of the earth in search for gold. Columbus sailed to America to find gold and riches. In America, states like California became populated because of it. The gold rush has been going on in many countries—for thousands of years.

While many have spent their lives in search of gold, so too have countless others spent their lives trying to make it. We are able to transform many things from one substance to the other. So why not gold? Metals are like the spectrum of light. They lie along a continuum, each with more atomic mass than the next. Just as the wavelengths of light can be altered and separated with a prism, cannot the same thing be done with metals?

Over the centuries many have claimed to have found the secret to making gold from other, lesser substances. Many theories have arisen as to how it can be done, and why it is possible. Gold is the ultimate metal. It will never tarnish. It can be pounded, and bent, and it will never lose its luster, or its malleability. Gold is eternal. Many have believed that all substances are in the various stages of becoming gold, and that one must only learn how to speed up the natural process of transformation to create it. Legends have been built upon the unique properties of gold. Men came to believe that there is a special substance that can make gold and when used by man, can give him the same properties as the metal: the physical and spiritual malleability to withstand change, and achieve eternal life. This mythical substance has become known as the Philosopher's Stone, the Elixir of Life. It is purported, but unproven, that a number of men throughout history have learned its secret.

Most of what I am telling you I have learned long after the day General

Swanson enlisted my services. As far as I was concerned, von Hoffenburg was but one of many men that helped Hitler in his rise to power. Yet, from the beginning, there were signs that this was far more than that. For some reason, I was chosen to play a significant role in the struggle for world domination. In so many words, Swanson told me that what I was being ordered to do was a treasonable act, in conflict with the oath of loyalty that I had pledged to our nation. So, from the outset, I chose to let myself be guided by the I Ching. Through the many years since, I have used it to determine my actions. I urge you to do the same. Because you must remember that we are only minor players in the Great Game. We are but one planet, surrounding one minor star, in a universe so large as to escape comprehension. With your I, you will be able to tap into the wishes of the Creator, and understand what it is that you are meant to do, and there is much that you must do. The future of our insignificant world has been placed in your hands.

The early Middle Ages were a period of cultural darkness throughout Europe. At that time, barbarians dominated much of the world, with little interest in art and philosophy. The focus of their existence was the militaristic control of as much of the world as possible. It was into this world that Baron Gustav von Hoffenburg rose to power. Von Hoffenburg was the ruler of a small fiefdom in Austria. In those days, such rulers exercised absolute control over the lives of their subjects. This even included the right of defloration—the barbaric right to deflower any virgin under their rule.

Legend claims that von Hoffenburg employed an alchemist who worked deep in the dungeons under his castle. In those days an alchemist was a blend between a modern day chemist, a doctor, and a religious mystic. Many of them were ascribed to have powers that extended far beyond those of normal, mortal men. Such was the reputation of the Baron's alchemist. A 'Merlin', if you will. Only, he was a Moor.

The alchemist had a daughter, who was taken (as was his legal right) by the Baron. She became his concubine, and she bore him a child.

As the story is told, one day (when his daughter was still quite young), the alchemist confided to her that he had solved the mystery of transforming base metals into gold. He told her that his discovery was so important that it should be kept from the Baron. Making gold was the province of alchemists, not of greedy kings. He began to secretly make the Elixir in the Baron's castle, and remove it to his own home.

Legend says that, after she was taken, the daughter let it slip that her father had made this discovery. Some said this had been deliberate, a bribe to elevate her to the status of wife, a position she reportedly craved. Others said it was a momentously inadvertent mistake that could not be reversed.

When the Baron became aware of the alchemist's discovery, he declared treachery. The alchemist was tortured and held captive until the Baron was able to duplicate the making of the Elixir, and ultimately, the transformation of gold. The alchemist was kept in chains for more than a year, deep in the Baron's dungeons, for it takes that long for the entire process to be completed. During this time he was under the care of his daughter.

As the process neared completion, it is said that the Baron told the daughter, 'Your father will have to die. He cannot be allowed to betray me and go unpunished. You are welcome to stay...You are ordered to stay.'

One day the alchemist called his daughter to his side and said, 'Tomorrow the Baron's transformation of the Elixir will be complete, and I will be killed. I do not blame you for what you have done. You are young. You could not have known the consequences of your actions. But the Baron is an evil man. He will not use this new power for good.'

My son, the Black Madonna has told me that this legend is only partly true—though she would tell me no more. Perhaps she will tell you.

Trance closed his eyes and envisioned life in the Alps a thousand years ago. How primitive it must have been, with no running water, no electricity—none of the modern conveniences of life today. Yet, here was a man that controlled a technology that had not been duplicated in a millennium—a technology that many men would gladly die or kill for. He pondered the extent of the wealth and power that von Hoffenburg must have accumulated in that time, and marveled at how he had been able to keep it hidden from the world. He read the rest of his father's words.

Legend says that the alchemist said to his daughter, 'You must promise me that you will not rest until the Baron has been stopped. You must see that the formula is returned to where it must stay—alongside the other myths, not among the realities. A power such as this can only lead to death and destruction. It was not meant to be among men. You must promise me that you will see that the formula is returned to the earth. Destroy it. Destroy the man who has it. Promise me!'

'I promise you, father,' said the Madonna

'Now you must go. The Baron may kill you, too. I have heard him talk. The gold has already made him lose reason. At our home, you will find a supply of Elixir. I have been storing it for years. Drink it when you are feeling weak and it will make you strong. Take it when you are feeling old and it will make you young...Promise me that you will not rest until the Baron is dead.'

'I promise you, father. He will die.'

The legend says the Alchemist's daughter left that day, the day before her father's death. She took with her a great supply of Elixir—a supply that has kept her alive to this day. You must see her. She is known as the Black Madonna. She will help you to destroy the Baron. Breitfuss will tell you how to find her.

Remember this—he will be a formidable adversary. For a thousand years the Baron has been using his gold in attempts to rule the world. He joined forces with the Great Kahn. His own son, Maximilian, ruled the Holy Roman Empire in the fifteenth century. He financed Napoleon, only to fall short at Waterloo. He tried again, killing his own son, Ferdinand, to start the First World War. Failing there, he financed Hitler to his rise, only to be stopped once more.

According to the Madonna, there is only one copy of the formula. Both the alchemist and the Baron considered it too valuable to be copied. You have the formula now, except for three missing pages, which Breitfuss will give you. I trust you will not be tempted, as I sometimes was, to use this for your personal gain. I took the formula in 1940 because the Creator told me that it must be done.

When I climbed into the Baron's castle my instructions were to obtain evidence of treachery. I knew that there was something else that I must obtain, although I did not know what it was. The Creator led me to the formula. The Creator told me that I should set it aside until I was dead. The Creator wants you to have it. You are his chosen one. What he will want you to do with it, only He can tell you.

The Baron is worse than a terrorist. He will kill indiscriminately. He has unflinching designs on global control. He is preparing another assault upon the world. Only this time, it will be aided by the rapid advance of technology— and by the enormous capability in the selective killing power of today's weapons. It is possible to unleash as much devastation in one hour as has been used in the entire history of warfare. It is possible to land a missile on a dime from a thousand miles away. No place is safe from the Baron. Not the U.N., not Congress, not the White House. Anyone could be his ally. This is why.

Through the centuries, the Baron has been sending family members to countries throughout the world. He has supplied them with gold, to create some of the largest companies on earth. I left you some of the financial records of these corporations. These are only a few. There were many more.

Trust no one, except for Breitfuss, the Creator, and your own instincts. von Hoffenburg's puppets have reached the highest levels of power in nations everywhere, including the CIA, and perhaps, even the Executive Branch of the United States. They are working together to bring about one final consolidation, the consummation of the Baron's grand quest. This will leave the world in ruins. They will stop at nothing, including global nuclear war, to bring about this end.

Trust no one.

And, in case you were wondering, Breitfuss does have the Elixir. One of us had to be alive to help you, so we agreed to take the Elixir ourselves, beginning many years ago."

The remaining part of the letter was a list of instructions and questions to ask Breitfuss. It also contained the answers that Breitfuss should give.

It took hours for Trance to translate his father's letter. He had to meditate several times to replenish his strength.

When he had finished the translation, Trance read and reread the letter. He looked for hidden words and images. He looked for signs that might point him in a direction other than where the apparent words would lead. His father was one to do that. "He's making this into some kind of cosmic treasure hunt." Yet, Trance could find no hidden meanings. Perhaps it was because he was weak and that his mind was at half power. He called for Gretel.

When she entered the room, Trance felt like the sun had emerged from behind a veil of thick clouds. The room, which had seemed so dark, looked brighter. His mood elevated, and he felt happy to see her face. How long had it been since he had felt this kind of hope?

"I hope this doesn't offend you," he said as she came walking vibrantly into the bedroom. "But you have an energy about you that is very appealing."

Gretel laughed, and said, "I feel it, too, about you...I don't know what it is. But you can go for years without meeting someone that matters—meet hundreds of people that don't affect you one way or another. But then, wham. You meet someone, and from the outset, the juices are flowing. It's something you don't understand. Something you can't explain. But it's there. I felt it the moment I saw your ugly, beat up face."

As Gretel spoke her green, diamond-cutting eyes looked directly at Trance. They strolled through his head, tweaking emotions that had long lain dormant. He could hear her words as she spoke, but he could also feel her plucking at his insides, pulling him apart like an artichoke, until his heart was bare and unprotected.

"Who are you?" he said, looking at her as he might the Mona Lisa, trying to fathom what mystery made her so appealing.

"Are we talking metaphysics here?" she retorted.

"I mean—" said Trance slowly, weighing each word as he spoke it. "I woke up and...when I saw your eyes I felt...comfort. I don't know the first thing about you, yet I feel a connection with you that I haven't had with anyone since...since...a long time ago."

"Since Janice?" she said softly.

"Yes." Trance's eyes slackened. "How did you know?"

"You called out her name this week. Many times. You must have loved her very much."

"She was my world."

"And you lost her?"

"She was a CIA recruit, sent to me for training. We fell in love, and we were married. She was quitting the Company—in less than a week's time. I was to quit soon after." Trance closed his eyes and fell silent. Gretel wanted to touch him, comfort him, but she let him emerge on his own.

"They sent her to meet a woman at the Washington Mall, a new informant with terrorist ties. My wife wasn't qualified to sense the danger. She was set up and gunned down by terrorists." He looked away. "But *we* killed her, as sure as I sit here."

"The CIA?"

Trance nodded. "I never knew why they chose her, or who she was supposed to meet. They wouldn't tell me. She was murdered, and I know at least one man who was behind it."

"It must be hard."

Trance closed his eyes and drew a sorrowful breath, in through his nose and out his mouth. "That was a lifetime ago. But I will never forget." He smiled half-heartedly. "Enough of that. Tell me, who are you?"

"Well, you know my name. My father was an industrialist in West Germany. Chemicals, steel, and pharmaceuticals. The Nazis took away his companies, but they were restored after the war. He survived the camps, but his first wife didn't. Later, he married my mother, and I was born. My father was actively involved in early Palestine. He moved to Israel in 1962, and spent his life seeking peace. I was sent to school in Switzerland.

"PLO radicals killed my parents when I was fifteen. My father's companies were placed in a trust for the State of Israel, with an annual stipend to me of two million dollars. I have been on my own since then. I continued my schooling in Switzerland until I was ready for college. From there I went on to Williams College in Massachusetts, where I majored in English literature. I took my Masters at Oxford." Trance's eyebrows rose at the mention of Williams—where his own father had lectured.

"I became a professional student. I tried living in the outside world, but found it too difficult. Too many people with too little to say—shallow men interested in sex or money, little else. It's not that I really have anything against either, mind you. But there had to be something more. I found it in books.

"I took my first Doctorate at the Sorbonne, in Paris. My letters were in philosophy. I suppose I was searching to find meaning in this crazy life we lead. When I finished my second PhD, I started coming here. I stopped in one winter when I was skiing at Zell. I enjoyed the people so much that, when summer came, I returned. I have been coming here every summer since. The Breitfuss's have become my family. I can't tell you how much they mean to me.

"When I am in school, I escape from the world. I see virtually no one, preferring to spend my time without pain. I just can't seem to meet anyone important enough to spend time with. Whenever I try, I begin to feel an emotional void, wondering where it's all leading. Then I see that it's going nowhere. So, rather than face the stress of a meaningless relationship—I choose to have none at all…

"When I am here, I change. There is something here that makes life fun. I go mountain climbing and summer skiing at Kaprun. I do my meditations and go to a dojo in Salzburg three times a week. I keep running—five to ten miles a day. I run with others here, not alone like I do when I am in Paris. There is a crew of us that run along the Salsaac River most mornings. During the summers, I paint." Gretel paused, looking embarrassed. "I am running out of things to say." Then she added nervously, "I am not used to talking about myself."

Trance thought of how much Gretel's attitudes and interests mirrored his own. She was an intellectual searching for meaning, finding solace in running, the martial arts and solitude. She also was an artist—Janice was an artist.

"I want to get to know you," said Trance softly.

"And I have wanted to know you—since the moment they carried you in. Even then, unconscious, there was a look about you that attracted me. In all those hours that I sat watching over you…hearing you cry for what you had lost…I feel like I came to know you. Somehow, I understand you. I feel your pain, and your sorrow. In those hours, when you would cry, I held you in my arms. You were crying in your sleep, and my heart embraced you. I felt sadness when you would speak the name of someone else…your wife and someone called Lauren. I felt sadness that you needed them, and sadness that it wasn't…" Gretel lowered her eyes. She had said too much, but she felt compelled to continue.

"Perhaps it was the childish dreaming of a lonely little girl who wanted to feel needed. Or, maybe it was because you were the man I was destined to meet, but never had. I was never very good at chemistry. But there was some kind of reaction in me when I saw you. Something…mixing all around inside. I don't understand it. But I am too old to deny it, and I feel secure enough about myself not to hide it from you." She looked into Trance's eyes. "Perhaps I will not feel this way, now that you are awake. But just as you want to know me, I too, want to know you."

CHAPTER 16

▼

"Well, well," said Breitfuss, as he walked into the room. "I see that you have finished the translation of your father's letter. A hell of a story, isn't it, Jackie? If I weren't part of it, I doubt that I'd believe a word." Both men looked at Gretel standing beside Breitfuss, each pondering if she should be included in their conversation. There was a risk in letting anyone get close to the information they guarded. There was a brief instant when their eyes met, each acknowledging the other. It was Trance who broke the momentary calm.

"Yes, Fred. But before we begin, there are several questions that I must ask you."

"Your father said there would be questions, although we never discussed what they would be."

"Where did you and my father first meet?"

"Ha! The Matterhorn. We couldn't have been more than eighteen then."

"And what were you doing?"

Breitfuss adjusted the suspenders of his pants. His eyes took on a faraway look. "Our fathers had taken us climbing."

"And was the climb successful?"

Breitfuss smiled. "That son of a gun. No. The climb wasn't successful."

"And why did it fail?"

"Because I fell, that's why. But I was as good a climber as he was. Did he tell you about the time when I saved his neck on the Eiger?"

"That was his next question."

"Well, at least he was fair."

"There was a girl that summer..."

Breitfuss nodded, closed his eyes and took a long deep breath. "Crystal. Yes, I remember Crystal." He looked at Trance, with a broad smile upon his face. "He was the first to kiss her. But I was the one to have her heart."

"And what was her birth mark?"

"That son of a gun." Breitfuss lowered his eyes. His face flushed with an embarrassed pink. "He never told me that he saw her naked." Breitfuss's eyes darted to Gretel, then to Trance. "She had a mole high on her inner thigh. Did your father also notice the large set of freckles that formed a heart on her buttocks?"

"Yes, I am afraid he did." Trance laughed.

Breitfuss guffawed with him. "We were young innocents then. The world seemed so simple."

"That is all that I have to ask you, Alfred Breitfuss."

"And so, it's my turn to ask you."

"Ready when you are." Trance winked at Gretel and smiled. He was beginning to feel alive again, and she looked so happy.

"You and your father carved your initials on a tree in Switzerland. What was the name of the town?"

"It wasn't Switzerland. He is mistaken. It was France. We were cross-country skiing near Mont Blanc. We may have skied into Switzerland. But the initials are in France. We were staying at an inn in Chamonix. At lunch we had too much glu wein and started acting a little silly. I had just met Janice and I was very much in love. I stopped and carved our initials in a tree, surrounded by a heart." Trance paused, and blinked his eyes several times. He lowered his head and also his voice. "My father did the same—with his initials and those of my mother."

"Good. Your dog used to be a retriever? "

"Kipper."

"And what peculiar talent did Kipper have?"

"Actually, he had several peculiar talents. When I was a child, I collected turtles. Kipper understood this, so he became a turtle retriever. We used to go for walks in the woods, and I would hear him barking. He would keep barking until I came to his side, and there he'd be with a new turtle for me." Trance's eyes crinkled into a smile. "I had a turtle retriever."

"And in Maine?"

"In Maine?" Trance had to think for a moment. "Ah! We used to fish the mackerel runs in the summertime. We'd fish from the docks, catching thirty, forty fish an hour. When we'd pull them from the water, Kipper would pounce on them. He was a fish retriever, too. My father once told me that Labradors were initially bred to be fish dogs, not bird dogs."

"How old were you with your first sexual encounter?"

Trance blushed. "I don't believe he said that," he said quietly. "It was his choice, not mine."

"How old? And where?"

"I was sixteen years old, for gosh sakes. I was a boy. My father sent me back to Japan, to spend a month with the ladies of the Willow World, like his mother had done for him."

"Japanese concubines?"

Trance nodded, and looked uncomfortably at Gretel. "My father was old school Japan. It was the concubines' job to teach me the art of lovemaking. It was part of my father's training for me—scholar, warrior, and lover. He was always preparing me—for this, I suppose."

"Welcome, Jack Trance. It is a pleasure to meet you." Breitfuss gave him a brief, but tender hug. "Now, we have some business to take care of." Breitfuss left the room, and returned several minutes later holding a plain manila envelope. He handed the package to Trance. "The final three pages," he said. Then he reached out his hand. "Let me see that letter, if you will."

Breitfuss read the letter reverently, pausing now and then to look into space, as if remembering the events from long ago. When he was done he said, "Your father called me the day he came down from the castle. I helped him get out of the country. He left the formula with me, and other important papers, too. I buried them under the snow where no one would find them. He left them with me for over twenty years. When he came back to claim them, he told me that he was going to leave them for you. He said some day you would be coming. I am glad I lived to see the day.

"Your father and I made copies of the final three pages; he left the originals with me. He said he was going to see if the formula actually worked. I know it did, because he brought me the Elixir. It has helped me stay young while I waited—for this.

"Your father said he would put the book in a place only you would find—without the final three pages. He planned to destroy those; apparently he did. He wanted to make sure that you came to me for help."

"I almost didn't make it."

"You mean the kidnapping?"

Trance shook his head and smiled. "My father's final message was destroyed. I didn't know you were involved. However, he had told me that someday I would need your help, that you were the best friend he had."

"You are damn right, I was. Your father was a hell of a man, God rest his soul. I never loved anyone as I loved him. He was...different, you know."

Breitfuss blinked several times and turned away. Trance reached over and patted his hand. "Yes, he was." After several moments of awkward silence, Trance continued, "So, how can you help me?"

"The Baron has a new champion—a new Hitler, if you will. He is preparing to launch the world into war and take over what is left. He has developed an intricate plan—moving his men like chess pieces, slowly guiding and cajoling world leaders to the brink of holocaust."

"Impossible," said Trance. "It can't be done. The man must be mad."

"Oh? Mad he is. But he can succeed, Jackie. He has had centuries to maneuver his family members into positions of power in Russia, China, Korea, Great Britain, France, Germany, even the United States. The minute he gets his formula, it all begins."

"I don't understand. Why would the formula be so important to him? I mean, with all the companies...the money...Why would that be the determining factor? Surely he can duplicate the process?"

"The book was his prized possession, Jack. It was something he possessed for over a thousand years. Why men become so attached to things, I don't understand. It happens with their spouses, their pets, art, cars, baseball cards, all sorts of toys. Men will kill for their prized possessions. But there are better reasons here, my boy. What thing over the span of man has fascinated him more than gold? Power? Women? Women grow old. Power becomes boring without more of it. Eventually it too, always fades. But gold is eternal. There is just something about it. Unlimited wealth, and the formula to make it? Priceless. This is the one known formula in the world. Men kill for rarities. This is the rarest of all. Would the Baron risk losing it in a nuclear holocaust? Never."

Breitfuss paused to lick his lips. He walked over to a table and picked up a bottle of Perrier water. He pointed the top toward Trance and whispered, "But the overriding factor is this, the Baron has used up his supply of Elixir, and without it he will die." He lifted the bottle up over his face and stared at the sparkling water. "Just like we would die without water."

"How do you know that?"

"You, of all people to ask. Spies, Jack, and the Black Madonna, of course. You will meet her soon. But that must be carefully arranged. She is closely watched by the Baron's men." Trance shook his head and bit his lip.

"He knows where she is?"

"Of course."

"And he lets her live?"

"She has done him no harm in a thousand years. He will let her live, although he has taken nearly all of her Elixir. She will be dead soon without it."

"Can we make her some?"

Breitfuss shook his head. "I have offered her what your father left me, but she refuses me. She is waiting for you to stop the Baron, Jackie. Then, I fear, she is ready to pass on."

"She knows about me?"

Breitfuss laughed heartily. "She knows more about you than anyone alive."

"Let me guess, spies?"

"They are everywhere. You should know that. You, my boy, are what you might call a...how do you say…a hot commodity. Just about every secret service in the world is after you—each for its own reasons. The Israelis want the formula because they need the money. They have high inflation, virtually no raw materials, little oil, and have to spend so much of their annual budget on the military—yes, they need the formula. They are also interested in preventing war. One of the triggering events of the upcoming war will be an all out assault on Israel by the Arab States."

"Do U.S. leaders know this?"

"As usual, your leaders have their heads in the sand—a funny country, America. Look at all the furor over weapons of mass destruction in Iraq. No one could agree about their existence. Did Saddam have them? Did he not? Your government *gave* them to Saddam when he fought Iran.

"You watch tens of thousands of terrorists roam the planet, while you keep your borders so open that millions of people cross them at will. Then you say, 'Oh my God, we've got a problem with terrorists inside our shores. How did this happen?'

"Americans are a peace-loving nation. You ignore world problems until they are prescient—until the whistle blows loud enough.

"There are people blowing whistles about the Baron. But there are hundreds of whistles blown every day. For one to be heard above the others?" Breitfuss shrugged. "The United States has too many things to worry about. Are they prone to believe that there is a man in a castle in Austria who has been trying to rule the world for a thousand years?" He laughed. "Imagine the fate of the politician who spouts that rhetoric. But, believe this, the Baron's own people hold high places in the American government."

"How high can they be?" asked Trance.

"These families have been in your country since its very beginnings—for hundreds of years. They have been given the money to form dynasties. How high have they have reached? The Congress? The Senate? Perhaps even the Presidency. Who is to know? We do know that Penwell, a man who was once the head of the British Secret Service, was the Baron's own son. When the Baron passed him in favor of Hitler, Penwell tried to get the formula for himself. That's how your father was brought into this mess. They say the British authorities had no idea of what Penwell was doing, and he was killed shortly thereafter. A bullet in the head, in the middle of morning traffic. So, who is to know? Perhaps the head of the CIA is one of them. Perhaps the U.S. Secretary of Defense. Who is to know?"

"You are saying that this is a well-orchestrated conspiracy of powerful men—"

"And women."

"—and women, in major countries, all working in concert to overthrow the world?" asked Trance. "That's a tired old story."

"They have been *at* it for centuries. This time they intend to castrate the major world governments, then rule what is left. Their nuclear arsenal rivals that of the U.S. They also have the means to deliver warheads on a dime."

"Incredible." Trance had been living with bits and pieces of the information for days. But it was now coming together. "And the formula works?"

"Your father left you gold, didn't he?"

"Enough to get my attention."

"You see my black hair? I'm over eighty." Trance smiled and Breitfuss continued. "You've seen the documents linking von Hoffenburg to Hitler. Now our sources say something immediate is in the wind."

Throughout the conversation, Gretel sat quietly in a corner of the bedroom. Her eyes had grown progressively wider as the conversation unfolded. She appeared to be in shock. Beads of perspiration had formed along her upper lip and across her brow. Her fingers trembled, and she clasped them together to make them still. These men were talking about World War Three—yet they were so calm. It was almost as if they were discussing a chess match.

"Are you all right?" Trance asked.

"Y...Yes. It's...just that what you are talking about is so...I mean you are talking about... war. I mean, as if it's going to happen."

"We will keep it from happening," said Trance. "Don't worry. Everything will be fine. I do this for a living. I've had practice."

Gretel looked at him strangely, wondering whether or not to take his statement as a joke. She didn't laugh. Neither did he.

"I helped form, and then ran a special branch of the CIA, called `T-Force'. The T was for 'task' or 'Trance', you take your pick. Our job was to diffuse international catastrophes before they occurred. We prevented hijackings, assassinations, and engineered helpful coups." He paused. "Sometimes we had to stop people like the Baron before they came to power."

"You mean kill them?" asked Gretel.

Trance pursed his lips and spoke slowly. "We don't kill. We eliminate. But, sometimes, yes. Most wars are not officially declared. Some undeclared wars are public, like our campaigns in Vietnam and Iraq. Others are quiet. Our government decides how to play it. If killing one man can save the lives of millions, the tradeoff is fair—according to them."

Trance shook his head. "I believed in what I did, although it often seemed that the men we put into power were nearly as bad as the ones we replaced."

"Except they play nice nice with America?"

"Yeah, sometimes." Trance sighed. "I don't mind when it's for our 'National' safety. But half the time, I swear, it's because someone's got a bug up his ass."

"But this time it's different?"

"You tell me."

"Yes. Yes, it is different. The man must be stopped. I...I would like to help you."

Trance lifted his eyebrows, and said, "No. I am sorry, but I can't let you become involved."

"What do you mean, you can't let me become involved? Who the hell are you to tell me how to run my life? And what gives you the right to tell me, that if I can, in some way, help stop another holocaust, you won't let me?"

"That's...not what I mean. I...lost...I just don't want to lose..."

Gretel's eyebrows knitted into a frown and she stared at Trance. She then walked slowly toward him and put her arms upon his shoulders.

"I'm sorry," she said. "That was selfish of me. But don't you understand?"

"We'll talk about it later, okay?" said Trance softly.

Gretel nodded slowly. "Okay."

Breitfuss watched as the two of them embraced. *When had this happened?* he wondered. Kids...

CHAPTER 17

▼

As the days passed, Trance and Gretel found that they never ran out of things to say. The most trivial events became sources of wonder, unleashing a wild, free sense animation in their new partnership, like prisoners released from jail. Still, each of them stood on guard, waiting for the magic to break and leave them picking up the pieces of something that could never be. Each was afraid to expose wounds that were covered with only the most tender of scars.

Two weeks passed before Trance was on his feet. He began taking short walks with Gretel. He was happy for the time with her. It was as if he were watching the unfurling of a rose from tiny bud into full bloom. Each new unfurling, each small facet he discovered made her only that much more beautiful.

"I feel younger when I am with you," he said one day, while they were walking alone in the mountains.

"Yes," she replied. "I feel the same with you. Since my parents died, I feel like I've become encrusted with the weight of each new year of living. The loneliness, the vague fear...of a life with no meaning. The years are like the rings of a tree, and I carry them around with me like dead pieces of wood—memories of a past that I hoped to forget...All those feelings are gone when I am with you. All I can think about is tomorrow, and I look forward to spending it with you."

"Hmm."

"You are a beautiful man, Jack Trance." Gretel turned toward him. She let her hair fall backward over her shoulders, exposing her lips and her neck to the air.

Trance looked into her half-closed eyes, and he felt a strange heat surge through him and a light charge of electricity tingling his fingers.

"I've got something for you," he said.

Gretel's eyes grew wide and she grinned like a young child on her birthday.

"A present? Oh, how exciting!"

Trance pulled a crumpled piece of paper from his pocket.

"I'm afraid I'm not too good at this, but I was trying to think of how my life has changed during these last few weeks and—well, I came up with this." Trance began reading a poem, one that touched the most guarded places inside him. He would give love one more try, if Gretel would have him.

"Oh, Jack," she whispered, as she put her arms around him. "In those lonely years after my parents were killed...I needed you. I cried out for you. But you were not there. So I built a world without you, piece by piece, until I could pass from day to day without the pain. Now...I don't know what to say. I am so afraid. Afraid to let myself love you, and upset the fragile balance I have worked so hard to create." Gretel wiped a small tear from one eye and dabbed at the other.

"But there is this feeling in me that has come alive. It is as if I have been reborn, being here with you. There is a whole new me, a completely different me than the one that existed only weeks ago. This new me feels happy—like a shining Cinderella, not the ugly sister I was before.

"I want so much to let Cinderella live out the rest of her days with her new prince, and forget all the past. There is so much that you don't know about me. Things that I have done that I cannot change..."

Trance could feel Gretel trembling. He felt the dropping of her tears against his neck. He could feel them fall, and run down along his chest, like warm summer rain.

They held each other without speaking. There was so much to tell about their past. Weren't they different people now? Couldn't those people be left to the world in which they had lived? Couldn't they just leave them behind?

"I don't care what dark secrets you have," said Trance softly. He stroked her hair. He pushed his nose into the silky strands and nuzzled against her ear. "I am in love with Cinderella. Not with an ugly sister that is no longer there to torment her."

"And if the ugly sister returns?"

"If she returns, we will let her make her own choice," said Trance. "I have faith that she will know what to do."

Gretel pulled her face back from the comfort of his closeness. She looked into his eyes, her mind blood-streaked from inner battle. Her eyes stared into his, unfocused, looking somewhere far away. They followed the contour of his chin, and finally rested on his lips.

"I have wanted to make love to you since the first moment I saw you. But I have been afraid, Jack. I can't tell you how afraid I am. My world—you will change my world, and if I give myself to you there will be—"

"We have plenty of time," he said softly. "I won't ask you to give yourself up until you are ready. No, I will not ask you to give yourself up at all. I want you to *become* with me. We can never be the same again, even now. I will make love with you when you are ready to accept whatever happens. I will do the same. I don't care what you were yesterday. I want you for today...and tomorrow. I am ready for you now."

Their lips were only inches apart. Trance could almost taste the moist sweetness of her mouth, like a fresh, ripe strawberry. He began to imagine what it would be like to take her into his arms and then take her completely. His stomach tightened, and he felt a spreading warmth run from his chest. Sweat broke out on his forehead, and he noticed himself growing hard at the thought of her.

Gretel swayed beneath him. Part of her pushed to let go, while the other stubbornly held fast. Was she ready for this? But what was the past without the future? And the future was mere moments away.

Their lips closed the distance, until they brushed ever so slightly. They touched noses in a tender caress. They touched again, except this time their noses stayed together, until their lips met hungrily.

Images raced through Gretel's mind like a pinball. Happy scenes when she was a girl, being held by her father and bounced upon his knee. He was holding her, saying, "Of course I'll never leave you..." She saw his bullet-riddled body. She had forced herself to look. She had taken him in her arms, kissing him, vowing to avenge the men that had caused him to die, and to carry on his dream. She had been a girl of fifteen then, young, innocent, and sheltered. Then, she was suddenly old, vengeful, and alone.

There had never been a man that could make Gretel wash away the memory of her father's death. It clung to her like car grease, thwarting any attempt to rinse it clean. She had been daddy's little girl. Her father was always larger than life—one of the richest, most powerful men in the world, and entirely consumed with the purpose of seeing that his daughter could live in a homeland that was safe, one where the persecutions of two thousand years would not exist, a free Israel. His death had branded her brain, scarring it forever.

There had never been a man that could make her let go, no matter how hard she had tried—someone to release her from the burden, someone to jolt joy into her life. She prayed that she had found that man, and she knew that she could never know for sure until she tried.

Trance lay beneath her, his chest bare, his taut muscles pulsing rhythmically with blood surging through them. Slowly he removed Gretel's pink cotton pullover. Her hair shimmered against the sun behind her, and as Trance lay back to look upon her naked chest, he groaned softly.

"Be gentle with me," she whispered. "I...I've never done this before, never all the way."

Trance began to speak. But she placed her finger against his mouth.

"No more words," she said. "I am ready now...for you. Only you. Talk to me with your body. Make me into the woman that you need. Hold me...love me..."

When they both lay exhausted, arm in arm, Gretel spoke in Japanese, "So this is what they call the 'clouds and the rain'. I've only read about it. Now I know."

"The Japanese also say that they are 'going', rather than 'coming'," replied Trance, also in Japanese.

"Either way, it's wonderful...I never knew..." They lay for hours together, watching the sun set into the hills, and then the stars as they marched across the sky.

CHAPTER 18

▼

The day broke hard and early, when Breitfuss strode purposely into Trance's bedroom.

"It is time to begin, Jack," he said. "The Black Madonna is weakening more quickly now. I am afraid your recuperation is over."

"We're ready," replied Trance.

Breitfuss arched his eyes at Trance's use of the word "we." So, Trance had accepted her completely, just as he had.

"But, we'll need money," continued Trance. "Unfortunately, I just gave away billions. I have other money, but it might be hard to get."

Breitfuss nodded. "We will leave in the morning. Will your friend at the Klug Bank be cooperative?"

"Depends on his orders. His sense of honor will make him ignore threats by the CIA or the FSB—even at the expense of his life. Swiss bankers have their own little brotherhood. The Swiss authorities could make Klug turn against me, but they interfere with great reticence. I am not a terrorist."

"Your accounts are not frozen," said Breitfuss. He winked at Trance's questioning look. "Spies. Remember, your bank is in Zurich. The Black Madonna's influence is strong there."

"It seems she has people everywhere."

"You would too, if you had been at it for as long as she has."

Trance turned to a notebook in his hand. He flipped through several pages, jotting thoughts in the margins as he read.

"Okay," he said. "I've been able to line up two Cobras out of Egypt, and an old B-29 bomber, from France, of all places. Another Cobra hit the market in Nicaragua. They'll cost us fifteen million, fully equipped. I am afraid I had to call in a few favors, as well as make a few...ah, promises...It seems that my reputation still holds in the black markets. I've got three 150-millimeter cannons, a transport chopper, and a hundred handpicked men on their way. I also have the best damn field general on the planet. These men are pros. They are the best. But they don't come cheap." Trance signed. "I know it's not much, but it's all I can afford."

"And your plan?"

"If the Madonna can furnish me the information you say she can, it will be complete within a week."

"She'll give you more than you can imagine," said Breitfuss quietly. "Including money, if you need it."

Trance gazed out the window at the summer flowers blooming in a square, brightly painted box that hung just below the sash. "I hope so..." he said from a far mental distance. What was the right thing to do? He already had the formula. Perhaps he should just destroy it and forget the entire matter. But, if his father had not done so, there must be a reason. Mustn't there? He couldn't trust the bastards at the CIA. He could trust the president, perhaps, but what about the men around him? Shit. The moment he called the president, they'd be down on him like flies on a pig. There was no one he could turn to. There was no one he could trust—except, perhaps, for one man.

Now that Trance had Gretel, he was losing his will to fight. He wanted only to escape into his own small existence, and to live a life of simplicity, relaxation, love...

"I still find this whole thing hard to believe, Fred, and I won't go through with this unless the Black Madonna gives me proof."

"She convinced your father, Jack."

"I don't give a damn right now, about what she, supposedly, convinced my father to believe. I'm getting tired of the killing. I'm tired of playing God—screwing around with the nations of the world as if they were toys. I'm sick of power hungry men in Washington who use the concepts of freedom and liberty to justify meddling where they have no right. For years I believed them—that we had an obligation to protect the innocents of the world."

"And you don't think so any longer?" asked Breitfuss.

"Christ, Fred. I just don't know any more. I believe in freedom. I believe in justice. It's... it's just become too goddamn much. I mean, preventing a hijacking is one thing. Assassinating a dictatorial tyrant might be justifiable, under certain circumstances. But the lines have become so hazy—the morality so arbitrary. I understand the arguments regarding terrorists. I can understand the willingness to see these men dead, to replace them with more levelheaded criminals. But everybody sees something wrong with *every* leadership group—including our own. Where do we draw the line? And who draws it?"

"Don't you think you are losing the point?"

"What is the point? I mean, what gives us the right to interfere in the affairs of other men, other nations?"

"Duty, Jack. We are talking about a man that has been seeking to dominate the world for a thousand years. He is about to start World War III—and create a new Reich to rule what is left. Is that what you want?"

"No." Trance sat heavily and sighed. It was a weary deflation of air, and all of Trance's energy seemed to be sucked out with it. "I just wish that someone else would stop him."

"Thousands have tried."

"It is all too much, Fred. If what you say is true, don't you think Washington would have done something by now? Hell, I spent six years operating T Force. There can't be more than half a dozen men in the entire United States with more classified information floating inside their brains than me. I've never even heard rumors about this Baron of yours."

"Your father told you..."

"Did he? Did he really? The only thing I know is that I received a coded letter that was supposed to be from him. There was never anything said, during my entire lifetime, about gold, the Baron, or the Black Madonna. How do I know that this entire matter hasn't been contrived to get me to launch an attack upon the von Hoffenburg castle? Christ, that would be a good one. I'm a civilian, you know. They would hang me so frigging fast..."

"You have to do what you believe is right."

"Don't you understand? I'm too confused. I don't know what is right anymore!"

"You've gone through a difficult time. Your wife. Your parents dying...people trying to kill you..."

"There is one man I can call. He'll know what is right."

Breitfuss's face took on a puzzled look, but then his eyes sharpened.

"He is a man I trust...a man I love...almost as much as I loved my own father."

"Hopewell?"

"How did you know?"

"Your father and I were very close. I know more about you than you might imagine."

"He'll know what I should do."

"Should you involve him in this?"

"Involve him? He was my mother's brother. He doesn't need more wealth. He's going to be the next goddamn president of the United States. You're talking about World War III and you don't want to involve the man who will be leading the nation?"

"Hopewell already knows about the Baron."

"What?"

"I said Hopewell knows about the Baron. Just because you've never heard about him doesn't mean that some of your nation's leaders have not. The Madonna has told them about the Baron before. But there was never enough evidence to bring him to trial—the story too fantastic to get a wary politician to believe, or even question. Besides, your father had the formula."

"So, I will deliver the formula to the president and let him take care of the rest. I'll wash my hands of the whole matter." Trance clasped his hands behind his back and began to pace the room.

"You can't do that," said Breitfuss after several long moments.

"What do you mean, I can't do it? I sure as hell can."

"There is no one you can trust."

"Are you saying that I can't trust Hopewell?"

Breitfuss shook his head. "No. But you don't know what people *he* would involve—and which of those can be trusted. No, Jackie. This is a matter that you were destined to handle on your own."

"I'll talk to Hopewell—just him alone. I'll ask his advice. I'll see what he would do, before I give them anything. I need a sounding board—one high up in the government."

"Jack—"

Trance stood to full height, pressed his chest against Breitfuss and said, "I am in control here. The formula was left to me—wasn't it? The financial documents were left to me, weren't they? I am the one who has experience in dealing with this sort of problem. You may not know this, but Hopewell created T Force. He and I shared the same dreams. He was always there to turn to. He was the one that helped me keep the politicians in check. You don't know him like I do. We must trust him."

Breitfuss held out his hands and smiled grimly. "I cannot force you to do anything. You know that. But remember what your father said—"

"Or what someone wants me to believe my father said." Trance stood for a while in silence, then sat down heavily. "First we see the Madonna."

The Black Madonna lived outside the town of Einsiedeln, Switzerland. She owned an entire mountain, much of it ruggedly uninhabitable. There were rolling hills and meadows along the base, and it appeared deserted, void of the usual farmhouses and animals that normally dotted the countryside. As the altitude grew, so, too, did the steepness of the mountain's sides

Trance was taken through an Austrian version of the French underground, by a small group of dedicated men committed to the downfall of Baron Gustav von Hoffenburg.

They were traveling the final few miles of their journey in a blue Ford when Breitfuss asked, "Did you know that Einsiedeln is one of the major pilgrimage cities of the world?"

"Whatever for?" asked Trance.

Breitfuss laughed. "Few people understand the significance that alchemy has played in the development of the world. It is not just the transformation of lead into gold, Jackie. Alchemy encompasses the entire art of transforming matter from one form to a different form. For instance, a thought put down on paper is transformed into something greater, a concrete image on paper, perhaps in a book, shared with others…perhaps into an entire new religion. Wood becomes pulp, becomes paper—"

"And?"

"Alchemy is a state of mind, Jackie. Not the simple transformation of base metals into gold. It is a religion in itself. Millions have come here from the world over, as pilgrims, to pay homage to the Black Madonna."

"They come to see her?"

"They come to visit the symbol—a statue of the Black Madonna. There are hundreds of them throughout Europe."

"A statue of a Black Madonna, as in the mother of Christ?"

Breitfuss nodded, then shrugged his shoulders. "Who is to know?"

"This is getting weird, Fred."

They were huddled in a small rented home on the outskirts of Einsiedeln. All lights were extinguished, except for a small kerosene lamp on the kitchen table. They sat quietly arguing over what they should do next.

"There are a hundred of the Baron's men guarding the grounds of the Madonna's home," said Breitfuss. "You must go alone. You can't take the risk—"

"I'm going with him," interrupted Gretel. She fixed her eyes on Breitfuss. They held no compromise, and her brows were furrowed into a determined stare. She shifted her gaze to Trance, and silently dared him to defy her.

Trance argued with himself. He wanted Gretel with him, no matter where it was. The thought of denying her something of such importance to her was distasteful. But how could he take the chance of losing her—just as he had lost the other love of his life?

"Gretel, please..." he begged.

"My darling," she said. "I am a grown woman. I have been making decisions for myself since I was fifteen. If I am to be with you, it must be one hundred percent. I live no other way, Jack. I can help you, and you are going to need it."

"Are you prepared to die?" asked Breitfuss.

"Completely." Her eyes took on the slanted look of a lioness protecting her cubs.

"Oh, no," groaned Trance.

"I'm not about to die," she continued. "I'll pit myself against any man. My father taught me to help defend a nation, and I will do so." She touched Trance's cheek. "Would you let me go if I were a man?"

Trance lowered his eyes.

"Let me tell you something about men," Gretel continued. "I can outshoot them, outrun them, and outfight them."

"I love you," said Trance softly. "And I don't want to lose you."

"So, can't I feel the same?" she said. "How do you think I feel with you going off alone? With me helping you, your odds are better, not worse."

"I don't know—"

"Trust me...sweetheart...trust me."

"I don't know what or whom to trust anymore."

"Then let me help you."

Trance drew a deep breath, then groaned.

The sky was overcast and the night was devoid of light. There was an eerie silence floating through the air as Trance and Gretel followed their guide through the darkness. The air smelled like damp dirt. Its musky scent worked deep into the nostrils like acrid smoke. A fine mist hugged the ground, weaving in and around the thick underbrush. It parted as they walked through it, only to close again behind them like ghosts as they moved.

The stone hut that housed the Black Madonna lay nestled in the trees, across a valley that could be approached on foot from three distinct routes. Each route threaded through the rocky hillside and dense groundcover in a manner easily guarded by the Baron's many sentinels.

The Baron's men were stationed in regular intervals along the approach routes. They stood at distances never exceeding two hundred yards. Three man patrols lead German shepherds around the grounds randomly to detect intruders.

Trance and Gretel wound their way up the peak adjacent to the Madonna's mountain, still several miles away. The climbing was steep but quick. Their guide, Jurgen Licht, knew the territory well. He was a third-generation guide and led hundreds of climbers through the region each year. He moved effortlessly among the rocks and trees, rarely stopping for breath, driving forward without looking back. Gretel followed him with focused determination, while Trance hung behind her, covering their backs.

Licht stopped suddenly and raised his right hand.

"We should rise above the fog soon," he whispered in English. "The mists hang in the lower valleys, where the cooler air meets the warm water and moist ground. As we climb, the mists will thin, until suddenly, they are gone."

Trance nodded. Licht looked at him through the corner of his eye. *So, he is the one*, he thought. When Breitfuss had called him earlier that week he had asked no questions. He had always known, always hoped, this day would come. The Breitfuss and the Licht families went back more than a century. They were bound by the comradery and trust that ran among climbing families—and by the great secrets they shared.

As their guide predicted, minutes later they broke through into the clear night sky.

"Do you want to rest for a moment?" asked Licht. He looked at Trance, then at Gretel. Trance smiled, while Gretel quickly shook her head. Licht shrugged his shoulders. Other climbers would have begged to stop long ago. Although he was still breathing lightly, he would have welcomed a break to rest his own tired legs. He shrugged his shoulders and said, "Then we will continue."

Half an hour later they drew even in altitude with the Madonna's mountain home. They could see two faint lights across the valley. Licht pointed toward the lights, and sat facing them, with his back against a large boulder. Trance nodded, but began to continue the climb. He looked like a strange apparition, with his hulking backpack hunched on his shoulders.

"I think we should rest," said Licht. He fingered his own heavy pack, supplied by Trance, and wondered just what was inside. "You must be tired," he continued. "If I am tired, then you must be."

"We have little time," said Trance. He looked at Gretel. She was breathing heavily, and sweat was dripping off her nose. She would make no complaint; Trance knew that. She would not slow them in any way. That had been part of their deal. If she couldn't handle the climb, Trance would leave her behind. "I suppose you are right," he said, seeing the anguish cutting across Gretel's face.

"We should go on," said Gretel. "Jack is right. We have little time." She started forward, but Trance reached for her shoulder.

"Stop," he said. "You've made your point. I won't leave you behind. By the way...I love you."

"Of course you love me," she said, exhaling with a grunt as she plopped her pack onto the ground. "I'm the best damn thing that's ever happened to you." She kissed his cheek.

Trance's eyes briefly shadowed, but he smiled. "You know, I think you're right." He pulled her against him, then nuzzled his lips against the hair over her ear and whispered, "You're a pain in the ass, you know."

Gretel let her head fall against his chest. "I need you so."

"I'm glad you're here."

"Are you ready to fly me away from this place?"

Trance laughed. "Baby, you are about to fly like you ain't never flown before."

Gretel's eyes glistened with apprehension. Hang gliding was one thing. But hang gliding for the first time, at night, in the Swiss Alps, off a cliff that stretched a couple thousand feet above the ground? This was a fearful indoctrination. She stepped to the edge of the mountain and looked down into a sheer chasm that stretched two hundred feet downward.

"What is life without new challenges?" she joked.

"Absolutely," said Trance. "Don't worry. It will be easy. Just hang on and I'll do everything. Do what I tell you and we'll live through it, okay? It will be like skiing in deep powder...floating through the air, a little wind in your face...guiding, not forcing…nothing to it."

After a short rest they climbed for another half hour and stopped.

"This should be enough," said Trance. He propped his pack against the ground, making sure not to bend any of the poles that protruded from the top. He walked over to Licht and helped him take the awkward pack off of his back. Trance quickly removed the contents, laying everything on the ground in neat order.

"Is that what I think it is?" said Licht.

Trance looked at his guide, wondering how much he knew.

As if to answer Trance's unasked question, Licht said, "My father told me that one day someone would come. He had hoped to be here himself."

"And when was that?" said Trance.

"Thirty years ago."

This is insane. What kind of people wait decades for someone they do not know—for someone who, himself, doesn't know what he is doing?

"You will understand it all soon," said Licht. He turned and began to walk down into the darkness. "The thermals are good here," he said. "You should have no problem reaching the Madonna's hut."

Twenty minutes later Trance was making the final adjustments to the assembled hang glider.

"Are you sure this thing won't collapse under our weight?" said Gretel as she fingered the thin fabric and the light pipes.

"I hope so," said Trance with a wink.

"I want to be on top."

Trance laughed and motioned Gretel to stand beside him. He clipped her onto the right side of the glider. After making sure that she was securely fastened, he snapped his own harness into the frame.

"Ready?"

"As ready as I'll ever be."

"Let's fly," said Trance. He began jogging and she moved with him. As they loped towards the mountain precipice Gretel could see only blackness rushing toward them. She saw her life pass before her in that one brief second. Then they were airborne.

How in the hell did I ever get myself into this mess? she thought.

"Ooohh," Gretel heard herself gasp, as their feet left the ground. As first, there was nothing. Then the wind rushed against her ears, with the opaque ground underneath them passing quickly by. The sense she was most aware of was that she was floating, drifting effortlessly through the air, but completely out of control. Trance caught an updraft and they swirled higher. Gretel could feel herself wanting to push them along, but all she could do was hang there motionless. She was suspended in mid-air, with no effort needed on her part to keep them aloft. She felt as if she were floating in water, but moving fast, with her stomach in her throat.

"Jack—this is great!"

Trance tried to whisper, "Ssshh," but the sound was lost in the wind. He put a finger to his lips and Gretel nodded.

As he drew closer toward the Madonna's small fortress, Trance caught as much air as he could. He knew he could always circle downward from above, but if they lost too much altitude they could land far short of the Black Madonna's home and lose their lives. This was all a long shot anyway. Even if they made it to the home, there was no assurance that they wouldn't be picked out of the sky by the Baron's men, like slow flying geese lazily drifting into range.

The valley was a boiling, milky broth, as the mist scuttled around the mountains. Shafts of the thick moisture stretched like bony fingers out of the valley floor and swirled below them, caught by the wind and lifted skyward. The mists rose nearly to the height of the Black Madonna's slate roof now. Trance wondered whether this helped or hindered their chances.

On most days there were just a few men standing guard at the hut. The rest were spaced in two broad circles fanned around the mountain and along the path. Trance hoped the fog would obliterate all skyward vision, and work to his advantage. However, the fog may have driven the men up from below, where they could see any intruders above. There could be many eyes glancing into the sky at that very moment. In that case they would soon be dead.

Trance waited for the crack of a rifle and the feeling of another bullet burning through his body. He could see himself tumbling out of the sky, like Icarus, crashing on a task he could not complete.

But Trance saw no one as the glider flew over the fortress. They circled and dropped beside the woods in front of the home, the landing perfect, with both of them standing. They unfastened themselves rapidly and carried the glider to the forest. Trance covered it with a thin, black nylon tarp, which he pulled from a bag attached to the frame. Trance had no time for more camouflage, and he prayed it would work. Moments later a voice came from the shadows.

"Grusse Gott," it said softly.

Trance raised his pistol and pointed it towards the voice. "Identify yourself."

"I bring you greetings from the Madonna."

"Then let us proceed." Trance lowered his gun. A man stepped from the shadows. He was dressed in black and moved with catlike grace. They followed him to the front of the cottage.

The man spoke softly into a small intercom and the heavy door opened. Inside the entryway stood a man who was at least seven feet tall. As the door swung forward, Trance stared at the man's massive chest. The man grabbed and lifted him by the throat. Trance made no move to stop him. Trance's nostrils flared, as they filled with the sticky-sweet smell of fresh blood. His eyes darted about, searching for the bodies he knew must be there. He saw them piled in a corner.

"The wildflowers grow well in this region," spoke Trance, in their pre-arranged code. The man grunted. "Nice to meet you, too," continued Trance, still hanging in the air by his neck.

"They had to die," said the man, following Trance's gaze. "If you were to make it in here alive, they had to die." The man spoke German, but with a dialect that Trance didn't recognize. "You have forty-three minutes before the guard changes and others return. Follow me quickly." The man dropped Trance to the floor and led them down a flight of stairs. They went far under the ground, to a level of the home many times larger than the modest living space on top. While the upper living space seemed like a hunter's cabin, the lower level could have passed as a penthouse at Trump Towers in New York.

"Nice digs," said Trance, switching to English. He looked at the perfectly preserved seventeenth and eighteenth century furniture that lined the room, and felt the lushness of the Persian rug underneath his feet. Along the walls hung paintings by Vermeer, Rembrandt, DaVinci and Picasso.

The man made no reply, but led them through a series of narrow hallways until the house came to an apparent end.

"Yes," replied the man in perfect British English. "Very nice digs. Over a period of years one tends to accumulate possessions. The Black Madonna sees no reason for living the life of a pauper."

"I see that."

The man removed a Rembrandt from the wall and tossed it carelessly on the floor. He pressed his hand against the polished marble surface. After a minute they heard a soft purring, as a motor began to move the entire stone wall inward. The man watched Trance intently, wondering what was going through his mind. He had been briefed on Trance's background, but had little faith that he could stop the Baron. He could see Trance ponder the security system.

"Very simple, really," he said. "Heat and moisture sensitive...Triggers the motor."

"Of course," said Trance. "No retina scan?"

The man scowled. "Of course. Highly sophisticated. It's already scanned all our eyes."

"Very clever."

The wall opened to an elevator. This took them another two stories deeper into the ground, to a room that looked like it belonged more at NASA than in a European mountain home. The room expanded into an immense command station. Several mainframe computers stood enclosed by glass at the far end of the room, linked into a massive neural. Along the wall flashed six wide, brightly lit screens, and, down a flight of four more steps, stood thirty or forty desks, each manned by someone monitoring a separate computer screen.

"Quite a playroom," said Trance. Gretel nudged him and he kept further thoughts to himself.

"As you see, Mr. Trance, we are far more serious about this than you appear to be." The tall man loomed over Trance with a menacing look on his face. His dark skin looked almost black in the recessed light. It was deeply lined and looked like tanned leather. His eyes were surrounded by deep sockets, and there was a cratered scar between them. "And if it were up to me—"

"Enough!" came a sharp voice. "Leave us."

The man turned obediently and walked quickly away.

"Hello, Mr. Trance. I have been waiting to meet you for many years. Hello, Gretel." A woman was walking toward them. She moved with an easy grace. Her manner was confident and sure. The woman was old, although neither of them could have guessed her age—she seemed almost ageless. As she walked toward them, both Trance and Gretel noticed that she was dressed all in black.

"I am the Black Madonna," she continued. She stopped in front of Trance and slowly surveyed him from head to foot. "I can see that you are all your father said you were. Yes, I believe you may be the one—it was prophesied centuries ago, but then you must know that."

"I am afraid I don't."

The Madonna peered into Trance's eyes. After several moments she said, "Really?" Without waiting for a reply she continued, "That does not matter. There is little time to explain—but please follow me." The Madonna led them to a large console desk with a wide monitor resting on top. She issued several verbal commands, pressed some buttons and the screen came to life.

Trance watched the Madonna closely. She spoke with the same foreign dialect as the hulk. The back of his mind was contemplating her speech when he remembered that this woman was, by legend, more than a thousand years old. Perhaps the accent was not from a different geographic region, but of a different time in history.

"I understand that Breitfuss has told you about me?" she asked.

Trance and Gretel nodded. "He spoke of a legend," said Trance.

"Do you believe what has been said?"

"I don't know."

"The gist of what he says is true. A few of the details are off, but that should not concern you now. What *is* important is that we move quickly." She paused. "If you cannot believe in me then you must relinquish the formula to someone who does."

"Why?"

"I told you, there is little time. If you do not believe in me, I can protect you no more. They will kill you." She took a wheezy and sighed wearily. "The formula must remain in your hands, but only if you believe. If not, you must pass it on, like an heirloom. Regardless of who has the formula, the Baron must be destroyed."

"Convince me."

The Black Madonna's face tinged red. He could see fury in her eyes; a fury he sensed could drive her beyond reason. Then, as quickly as it began, her face slackened and she smiled.

"Yes. Of course. You are entitled to an explanation. Your father should have told you—"

"Enough of my father, please."

The Black Madonna raised one eyebrow, yet made no protest to his remark. He was young, and the young were prone to insolence. She had already decided that if he did not believe her she would kill him.

"My father did, indeed, discover the secret to the transformation of gold, and with it, the key to immortality. But he was not the Baron's alchemist. The *Baron* is my father. Centuries ago he began seeking power, and he has been at it ever since. During that time I have done all I can to stop him."

"You want to see him dead?"

"He has to die."

"And if he doesn't?"

"Then half the world will perish."

"I can't believe you."

"You can't believe me?" The Black Madonna closed her eyes and chuckled softly. When she looked back at Trance there was no mistaking the truth.

"My father has been trying to rule the world since the earliest days of his reign. Even then, he understood that he could not reveal his secret to the world—or surely he would be killed. He has been forced to remain behind the scenes…until that final moment when world power has been consolidated into his hands. My father knew that he could outlive any ruler. He also knew that the power of gold could usurp even the most powerful man's reign on his kingdom. He has helped support many men that have sought to rule the world. He avoided the early Romans. Their power was too great in its day, and he hated the Caesars. He financed the Crusade of Richard the Lion Hearted in 1190. He supported the Mongol king, Kahn, in 1206. One of his own sons, Maximilian, ruled over the final vestiges of the Holy Roman Empire, beginning in 1493. The list of minor rulers is endless, his quest for power uninterrupted for a millennium. He was a great friend of St. Germain. He gave the man small portions of his Elixir to let him live longer. In return, Germain lent his own support to the conquests of Napoleon.

"When Napoleon failed, he switched his efforts to the Germans, and even sacrificed his favorite son, Ferdi, to launch the First World War. Then came Hitler. Now…" The Black Madonna took another wheezy breath. Then she motioned to Trance and Gretel. "Sit," she said. "I am tired, and we have little time."

CHAPTER 19

▼

"We've located him, Sire."

"Where is he, Major?"

"He's with the Madonna."

The major watched as the blood drained from the Baron's face. He watched as the old man's eyes clouded gray, and his lips began to quiver.

"What? With that bitch!"

"None of the six men stationed outside the Madonna's compound reported last hour. Everyone else checked in. The fog is so heavy that we can't make a visual of the house. The men are using infrared until it lifts. When we couldn't reach any of our guards on the radio, I had Claus survey the grounds."

"And?"

"He found blood leading up to the house...and a glider hidden in the woods."

"A glider?"

"Trance must have flown in above the fog."

"Get him, Major." The Baron's eyes slit in response, and he looked like a python ready to coil around its prey. "Perhaps I have given you too much autonomy in this matter. Remember, with power comes responsibility...You will get him...or you will not live to enjoy the money I have been paying you. I will kill you myself."

"Yes, Baron."

"Any progress in finding the formula?"

"Perhaps. We traced Trance to the skier, Alfred Breitfuss, on the Smittenhohe."

"That has-been innkeeper? Why wasn't I notified?"

"I saw no reason to tell you, until there was something significant to report. We have him. We've bloodied him up, but we are getting little information from him. We did learn that he had the formula for a long time after the war. We knew that, until recently, parts of the formula were kept in two places, one part in America, the other with Breitfuss. Several weeks ago Trance took the pages from Breitfuss and sent them somewhere else."

"Where?"

"We don't know."

"The formula has been here in Austria since the war?"

"At least part of it, Sire."

"All that goddamn time? Under my goddamn nose all that goddamn time? Kill the son of a bitch. Now!"

"We can't kill Breitfuss, not until you get the formula—"

"I said kill him!" the Baron stopped, and then grinned like a hyena resting beside a fresh carcass. "No…wait a minute...Bring him here. I will do it myself." He shuffled off mumbling to himself. "Yes, yes, I will do it myself…"

Three hours later Breitfuss was led into the Baron's chamber. His left eye was swollen shut. His face was mounded and speckled with dried blood, and it looked like a rotten apple. As he walked into the room he smiled at the Baron, revealing a bloody gap where his two front teeth had been.

"Good evening, Baron. At last we meet," he said cheerfully. He watched the much taller Baron warily through his one good eye.

The Baron peered at the approaching apparition. Was this also the one who helped Trance escape Penwell years before? Was that the role this man had played?

"Yes," he said calmly. "We finally meet. I remember your brief but impressive skiing career. You let your nation down by leaving for America."

Breitfuss shrugged. "Fate." He gave a sly smile. "I have always wondered when I would get the chance to look you in the eye. I was hoping that it would be at your funeral."

"I am afraid this is to be yours."

"Perhaps we will be buried together."

The Baron laughed. "You amuse me, Herr Breitfuss. I have cheated death for hundreds of years. I do not plan to die now. In fact, I intend to rule the world for a thousand—"

"Your killing days are over, Gustav," said Breitfuss with a loud but measured voice.

There was no point in arguing with Breitfuss, so the Baron decided to play his game. "I see...Then will you grant a dying man his last request?"

A clever man, thought Breitfuss. "And what might that be, Baron?"

"I know that your friend, John Trance, disobeyed his orders during the war. He cheated. He lied. He stole from me something to which he had no right. But then he did nothing with it. Why?"

The Baron waited for an answer but received none. "And now...now that he is dead...suddenly his son is trying to kill me. Why?"

Breitfuss laughed. As he laughed a glob of bloodstained spittle dripped from his lips. "I'm sorry. I seem to have messed on your rug."

The Baron rushed forward and slapped Breitfuss with a full, open hand. "Why do these men haunt me?"

"Would you believe that it was all decided with a roll of the dice?"

"Dice?"

Breitfuss smiled again through the gap in his teeth. "Are you familiar with the *I Ching*?"

"The bullshit game played in China?"

"Many say that the *I Ching is* China. One cannot explain or understand China without a complete understanding of the *I Ching*."

"They are not Chinese. They're Japanese."

"Many others use the *I* as well."

"So?"

"John Trance consulted the *I Ching* and it told him what to do."

The Baron stood without comprehension. Breitfuss continued.

"His reading of the *I Ching* told him to steal your formula. It told him to contact me, an old friend of the family. He left it with me for over twenty years—buried less than a hundred kilometers from here."

The Baron's eyes narrowed. He looked like a jungle cat ready to pounce.

"One day he came and took it with him, back to the United States. You let him live all that time. Why?" asked Breitfuss.

The Baron answered softly. "I could not take the risk of losing the formula forever. I was never sure that Trance still had it...although I suspected it enough to...Never mind."

"Yet you killed John only now. Why?"

The Baron looked into Breitfuss's single open eye. This man was asking questions that a man could never know the answers to—and live. No matter.

"I have had people close to him for years. Closer to him than you can imagine. But he never let it slip...until a few months ago. He told someone, Herr Breitfuss...about his plans for the formula and his son. That is what led to his death. Once I knew he still had the formula, and that he intended to leave it for his son, I could not wait to see him die. Only once he was dead could I hope to regain it."

"You'll never get the formula from Jack Trance," said Breitfuss. "He is better at this game than his father. John was able to get the formula. Jack will keep it from you; then he will end your life."

"I think not, Herr Breitfuss. At this very moment he is surrounded by over a hundred of my men. Within minutes they will have him in chains." The Baron paced the chamber. "I'm going to let you live, just so you can see me rip the head off of your Jack Trance—after, of course, he has delivered the formula to me."

"He won't tell you where it is."

"Oh, yes he will." The Baron rose to his full height and stood menacingly above Breitfuss. He took a few quick breaths and continued. "Did Trance tell you about his wife?" Breitfuss was silent. "How do you think she died? Her name was Janice. She was a pretty girl, dedicated, but so naive..." The Baron stopped speaking for a moment, leaned against his desk, and continued. "If that Starr woman hadn't killed her, then we would have, Herr Breitfuss. We wanted him in a position where we could control him." He laughed. "Oh, yes. We controlled him through the CIA, even after he left. We kept him unbalanced, filled with conflict....What will he do now, when faced with losing the new love he has found? Will he stand and watch as we torture Gretel in front of his eyes? I think not. The formula means nothing to him. How convenient it was for him to fall in love again. We had thought that we would need to use his American banker friend—"

Breitfuss looked startled. "Who?"

The Baron chuckled. "There is so much you do not know. Until now Trance has been close to two women, his dead wife, and, uh, I have her here now. Lauren Haverford."

"Lauren? You're an animal."

"Aren't we all?"

The phone buzzed on the Baron's desk. He reached for the receiver and held it tightly against his ear. He nodded a couple times, then broke into a wide smile and said, "Go." He hung up the phone, looked at Breitfuss, and said, "It will be any moment now."

Back at his CIA offices in Langley, Virginia, Jacob Miller stood feeding his ulcer. He lifted a tall glass of goat's milk, mixed with Pepto Bismol, to his lips and took a pained swallow. He peered at the thirty lights that were lit on his phone console and took another deep draft. Every phone line was in use by his staff. Miller lifted the receiver and yelled a set of orders.

"Bring me every piece of intel that might relate to Trance, in hard copy. I don't care if you have to bring it here in a frigging wheelbarrow. You hear me?"

"Yes, sir."

"Now!"

Thirty minutes later a forest of papers standing four feet high was dumped onto Miller's desk. On top of the pile were index sheets, which he perused as he took a few more swigs of his goat's milk shake.

Miller's assistant said, "We were able to trace Trance to Austria, and finally to Breitfuss in Zell am See. But when we raided the Inn to acquire Trance, we found everyone gone. The doors were unlocked and a sign on the door read simply, *The Smittenhohe Inn is closed due to an emergency in the family*."

Miller's phone rang again. He reached for it angrily.

"What?"

"It's the President, sir."

"Tell him I'm not here."

"I'm sorry, sir. I've already told him you're not here. He said to get you anyway."

"Of all the...Hello, Mr. President. What do you want...sir?"

"You can tell me what the hell is going on, Miller."

"This shouldn't concern you at this time, Mr. President."

"Concern me? You got me to issue a blank authorization for you to requisition information, men, money, and machines throughout the U.S. and Europe. You said I shouldn't concern myself, so I went along with you. You asked me to ignore my Defense Secretary *and* my Secretary of State, so I did. Now you are stirring up a ton of dust, Miller. Do you know how many calls I have had? What the hell are you up to?"

"Sir, I could explain, but—"

"Don't give me any buts!"

"Sir...are you in your office?"

"Yes...why?"

"We need to meet in a place where our conversation can't be overheard. I am afraid the Oval Office won't do."

"Don't give me that shit, Miller."

"Really, sir. It's not safe."

"Are you telling me—"

"I am sorry, Mr. President. I am very serious. You or your office may be bugged. You know as well as I do that it is possible. The Russian technology is—"

"Now it's the Russians?"

"Or the Chinese. It's more complicated than you might imagine."

"They sweep this office everyday. There are no bugs."

"Yes, but—"

"I am going to give you one minute to convince me that you haven't lost it, soldier. If you can't, I'm going to fire your sorry ass and put someone in there who can do things right."

"All right, Mr. President. You want to know the truth? This may be our last chance to save the nation." *You shithead. You pull me out of here and your ass is grass.* "There is a global conspiracy—"

"Dispense with the crap, Miller," interrupted the President.

Jacob Miller took another gulp of his chalky, Pepto Bismol shake. "Have you got a hammer? Scissors?" he said.

"Scissors. I can have a hammer here in thirty seconds."

"Good. Snip off every button on your shirt and coat."

"What the—"

"Do it."

"Hold on." The phone went dead for thirty seconds, and the President returned saying, "You have less than a minute."

"Are you clipping the buttons?"

"Yes."

"When you get the hammer I want you to smash each of the buttons. Do it carefully."

"Smash my coat and shirt buttons? You think that one of them is a bug?"

"Something just hit my desk that would lead me to think so, Mr. President," lied Miller.

Miller could hear the cracking of the hammer, one pounding after another. Then there was silence. The President came back on the line. "I'm no spy, Miller. But one of the buttons of my coat didn't shatter like the rest..and there's..."

"That is just one bug, Mr. President."

"There may be more?"

"I'm not sure. An efficient bug can be smaller than the head of a pin. It can be dropped into the fabric of a couch, a rug, the frame of a painting. The only way to detect it is when it is transmitting data. Technology has become so advanced that bugs can be turned on and off at whim. They can store conversations and zap them in microseconds to a receiver on the outside— I have reason to believe that several men high up in your administration are linked to a plot to overthrow the U.S. and start World War Three."

The President laughed. "Jesus, Miller. You spooks do let your imaginations run wild."

"That bug wasn't my imagination, was it?" *Of course I had that bug planted on your coat this morning, Although, I wouldn't doubt there are others.*

"What is it you want?"

"Let me do my job."

"I'm getting pressure from Senator—"

"I don't care about any goddamn Senators. I am talking about the whole frigging free world here. If some Senator gets his feelings hurt—" Miller paused, then pleaded, "Just let me do my job."

"I have a mind to yank you out now, Jacob. It's men like you that can screw things up to the point where we *will* start a war." The President remained silent for several long moments. When he spoke again, it was with weary resignation. "Still, I have to trust you. You've got twenty-four hours. No more."

"But I need—"

The phone went dead. Miller threw his headset onto his desk and returned his attention to the piles of paper before him. He let his eyes run down the index file, still not sure what he was looking for. He just hoped that he would find it, whatever it was.

Three hours later Jacob Miller was still shuffling through the pile, searching through all of the reports he had noted on the index as having relevance. His phone rang.

"What?"

"Did you want dinner?" said his long-time male assistant.

"Don't have time."

"Don't have time? You didn't eat breakfast, didn't eat lunch, unless you call that goat piss and pink shit food. How do you intend to—"

"I'll eat on the plane."

"The plane, sir?"

"I'm leaving for Europe, in two hours."

"I see."

"Now leave me alone."

Miller returned to the papers. He entered figures and names into his computer and watched as the screen fed him more and more data. He was tapped into a supercomputer that could search through the entire government database, then out through portals to a plethora of sites requiring the highest security clearances. His search power was extraordinary, but he kept coming up dry. There is much a computer can do, but it is only as good as the data inside, and the skill of the person retrieving it. One or both of these factors were missing today.

Miller would have to put his faith in his own ability to reason. As he read the files further, several items kept popping back into his mind.

Miller knew Trance better than any man in the CIA. He had studied him, partly in awe, the rest out of fear. He had spent years pondering the secrets to Trance's success. He knew of the information Trance kept hidden from the Company. He knew the names of highly skilled mercenaries that Trance had covertly hired over the years. He had the numbers to unauthorized Swiss Bank accounts, accounts Trance used to disperse funds to these men. Every known CIA dollar had been accounted for—but he knew there were millions more. Miller found it interesting that the man could be so subversive to the CIA, but never to his country. Trance had never taken a dime for personal gain. To Miller,

this was most unsettling. Morals and convictions were extraordinarily dangerous in his line of work.

Miller had unearthed many of Trance's contacts, and followed multiple links
to black markets throughout the world—places where a man could buy anything if he had the guts and the money.

Miller had tagged Trance's favorite independent soldiers for surveillance,
and he knew they were now converging on Europe. Trance was actively buying
weapons and hiring men.

"I'll stop that sucker if it's the last thing I do," he said. "Whatever he is
doing."

No source could locate Trance, yet. But Miller had more than a dozen mercenaries under surveillance—warriors he knew were loyal to Trance, and he
would find him through them. He would let Trance play his game, then nail
him unmercifully in the end.

CHAPTER 20

▼

"The Baron is about to start a full-scale nuclear war between the United States, China and Russia," said the Black Madonna.

"No single man could start World War Three," said Trance. "There are too may intertwined interests. He can't act alone."

"Who says he is alone?" replied the Madonna. She let the words hang in the air, then continued. "Let's assume that you are the United States president and you learned that a nuclear missile was launched from ten miles off the Eastern Seaboard, the Gulf Coast, or California—and that before anyone could react, it laid waste to New York, Houston or LA. Suppose the minute you hear this you are told that there are several more missiles in the air coming from Russia, and that each is heading toward a major US city. You get on the phone to Moscow and they vehemently deny that they are behind the massacre. Then, while you are on the phone, the Russian president announces that a nuclear missile has just leveled St. Petersburg. Then he tells you that six other missiles have just been launched from Idaho. You begin your denial and he yells back into the phone that others have now been launched from the Baltic Sea and that they are on their way toward Moscow. As you deny, your Chief of Staff informs you that a missile salvo is coming in from Cuba and that within seconds one may penetrate the U.S. defenses and obliterate Cape Canaveral. There are more missiles heading towards San Francisco and Chicago, and unidentified aircraft converging on the Silicon Valley. To make matters worse, you get a call from the Chinese Premier and he accuses you of doing the same to his country. What would you do?"

"It couldn't happen."

"Oh? Do you know what organizations the Baron controls? His companies make submarines, fighter jets and missiles. They make nuclear warheads and have government contracts with a dozen nations. They have oil and gas operations around the globe...offshore drilling rigs, ships, storage facilities...

"Imagine a terrorist network that uses H bombs rather than car bombs. What is to stop the Baron from making a few for himself and placing them strategically around the world?"

The Black Madonna walked slowly to the wall and placed her index finger in a small slot inside. Immediately the walls began to shift, until they were looking at a bank of high definition screens. The Madonna pressed several icons on one screen and they all came to life. The wall revealed a flat map of the globe. On it were dozens of other icons—ships, submarines, and planes. There were many other symbols Trance could only guess at. Trance heard a small rumble behind him, and when he turned, he saw a holographic image of the Western Hemisphere. Missiles launched out of the ocean and were converging on America.

"The decision to launch a full scale defensive attack will have to be made in minutes...seconds...Mr. Trance. Imagine you are the American president and your intelligence sources have been warning you for weeks that the Russians and Chinese are up to something. Imagine that you are looking at a map like this, and it shows danger everywhere. Your military analysts are going bullshit. The Russian and Chinese leaders say you are mistaken—that they have no assets in the areas you claim. Then suddenly things begin to happen. What do you do? What would you do if missiles started launching from *inside* the United States, on their way toward Russia and China? Would you call the Russian president and say `Ah, I know those missiles look like they are from us, but it really isn't us.' What would you tell him? Tell me."

"Only the president can start the launch."

"You are talking about *your* military. What if they come from the Baron's own forces? Do they listen to your president? I don't think so. Besides, you and I know that your military can launch without the president."

They heard the pounding of feet coming toward them. The Madonna briefly clenched her fist, and then shook her head.

"This is what the Baron will do the moment he has the formula in his hands. You cannot stop him then. You must stop him now, before he has it."

"They're here!" came a shout.

The Black Madonna patted Trance's shoulder, and said, "Our time is up, my dear." She handed Trance a thick leather briefcase fitted with shoulder straps and said, "Here. Take this. It will explain what you need to know and how to communicate with me. It will not tell you everything, but some things are better left unsaid. If you need more money, let me know."

Trance stared numbly at the overstuffed briefcase. There were still so many questions. What did she mean, some things are better left unsaid? What other secrets could she be hiding?

But Trance found himself being pushed forward by the giant man, who had suddenly reappeared. "They have surrounded the house. You will have to follow me," he said.

The giant led them down a set of stairs to a well-lit hallway where they passed the opened doors to several offices. At the end of the hall they faced two paintings. One was a Rembrandt self-portrait. The other was a DaVinci of the Madonna, as a younger woman. It looked strikingly like the Mona Lisa, except for the coffee colored skin.

"That is the original," said the giant. "The painting in the Louvre is a copy, one Leo made at the Madonna's insistence."

The big man took the painting off of its hooks and dropped it to the floor. Behind it they saw nothing but wall. He placed his large palm against a spot in the center between the hanging hooks. Fifteen seconds later a small buzz could be heard from behind the wall. The man moved his hand a foot lower. Ten seconds later the wall began to give way. It was like the door to a vault, over a foot thick of solid steel. It opened to another hallway. This one, too, was well lit. But there was nothing along the walls except for one door. The floor and walls were of polished gray marble. The hallway stretched as far as they could see, and it appeared to narrow like train tracks as it drew farther away.

So many questions, thought Trance.

"This is a tunnel…" said the big man, "…that will take you to the far side of the mountain." He handed Trance a key, opened the single door and pulled a Yamaha motorcycle from inside.

"I trust you can use this?"

Trance looked at the dirt bike and nodded.

"You are on your own from here. I cannot go with you…I must protect her."

"How long is the tunnel?" asked Trance.

"Over two kilometers. Built many years ago, just for this day. You will come to a dead end. Stand with your feet one foot from the center of the wall before you. Then turn to your right. Against that wall you will see a small black dot. Press your palm against it. It has been programmed for your hand…and your hand only. Ten seconds later the door will open. Do not fail, Trance. If you do, the weight of hell will fall upon your shoulders." The man extended his hand. "And if hell doesn't get you, I will. Good luck." He looked at Trance with a wry smile.

"One question?" asked Trance.

"Perhaps."

"Are you her son? The Madonna's son?"

The giant lowered his head and smiled slyly. "She did have one son. But it isn't me."

"What is your name?"

"You know who I am," said the giant. "Deep down, you know who we are." Then the giant vanished like a puff of smoke.

Trance and Gretel stood silently, looking at each other, thinking about the enormity of their task.

"Seems like our day for excitement," said Gretel. She strapped the briefcase to her back.

"Don't worry," joked Trance. "I'm used to this."

Navigating through the darkness of the mountain on a motorcycle was the least of their worries. When they emerged, the Baron's men would be everywhere. If Breitfuss wasn't waiting at their prearranged rendezvous point, Trance would not know where to go for safety. He would worry about that later. He stood with the bike between his legs and strapped on a helmet.

"Ever ridden one of these before?"

"Sure," she replied. *Many times*, she thought. *I am prepared.*

"Hop on and hold tight, mama," said Trance. He was back in his element. It was moments like these where he felt truly alive. He wasn't thinking of the enormity of his task, the consequences of failure, or the loss of his wife. At this single moment he thought only of what must be done.

"I love you," he said.

"Oh, Jack."

Trance couldn't see through her helmet's visor, to the painful look in her face.

"Soon," he said.

"Then can we go away? Far away?"

"We'll go where none of them will find us. We'll be happy. I promise."

"There is so much that we need to learn about each other."

"We'll have time."

"Oh, how I hope so. Now get our asses out of here."

Trance jammed the key into the motorbike and fired it up. Despite the bike's custom muffler, the loudness roared through the tunnel with an almost unbearable blast in the tightly closed space. Gretel wrapped her arms around Trance and they ripped toward the end of the tunnel.

A minute later they had reached the end and Trance shut off the bike. Trance did as he had been instructed and the hidden door began to open into the darkness.

"Open sesame," said Trance. Gretel knocked him playfully on the helmet.

As the door yawned, Trance spread himself against the wall, peering around the edge of the opening for men who might be laying in wait to capture them. No sign of anyone lurking, but he could hear rapid shots being fired at the top of the mountain near the Madonna's home, more than a mile away. Trance slipped back into the tunnel, hopped on the bike, and they tore off into the night.

Trance rode without lights, trusting his senses to guide them. He headed south toward a thicket of trees. When they were inside the trees he turned the engine off and listened. He heard nothing, but the distant noise of the fighting. He looked to the sky and fixed his eyes upon the stars, which could now be seen through the rapidly thinning ground fog. He looked at a small GPS display on his wrist and pointed.

"We've got to head south to meet Breitfuss. It should be this way."

Trance started the engine and began to navigate through the woods. He wondered if he should ditch the bike and continue on foot, or risk the chance of being heard. The chances of meeting a patrol on the mountain were strong, and they could evade them more effectively on foot. But there would be teams of dogs, and men on motorcycles and ATVs chasing them whenever they were found. He might be able to outrun them on his own, but with Gretel he wasn't sure. She had no training. She had a better chance with them both on the bike.

They had five miles to cover before reaching their rendezvous point with Breitfuss, and were crossing a rugged field when their luck ran out. With the din of the motorcycle's engine in his ears, Trance didn't hear the whirr of the rotors approaching from the backside of the mountain. Before he could react, he was covered with a bright beam of light.

"Shit," he said. "Hold on." Trance revved the engine and crashed headlong toward the far off shelter of the trees. Gretel clenched her teeth to keep them from chipping from the jarring movements of the ride. The bike flew off a grassy mound into the air and hung there like a dancer, as if frozen in motion. Gretel couldn't tell when they would land, and when they did, her head slammed into Trance's back. She loosened her grip around his waist, but caught herself in time to stay on.

"You all right?" he yelled.

She squeezed him and said, "Yeah. You're a maniac!"

"They could begin shooting any—" Shots came from the helicopter hovering above them. They were in rough terrain, but there was no cover from above. Trance weaved the bike along a dry streambed. He nearly fell several times, but each time he stopped the fall with an outstretched leg. The shots came from a single shot rifle every two or three seconds. That was a stroke of luck. A machine gun would have sprayed them into pieces.

Trance zigzagged west toward a thick set of pine trees jutting between the wide valley walls. He had just seconds to go when another helicopter emerged in front of him and splattered the ground with a burst of gunfire.

"This one's got firepower," he muttered. The helicopter swooped low in front of him and shined another bright searchlight in his eyes. Bullets rained about them again, so close that Trance could feel them whistle by his head. He jerked the bike to the left, back towards the south. He would have to maneuver the chopper away from its position between him and the woods. If he couldn't, they were dead.

Trance reached to the small of his back and pulled out his father's old Colt. It was useless against the helicopters, unless he got lucky and hit the gas tank, pilot, or the hydraulics. Even then, he wasn't sure his gun could penetrate the windshield or the steel. He snapped a bullet into the chamber against his leg and turned towards the helicopter that was floating between them and temporary freedom. He raced the engine and continued to zigzag forward toward the chopper. He felt no fear of death. He was consumed only with thoughts of dismembering the enemy, his mind running on automatic. He no longer thought, just reacted.

Trance was nearly blinded by the piercing light. He pulled down the visor on his helmet, which dulled the brightness enough to let him see. He could hear the popping sounds of automatic gunfire and saw spits of dirt fly into the air as the bullets sprayed a path in front of him, then to his side. It was all he could do to stay out of the line of fire. Then suddenly, he realized that the bullets weren't meant to kill them, just contain them until other forces, ground forces could capture them. "They're trying to take us alive," he muttered. "Well, hallelujah."

Trance called their bluff. It was his only chance. He picked out a beeline toward the helicopter in front and ignored the one hovering behind him. As the distance closed Trance began shooting, doing his best to adjust to the jarring of his body. The helicopter stopped firing but still hovered within a few feet of the ground. It began to move toward Trance in a deadly game of chicken. He heard one of his shots ping off of the chopper as the distance closed to within fifty yards. Just a few more seconds...The helicopter seemed to hesitate, then pulled into the air as another of Trance's shots smashed against the cockpit.

That was all he needed. Trance and Gretel plunged into the dense canopy of trees.

When he was sure that they had escaped the pursuit, Trance stopped to assess the situation. "It won't be long before they swarm this place," he said softly.

"We'll make it," said Gretel reassuringly, although inside she was beginning to feel a dark, foreboding desperation.

Sensing this, Trance spoke again. "If we can reach Breitfuss, we have a chance. We took delivery of an Apache gunship this morning, and the best renegade pilot around should be flying it. If we're lucky, they'll be waiting for us."

"How did you pay for it?" asked Gretel. "Your money is in Zurich in a signature-only account. They won't release funds without you there."

"I charged it," replied Trance.

"Master Card?"

"American Express," joked Trance. "Good as money." He laughed. "These are old friends, sweetheart. I've dealt with them for years. I've bought...Uncle Sam has bought a lot of toys. We've put billions of dollars into their pockets. I know who they are and I've protected their asses like a mother hen protects her eggs. Arms dealing isn't exactly the safest of professions, so, when you have someone you can trust..."

"Do they know that this isn't a U.S. operation?"

Trance cocked his head and shrugged. "The less they know the better. Wouldn't you say?"

"They'll kill you if you don't deliver. Won't they?"

"Honey...If I don't deliver I'll already be dead."

"Will we survive, Jack?" Gretel grew serious. For once in her life she was on the verge of happiness, of having the family she had lost as a child. For once in her life she harbored hopes for the future. If only—

"Of course," said Trance, kissing her gently on the forehead. "Don't worry."

The helicopters buzzed overhead and the searchlight passed within yards of where they stood.

"Got to move, now," said Trance. "Breitfuss should be waiting."

"And if he's not?"

"Let's just get there first."

Trance stopped the bike a quarter-mile from the rendezvous point. There was no telling what they might find in front, so approaching on foot was safer. The Baron's helicopters continued to sweep across the mountains in search of them, and they could hear them whirring in the distance to the north. Trance wondered if they had lost them, or if they were just staying out of his way while he walked into a trap on the other side of the ridge. There was no end to the psychological games that could be played in this type of situation. Trance could only hope that Breitfuss and his pilot were waiting.

Trance could see the faint glow of a cigarette from his position in the trees. Breitfuss didn't smoke. Neither did the pilot that Trance hoped would be there.

"Stay here," he mouthed with an almost silent whisper. Fifty yards lay between Trance and the smoker, and he could see the man's silhouette against the opaque sky. He was leaning against a tree, peering casually about, more concerned with the final drags on his cigarette than catching Trance. Trance crept toward him. He pulled a thin rope from his pocket and fingered a knot tied only inches from one end. He tied this end of the rope to a small metal shaft he pulled from a sleeve in his pant leg. Trance wrapped his hand around the smooth steel and inched forward. He shadowed himself with the trees, passing between them like the wind...unseen and noiseless. Within moments he peered around the same tree as his victim. In a blur he wrapped the end of the rope around his left hand, pulled it taught and wound the rope under the man's chin. He yanked up, the knot stifling any sound until he felt the man go limp.

"One move and you're dead," he said in German. The man waved his arms. Trance released the tension on the rope, just enough to let the man whisper.

"I...I can't understand you." The man's response was in English.

"Make a sound and you're a dead man," repeated Trance. "Who are you? Where's Breitfuss?" As he spoke, Trance pulled up on the cord. The man choked.

"Aarrgghh...Th...They have him."

"Who?"

"I don't know."

"Who are you?"

"I can't tell you."

Trance tightened the rope. He saw the man's eyes pop wide and gloss over, and he continued to pull at the last remnants of the man's life. Then he relaxed.

"Don't make me kill you...Who are you?" The man couldn't speak for a few seconds. Then he replied in a raspy voice.

"Are you Trance?" Trance stared at him and the man continued "You can kill me, whoever you are. All I can tell you is that, *You're no drinking match for the big stick, Batman.*" Trance released his grip. Stick Granger was his closest friend, and a freelance mercenary, working only for the good guys in places too sensitive for the U.S. military.

Granger had challenged Trance to a drinking contest one night in Nicaragua and drunk him under the table. He had never let him hear the end of it, and took this chance to remind him again.

"Who told you to say that?"

"That's all I can say," said the man. His eyes had cleared but they were filled with fear, and still unfocused.

"Granger tell you to say that?" said Trance. He watched as the man's eyes focused briefly with the mention of Granger's name.

"I can't say," he said.

Trance looked at the man for a second more, and then completely released his grip. He stuck out his hand and said, "The name is Trance...Jack Trance."

The man looked at him, blinking, but without words. Then he finally croaked, "Berringer...Clay Berringer," and stuck out his hand to meet Trance's. He managed a smile.

"You're a good soldier," continued Trance. "I commend you on your bravery. I pay well for that. But that smoking...Didn't Granger warn you not to smoke?"

"I...Yes, sir. But I'd been here for hours—"

"You've had your one free mistake, soldier. You're lucky it was me."

Berringer nodded, rubbing his mottled neck with his left hand, while leaning against the tree with his right. "Yeah. Lucky."

"Take me to Granger."

The man nodded, turned and led Trance toward a nearby clearing.

"Where's Breitfuss?" asked Trance.

"The Baron."

Trance looked at him grimly. "Just you and Stick?"

"Here, yes. But the others are in country."

In the clearing Trance could make out the AH-1W Super-Cobra with its missile pods hanging below its stubby wings like vipers. It was covered with thin camouflage netting and cut branches that made it almost unrecognizable, even from the ground. Standing to one side, with an Israeli Uzi machine gun hooked to his belt and an M-16 in his hands, stood the imposing figure of Stick Granger. At six foot four Granger was large for a pilot. His arms bowed slightly as they hung from his side, forced outward by the slabs of solid muscle along his chest and back. The arms were long, almost ape-like, and his hands were huge, like baseball mitts. His reddish hair was long in the back, flowing down to his shoulders in a mullet. It was cut short on the top and sides, revealing two gold-looped earrings. His face was tanned, with crow's feet along the sides of his eyes from an ever-present smile. From the edge of the clearing Berringer lit his Bic lighter twice. Granger responded with three. They walked forward.

"Hello, you son of a whore," said Granger with a wide grin.

"How'd you get yourself into this mess, Stick?" laughed Trance.

"Some asshole said he needed my help."

The two men embraced in a hug lasting several seconds. They had a friendship spanning many years. Each had saved the other's life more than once. There was no debt between them, yet each would die for the other without a second thought.

"What did you do to your face, Jack? Butt heads with a bull?" Stick fingered the lump on Trance's nose and looked closely at the scars that were still fresh on his face.

"Had a little excitement. I'll tell you all about it after you get us the hell out a here." Trance pointed at the helicopter. "Get that bird ready to fly, will you? I'll be back in two mikes." Trance vanished into the woods.

When Trance reappeared with Gretel, Stick smiled from the cockpit. "Well...well..." he muttered to himself. By the time Trance had reached the door, the rotor blades were spinning. Seconds later they were airborne.

"There are two uglies to the north," said Trance through the microphone built into his helmet. "We could be in for a fur ball."

"Yeah, we heard," said Stick. "You want to run or gun?"

"See if you can sneak out, Stick. But if they make us, then turn and we'll burn 'em."

"You got it, boss." Stick nodded his head toward the back. "Who's the babe?" Gretel sat behind them, with no earphones to hear them above the noise.

"That's my future, Stick."

Stick looked at his friend and felt happy for him. He had known Trance in the early days, fought with him in nearly every Godforsaken place known to man. Trance had always been complex. He was sensitive and thoughtful, a side seen only by his closest friends. But when fighting for his country, he was as ruthless as he had to be. Trance was consumed with a ferocious commitment to his nation. He needed something to believe in, and Trance had found it in America. America had become his mother, his lover, and for years he had fought for her like no soldier Stick had ever seen before, or since.

In the CIA Stick had watched his friend grow increasingly disillusioned, not with America, but with human nature. The job of ensuring peace was a dirty one—fraught with corruption and the necessity for deceit. Freedom was paid for with bullets and blood. The price of freedom came high, and Trance had paid dearly. Stick had seen his own marriage fail, as his lonely wife had sunk deeper and deeper into a bottle, then into the arms of men she didn't know.

Stick had escaped, by becoming an independent soldier of fortune.

Trance got lucky. He found Janice. The melancholy disappeared, and Trance grew happy, almost free-spirited. Then the assholes killed her—the underbelly of the world who cared for no one. Who it was and why it happened, he never knew.

"She anything like Janice?" he asked. No other person, except Lauren, would dare to ask him a question like that. Stick saw Trance stiffen briefly, and then relax.

"Yes, 'ol buddy. She is. When I am with her I feel whole...alive...I want nothing more than to get this mess over with and fly away to someplace where the world won't find us."

"You've had it tough."

"No more than you, my friend." Trance chuckled. "Who says we've had it so bad, hey? We're alive. That's better than many."

"How 'bout the time they nearly starved and beat you to death in that Iranian prison?"

"Water under the bridge."

Stick laughed and shook his head. "Man, you're whipped."

The sky lit with fire.

"Oh, shit," said Stick. "The fur's flying. Bogeys at ten and two."

"Roger that," said Trance.

Stick pulled out of the gunfire and swooped low toward the valley to pick up speed and evade their pursuers. They were in for a ride.

"A hundred bucks says we get 'em both within three minutes. No Hellfires," said Stick. Firing a missile would be cheating in this private game, like shooting ducks on a pond. They'd take them down with machine guns only. Trance smiled, shook his head and looked to his friend. Trance heard a voice in his head say, *Does the fate of the world rest in the hands of two irresponsible children who can only play games?*

"Some kids never grow up. You're on." He reached down and pressed a button on his watch. "Go." Trance knew what Stick was doing. Making it a game would keep him loose, so he wouldn't choke like some Super Bowl quarterback or a World Series pitcher when all was on the line.

CHAPTER 21

▼

A black Mercedes limousine spun its way through the Swiss country roads. It would be dawn soon, and the driver had been ordered to reach his destination before daylight. It was a close race, and the limo used the entire road as it swerved around the corners. Inside, the single passenger sat impassively viewing a computer screen built into the back seat of the car. He nodded as he reviewed the figures, the ship positions, and the itineraries of several dozen men—the pieces that would have to be in place before it all began. Everything was perfect. He switched off the machine as the car made the final turn into the private drive of the Swiss castle. Then he looked at his watch.

"Very good, Alex. You keep your job for another day," he said without humor. The driver gave shiver of relief.

"You will wait here," said the number two man in the Russian FSB, which now housed the former KGB. The driver gave a slight nod, but continued to stare forward, his face devoid of expression. The director was the youngest man in Russia to hold such a position, and it was accepted in Russian governmental circles that he would soon climb the stairs to the pinnacle of power, assuming he wasn't assassinated first.

The driver watched out of the corner of his eye as the man walked the final steps to the underground entrance of the fortress. His man oozed power and confidence. Over the years he had driven for many of them...Putin, Yeltsin, Gorbachev, and none of them could match this man's presence.

Vladimir waved his hand at the guards and proceeded through the metal doors. Moments later the Russian sat in one of the plush chairs of an elevator that took him to the top of the schloss. His eyes closed in preparation for his meeting with the one man in the world he considered to be nearly his equal— the Chosen One.

The door opened to a broad room, amply furnished with ultra-modern furniture. He thought how ironic it was that a castle five hundred years old should be furnished in the newest fashion. He walked across the floor toward the far end where a bright flame was burning in a wide fireplace.

"Hello, my brother," he said as his counterpart turned to face him. He spoke in German.

"Sorry to call you on such short notice," was the reply, also in German.

"It was no trouble to advance my schedule two days. But I am curious—"

"I want to push the date forward. I thought it should be a decision we made together. So I asked you here." *I will force you to make a choice*, thought the Chosen One.

"And what does father think?"

"He won't know."

"Ah, the prodigal son—"

"Father is old. He is consumed with his damned formula, and he has lost sight of the true goal."

"But he is in control."

"Not if we work together."

"Perhaps," said the Russian, switching to his native tongue. "But what difference will a few days make?"

His half brother effortlessly changed language with him. "A few days could make all the difference. He is up against Trance. Trance has the formula, and the old man will not begin until he has it in his hand."

"Which will be at any moment."

"Will it?" asked the Chosen One. "You don't know Trance, then. They say there is something mystical about him. They say he's done things—impossible things."

"But we have found him. My people found him. It is just a matter—" said the Russian coldly.

"And how many times have you lost him?" interrupted the Chosen One.

"I've had to limit the use of my men." The Russian sneered at his rival. "And what about your forces? Useless."

"You could send your whole damned army, Vladi, and you still might not capture Trance. He's eluding us, and I've got teams of men." He paused to collect his thoughts. "But that's not what concerns me. If Trance deduces our plan he might abort it. If forewarned, your leaders and mine may not fall into place. If they know the missiles come from us, and not from each other, they may stop the war from ever taking place, perhaps take down the whole family."

"They could never stop the warheads we already have in place. The bombs under the Potomac and the Hudson Rivers...the ones loaded into our suicide squads of private aircraft in the U.S., Russia, Europe, and China, the missiles hidden in our drilling rigs and inland silos."

"By the way...Nice touch...flying a bomb-filled plane right into the Washington Mall."

The Russian smiled. "Just wanted to raise the tensions a little. It was beautiful on the news. The fireball lit the entire sky when they shot it out of the air. Just beautiful."

"Yes...very effective...But, we have a serious problem if our leaders are warned. They won't take the bait. We both agree that the only prize worth such destruction is power—world power. If we cannot render all nations defenseless against us, we will have no prize...and the price, my brother...the thought of destroying New York...Moscow...with no reward is—"

"Meaningless," interrupted the Russian. "I agree."

"I fear that Trance will evade capture and gain a confrontation with father. When he does, he will uncover our identities and our motives."

"Impossible."

"When he challenges father, he will pull out the information—" continued the Chosen One.

"Trance won't live," interrupted the Russian.

"We cannot take that chance."

"Your recommendation?"

"Begin now."

"What's in it for me?" asked the Russian.

"We both know it was a close choice between us."

"But you were chosen."

"As a figurehead only. Do you think that father will ever let me rule? Let *us* rule? If he gets that goddamn formula, he'll live another thousand years." The Chosen One let the thought hang in the air. This was the moment he had been waiting for, the one that would seal their fate.

The Russian stood silently for more that a minute. He looked at his brother with a cold, calculated stare. "So, we keep the formula from father, let him die, and have the world for ourselves?"

"Exactly."

"So, what's in it for me?" asked the Russian again.

"The world is a big place. Perhaps it could be split in half."

"Would you be satisfied with only half a world?"

"It is better than none at all."

"You get the West and I get the East? What is to stop us from fighting each other?"

The Chosen One laughed. "The world may not survive the first nuclear war, let alone a second one. "

"True," mused the Russian. *He's making a fatal mistake, but I'll let him. It'll make it that much easier for me.*

"The world will survive and we will be brothers, always."

The two men embraced and said, "Brothers."

While the Baron's sons were plotting against him, Lauren Haverford was being driven from an airfield outside of Salzburg to the Baron's castle. She had been kidnapped from her Boston brownstone on a Friday night and then flown by private jet directly to Austria. No one would miss her until Monday. By then the trail would be as cold as a dead fish, and she would never be found.

"You can't do this," she said. "I am an American citizen. I have friends in the government."

"Miss Haverford," replied her escort. "We know exactly who your friends are. There will be no government to come to your rescue. You have simply vanished."

"But my bank—"

"Soon your bank will cease to exist, Miss Haverford," interrupted the man. "Still, your life may be spared, if you cooperate."

"Cooperate? The hell I'll cooperate."

"We'll see, Miss Haverford...We'll see."

In the United States, a phone rang at CIA headquarters. It rang for a long time, but was finally answered by a tired female voice.

"Yes?"

"Get me Miller."

"I am sorry, but Mr. Miller is not available at the moment. Neither is his assistant."

"Make him available. The President wants to speak with him, now.

"I'm sorry, sir. Mr. Miller has left the country and cannot be reached."

"What do you mean he cannot be reached? Hold on..." There was silence. Seconds later another voice came on the line.

"This is the President," he said. "Patch me through to Miller."

"I am sorry, Mr. President. But I can't." The woman's voice wavered. "Mr. Miller said that if you called I was to tell you that he will contact you when he can."

"I'm going to give that sonofabitch a piece of my mind. Where the hell is he?"

"He's out of the country, sir. Somewhere in Europe, near you, I believe. Haven't you gone to Europe?"

"This is nothing personal against you, miss, but you tell the ass wipe to call me. I mean now!"

"And how can you be reached, Mr. President?"

"Just tell your boss that I'm over here doing *his* job. I shouldn't have to clear up this hornets' nest...like I don't have other things to do. He'll know how to find me."

CHAPTER 22

▼

The helicopter was a flying arsenal. They had enough weaponry to level a small town. But all the firepower in the world wouldn't help them if they took a hit.

"They had orders not to kill before," said Trance.

"They're out for blood now, buddy," replied Stick. "We could beat feet, but those Apaches can outrun us by a hundred knots. They will be on our six in no time. I can outmaneuver and outgun them, but we sure as hell can't outrun them. We have to fight."

"You've got two minutes and thirty seconds," said Trance.

Stick smiled. "Double or nothing?" He plunged the helicopter along a dirt road through the trees, flying just a body length from the ground. The countryside whooshed by in the faint light of the coming dawn. The pursuers hovered above them, content to wait them out.

"You know, I do believe their orders haven't changed," said Stick. "Poor suckers. I feel sorry for them." With that he pulled on the stick and sent the chopper screaming into the air so fast that, by the time the enemy could react, Stick was behind them, with both in his sights.

"Nice move, Pirate."

Granger gave a sideways glance toward Trance. His friend hadn't called him Pirate since the old days, days when things were simpler, and happier.

"Which one first?"

"Your choice," said Trance. "But make it fast or they'll jump out of range."

Stick tore the gunship toward the one on the left and pulled behind and above the air wash. "Your baby," he cried.

Trance took aim and shot a quick burst of fire. A second later they saw the helo spin into flames below them. The other helicopter veered to the right and was beating a path out of range. Stick pulled at the nose of his chopper to get him in his sights.

"Go!" he cried and another burst of bullets let loose from the guns. The second chopper exploded and dropped out of sight.

Trance looked at his watch. "Three minutes and eighteen seconds," he said. "You owe me two a hundred bucks."

Stick smiled and shook his head. "I save your ass, *again,* and all you want is my money." He paused. "Speaking of money, your message made no mention of it. Not your standard procedure."

"This one has nothing to do with the U.S. government, Stick."

"Always wondered if you would go into business for yourself. Really didn't think you would."

"It's not what you're thinking."

"Jack, I've got a hundred men that will be asking me how they're getting paid."

"And I suppose you want something too?"

Stick laughed. "Nah. I do this for fun."

"You get half a million to lead the operation. I'll give you another five million to distribute among your men, as you see fit."

Stick whistled softly and said, "Must be quite a prize we're after, ol' buddy. I could just imagine what they're paying you on this one."

"This is all me, Stick..." Trance continued his explanation, leaving nothing out. He would be placing his life in his friend's hands, so he would have to know it all. When Trance had finished Stick looked at him and said, "Jesus, Jack. If this had come from anyone else I'd tell 'em where to shove it. But from you?" He shook his head again.

"Ol' buddy, for once in your life you are going to get the opportunity to do a real service for your country." Trance patted him on the shoulder.

"Who would ever have thunk it."

Trance reached back and put his hand on Gretel's knee. She grasped it and squeezed. She prayed it wouldn't be long before they reached Trance's safe house in the mountains of Switzerland.

"You short on money, Jack?" asked Stick.

"Nah. I've got about twenty million liquid of my own. I've got stock in a little film company I could sell. I'd rather keep it though. Then, of course, there's the Freedom Fund."

"What about your parent's money?"

"I put it all into a charitable trust."

"Damn stupid of you, JT."

Trance shrugged. "Perhaps I should have kept some."

In his years with T Force, much of Trance's operating budget came from monies recovered from despotic dictators, drug runners and rogue arms merchants. He never mingled this money with his own, nor did he repatriate it to America. Trance kept it to fund covert operations that never made the news, the ones required to keep Americans free. This money rested in a labyrinth of bank accounts, totaling well over one hundred million dollars—most if it sitting safely within the vaults of the Nicolas Klug Bank.

"I've got about two million stashed in Zurich," said Stick causally. "It's just sort of sitting there. It's yours if you need it. Consider it a donation to the cause."

Trance felt a tingle run through his spine. He looked at his friend. Granger kept his eyes looking forward. Silence passed between them, their bond of friendship reaffirmed. Trance knew how many times Stick had risked his life to earn that money, and how much his friend craved security.

"Thanks," said Trance. "The Freedom Fund is fairly flush. We'll probably be okay. The Madonna has more if we need it. Don't want to use it though…Can't be indebted."

Trance guided them to a small wood and stone home deep in the Swiss Alps. It rested on the edge of a glacial lake, surrounded by dense forest.

"This was my father's," said Trance. "He called it his secret place. Even my mother didn't know about it. Dad said I would need it someday, and I guess this is the day he meant. I've only been here once."

"Looks peaceful," said Stick.

"Gretel and I might settle here when it's all over."

Stick looked at Trance and saw him covertly dab at some mist in his eye. His friend was *wired*. Stick said, "I prefer the islands myself. Nothing like half naked native girls to help you forget the pressures of the outside world."

"You've always been a horny son of a bitch." Trance noticed a faraway look in Stick's eyes. He knew his friend was remembering his own wife and kids. He had never been the same since he lost them.

"Suppose so," said Stick wistfully.

The house was built as a hunting lodge. It had been used as one for many years, before being purchased by Trance's father. The home had a large living area with a rustic stone fireplace that dominated the room. Along the walls hung a herd of heads from big game animals, exotic trophies from days long since past—lion, tiger, antelope…boar. The dining area was an extension of the room, separated by a long rough-hewn oak table and hatchet-carved oak chairs. Behind it stood the kitchen, housing an iron woodstove and a baking oven made of stone. There were no electrical outlets in the lodge, but there was indoor plumbing, and a wood-fired furnace.

"This place is beautiful," said Gretel. She walked into the kitchen. "Look at this oven. I haven't seen one of these in years. Is there anything to cook with?"

Trance put his arm around her and said, "You must be tired. It's okay if you take a break. I'll get the furnace going. It will take an hour or so to heat up the water. Why don't you catch a quick nap, then take a warm shower?"

"I thought we were partners?" she asked.

"Yes, but—"

"Don't you *Yes, but* me, Jack Trance. You men have a lot to talk about. I'll do the cooking. I'll heat up the water. If I can find some flour somewhere, I'll bake you the best bread you've had all day."

"The only bread," muttered Stick, good-naturedly.

"Picky, picky, picky."

Trance looked at his friend, then at Clay Berringer and shrugged his shoulders.

"Women," said Trance. Then he smiled at Gretel. "I better quit now, before Stick and Clay figure out that you're the boss."

"I am the boss." Gretel paused. "At least in the kitchen I am, and perhaps in the bedroom."

Stick and Clay laughed loudly. Gretel walked to Trance and took his head in her hands. "I love you so." She kissed him on the lips. "Now get to work." She turned and walked through the kitchen into an expansive food storage closet filled with canned goods and containers of flour, rice and sugar.

"She'll do," said Stick.

"She hasn't slept all night and look at the energy she has."

"She loves you. I can see that," continued Stick. "And she's got a great ass."

The men chuckled and sat down at the table.

"I heard that!" came a voice from the closet.

The men began to talk.

"Where're you from, Clay?" asked Trance. The man looked vaguely familiar.

"San Diego," said Clay. "Did ten years in the Navy. Then got hooked up with Stick."

"I've seen you before."

"I was wondering if you'd remember. I was a Seal and a zoomie. Seven years ago you gave a seminar at Miramar. God you were good."

"I remember now," said Trance. "It was June. You were in the second row during the self-defense demonstration."

"You made our men look like pussies, sir."

"I was lucky," said Trance.

Clay turned to Stick. "He took on ten men. Leveled 'em all." He looked back at Trance. "They told us you were the best."

"Just hype, Clay."

"Bullshit," said Stick. "He was the goddamn world champion in ultimate fighting. Undefeated, he was, 'till he retired."

Trance put a finger to his lips, glanced toward the kitchen and whispered, "That was a lifetime ago, Stick. I was angry then." Trance stood and walked into the kitchen to see how Gretel was coming along

Clay turned to Stick as Trance vanished through the door. "I follow that ultimate shit. I've never heard of him fighting."

Stick wrapped one of his huge arms around Clay and spoke quietly, so no one would hear. "There's a Chinese businessman in New York, goes by the name of Robert Yang. Every year Yang holds a contest in his Park Avenue mansion. Only the world's best are invited to compete—most of them men you have never heard of, and never will.

"Yang broadcasts the competition around the world in a secure webcast. Only catch is—you've got to pay a hundred thousand dollars for the live feed. To attend the event in person, you need a proven net worth of a hundred million or more."

"No way."

"Yes, way. Bettors have to secure a minimum betting line of credit of one million dollars, in advance, just to have the opportunity to wager."

"The take must be enormous."

"Dwarfs any boxing match. Even the Super Bowl."

"And the stakes to the fighters?"

"Ten percent of the take on each match, twenty percent if you kill your opponent in the ring. It takes six wins to get to the final—sort of like March Madness."

"That's crazy. How can you live through six matches?"

"Some don't. Men have been known to walk away with twenty million or more from a finals match alone."

"And Trance?"

Stick laughed. "He didn't do it for the money."

"Then he's crazy, too.'

"Jack was in a bad place then. His wife had just died. He needed to feel alive…or die in the process." Stick motioned with his head and both men fell silent as Trance returned.

For the next hour the men went over his plan. They were hunched over one corner of the huge oak table when Gretel came in from the kitchen.

"Breakfast is served, if you gentlemen care to take a break."

The men leaned back in their chairs and stretched. Before them sat the Black Madonna's open briefcase, with a islands of papers strewn across the table's length. Gretel leaned over Trance's shoulder and looked at the mass of documents.

"He's got major interests in more than four hundred corporations," said

Trance. "His companies are dominant in finance, energy, weaponry; you name it. Many of them are household names. Others are privately held, little known, but just as big and powerful. This guy has access to nuclear missiles, submarines, biological weapons of mass destruction—anything needed to destabilize or terrorize the world.

"He's got an army of twenty thousand men inside the mountain beneath his castle, and an underground military compound with a hundred thousand more, less than a hundred kilometers away. This single man could take on almost any nation, one-on-one, and win." Trance pointed at a neat stack of papers to his right. "These documents provide a breakdown of the Baron's castle defense systems—his weapons, manpower, positioning."

Gretel reached down to the table and lifted a folded document made of thick bluish paper. Trance motioned toward it. "That's a blueprint of the castle. It details an array of passageways and tunnels boring deeply into and throughout the mountainside." Trance held up a similar set of papers. "These are the schematics for the Baron's nuclear reactor, built more than a mile beneath the castle."

"This man is insane," said Gretel, in a barely audible voice. "You can't even think to take him on. You'll be like…like a gnat on an elephant."

"More like a rattlesnake," said Stick.

Trance clapped his hands. "Enough of this for now. What earthly delights have you prepared for these hungry men?"

"Fillet au Spam, corned beef hash a la Bordelaise, and hash browns mitt schlag."

"Schlag? Whipped cream?" asked Trance.

"Actually, powdered eggs. But they look like whipped cream to me."

"A veritable feast," said Stick.

"Not the Four Seasons. But given what I had to work with—"

"Did I ever tell you that you're amazing?" asked Trance.

"Not in public." She smiled.

Stick took a bite of food and waved toward Gretel. "I must compliment you on this one, JT. Not only does she have a great ass, but she can cook."

Gretel snapped at Stick playfully with a dishtowel. "I do windows, too."

"And she could probably drink you under the table, Trance." Stick winked at Gretel.

When they were done with breakfast, Stick said, "The next order of business is securing the money to pay for all this. Once you've made final arrangements, we can wire funds to most of the arms dealers. A few take only cash or gems. My men expect cash. How, may I ask, do we get to Zurich?"

"There's a Volvo in the shed," replied Trance. "Our caretaker keeps it in running condition. The registration's current; and I've got a Swiss driver's license."

"So you just walk into the Klug Bank and ask for thirty million?"

Trance laughed. "Not quite, my friend."

Zurich would be crawling with people searching for Trance. His personal banker, Koenig, would be followed night and day. They would have someone on the inside monitoring his accounts, and any large withdrawals from any one of them. If the Swiss authorities or INTERPOL had become involved, there was no telling what the security might be like.

"So what is it that you plan to do?" asked Stick.

"Well, Stick, let me tell you…"

Koenig left his office at precisely 5:45 PM. He hailed a cab, which he took to the Zurich airport. From the cab he walked in a stiff and deliberate manner, directly into the main terminal, then into one of the travelers' lounges. He took a seat at a dark, corner table. Koenig glanced repeatedly at his watch, as if impatiently waiting for someone to arrive. He looked around nervously, wondering which of the innocent looking men and women surrounding him were paid to keep him under surveillance.

Koenig finished two glasses of white wine. At exactly 7:45, he got up with his briefcase and walked into the men's bathroom. He took a seat in the third stall, stayed there for exactly five minutes, then left.

Anyone watching Koenig could not help but notice his nervous, suspicious behavior; he was playing his part well. Koenig had already received his instructions and authorizations from his taxi driver, Stick Granger. The nervous attention to his watch, the precise timing was all cover for an event that had already taken place.

Ordinarily, Koenig would never do such a thing for a client of the bank. In fact, he was acting in strict contradiction to the stringent banker's code in Switzerland. But years ago, when he had been a rookie clerk, Trance had singled him out for favors. He remembered that first day, when Trance introduced him to an oil sheik that promptly deposited one billion dollars at the bank.

Koenig's bonus on that account provided the down payment on his first car, a used Mercedes diesel with two hundred thousand kilometers on its engine. Over the years there had been many such accounts. Trance had asked for nothing in return, until now. The only thing he knew about Trance were his account numbers, and that he was somehow connected to the American government. He had always been protected and sanctioned by the Swiss authorities.

Trance's first request, being picked up at the airport, was not uncommon in a nation that served as the world's banker. But this—what he was doing now was highly unusual. He might have felt uneasier, but he was sure that this was important government business. So, he bent the rules.

As Koenig left the restroom, he heard a voice say, "Excuse me, Herr Koenig. We would like to speak with you." An airport security guard came up from behind him and pinched him at the elbow.

"Of course," said Koenig nervously. *How should I handle this? Will they search me and find the handwritten list of account numbers hidden in my shoe?* These handwritten numbers served as the account holder's signature; there was no name, no identity at all.

The security guard ushered him into a private office. It was cramped but clean. Seated behind a small metal desk was a man with thick shoulders and a pug nose the texture of an avocado. He was cleaning his fingernails with a pocketknife. Another birdlike man stood behind him, his head twitching sporadically in a nervous tick. They looked like characters from an American silent movie.

"Herr Koenig," said the man with the knife. "Please be seated." The man pointed his knife at an old chair with a ripped, clear plastic seat cover.

"I am told that you are an important banker in this city," he continued.

"I—" Koenig started to protest.

The man held up his knife and continued, "Herr Koenig, if you had no other client than Jack Trance, you would be an important man in the banking world."

"Who are you?" asked Koenig, still struggling to get his wits about him. "And who is Jack Trance?"

"I represent private clients that are interested in information." The large man continued to clean his fingernails. He didn't look into Koenig's eyes.

"I am afraid that I can be of little help to you," replied Koenig. *Who are these men? Are they Swiss banking regulators trying to catch me giving private bank information to people who shouldn't have it?*

The thick-shouldered man looked up at Koenig. His wide, black eyes narrowed and he smiled coolly. Koenig only sensed the movement as the man's wrist flicked his knife toward Koenig's head. Before Koenig could react, the blade stuck into the wall, only inches from his right eye. He looked at the airport security guard, who pretended not to notice.

"I believe you have information we need."

The man pulled another knife from his pocket and began to clean his nails once more. He didn't look in Koenig's direction. He said nothing more; he just let the air grow heavy with silence. Koenig's eyes moved to the first knife, which still quivered in the wall. Then he looked back at the passive face of the big man seated across from him, who was intently watching his own hands. Koenig envisioned the blade in the man's hand slicing through the air and into his forehead as he tried to run. He couldn't run. What would happen if he screamed for help? Was the airport security guard standing at his side a fake? Or would he be joined by others who would support this brutality? He didn't think so. No, Koenig couldn't call for help. If he did, and there was publicity over the matter, he would lose his job, his life.

"What is the information you need?"

"Tell us all you know about Trance."

"Trance? I know no Trance. I only know account numbers."

The man's eyes narrowed.

"I swear!" screamed Koenig. "I know of no one named Trance! In my department we don't ask names."

"You met him at the airport a month ago. You helped him enter your country after he had killed ten men."

"I knew nothing of that. I only know that I was asked by an important client of the bank to meet him at the airport and speed him through customs. I only know his account numbers."

"Which are?"

"Oh, God—"

"Come, come...Herr Koenig...Surely you can tell us the numbers of his accounts? Or perhaps your banking authorities would be interested in learning about the little financial tokens you have been accepting from clients over the years."

"I have never taken anything from a client!"

"Do we really need proof, Herr Koenig?"

The accusation alone could ruin his career. During the next thirty minutes Koenig told the man just enough about Trance's accounts to stay alive. He told him where they were to meet next, and when. He told the man about three of Trance's minor accounts and told him about the money Trance had asked to be delivered. Koenig didn't reveal the existence of accounts that still held over one hundred million dollars.

The telephone rang in the Baron's study

"Trance has escaped again, my Lord."

The Baron held the phone away from his ear and closed his eyes. "I see," he said softly. "And your excuse this time?"

"He escaped through a tunnel. We had no idea—"

"You are paid to have ideas."

"And...we lost two helicopters," said the voice.

"And my son, Gustav?"

"Dead, my Lord."

The Baron inhaled deeply and arched his face toward the ceiling, staring sadly at a broad wooden beam. So many of them dead. How many of his own would it take? "Are you prepared to die, my friend?" he said.

"At any moment you choose." The reply from his commander was clear and without hesitation.

"You may yet live, then. Find him. I will string him from this ceiling myself."

"Look," said the President. "I know this is not your fault. But, I don't have the time or the patience to put up with Miller acting like a spoiled diva. You tell Miller that he will return my call or I'll have him sent to the most dusty, flea-ridden, water-starved, outpost in the Sahara." The President slammed the phone into its receiver. "The bastard has turned," he said. "Of all the people, I never thought it would be Miller...Jesus...With what he's got, we're sitting ducks for the Russians, the Chinese. Spies...Spies...The whole frigging world is filled with spies." He reached again for the phone. "Get me Hopewell in Vienna," he barked to his Chief of Staff.

"Actually, Sir...Senator Hopewell has come here to Salzburg. I will bring him to you shortly."

An hour later Senator Hopewell was led into the room.

"Mr. President."

"We've got big problems, Winner."

"I'm doing all I can, Mr. President. I'm getting close—"

"You better double your efforts. Rumors are buzzing that the Russians are about to launch a nuclear first strike. My Defense Secretary tells me that their subs have scattered. Planes armed with warheads have scrambled. I can get no solid data from anyone, and they won't answer the goddamn hotline. China has mobilized a million troops. Their silos are primed. I just got word that someone has been hacking into our computers, for several weeks now. Someone has files of every damn strength and weakness we've got. Do I call the Kremlin and tell them I know what they're doing? Do I call Beijing and tell them to knock it off? They think it's us! And then Miller disappears. Christ! Can you imagine? Miller? With what he knows?"

"We've declared him beyond salvage, Mr. President. He'll be shot on sight. I've taken control of the intelligence forces here. The Secretary of State is on his way to Moscow."

"What the hell is Miller up to?"

"From what we can piece together, he plans to meet with Trance."

"Oh, Jesus." The President put his hand to his head and maneuvered himself into a green reclining chair.

Hopewell walked to the edge of the room, to a dark wooden high boy, and poured a glass of bourbon into a paper cup from a crystal pitcher. He sighed and shook his head slowly. "I know. I know. Our top field agent goes on a murder spree and vanishes. Now the evidence says that his handler, Miller, was working with him. Some have suspected Trance for months, but I still don't believe it. I've known him since he was a boy. He's my sister's kid, and he's like a son to me. Hell, I've made him heir to my estate. I can't believe he'd do something like this. There must be some explanation."

"So, what do we do?"

"I've got our men searching for both of them. Miller's a dead man. Trance, we need alive. I want to meet with him before anything's done. I...we owe him that much."

"Not if he's committing treason, we don't."

"What's happening is far bigger than any two men, Mr. President."

"You bet your ass it is. I'm flying to Geneva within the hour to summit with the Europeans. Then I'm returning to the States for a briefing at the Pentagon. I'll have more information for you then..." said the President with a bone weary voice. "...provided we're all still alive."

"Are you going to put our forces on DEFCON 1?"

"I'm trying to avoid it. That alone might provoke the Russians or the Chinese." The President shrugged his shoulders, and he seemed to shrink like plant leaves withering in a drought. "But it's probable, Senator. Too much is happening to sit back with our eyes closed, to wait for our adversaries to blow us to pieces."

"I'll call if I hear something, Sir."

The President rose from the chair, stretched his legs and arched his back. "I'm getting too old for this. I'll be glad to hand this job over to you, Winner. I just hope we have a country left when I do."

Hopewell took a long, measured sip of his drink. "There's got to be some logical explanation for this. What purpose would a first strike by the Russians or Chinese serve, but to kill a hundred million people?"

"We're more vulnerable than you know, Winner. If they strike first we could lose a hundred million. Yet we might only kill ten or twenty million in retaliation. Hell, I might not even retaliate at all. How could I, knowing that millions would die? They could have their entire nations intact, and America, it would be uninhabitable. The world could belong to the Russians, the Chinese or both. Unless we strike first—"

"Don't let it happen, Mr. President. We don't need Armageddon."

"Then pray for us, Senator, because I just might have to start it."

CHAPTER 23

▼

Trance blinked until the contact lens felt comfortable in his left eye. Then he inserted another into his right. After blinking several more times he looked into the hotel mirror, pleased with what he saw. His eyes were no longer brown, but a deep shade of green. His eyebrows were noticeably lightened, as was his hair, which now fell across his forehead in thin wisps. Trance parted his hair to check the color of the roots.

"Perfect," he said.

Trance reached to a silver metal case sitting beside him on the bathroom sink. He chose a blond mustache, one of three that were set side-by-side in a plastic folder. He applied a thin film of adhesive to the mustache and to his upper lip, then pressed the base of the mustache against it. In less than a minute the mustache became part of his face. He pulled at it firmly, but it wouldn't budge.

Trance stood back to view his handiwork. The hairs on his lip matched perfectly with the rest of his face. He took a pair of tweezers and gave his eyebrows a more rounded, manicured look. These subtle changes made all the difference. Now, with a little makeup, cheek inserts and a change of posture, he was an entirely different man.

"Well, what do you think?" he said to Gretel as he walked back into the hotel bedroom.

Gretel regarded him, then said, "I liked the old you better."

"It's good, isn't it?"

"Very good. Even I wouldn't recognize you." She smiled. "Perhaps if you were naked I might." Gretel put her arms around Trance's neck. "Jack, I want to go with you."

"No."

"But—"

"No!" Then Trance continued softly, "You will be safer here."

"They wouldn't recognize me—"

"I can't take that risk. They know who you are by now. For all we know, each one of them has your picture tattooed to his arm. I need you here."

Trance held her face in his hands. "Listen, kid, you're my second chance. I want nothing more than to live, and for you to live. So, do what I say and keep your butt here. Please."

"You come back to me, Jack Trance. Or I'll ring your neck." Gretel turned away. "Until you came into my life, it was all so simple. But lonely, oh, so lonely."

"It will be simple again, Cinderella."

"Jack, there are things about me you do not know—" Gretel stopped speaking. She looked at Trance, as if pleading for her life. She bit her lip, lowered her eyes and whispered, "I'm afraid that Cinderella will vanish, and in her place the ugly sister will emerge...Jack...I've got to tell you things—"

Trance drew her into his arms. He didn't want to hear. What was it that kept him from listening to the words she wanted so desperately to say? Or from looking more closely into her background. He knew he was avoiding anything that would take his hope away. Was he afraid? Afraid there was something she could say or do, that would imprison him again? Yes, he would rather cling to the dream than face any reality right now. Besides, things change.

"There, there," he said. "We'll have plenty of time to rid our demons later. There are things about me that you don't know, too. Things of which I'm not proud. But we'll work all that out. I know we will."

"I love you. Whatever happens, Jack...Please remember that I love you."

Trance let her go. "Got to go now. We'll talk about it when I return with the money. We'll talk about it then." He stroked her soft hair with a lover's caress. "I don't care what you were before. I know what you are now, and I love you for it."

The sky was overcast. There was no moon, and there was a ponderous stillness cloying the night air. Stick drove the Volvo slowly through the quiet side streets of Zurich, past the outskirts of the city into the countryside. The land was dotted with lights that shone from the scattering of small houses that fanned out from the road. Except for these lights, the night was deathly black. Trance rode in the passenger seat with his eyes closed, saying nothing.

After a while they approached an ancient cemetery, where Stick stopped, put the car in park and stepped onto the gravel drive. Trance got out and stood beside him.

"Thought this might be a good spot to meet with Koenig," said Stick.

"Tough choice though, isn't it?" replied Trance. "This could be the perfect place. The cover of darkness. No one here to see us meet. But if Koenig's followed, or if the details of our meeting fall into the hands of the wrong people, we could be sitting ducks here."

"So what's your suggestion?" asked Stick.

"Let's make the pickup in the city. We send Koenig running around town with no idea where the drop will be made. We use him to flush out unfriendly elements, we neutralize them, then the deal goes down. We bring the money here. We can station our men along the route to protect the currier."

"How much cash will he be carrying?"

"Five million in Euros. The rest in diamonds." said Trance. He laughed. "You know, in the work I did—" They both noticed how Trance described his work in past tense. "Money flowed freely. A dictator whose life I saved, in the name of freedom, of course, might offer me a small token of his appreciation—a hundred thousand here, five million there. At first I refused them. Then I realized that their money would be spent in some profligate manner, rarely getting to the citizens that the leader so publicly might care for. So I began to accept them, the tokens, the bribes, the excess recovered funds. I used them to start the Freedom Account. It was better than dealing drugs to raise covert cash. When the U.S. government fell short on funding, I dipped into the account. When our leaders refused to support a man that truly stood for good, I might help him along with a little contribution. The balance in this account would fluctuate— a hundred million at times, almost nothing at others. Never used it for myself. Right now the account is flush."

"And Koenig controls this account?"

"He is the only man I deal with...and the business I've sent his way? Billions. The name of a trustworthy banker, jotted down on a piece of paper and handed to a dictator who wants to hide money from his country—" Trance stopped. He felt the familiar mixture of guilt and anguish that could incapacitate him for weeks after one of his missions. Then he continued, "Yeah. Koenig runs these accounts, and he knows the influence that I can exert. I made him, Stick. In ten years he's risen straight towards the top, showing an uncanny ability to attract large depositors."

"And can we trust him now?"

"I have helped Koenig, but I've never used him as an asset." Trance shrugged his shoulders. "Can we trust him? He accepted the deposits of despots, never breaking the rules, but bending them nonetheless. Someone can pressure him, so you tell me. Will he break?"

"Do you trust me, JT?"

Trance laughed. "Stick, you're such a stupid shit; if you decided to betray me, you'd tell me first."

"And the lady?" Stick noticed Trance's eyes focus in the distance for the briefest of moments.

Trance smiled. "Love distorts all reason, so we must suspect even those we love," he said quietly. He turned back toward the car. "Let's go. This will do."

Koenig was standing alone in his office, gazing out the window at the busy Zurich streets, when a private messenger delivered a folded white note. When he read the note his throat tightened and he found it nearly impossible to breathe. Trance was withdrawing everything from three of his accounts. Koenig was to provide five million Euros in Euro 500 notes. The rest was to be converted to one and two carat D flawless diamonds. He was to place all of it into a briefcase and walk with it into the evening rush. How much money did his client have in these accounts? It had to be thirty million U.S. dollars. At least. Would that many notes fit into a briefcase? He did the mental math—that was ten thousand notes. They'd fit. But what if he was robbed? What safety was there for an unarmed man walking the streets with that kind of money? And what about the killers, the ones that had threatened his life unless he told them everything he knew about Trance? Was that his true name? Trance could kill him, too. Somehow he had always known this. When they were together, he had always had the feeling that his client could reach right out and snap his neck in two. There was that kind of power in the way he carried himself...and his hands...his hands were like iron. Koenig had never felt hands like that. Still, he had never been afraid. There was something honorable about the man. Even so, some of the men referred by Trance were killers—that he knew. Was Trance a killer, too?

What sort of game were they playing? What if he went to the police? Trance's enemies had promised him instant death, perhaps worse. They would frame him for illegal acts he had never committed. What would his young son think of him then? And his lovely wife who thought he was the best husband a woman could ever have? What then?

The messenger stood waiting for a reply to the note. Koenig stared at him, not knowing what to say. What was the right thing to do? He sat down at his desk and began to compose a note with his Mont Blanc fountain pen. After writing several lines he tore the paper from its pad and ran it through a shredder. He started another, and this one, too, soon rested in pieces. Finally, he followed his instincts and wrote a simple message.

"Your package will be delivered as requested. It has generated much interest here at the bank." There. He had done it. He had fulfilled his obligation to the man they called Trance, the man who had helped him to earn the kind of life that he and his wife had dreamed of living. He had warned the man that had never asked anything of him, except this once, in ten years of business. He turned to the messenger and said, "Take this to him."

Clay Berringer took the message, turned silently and left the office. Koenig picked up his phone and dialed.

"Hello," said a voice on the other end.

"It's time. Today at closing."

"Good. You know what to do."

The phone went dead. Koenig had covered his bases, provided his message to Trance didn't fall into the wrong hands. He began to sweat, even though air conditioning kept the air cool and light. His mind jumped from one thought to another like a water bug. What should he do?

Koenig walked out of his corner office, the one he had worked so hard to achieve, the one he hoped he would be able to keep. He walked slowly down the hallway of the bank's executive offices. Not many men his age had been able to achieve such a position of power in so few years. He was proud of his accomplishments.

Among Koenig's clients a capital shift of a hundred million was commonplace and he didn't need authorization to complete this transaction. As he walked along the hallway, he passed several secretarial stations. At each one he was greeted with a "Good afternoon, Herr Koenig." Yes, he was a man that drew respect at the bank. A rising star that someday, soon, would be the ranking non-family member in the entire organization.

Koenig took the elevator deep into the vaults of the bank. U.S. banks often keep little actual currency in their vaults. Cash is a useless commodity in the U.S. It must always be working. U.S. cash doesn't sit around waiting for someone to claim it, because U.S. depositors don't ask for millions of dollars in currency and perfect diamonds at a moment's notice.

In Switzerland, banking could be different. Many of Koenig's accounts paid no interest at all. Why would a depositor accept such an arrangement? No interest, no trail. That was why he was walking into the vaults himself. His clients craved anonymity, secrecy, stability and service. A depositor could walk into his bank, demand that a few million dollars in cash be placed into a paper bag, and the only response to his request would be, "What color and shape would you like the bag, sir?" There was a great store of cash and gems in Koenig's bank, and some of it was about to leave—all of it untraceable.

Koenig could have forwarded the request to a team of clerks. But, for his important clients, he took it upon himself to do such work. There could be no mistakes.

Koenig passed through the elaborate safety systems and was soon standing within a large vault filled with neat stacks of carefully inventoried cash, in both Euros and U.S. Dollars. The money was banded into what his bank called units, so that large withdrawals could be quickly completed. Koenig began to pluck units of Euros and lay them neatly into thin nylon bags. Then he placed the bags in his Halliburton briefcase. He put exactly five million Euros into the bags. Koenig then went to the section holding gemstones. He checked the computerized daily diamond fixings and assembled the stones—nearly five hundred of them—and put them into bags worth around one million each. He placed these bags into a second briefcase. He could retire with a couple small bags, he thought with a rueful smile.

Koenig took one last look at the money. He thought about the kind of world where assets like this belonged, and he wondered what it would be like to live such a life. A life where he could carry such wealth for himself. He closed the case and negotiated his way through the intense security system. Twenty minutes later, he was sitting alone in his office.

Koenig placed the case under his desk. He could feel heat around his legs. Handling that kind of money always raised his temperature. This time it was different. His job was on the line, possibly his life. Perhaps that was why he enjoyed being a banker, particularly in Zurich—the understated danger, the occasional intrigue. He turned in his chair to look out his window over the city. How many men his age, not even thirty-five, could boast of such a view? But there was fear in the pit of his stomach, a fear that warned he wouldn't live to enjoy his view much longer. What would he do if he survived? Would his reputation be destroyed? Would they send him to prison? Would they even know? He was startled by the phone.

"Herr Koenig?"

"Yes?"

The man gave a series of numbers and said, "You will now walk out the main doors of your bank, turn to the right, begin walking, and wait for further instructions."

"But—" The line went dead. "Oh, God," said Koenig. "This is it." He quickly dialed the phone.

"Yes."

"I am to walk out of the bank at this very moment."

"Very good, Herr Koenig. Now do as we planned."

It was late afternoon when Koenig emerged from the fifteen-foot doors of the Klug bank and began walking along Bahnhofstrasse. The street was filled with people on their way home from work. The sidewalk was bustling with travelers rushing in every direction. As he passed through the doors, he had a strange, sinking feeling, as if he were a gladiator walking into a sweaty coliseum for a fight to the death. Where was his enemy? Who was his enemy?

He peered into the crowd, trying to find a familiar face. There were none he recognized. He wiped sweat from his brow onto his pants. Then he began to walk.

Trance was several blocks away, sitting in a line of traffic, waiting for the light to change. Clay Berringer was a hundred feet behind Koenig, walking slowly but keeping pace. Stick Granger perched upon the roof of an office building high above them with a Fujinon Stabiscope and a sniper's rifle.

Men from Trance's private army waited for his instructions. These were men who had worked for Trance before—all men he had trained, men he could trust.

These men came from all walks of life. One was a construction foreman from Los Angeles. Another sold lighting fixtures in Paris. The third managed his family fortune from a chalet near St. Anton. The fourth was a rock music promoter from New York. Another was a minor public official in Mexico who secretly made a fortune smuggling illegal aliens cross the border into Southern California. Each of these men had their own reasons for helping Trance, but none of them did it for money.

These men were highly trained professionals, spread throughout the crowd, blending into the bustle of the afternoon rush. Their job was to identify anyone following Koenig. Depending on who and how many there were, they were to take them out of play, preferably alive.

Trance's men knew where Koenig would be going. What they didn't know was where and when Trance might surface.

As Koenig approached Paradeplatz, he passed through a thick group of people waiting for the bus. A passerby gently bumped him. Few could have noticed the exchange; it was done in such an innocuous manner. But when Koenig reached the corner, he withdrew a piece of paper from his trousers. He read the note quickly and put the paper back into his pocket. As he waited for the light to change he began to sweat freely. He felt the wetness spread under his arms and collect on his brow. This wasn't going to be easy.

The light changed and he started across the street toward the river. As he trudged ponderously forward a walker pulled beside him and said, "What was the message?" Koenig handed him the note.

Across the street one of Trance's men raised a small communicator to his lips and said, "Bravo, here. Tall man, black hair, brown glasses, gray suit, blue striped shirt, red tie, black shoes…"

"Alpha, here. You on his six, Echo?" said Trance.

"Roger that, Alpha."

"Proceed."

"Omega, here. Short man on the corner. Brown suit, heavy beard, white shirt, brown tie, brown shoes…."

"This is Gamma. I got you covered, Omega. You peel off and I'll follow Sparrow."

Trance drove along in the Volvo listening to the chatter of his men with a receiver, while monitoring all other frequencies with a sophisticated scanner. Anyone following Koenig would have to remain in contact. There was no telling what encryption or frequencies they might use, or to which ones they may change. His receiver scanned the entire frequency range, filtered each conversation through a computer and locked onto the ones most likely to be his pursuers.

For the first few minutes there was no enemy communication. Trance prayed his equipment was good enough to sift through the encryption and chatter and produce results.

Shortly after his team spotted the tall man with the gray suit, the enemy began to buzz.

"They've made you, Johnson. Pull back and we'll cover."

Definitely American, thought Trance. He sent a coded message to warn his men.

"You have been spotted Dimitri," said another voice, this time in Russian.

"Shit," said Trance. Two languages. Were these men together, or was he dealing with multiple adversaries?

In the next thirty minutes Trance heard messages in German, Russian, American English, heavily accented English, and finally, one in French. It was a goddamn convention.

"You are one popular man, Herr Koenig," Trance said quietly. "I wonder if you really have the money." How much risk should he take? Should he risk it all, knowing that any mistake could end in death? Trance nodded. He knew. He must take any and all risks, because without the money he could do nothing, and the Madonna's money would come with obligations he wasn't sure he could meet. He pressed a button that sent one long beep over the airwaves. Proceed with caution.

Koenig continued to walk forward, block after block after block. The complexion of the city changed from the elegant financial district to a combination of lower-rent office buildings, small shops and neighborhood pubs. The street traffic thinned, but there were still many people about. Koenig walked slowly, his eyes darting from side to side. Then suddenly, before he could react, he was thrust into the open door of a large, rowdy beer hall. He was greeted with a punch in the face, while his briefcase was ripped from his hands. He went down in a heap before he could lay eyes on his attacker. As he drifted into unconsciousness he wondered if he had failed.

The attacker ran through the hall and carried the briefcase into the bathroom. Inside, he stopped, tore it open and pulled out the nylon bags filled with cash and gems. He stuffed these bags into one large sack and threw it out the opened window. He threw Koenig's briefcase behind it, then climbed out the window himself. Before his feet hit the ground, another man took the bag and threw it over an eight foot wall separating the back of the tavern from a small bakery. The bag was caught by a large man on a motorcycle, who removed the smaller nylon bags and fitted them quickly into two oversized saddlebags. Exactly fifty-five seconds from the moment Koenig was rendered unconscious, all of the money was safely on its way to Trance.

After Clay Berringer jumped from the beer hall window, he reached down and grabbed Koenig's empty briefcase from the base of the fence and began to run down the narrow alley toward a busy street behind the beer hall.

The surveillance teams following Koenig sprang into frenzied action the second Koenig disappeared into the bar. Men sprinted from every direction. Six men fought for the entrance—yelling and swearing in a mixture of languages. The first man through saw Koenig lying face down on the floor. He stood above him staring, but didn't offer help. Three other men bolted for the back of the club, while one returned out front. One other man remained inside the hall and searched through the hundreds of patrons who were still talking, laughing, and singing merrily—oblivious to anything else.

Clay Berringer covered two hundred yards before he heard men screaming behind him. Gunshots rang out, and he saw two puffs of pavement as the bullets missed his feet. He veered to the right and hailed a taxi as he ran. A cab pulled lazily to the curb beside him. Before the cab came to a stop Clay threw open the door and jumped in. A moment later the cab roared out of sight.

"We've got him, sir," Trance heard over the speaker. "He just jumped into a cab... license number...heading..."

Trance closed his eyes for a moment, turned the wheel of his car into the traffic, and began heading toward the cemetery on the outskirts of town.

Clay Berringer lived just a few minutes more. Cars converged on him from every direction. Men jumped out and sprayed the air with automatic gunfire. Thunder shook the ground. Men began dropping all around the cab. The cab itself shuddered with bullets. In his final seconds of life, Clay Berringer smiled. He knelt in the backseat to pray one last time—just as bullets punctured through the window of the cab. He was content and died with grace, like so many other brave soldiers, for the cause of freedom.

CHAPTER 24

▼

"I'm sorry, Senator. Word just came in that Trance got his money."

"Impossible. We had a dozen men following Koenig. Where's Trance now?"

"We don't know, Senator."

"You don't know? You don't frigging know? Let me tell you something, soldier, your job is to protect your country, and every goddamn moment that Trance is on the loose is a dereliction of your sworn duty. Now you find that son-of-a-bitch, or I'll find some very sick reasons to get you and every one of your men busted out of the goddamn army."

With support from the Austrian government, Senator Hopewell now occupied the top floor of a small but elegant hotel on Franz-Josef Strasse in Salzburg. He had turned his suite into a command center. Banks of phones lined the walls and people were running in and out of the room like ants. A low hum permeated the room from the phones, the radios, transmitters, and jamming devices. Computers whirred and spit out reams of data through rows of printers that worked non-stop.

The Senator paced the room nervously, with a cigarette hanging from his mouth. Hopewell was known to the world as a non-smoker, and he stayed away from cigarettes, except in times of great stress. During these times he would chain them together at the rate of four packs a day. He used the tip of his cigarette to light one more, then took a long, deep drag.

A young lieutenant approached Hopewell carrying a sheaf of papers. "What is so important about this Trance, Senator?"

Hopewell took one step backward and stared, red-faced, at the innocent questioner. This patriot had been called into duty with no hint of the mission's purpose—just like every other soldier in the room. Hopewell felt anger spread through him, but let it dissipate before he answered.

"Has it occurred to you that you were not informed about him for a reason?" Hopewell moved his cigarette to one side of his mouth and pressed his nose against the soldier's face, dropping ash on his lapel. "Quite frankly, Lieutenant, it's none of your goddamn business." *Goddamn incompetents. The world is filled with frigging morons.*

"I'm sorry, Senator. Just thought that I'd ask."

"You ask your superiors why they haven't found Trance. That's the question you should ask."

"Yes, sir." The lieutenant saluted, snapped his heels, turned quickly and walked to the far end of the room. "Asshole," he muttered under his breath. To think that this man would soon be his Commander and Chief…

"How much longer before Trance is here, Major?" asked the Baron. He was wringing his hands in a fruitless effort to hide his excitement. Soon he would have his formula. Then he could begin to live again, and take control of the world that should have been his long ago.

"I...We've lost him...But..."

The Baron stood, stone-faced, looking malevolently into the eyes of the major. "Someone will have to die over this," said the Baron. "There has been an appalling breakdown in discipline. The only thing that will restore discipline is fear. Wouldn't you agree?"

"Yes, Baron."

"It is your choice who you kill to set the example. Be careful not to get any blood on my rugs." With that, the Baron dismissed the major with a wave of his hand and turned his attention to his computer.

Major Wilson stood his ground. "We may have found the girl, Koppleman."

"Bring her!" screamed the Baron. The loudness startled the major. It was an animalistic cry that sent his skin crawling. He could feel the hair rise on the nape of his neck and he knew he better produce the girl or *he* would be the one to die.

"We've lost Trance again," said the radio operator at the Israeli command center.

"No problem," said the Israeli general, Swartz. "Viper is still in place." Swartz sat back in his chair. He hadn't slept in two days, knowing the fate of his nation was at stake. He would remain awake for a week if he had to. "Trance should have joined us when he could," he mumbled to himself. "Now he will die...He was a good man...such a waste."

Darkness had settled into the secluded valley. Trance stood alone at the entrance to the old cemetery. It would be an hour before he would see the light of the motorcycle begin to wind through the valley. He would wait here for its rider.

Trance looked to his watch and spoke quietly into his transponder. "Are we clear?" Trance, Stick and one of his men had spent the last hour scouting the area. This part of his operation had to go smoothly or everything would be lost. Once he had cash for his men, they could return to Austria to make their assault of the Baron's castle. If his calculations were correct, he would have just enough to pay for the remaining weapons. He had secured an A-4 Mighty Midget Skyhawk. It was old, left over from the Korean War, but it was agile and could land on their rough, 4000-foot makeshift runway. He was still negotiating the use of a British Harrier, a jet that could land and take off vertically. But the arms dealer was holding out for three million more than Trance would spend. The Skyhawk would be flown by one of his father's cousins, an aging Samurai with youthful reflexes and a willingness to die.

Trance had secured six cannons mounted on railroad wheel cars—enough to air-condition the Baron's castle walls and distract his men.

Waiting in the cemetery, Trance felt like he was in an old Bela Lugosi film. Everything was black and white. The tombstones were pale in the darkness, drab shades of gray from near white to charcoal, and in various stages of decay. Many of them leaned backward, pounded by the elements over the centuries. Trance thought of how odd it was for the Swiss to leave them this way. Must have been the end of the line for these families, he thought. Was he about to become the end of the line in his own family?

Trance edged carefully toward the center of the cemetery. In the middle, on a rounded hillock, stood three stately tombs arranged in a tight triangle. Together they ruled over the surrounding space, as if seated atop a throne for the dead. Just why he had chosen to use this place for the final transfer of the money, Trance wasn't sure. It was just something he felt, deep in his gut.

Trance was surprised to hear his body speaking to him so loudly. How long had it been since he had listened to this inner guidance? Trance thought of his father and smiled. His father had been so sure that one day his son would find inner peace—through the release of ego to the great power of the Universe. Trance had always been sure there was nothing more powerful than the intellect, the conscious. Now he was dealing in matters his intellect found difficult to fathom. In the silence, Trance realized that for the past few days he had been following the fates more than his head. Perhaps he was learning. Or was he losing his mind?

Trance thought fondly of his Grand Master in Japan.

"You must allow yourself to *become* one with your surroundings..." Trance felt warmth stir in his lower belly, his "hara" suddenly came alive. This was the place where all power dwelled. It all came back to him—how he used to sit for hours thinking of nothing, while experiencing everything. He remembered the breathing, the balance and form of the Universe, and the peaceful sense of "knowing" what was right. Slowly, he reached into his blue gym bag and withdrew his father's special coin from its soft leather pouch.

"This coin has magic in it," his father had told him when he was a boy. Now he weighed it in his hand. In a reflexive way he began to toss it, and in the back of his mind kept track of the heads and the tails until he had formed a hexagram of the *I Ching*. Trance had found it fascinating in Japan, how his elder aunt, Yuko, would use it before she made any big decision. In America it had never been more than a game, so foreign to the American way of thinking. In Japan he had been encouraged to memorize the *I*, and he remembered it to this day. As the tossing continued, Trance felt a growing excitement. With each toss the choices narrowed as to what his hexagram would be. With the fourth toss he felt his heart begin to accelerate. What would his message be? And what was his question? There were so many questions.

For the next thirty minutes Trance asked question after question of the *I*. Answer after answer made it clear that he was on the right path. The Baron must be stopped. Treachery was all around him. Death was everywhere, and the deaths wouldn't stop until it was over.

Trance's mind ground around his problems, like a molar on an exceptionally tough piece of steak. Over and over, his options twisted in his brain. There was so much he could do. So many options he could take. He could hand the notebook over to the United States government. But who could he trust? So much power in the hands of so few? He could call Hopewell and let him make the choice. Or, he could destroy the formula and let the world pass him by. He could move to some quiet country villa and spend the rest of his life in quiet comfort with Gretel. Perhaps he could negotiate with the Baron, and reach some kind of compromise. Or, he could attempt to destroy the Baron and his forces entirely. Then what would he do? Would it be over? Must he then destroy the formula? Should he? And would the world ever leave him alone? Would his conscience leave him alone?

Trance pushed the light button on his watch. He set the alarm for twenty-nine minutes. Then he then sat on the ground and closed his eyes. He breathed deeply, allowing himself to drift into pleasant relaxation. He envisioned himself lying on a beach, with the warmth of the sun spreading through his body. Rather than become dull, his senses heightened and he began to feel his surroundings. His body and mind became part of the great Universal Order. The seconds passed in growing harmony. Trance's mind began to drift, and he found himself standing before his father. In the vague recesses of his mind he was aware that this must be some sort of vision. But at that moment his father was very, very real.

"Hello, my son," said his father. "It is good to see you again." They were in bright sunlight, on a beach. Trance recognized the place—Naples, Florida. They were walking to the south, and the afternoon sun was skipping across the ocean to their right. The water was a frosty blue and clear as a swimming pool.

"I was wondering when you would find me here," said his father.

"I'd be lying if I said that I came here looking for you," said Trance.

"Ah..." His father shook his head slowly. "Always the skeptic. Perhaps one day you will come to realize that there is far more to life than what we see."

"Did you call for me, father?" Trance watched as sandpipers skittered up and down the shore.

"Perhaps I did. Or, perhaps you called for me. What does it matter? We are together." They walked on in silence. The older man continued. "You know, there is one thing I regret that I did not do while I was alive." His father's voice was barely audible, and Trance had to lean close to hear him.

"And what is that father?" His father with regrets? So unlike him to express regret.

"I regret that I didn't tell you how much I loved you. I didn't show my pride. I never hugged you. Why do you suppose that was?"

"I...I don't know. I guess that was just the way that it was between us."

"Ah...Wise words, my son. But must things always remain the way that they have always been?"

Trance laughed softly. "What in this world remains the same? Except perhaps for the constancy of change."

"Does that mean that I can hug you now?"

Trance felt a sudden rise of tears come to his eyes. "Yes," he choked. "I suppose it does."

The old man stopped and faced Trance. He stretched his arms wide and then wrapped them around his son. "There are so many things I should have said." The two men stayed embraced for a long time. There had always been an unspoken love between them. There had always been an underlying respect. But there had never been closeness. Trance's father had always remained aloof until now, in death.

"You were a fine father," said Trance. "And I always loved you. Do not apologize for things being the way they were. What was, was...and what is, is."

"Since when have you become so wise?"

"Wise? Perhaps I finally accept the world as it must be."

"And what would you change, my son?"

"I would change what I can, for the better."

"And should you punish yourself for not changing that which you cannot change?"

Trance stared at his father and blinked. He felt his face flush, as if he had just caught a glimpse of something he had been forbidden to see.

"No. Must you ask such a question?"

"Hasn't that been the way you have lived? Punishing yourself for the sins of others?"

Trance chuckled softly, as he realized where his father's mind was heading.

"If someone doesn't take responsibility, who will?"

"Must someone always take blame?"

Trance stood motionless. Was this the crossroads of his life, where duty and happiness branched in separate directions? Or was it where they merged? "I guess not," said Trance softly. "But someone must take responsibility."

"What is yours? Surely you're not responsible for all mankind?" Trance's father waited patiently for his son's reply. He could almost hear the thoughts rumbling inside Trance's head.

When he finally spoke, Trance said, "I must have been searching for you. Because you have provided me with the answers I need."

"Perhaps," said his father. "Perhaps. But there is still too much that you do not know…" The image of his father slowly faded away.

Trance was pulled out of his meditation by the beeping of his watch. For the first time in months he felt refreshed, his mind clear about what he must do.

Gretel was lying in the bed of her hotel room, engrossed in one of Voltaire's essay's on religion, when the door slowly swung open. She heard no sound; there was no warning. As she lifted her head from the book, she found herself staring into the barrel of a Berretta 9mm pistol, and four men surrounding her.

"You are coming with us," said the man with the gun.

"But—" Gretel began to protest, but one of the men punched her in the cheek. Her words choked, and she felt her mind waiver under the force of the blow. Blood dripped from the corner of her mouth and she spit it at the man.

"Don't resist us." The man's voice had an odd German dialect.

"I will tell you nothing."

"You do not need to, Miss Rebecca Gretel Koppleman."

"But—"

"We know all about you. Now shut up! We must go. Come quietly and you may yet live. Resist, and I will hit you again."

"So nice of you to meet with me, Comrade," said the Chosen One.

"Much has happened, my brother," replied the Russian.

"But all goes well?"

"Everything is in order in my country. Another day or two and we can begin.

The old fools are ready to begin launching missiles at the slightest provocation. How goes your part?"

"According to plan. Everyone is properly programmed. Our leaders are paranoid as hell. The first detonation will send them scampering like lemmings. Yes, all is on schedule, except for Trance."

"Your man is illusive. Very resourceful. He would make a fine Russian oligarch." Both men chuckled.

"Of course," said the Chosen One. "It's in his blood."

"He still doesn't know?"

"She never told him. I don't think his father ever knew, until the end, perhaps."

"Such a shame. Still, Trance must die," said the Russian. "And the Jewish girl?"

"We have her, and the banker, Lauren Haverford, too."

"He will sacrifice it all for them?"

The Chosen one laughed and replied, "We have worked upon his mind for years, Comrade—always keeping him off balance, questioning himself and his country. Until Koppleman appeared, Haverford was his best link to normalcy, his only tether to a world that no man should be forced to endure. Haverford means more to him than he lets on, but he is a fool. The Jewish girl is another matter. She has been working for the Israeli government since we assassinated her father. She is intensely committed to her nation. We don't believe Trance is aware of her loyalties. Nor do we expect that he is working with her. We believe he is in love with her."

"How convenient."

"Yes. An unexpected stroke of fortune."

"Now only Trance can stop us?" asked the Russian.

"No one can stop us, my brother. Now it appears that the great Senator Hopewell may be about to locate our renegade soldier. Once he does, we are home free."

The Russian smiled. "There are rumors that Trance has assembled an army."

The Chosen One dismissed this with a wave of his hand. "What's a ragtag group of outcast mercenaries against a force that can rule the world?"

"Just a fart in the wind."

"Not even that. Good day, Comrade. I will see you at the Schloss." The two men parted.

When Trance emerged from his meditation, he was trembling to his fingertips. "I will not fail you, father," he said resolutely. He looked out over the valley and saw the solitary light of a motorcycle winding and bouncing its way along the country road. There were no other lights behind it. Trance gave two short flashes from a small, but powerful, light fastened to his belt. There was a red lens on the flashlight and only someone watching the very spot where he stood would have noticed the signal. Eight pairs of eyes actually witnessed the sign.

Trance waited from his vantage point. He could see the entire cemetery, and a long distance down each of the two roads that forked at the entrance. He watched as the motorcycle's light was extinguished a few hundred yards before it came to a stop. He followed the solitary rider as he got off the bike and began to walk through the weatherworn headstones. The man walked without haste, a leisurely evening stroll through a graveyard. A large pack was slung across the man's back; one Trance prayed was filled with thirty million Euros.

Michael Shaw was still fifty yards away, but Trance could see the gleam of his smiling teeth in the pale moonlight. Success.

Then Trance heard a soft spit from below him and to the right of Shaw. He watched in horror as Shaw stopped in mid-step, staggered, and fell face down to the ground.

"Don't move, Trance," came a loud and powerful voice in heavily accented English. Trance spun into the shadowed safety of the three crypts.

"Russian," said Trance to himself. How many were there?

"You are surrounded. Give yourself up and you may live."

"What do you want with me?" replied Trance in fluent Moscow Russian.

The unseen man was startled by Trance's reply, and took a moment to answer. "It is of no concern to you," he replied in Russian.

It was a small victory for Trance, but one nonetheless. The answer confirmed his suspicions about the nationality. He had taken control by switching languages. Now if the man would continue to talk. *Keep talking,* thought Trance. *Soon my men will have a lock on you and you will be just a memory.* As the Russian spoke, Trance crawled noiselessly toward the opposite side of the mound.

"Why we want you doesn't matter."

They don't know, thought Trance. *They are following blind orders.* Another small point in his favor. Just a tad less conviction could mean the difference between life and death.

"Your orders are incorrect, my friend. I work for the same employer as you do. We are allies, not enemies. So why do you approach me as such?" Confuse your enemy...distract him if you can. He reached into his bag for a small radio transmitter. The earpiece was already in his right ear.

"But we...ah—" The man was attacked in mid sentence by some unseen figure. Trance heard the sounds of the man's fight, then watched as the struggle drew both men out of the shadows. Peering through a set of boulders Trance saw the tall Russian clinging against his enemy as they stumbled toward the dead body of Michael Shaw. Then both men were cut down by a loud burst of machine gun fire exploding from Trance's left.

"Aw, shit," said Trance. Two of his men were down. There was only one other left on his team. How many enemy men were there? Were reinforcements on the way? He pondered whether it was better to flee or to fight.

"Who's down?" he said into the transmitter, as he strapped it over his head.

"Delta down," said a voice.

"I'm going for the assets, Beta. Can you cover?"

"Go, Alpha." Trance jumped from the safety of his perch and began to roll down the hill, carrying his blue gym bag in his outstretched hands. There was fifty yards of open space between the tombs and the nearest gravestones. If he could get to them safely he could use them to shield himself from fire, hopefully long enough to reach the backpack—which still lay in plain sight on the ground.

Machine gun fire split the night as Trance began his roll and bullets whistled only inches above him. More shots rang out from at least three other automatic weapons and the air roared like thunder.

Trance heard two quick reports from Beta's gun, recognizing the distinctive sound of an M-16. Then the shooting stopped. Trance cursed himself for not insisting that Beta bring a more accurate weapon, like he had by holstering a Heckler and Koch P2000 beside his Colt 32. He took note of Beta's position and guessed which way his partner would run. Then he sprang forward toward the gravestones on his hands and knees, rolling, then running where he could. He was barely a shadow in the dark and none of his attackers could follow him enough to fire.

In seconds Trance covered the distance to the two dead men lying on the ground. The backpack lay between them and Trance threw himself beside it. He nearly gagged at the odor of blood mixed with the pungent smell of bowels freshly released. Trance pressed his cheek against the wet grass and the metallic taste of blood ran across his tongue. Bullets thudded into the two bodies and both corpses twitched as the slugs peppered their remains. Trance heard the popping of Beta's rifle and the shooting stopped for a brief moment. Trance leapt from safety and rolled into a small depression of grass between two large headstones a few yards away. He was now half way to the entrance, and half way to his attackers.

Trance reached into his bag He withdrew his wide leather belt and wrapped it around his waist. He carefully placed two throwing knives into the folds of the belt. He wedged the Heckler and Koch into the small of his back. Trance then removed a small metal vial of liquid and dipped the spikes of several shuriken throwing stars into the same deadly nerve toxin he had used on the plane. He worked quickly, but cautiously—for he knew that an inadvertent cut would kill him in seconds. When done, he put the throwing stars carefully into the belt.

Trance saw muzzle flashes from behind two headstones near the cemetery entrance. He saw the edges of two heads peek around the stones, staying just out of the line of fire. A flawless shot might graze their faces but a kill shot was impossible. With a shuriken though, he could change the angle of attack.

Trance could feel Stick making his way to his left. He was almost behind him now. He suspected that there were two more Russians in that direction, but he couldn't risk calling Stick to find out.

Trance was pinned but sheltered from fire. Stick would cover his back. He knew this instinctively. The two had worked together for years, and they were like a great football quarterback and his favorite receiver. Together they would kill them all, or die trying. That left two for each of them.

Trance inched his way around one of the headstones and took a quick look toward the men waiting to gun him down. They were ten yards apart and only thirty yards away, close enough for him to hear them breathing in the still night.

Trance let his mind float into higher consciousness. He became a part of his surroundings and felt himself grow in harmony with the great order of the universe. What Trance must do could not be accomplished alone. It could only be done with the help of the Creator.

When a master Zen archer shoots one arrow after another into the center of a target he does not aim each arrow. He learns to *allow* each arrow to find its mark, the ego subjugated to the knowledge that, on our own, we can never reach perfection. Only with the help of the Creator can this be done.

Just as the master archer "allows" arrows to find their mark every time, Trance had to allow his shuriken blades to curve around the headstones that shielded the Russians from sight. Throwing stars can be made to curve in flight. Judging the curve perfectly, so that a throwing star can hit a mark that is out of sight, can only be done with the greatest of powers. The Creator's powers. Trance gave a wan smile. His father would be proud.

Trance grasped one of the deadly discs between his thumb and forefinger. He held it before his face and remembered the tedious hours of practice, entire days when he would throw the stars against a flat wooden target until his hands would bleed. These blades had rewarded his efforts and saved his life. Perhaps they could do it again.

Trance blocked the sound of crickets and the incessant *creee* of tree frogs in the night, until he floated into his surroundings. He closed his eyes and slowed his breathing until there was nothing but blankness in his mind. He allowed the star to reach behind his ear, his mind detached from his body, watching the movement of his left hand as if from above. His eyes stayed closed as his arm made a swift motion forward. He could see the blade whistle through the air, dart to the right and strike its target squarely between the eyes. With another swift motion he drew the other disc from its pouch on his belt and flung it forward with his right hand, without opening his eyes to view his foe. His mind saw it sail in an arc to the right, then quickly dart to the left and strike the Russian in the base of his ear. He saw the man's eyes grow wide with shock, and felt a tinge of sadness, as his own stomach felt the man's pain.

Trance heard four quick gunshots behind him and smiled grimly.

"Alpha clear," he said quietly into his wrist.

"Beta clear. Area secure."

"Get your ass down here, old friend."

"Yes, boss."

CHAPTER 25

▼

The Volvo turned down a decaying alleyway that led to the small, nonde-script hotel where Gretel would be waiting. Such places were common through-out Europe—places that had once been gleaming and modern, and near the heart of the city years ago. But as cities evolved, hotels like these remained frozen in time. The carpets were threadbare, the walls lined with paper that was peeling down to a dingy layer of smoke-stained white underneath, like a bride left at the alter, growing old. There were no individual bathrooms, only holes in the floor at the end of each hall, to be shared by all boarders. Trance had stayed in dozens of these over the years. They were all alike, as if cut from the same dented cake mold, the only differences the stages of decay and the amount of dust covering their hallways. This one, however, was clean.

As Trance began to pull the car into the hotel parking lot the spit cloyed in his throat. His mouth went dry. His stomach tightened and quick stabs of pain shuddered through his chest. He reversed his direction and jabbed his foot onto the accelerator.

"What's up, JT?" asked Stick.

"Don't know yet," he replied. "It's just a feeling. We better park a bit farther away." Trance drove the car several blocks, into a dark alley between two three story buildings of weathered brick. He got out of the car and drew his pistol. Then he reached into his bag for a silencer.

"Is that your old Colt?" asked Stick. He knew that Trance had an almost reli-gious attachment to the pistol.

"Yeah," said Trance as he screwed the smooth black cylinder onto the barrel.

"Where's your HC? Shit man, why don't you use a real gun?"

Trance laughed, "Like you and your M-16?"

Stick smiled. "Touché. But it worked pretty damned well at the cemetery, didn't it?"

Trance held the gun barrel against his cheek. "Uh, huh. Bullets from this gun have eyes."

Stick knew enough not to question Trance. "You flew commercial into Zurich, didn't you? How'd you get all that gear by security?"

Trance smiled. "Compliments of the Pentagon." He wondered if his friend, Jesse Tompkin, had lost his job, or his life. He made a mental note to reward him for his efforts.

The men split and circled the hotel from opposite sides. Trance still wore his dark, charcoal gray cotton clothes. A gray cap covered his dyed blond hair. He had removed the camouflage paint from his face, but was still able to pass almost unseen through the dimly lit streets. The closer he came to the hotel, the stronger the ache grew in his stomach. As the distance closed to within half a block it was almost impossible for him to swallow.

"There's someone here, Beta," he said into his headset.

"Roger." Stick sensed the anxiety in Trance's voice, and his heart reached out for him. He knew the pain Trance had endured over the loss of Janice, and he hoped he wouldn't have to see him through it again.

"Let's go get her," said Stick. *She's gone*, he said to himself. *They've taken her...I know it. We both know it.*

Trance and Stick met at the entrance to the hotel. There where four broad steps leading up to a pair of creaky brown doors. They climbed the steps slowly, looking around as they moved.

Trance went through the possibilities. Gretel was dead. She had been kidnapped. Maybe they were holding her in the room. Perhaps there had been no one here at all. Perhaps she was reading a DeMille or Cussler novel, calmly waiting. Was she out for a walk? Would a sniper's bullet cut him down as he walked up the steps—spray his face with bullets as he peered into the foyer? Maybe there would be an explosion. Or they could wait until he had climbed the stairs, took his first tentative steps to enter the room... The possibilities were endless, few of them appealing.

Trance's mind suffused with his surroundings. It became part of everything around him. The space between his ears became an echo chamber, listening for the sounds he knew would tell him what to do.

"I'll lead," said Trance. Stick motioned him forward with his Walther PPK.

Trance listened to the mental echoes as his hand gripped the doorknob. He pressed the door forward and into the small lobby. He looked at the clerk behind the desk. He was a short man in his mid-forties. The clerk wore a pair of crescent-shaped reading glasses with unusually thick lenses. As he glanced nonchalantly at the door, he looked like a fish with its head half outside its tank, with the glass distorting the look of the bottom part of his eyes.

"Guten tag, gentlemen," he said with a bored drawl. He returned to whatever he was doing when they entered. Had he seen their guns? Had he seen men taking Gretel? He was either a very good actor, terribly blind, or a man who went out of his way to mind his own business. Clerks in this type of hotel were often all three.

Trance avoided the elevator and slid to the back of the hotel lobby, to a set of narrow stairs that crisscrossed seven stories to the top of the building. He pressed his back against the edge of the stairway and leaned his head forward to look above. He breathed deeply and allowed the energy of the stairway to flow within him. He could feel no life in the space, so he went in. He walked up the steps using just his toes, until he reached the seventh floor landing.

When he entered the hall Trance would need to pass six rooms until he reached his own. Any one of them could be hiding enemies, or Gretel. He pressed his face against the hallway door and felt for the presence of anyone on the other side. It would be so easy to capture Trance in the hallway. With a few men on top and a few men below, they could trap him inside the hotel. He could feel danger through the door, but it was diffuse. He wavered, not sure what to do.

"Someone has been here," he whispered to Stick.

"They gone?"

"Not sure."

"Let me lead."

Trance shook his head. He took a tiny can of silicone spray from his bag and sprayed the hinges of the door. Then he withdrew a square mirror the size of a thin pack of matches. He unfolded a small metal handle that was attached to the mirror. He swung the door open and thrust the mirror into the hallway. There was no one. Trance stepped through the doorway and walked quickly down the hall, with just the balls of his feet hitting the floor. When he came to his room he heard no sound, except for the building's own tired groans.

There was turmoil inside the room, Trance could feel it. He motioned Stick to the other side of the door. The men stood facing each other. Stick watched the tenseness in Trance's cheeks drain them of color. He watched his friend take several deep breaths and then begin to feel along the door with his hands and his face, stopping for seconds at a time. He was listening for sounds, feeling and looking for signs of a trap.

Stick thought of how Trance had taught him that all matter has density, that each thing with mass has gravity, and a being of its own.

"Every object puts out a force that co-exists with all others. Although one cannot easily measure the gravity emitted by a plastic explosive or a shotgun rigged to shoot an opened door, one can, with the right instruments, with the right senses, determine that it exists. Scientists use machines. We can use our minds." Trance had told him how mere thoughts have a charge, and an aura that can be felt or measured. "Thoughts exist in a dimension that defies measurement by man-made instruments. But they can be *felt*, sensed. Man can sense fear, hatred, and lust in others without being given scientific proof. Although there may be no way to measure such things with machines, they can be felt, and measured by what they do to man."

As Trance stood by the door, he felt nothing. He couldn't feel the loving affection, and the ripe confusion that so characterized Gretel. Trance would bet that there was no one on the other side of the door. But Trance wouldn't bet on someone's life. Not today.

Trance sprayed the dry door hinges and the key. He inserted the key slowly, turned it, slipped open the door and jumped into the room. His eyes saw everything at once. Then he stood staring at the floor. His shoulders slumped as he realized that Gretel was gone.

There was a note.

Your precious bitch is with me. Now I have something of value to you, as you have something of value to me. I also have others, your banker from Massachusetts and your Austrian friend. Perhaps we can arrange some sort of trade?

The note was signed simply with the letters *vH*.

"The Baron has her," said Trance. "Lauren and Breitfuss too." Trance handed the note to Stick, and continued, "We knew about Breitfuss. But Lauren and Gretel? I am beginning to dislike this man, Stick."

Stick had always wondered why Trance never let down his guard with Lauren. They fit like hand and glove. It was obvious that she loved him. Why, the woman still waited for him after all these years…Trance was a fool to let her get away...and now...Gretel, too.

"Son of a bitch, ain't he?" said Stick.

"What would you do, Stick?"

"I'd waste the sucker. He's earned it."

"And what kind of odds would you place on us? Two men versus a hundred thousand."

"I'm not a bookie, JT. You and I both know the odds called us dead a long time ago. Always beaten the odds, so I don't play 'em."

"You ready to die?" asked Trance.

"Not planning on it. But I'd die for you. You know that. Shit, you know what that megalomaniac will do once he has the formula. Say goodbye to the earth as we know it. It's not the kind of world I'd like to live in anyway. So, I guess I'd rather die. I say waste him."

"And if we waste him, and Gretel still dies? Lauren, too?" asked Trance.

"Not to sound cruel, ol' buddy. But that's more your problem than mine. I told you what I'd do. But I'm not you." Stick watched Trance's eyes cloud, but didn't turn away. He would not embarrass Trance by turning avoiding him.

"Why?" said Trance. "Why did this all have to happen? Why did my goddamn father have to steal this formula? Why did he leave it with me? Why did they kill Janice? Tell me Stick, why?"

Stick placed his hand on Trance's shoulder. "Perhaps it was Divine Will."

"All my life I have taken on the burdens. Hell, I even blamed myself for the coolness in my parent's marriage. Oh, they traveled together, stayed together. But there was no love between them. My mother...she didn't love me. At least I never felt like she did. I blamed myself for that. How could a mother not love her son?"

"It's all right," said Stick.

"No, it's not all right. I failed my parents. I failed my country. I...I couldn't stand the pressure of the job…so I quit."

"They killed your wife."

"*Miller* killed my wife."

"It wasn't Miller. But that's beside the point. You didn't let your country down, Jack. Your country let you down. You stood for higher morals than the politicians and the criminals. You wanted more, and when mankind couldn't live up to the ideals you set for yourself, you let someone else be the hypocrite."

"But, I didn't. Don't you see? I kept going back. Every time they asked me, I went back. I became a whore. Charging money for things others would do for an Intelligence Cross and a patriotic pat on the back. I'm not a patriot, Stick. I'm nothing but a hired gun."

"Really? Are you prepared to sacrifice your life for your country now?"

Trance remained silent.

"Deep inside you know—that what you have done has been good. You have paid a heavy price—physically and emotionally. They wouldn't have paid you, if you hadn't been worth it."

"I didn't do it for the money. Hell, my family oozed money. If I wanted money all I need do was ask. I…I just thought that if they paid for it, it would justify what I did. They wouldn't pay if it weren't right. But…all the blood on my hands...I'm...I just don't know, Stick."

"Blood that has saved the lives of millions. I know you're confused. But it looks to me like your job is simple. Just stop the Baron, before he puts an end to freedom. That will even any score. You'll sacrifice your life for that, won't you?"

Trance nodded. "And the women I love? Are the needs of the precious few more important than the needs of the many?"

Stick lowered his head and his eyes searched the ground. Trance waited for an answer which didn't come, then said, "We sacrifice some to save the rest. It always works that way. Send a few good soldiers off to death so the rest of us can eat roast beef on Saturday and worry about our tee time on Sunday."

"No one said the world was fair, Jackie."

"I wish that for once in my life I could be happy. That's all."

"Happiness is a state of mind, Jack. You should try it sometime."

Trance's eyes darkened and his jaw hung open, like it had been pried fully open with a dentist's tool, hanging motionless as if waiting for the words that wouldn't come.

Stick continued. "Why don't we save the world…rescue the girls…and then be happy?"

Trance's eyes brightened and he smiled. "Yes, you brilliant son-of-a-bitch. That's just what we'll do." He slapped Stick on the shoulder with an unconscious blow that nearly knocked Stick's teeth out. "My father *was* right. Let's get the hell out of here."

Trance walked through the hotel room door with a fresh, light step. He glided down the hall to the stairwell. As his head bent around the door he caught the flash of a gun barrel. He twisted to the left and reached upward with his right arm to grasp his attacker's arm as it swung the gun down toward his head. With a quick flip he turned the wrist back toward his attacker. With the same motion, he spun the gun out of the man's hand and flung it to the floor. He leaned his weight against the wrist until it cracked. He kept hold of the wrist with his right hand and hammered against the elbow. It snapped like a carrot.

Trance moved in a blur. The attacker followed the pain, as Trance drew the man's back against his own chest. Trance pinched a spot on the man's neck and he went limp. Trance then turned the man to use as a shield against any attackers in the stairwell. There were none. He yanked the man back into the hallway, released him and said in German, "Let's have a talk."

The man fell to his knees and rasped, "We have nothing to discuss." The man spit on Trance's shoes. "You make me sick."

Trance ignored the spittle. He placed a gentle hand on the man's shoulder and said, "Who are you? And what have I done to you?"

The man struggled to his feet and Trance gripped him harder. He still had hold of the man's buckled wrist and he pressed against it slowly. His enemy ignored the pain and tried to jam his heel against Trance's instep. Trance sensed the movement and stepped back easily. As the man's foot rose into the air and began to come down, Trance twisted him by his useless arm and spun him back to the ground. The man's body struck the floor. Trance kept hold of his arm with his left hand and lashed out with his right. His fist rammed into the center of the man's chest. The man's eyes fluttered as the air rushed out of his lungs. He was paralyzed for an instant, then gasped spasmodically for breath.

The man's shirt fell open. Trance could see the gold pendant hanging around the man's neck. The Star of David.

What the hell, thought Trance. *I have done nothing against Israel!* How many times had he worked with them to neutralize the terrorist leaders of HAMAS, the PLO and Al Quaeda? How many weeks had he gone under cover in the Bakka Valley, knowing that any breath might be his last?

If the Baron had financed Hitler, the Israelis would want *him* dead. Trance was fighting *against* the Baron, not with him.

"But why do you fight against me?" said Trance. "I am trying to stop him. You must know that. You should be helping me."

The man spat again. "You are one of them," he said. The man's eyes bled hatred. "And we will stop you. We will stop you all."

What is this man saying? Surely they know I am not—

The man continued. "*He* killed your mother and father. But we will kill *you—*"

Trance lashed out with a spear-hand poke to the man's throat. The man's head buckled forward and he made a sickly gagging sound. Then Trance hit the base of his skull with a cross-hand knife blade that crumpled the man into unconsciousness.

"Let's go, JT," said Stick. "He won't wake up for hours." Stick pulled at Trance, who was now standing above the unconscious man, his chest heaving. Trance's eyes were smoky, staring blankly at the prone frame below him. His lips were trembling and his face was beginning to drip with sweat.

"What was he saying?" asked Trance.

"The man's a fanatic," said Stick. "C'mon. We've got to get out of here." Stick pulled Trance by the hand, leading him like a young child. Trance could not get the words out of his head. "You are one of them..." They kept repeating loudly, pounding in his mind. "You are one of them..." What did he mean? Would he exchange the formula for the lives of Gretel and Lauren? Is that what he meant? No, this man had hatred in his eyes. It was something stronger than hatred. It was the look Trance searched for in recruits, a look he had seen so many times in his own reflection. It was the look of unwavering commitment, unquestioned patriotism. Why?

Trance regained his concentration as the men walked down the stairway. He began to respond to the danger, his mind growing clear. But Trance could still hear the soldier's voice.

"He's got to have a backup," said Stick.

Trance focused. "He's outside." He locked eyes with Stick. "He's waiting in the shadows. I can feel him, and he is scared shitless."

They found a young man huddled against a wall, seeing nothing, hearing nothing. He couldn't have been more than nineteen. Poor kid, thought Trance. He stalked behind the boy with a knife in his hand, ready to throw. The boy stared inwardly at his own life. *It must be his first time in the field*, thought Trance. If it was anything like his own, this kid wouldn't hear him if he were playing the trumpet—because every small sound would already be ringing loudly in his head.

Trance grabbed the boy's gun with ease. At the same time he cupped his hand over the boy's mouth.

"Don't make me kill you," he whispered. The boy nodded, his eyes wide with fear.

"Your friend upstairs can't help you now. Are there others?" The boy shook his head.

"What are your orders?"

"We are to capture you, if possible. Kill you, if we need to." The young man stuttered. Trance couldn't believe they would send a boy.

"Why did they send you?"

"I...I...was the best in my class..." The boy could probably shoot the eye out of a flying eagle at four hundred yards and disarm five men without sweating. But until you've been under actual fighting conditions you don't know how you'll react. In the field the clumsiest man may become an efficient machine. The most qualified can crumble. No one can understand, or predict what will happen in the field.

"You a spook?" asked Trance.

The boy nodded.

"First time out, huh?"

The boy nodded again.

"How old are you?"

"Twenty, sir."

"Don't worry. You've just seen the elephant. It was a small glimpse; you'll get over it." He patted the boy's shoulder with a fatherly gesture. He remembered his own first night—the night his SEAL team had been dropped behind the lines into a jungle delta to assist a team of Army Rangers. They had made camp that night and he had been ordered to a lookout post thirty yards on the perimeter. It had seemed like miles. His first night...the reality of the jungle...against a real enemy that could be shooting real bullets into his face. He had sat there shaking, with sweat running into his eyes, sure that every small noise in the jungle was the enemy, fighting adrenaline surges, which only heightened the anxiety. His mind had been so alive with visions of the enemy attacking that he had not heard them approach. He was so busy killing terrorists in his dreams that he didn't hear the dry cracking of footsteps. When an enemy soldier stumbled upon him, he had frozen as the man drew his rifle, pointed it at his head and smiled. All of those years of preparing and he had let himself get killed on his first night out.

But Trance wasn't killed. The man had waited there grinning at him, letting Trance soak in fear. He had been so content upon making Trance shit in his pants that he hadn't heard the American soldier sneak up behind him and calmly slit his throat.

"You can't kill these guys by staring at 'em," his savior had said to him in the darkness. Trance fought off his shame and had the presence of mind to say, "Yeah. Thanks."

"First night out, ain't it?" said the soldier.

"Yeah."

"I remember mine. It won't happen again…By the way…don't believe we've met." He stuck out his hand. "Name's Granger. They call me Stick."

"Trance. Jack Trance."

"Nice to meet you."

"I owe you one."

"Don't mention it. You'll pay me back." And he had, too, many times.

Trance looked at the boy before him. How many recruits had he trained? And how many times had he told them the story of his own first night in the field?

"Same thing happened to me, son," he said. Trance smiled. "I got lucky, too." He paused, then said, "Why do they want me?"

"Because you've turned. You've turned and you have something you will deliver to our enemies."

"Do you know what that is?" asked Trance.

The boy shook his head. "My partner knows more…knew…is he dead?"

"Don't your superiors understand that I'm one of you? We're not enemies, but allies."

The boy shook his head again. "They say you will never go against the Baron."

"What the hell are you talking about?" Trance shook the boy.

"There is talk that you are joining him."

"No!" Trance's scream echoed into the night. "That can't be." He focused on the boy and said, "You're Mossad. You work for Swartz, don't you?" The boy nodded.

"You tell him I want to meet with him. Alone. You got that?" The boy nodded again, a hopeful look spreading across his face. "Tell him I'll be reading the paper."

Over the years, in sensitive situations where other forms of communication had been dangerous or impossible, Trance used the newspapers or encrypted websites for sending and receiving messages. An article inserted, a message sent through the personals, or the help wanted... Swartz could find him that way.

"Get out of here."

The next morning Trance found a message. But it hadn't come from Swartz. When Trance read the London *Times* the first thing he saw was the main headline. *AMERICAN PRESIDENTIAL FRONTRUNNER VISITS EU.* The article was about the American Senator, Winthrop Hopewell, on a goodwill tour of Europe. Trance read within the quotes from an interview with the presidential favorite.

"I am here on business for the United States. I am also hoping to meet with some old friends in Austria." Further on in the paper Trance read in the personals

"T. Need to meet. W."

"My uncle is here to meet with me," said Trance, as he and Stick walked along the ambling river that bisects Salzburg.

"Yeah, I read it too."

"What do you think, Stick?"

"Don't know."

"If there's anyone I trust, it's him. The man knows more about foreign policy than anyone in Washington. Perhaps he can help us take down the Baron without a fight." Trance paused. "But what about the formula?"

"He'll be running the show soon," said Stick. "He doesn't need the money. What better caretaker?"

"What would he do with it, though? Destroy it? No politician could destroy it, Stick. It has *legacy* written all over it. He'd have to do something. So what does he do? Give it to that son of a bitch Miller at the CIA? Call a press conference? Make it free to the world? Could society handle it? Hell, he wouldn't live a day if I gave him the formula. Assassins would be everywhere. They *are* everywhere."

"Maybe he's got information for *you*. Maybe the government knows all about the Baron. Maybe they've got a plan. He is a good friend of the president. Maybe he's got a message."

"Let's hope so."

"You going to meet with him?"

"I'm not sure."

"When will you know?"

"Soon," said Trance as he pulled a penny out of his pocket. "My father told me that we cannot make our most important decisions alone. We must allow the

Creator to make them for us." Trance smiled.

"Your father would be proud," said Stick reflectively. "Me? I think you've got too many loose screws."

Yes, thought Trance. *My father would be proud. But what would my mother think?*

It was early morning. Trance stopped the Volvo in a quiet, middle-class neighborhood in north Salzburg. He got out of the car and entered a small market on the corner. He walked to the butcher in the back of the store and selected the choicest cuts of beef. He grabbed two bottles of the finest wine he could find and took it to the front. As the crusty woman working the register began to ring up his purchase he said, "Excuse me. But may I use your phone?" His German was spoken in flawless Salzburger dialect.

The woman's eyes moved to the expensive food he was buying.

"Don't you have a phone?"

"I left it at home. I need to call my wife. She's pregnant—due any minute."

The woman pursed her lips as she regarded Trance, then motioned towards a door at the back of the store.

"It's in the office."

Trance handed her a pair of hundred Euro notes and said, "Thanks. I hope this pays for any inconvenience."

The woman examined the money carefully, smiled and stuck them into her bra.

Trance dialed a U.S. number, which was routed through several more before it came back to the exclusive hotel where the Senator was staying. It rang twice and was answered briskly by the State Department operator.

"Senator Hopewell, please." Trance looked at his watch, counting the seconds. He couldn't give them time to trace his call.

"The Senator has asked that we take messages on all calls."

"Tell him 'T' called. I will call back in exactly one minute." Trance hung up the phone. In sixty seconds he redialed.

"Senator Hopewell, please. This is T." He was put right through.

"Jack!"

Trance relaxed. "Hi, uncle Win. Good to hear your voice."

"Jack...what the hell have you done?"

"It's a long story, sir."

"I've got time."

"Not over the phone. Tonight, at precisely six-fifteen, I want you to walk alone from your hotel into the Alt Stadt. I'll find you there." Trance hung up the phone.

The Alt Stadt was a near perfect place to meet. The old part of Salzburg, with its narrow cobblestone streets and small shops packed one against the other like playing cards, would make it safer for Trance. The streets were crowded with people on foot. It would be easy to blend in—and much easier to spot anyone wishing to harm him or the Senator. Hopewell also had more than a mile to walk. He would have to cross the river on an open bridge to reach the Alt Stadt. There would be plenty of chance to view him along the way.

Trance paid for his food and walked out of the market.

Trance grinned at the eight men Stick had chosen to lead the thirteen-man squads into the Baron's castle. Trance knew each of these men personally. Three had worked with him in Southeast Asia and the Middle East. Three were early members of T Force, and two were part of Stick's own team of highly skilled mercenaries.

"Good morning, gentlemen," said Trance. "So nice of you to join my little lunch party."

The men laughed. They were in a small, isolated restaurant in the Austrian mountains. Trance had reserved the entire Inn for the day, paying the waiters to take the day off. Stick was serving Jäger Käse, made with a heavy pan filled with a spiced cheese that produced a deliciously savory grease. He placed baskets of freshly baked bread on the table, for dipping into the cheese. He added wiener schnitzel, sauerkraut, and various other dishes, including Trance's favorite—Bosna. Trance placed one of the thin red sausages on a bun, then layered on a mixture of onions, curry powder and pickles. He took a large bite and chewed with relish.

Trance pulled eight packets of crisp, 500 Euro bills out of his blue gym bag and tossed one to each of the men.

"There's fifty thousand Euros in each of these stacks, boys. Nothin' like a little green in the jeans to comfort you in the field. Stick wired another fifty thousand US dollars into each of your accounts this morning. There is a hundred thousand more for each of you, or your loved ones, after we are successful." Trance looked into the eyes of each man, stopping for several seconds to gauge the reaction of each. "You are about to risk your lives, so Stick and I thought you should be paid well. Does anyone have a problem? Suggestions?" The men looked at him in silence.

Trance didn't demand respect from anyone under his command. He believed in earning loyalty through action. He was not afraid to mix it up with his warriors, and never shied from the thick of battle. These men knew that he would do everything he could to ensure their safety, even if it meant risking his own life. They trusted him implicitly, but knew that he was always open to suggestions. Trance's mind was well tuned to strategy, from his days at the Naval Academy, his battle experience, and years with covert CIA operations around the world. His men had difficulty thinking of better strategies, but they always tried.

"This is the most important mission of your lives, and the fate of modern civilization rests in your hands." Trance let his words float in the air. "Never thought that I'd be saying this to such a bunch of jive-assed turkeys in my life." Trance smiled. The men sitting around the rough wooden table broke into relaxed chatter. Smoke filled the small private eating room as three of them drew on fat Cuban cigars. "Here's what we've got to do, guys...."

That evening Hopewell left his hotel at precisely six fifteen. He meandered from Franz Josef Strasse until he came to the Kurgarten gardens, where he turned toward the main street that leads towards the Salzach River bridge. Hopewell did not spot the men trailing him. Even an experienced field agent would have found it difficult, since his followers knew the precise route he must follow. They were spaced innocuously along the way, in the streets, the gutters, on bikes and in cars. During the quarter hour that it took Hopewell to reach the Altstadt, these men isolated and neutralized six other men who were following the Senator.

When he reached the old city, Hopewell walked nervously along the Getreidegasse. Without warning, he was pushed into the open doorway of a small bakery and coffee shop. There were six tables in the room, but it was nearly empty. An elderly blind man with a cane was using one table. Beside him lay a haltered German shepherd, who watched him intently, as if waiting for a bone. Another table was being used by a middle aged Austrian dressed in rough clothes—perhaps those of a plumber or electrician. As the Senator half stumbled through the door, a woman behind the counter said, "May I help you?"

Hopewell began to apologize and say 'no' when the blind man said, "The coffee here is quite good, Senator."

Hopewell turned and stared at the man with the dark sunglasses. The stranger lowered the glasses. Hopewell's eyes narrowed as he looked at Trance.

"Who are you?" he said.

"Look closely, Winner."

Hopewell stared at the white beard and weathered eyes. There was no recognition, except the voice.

"Jack?" There was a quizzical look on Hopewell's face.

"Have a seat, uncle Win." As Trance spoke the woman walked out from behind the counter, locked the door to the shop and drew the shades. She walked into a back room and was followed by the tall plumber, who looked back at Hopewell and grinned.

"Jack...I—"

"Thank you for coming, Senator. So good to see you." Trance's manner was cool, his eyes noncommittal, but his hand was outstretched.

Hopewell hesitated, glanced behind Trance at the closed door, shrugged his shoulders and grasped Trance's hand. He gave his best politician's smile. "It's so good to see you, son." There was worry in his eyes. "Jack. What is going on?"

"It's rather complicated, sir. Perhaps you should tell me what *you* know." Trance's voice was firm. He was going to dictate the terms of this meeting. The Senator looked from Trance back to the door.

"We are alone, Senator. Anyone that might interrupt this meeting has been...shall I say...diverted." Trance's eyes were now even colder, and he and stared unblinkingly at the Senator.

You little snot, thought Hopewell. *How dare you leave me unprotected in this city, with treachery everywhere You know what I mean to America, and the risks I am taking for you.* "Good," said Hopewell.

"Uncle Win, I've got to ask you a question." Trance paused, but Hopewell remained silent. "Why have I been shut out?"

"Shut out? I don't know what you mean, Jack."

"Don't play games with me. I know I've been tagged as a rogue, declared beyond salvage. My ass is grass with the first asshole that catches me off guard."

"Who told you this?"

"What the hell does it matter who told me? What I'm asking is, why?"

Hopewell leaned forward and spoke in a hushed voice. "How could you join von Hoffenburg?"

"Excuse me?"

"Our intel says that von Hoffenburg has accumulated vast stores of wealth. We've also connected the dots, Jack. We know the Baron helped finance Hitler. We know he has put together one of the largest and most effective terrorist networks in Europe." Hopewell shifted uncomfortably in his chair. "Miller told us you went solo and sold out to von Hoffenburg." The Senator's eyes were deadly serious as he stared at Trance. Then they softened, as if to plead.

"He's wrong."

"Miller linked your parent's death to the Baron. Did you help kill your father and my sister, Jack?"

"That son-of-a-bitch, Miller. My father had nothing to do with von Hoffenburg."

"You telling me they were strangers?"

"I don't—"

"Miller has damning evidence, but I'll support you, Jack. Come in with me and I'll give you all the help I can. Don't make this your own personal war, son."

"I can't, Winner. This thing is a hell of a lot more complicated than you can imagine."

Trance told Hopewell how his father had been sent to infiltrate the Baron's castle during the war, how he had taken the formula that could make gold out of any metal, a formula that had kept the Baron alive for a thousand years.

Trance gripped his hair on both sides of his head. He pulled at it in frustration. When he let go, the hairs angled in a confused mess. He said, "That formula can't get into the hands of a private individual, or even the wrong government. Do you know what it would do to the world's financial structure? Do you know what it would do to society?"

Trance tried to smooth his hair. "What else do you know?" he continued. Trance searched Hopewell's face for any sign of deceit. But Hopewell seemed sincere.

"I was told that your father was ordered to get information from von Hoffenburg during the Big War. He was sent by Bulldog Swanson, and he acquired some documents that tied the Baron to some of the world's most powerful companies. That's what I know."

"And what do you know about my mother?"

"What do you mean?"

"My mother was your sister."

"Yes. That's true. What of it?"

"Was my mother a von Hoffenburg?" Trance watched Hopewell closely as he spoke. He saw blood rush into the Senator's cheeks as he fumbled for words.

Hopewell spread his hands apart. "Look…she *was* adopted. But your mother was a Hopewell, just as I am. To insinuate that she was related to that scum is unthinkable. Who the hell told you that?" *Miller?* wondered Hopewell. *Miller is a madman and he has to be stopped.*

"It doesn't matter."

"If you've got the formula, Jack, give it to me and I'll see that it gets into the right hands."

"And whose are the right hands, Winner?"

"I'm not sure, yet. I'll have to meet with the Federal Reserve, the Treasury Department, the President, and consult with Congress. But I'll see that the right thing is done. You can count on it."

"von Hoffenburg is trying to start World War III," said Trance softly.

Hopewell's face turned white. "Impossible."

"Oh?"

"No single man or organization could begin that war. Too many things would have to happen. Hell, I don't even think that two or three direct nuclear hits into the center of New York City would get this president to fire back. No, Jack…don't you worry about von Hoffenburg starting a war. Just worry about the formula. That could set off a war more easily than anything else I could think of."

"So, you won't listen to the proof? Proof of what he plans to do?"

"We'll listen to any proof you have. But you've got to turn over the formula. The longer it is on the outside, the greater the risk. At least let us protect you."

"Will you give it to Miller?"

"Of course I won't give it to Miller. I hate him as much as you do."

"How is he, by the way?" Trance let the words hang. It took several long moments for Hopewell to respond.

"Same bastard he always is."

The moment the words left Hopewell's mouth, Trance stood abruptly and offered his hand.

"Thank you for meeting with me, uncle Win. I've got to go."

Hopewell stared at Trance's outstretched hand and frowned.

"What do you mean, Jack?"

"This meeting is over, Senator."

"But you've got to give up the formula. You've got to keep it safe."

"I'll think about it," said Trance. He stared at Hopewell for several moments more. Then he shook his head and walked out of the cafe.

CHAPTER 26

▼

After Trance was gone, Hopewell rose heavily from his chair and left the café. He walked back along the Getreidegasse, taking little notice of the bustle around him. His eyes stared forward, his mind far away in another time and place. He walked slowly over the Staatsbrücke, the old stone bridge, and back toward modern Salzburg. When he had crossed the bridge, he ambled along Linzer Strasse. He walked up the little hill until he reached Franz-Joseph Strasse, then angled left toward his hotel. His mind churned over Trance's actions. How could he get Trance to turn the formula? He laughed. Only Trance would tell him to take a hike. Who else would have dared? He came to a decision. Trance was committing treason and he would have to die.

Trance walked to St. Peter's, the twelfth century church, which still stood quietly in subdued splendor on the edge of the Altstadt. He thought about von Hoffenburg, and tried to imagine spending a thousand years on the planet. He wondered if von Hoffenburg had been involved with the construction of this gnarled church, or with its restorations five hundred years later. Time, such an odd thing, he thought. The restorations of this church took place two hundred years before the American Revolution.

Above the church rose the Hohensalzburg, the Schloss that dominated the city. Construction of the festung started in the year 1077, and Trance wondered if this too, was a monument to von Hoffenburg. Would the Baron survive another millennium, with Trance and his men long-since buried and forgotten? He was hoping the old church would help him find the resolve to fight such power, and accomplish what had to be done.

Hopewell had lied to him without blinking an eye. Trance's CIA contacts had warned him that Miller had gone to ground and was out to stop him. Hopewell knew this too, so why not warn him?

Trance sat in the church's small graveyard and pondered the problem. What would he have done were he in Hopewell's shoes? Hopewell *could* be acting in Trance's better interest, at least in a way he thought was right. Or, he could be under orders from the president.

He knew Hopewell was frantically searching for Miller. Why? Had Miller turned, gone to the other side? Was the Executive Branch afraid of what Miller might do? Were they finally aware of the true problem at hand?

Then there was his mother. Had Hopewell lied to him about her, too? Was his mother really adopted? He'd never heard that before. Was Hopewell under orders from the government to lie? Or was he acting on his own? Who could he trust?

Trance sat for a long while among the monuments of St. Peter's. He thought about how the von Trapp family had hidden in this very same place—during a war that von Hoffenburg had helped to start. Less than fifteen miles away was Hitler's Berchtesgaden. *Has the Baron really done all that they say he has? What kind of man could do such things?* He'd find out. Soon...

"I need to know how Trance plans to get inside the castle," said Miller. He studied the Black Madonna's coffee colored skin and wondered just how much she had seen in her long life.

"How would I know?" she replied. The Madonna appeared feeble, and she spoke with great effort

"Tell me what you told him," continued Miller.

The Madonna remained silent.

"How can you hesitate?" said Miller. "After all of the information I have funneled to you over the years?"

"I don't trust you, Mr. Miller. That is why. Power does strange things to men. I have watched it change good men, in so many ways...They are never the same, once they taste its nectar."

"But I must know. He'll need my help. I know things about von Hoffenburg that Trance must learn. I could save his life." Miller's eyes begged the old woman.

"Did you kill his wife?" asked the Madonna, softly. The Madonna knew that she was pulling hard on a mental spring inside Miller, one that was already tightly coiled, one that could snap at any moment. Miller turned pale.

"No. I carried out orders to arrange a meeting. That's all I did. Our operatives had turned a female terrorist. She wanted a meeting, that day. She had information of vital importance...and she demanded a woman...she demanded Janice Trance."

The Black Madonna held up her hand. "Enough," she said. "I will tell you what you need to know."

The warm sun hovered just over a cloudless ridge of the Austrian Alps. There was a slight breeze blowing from the south. The air smelled fresh and moist as it carried the rapidly evaporating dew from the southern valleys. Ten men sat drinking coffee around a weathered pine picnic table in the middle of a meadow of tall grass, far away from listening ears.

"How are the procurements coming, Stick?" said Trance.

"The choppers came in late last night. They should be reassembled by noon tomorrow. We got the Harrier, because I promised to sell it back to them next week at a deep discount. The F-4 is safe and under control. Our last shipment crosses today. The border guards cost more than we expected, but there should be no problems."

"See that the guards disappear for a few days once the transfer is completed."

Stick looked down to a plastic clipboard and made notes on a yellow pad that was clipped to the front. "Roger. The guns are in working order and resting in the Salzburg rail yard. If the Baron doesn't have any counter battery capability they might do us some good."

"Any problems?"

"None. Got everything. We're ready to go."

"Good job, Stick." Trance stood, then walked around the table and shook hands with each of his men. "We're almost there, guys. See you at Innsbruck."

Two days later Trance, Stick and their eight squad leaders sat inside a rented chalet near the base of Igls Mountain at Innsbruck. With the late summer grasses blowing in the breeze, the mountain looked tame, not nearly as imposing as it would during the winter when it would be covered with ice, snow and a field of angry moguls. Today it made a relaxing backdrop to their discussion. The men sat at an imported California Redwood table in the middle of a large, rustic kitchen. Trance pulled a thick set of blueprints and rolled up photographs from a cardboard cylinder and set them onto the table. He pulled down the window shades and turned on a notebook computer that was wirelessly linked a plasma screen monitor hanging against the wall.

"I'm going to familiarize you with the topography surrounding the castle. Then we'll move to the grounds inside the walls. Once we're comfortable with the outside I'll take you inside the castle itself, then into the extensive system of catacombs and tunnels down below. Any questions?" There were none. Trance ran them through a set of computer slides, then spread a large photograph on the table and held it down with a red brick on each corner. "This aerial shows the rail system that runs along the mountain." The photograph was marked with red circles in several dozen areas, each of them numbered with different colored inks.

"The areas marked are critical to the operation. Numbers one, two and three green are locations that will allow a clean line of fire from the tracks to the castle. This rail spur is rarely used, just once or twice per week. We have the schedule, and our attack will commence during a down time. The 150s will be mounted on motorized flatcars and moved into place after the last train. "Numbers four and five blue are hidden entrances into the castle catacombs. This is all the Baron's land, by the way. He owns twenty miles in all directions. These train tracks run through his property with an easement he can revoke at any time. Consequently, it is well guarded with barbed wire, patrol dogs and electrified fences. Fortunately, we have assets in place that can help us bypass his security." Trance paused, then looked from face to face before continuing, "These entrances here are used sparingly, and only at night, for the transport of heavy machinery and the export of gold. They are well camouflaged. You can stand right next to one and not know it exists. As you can see on the aerial, they blend into the wilderness." Trance passed reduced copies to each of the men.

"The Baron's life runs like clockwork," continued Trance. "He manages everything with precision. This includes the armies he controls, the plans he makes, the defenses he creates. You need to understand this, men. The measures taken to ensure the safety of this fortress are like no others in the world. We'd have an easier time taking over the White House, Fort Knox, or the New York Federal Reserve Bank. I'd rather lead an attack against the Kremlin, or engineer a coup in North Korea than go against this place." Trance pointed to the circles numbered six and seven orange.

"See these two rock faces?" His men nodded, as Trance touched them with a wooden pointer.

"Behind these rock walls, deep inside the mountain you'll find more firepower, more jets and more helos than in the arsenal of most nations. There is a door here, with a hundred feet of solid rock that slides on rollers into the mountain. Behind the rock is another series of rock walls, then thick strips of lead, coated ceramics, and steel. The complex is radiation proof, and can withstand twenty-megaton detonations. When opened, these walls leave a path wide enough for F-16s to take off and land simultaneously. Do you understand what we're dealing with?"

Trance regarded the consternation on the faces of his men. "Anyone want out?" He looked from face to face, meeting the eyes of each of his leaders. The last man to meet his gaze was Brian "Boomer" Caldwell. Caldwell had been a punk thief in the Bronx for most of his childhood. When given the choice between hard time and the Navy he had chosen the latter. He was six foot two inches of solid muscle, with a razor wit and curly red hair.

"No," said Caldwell. "But I sure as hell would like to know how in the hell this guy built such a place, and what the hell he plans to do with it."

"Good question, Boomer." Trance looked at his men to make sure they were listening. "It's time you knew." Trance paused. "von Hoffenburg has hundreds of billions of dollars, maybe more. His motive is simple. He wants to rule the world—"

Boomer Caldwell snorted. "Who doesn't?"

"—and he is willing to start World War Three to do it."

Caldwell shook his head. "There would be nothing left to rule, what, with all the fallout."

"He's got time to wait it out. He's immortal." Trance watched the vague disbelief spread across the faces of his men. "Anybody hear of the Philosopher's Stone, the Elixir of Life?" The men looked at Trance, waiting in silence for him to continue. "He's had it since the Middle Ages, perhaps longer."

"You've got to be shittin' me," said Boomer.

"Thousands of books have been written on the subject of alchemy over the centuries, boys. Scores of men have attempted to unlock the alchemist's dream. Is it any wonder that someone actually did? Far stranger things have happened." There was a hum among them, the shaking of heads, and finally full attention to Trance's next words.

"My sources tell me that within days he is going to force the U.S., China and Russia into a game of nuclear chicken that none will win. When the dust settles, all three governments will be obliterated. I intend to stop him with your help." Trance laid a new blueprint on the table.

"These circles denote the ordinance and manpower placements. He's got Tomahawks, SAMs, RPGs and heavy battery everywhere." Trance fingered the hot spots, while his men looked on. "Then once you get inside the perimeter of the castle walls, the going gets tough."

"He's got a neat little package," said Caldwell. "And how much you payin' us?"

"Low pay, no women, no glory," said Trance.

"Sounds like the Bronx," said Boomer with a sarcastic New York accent. "Except for the women, I mean."

"Isn't this like takin' on a lion with a pea shooter?" asked one of the men.

"It's been done before." Trance placed his right foot on the edge of the table, leaned forward and began to tell the story. "My father went in and out alone and unharmed during the Big War. If we can get in, we might stand a chance. I'm going to show you how..."

CHAPTER 27

▼

The room was like a meat locker, and made entirely of rough granite stone. The walls were sweating, with moisture pooling sporadically on the floor. The air was dank, with the musty smell of mildew hovering above the floor. Lauren and Gretel huddled before a large fireplace with a struggling fire, trying to stay warm. They were in a bedroom chamber. The sheets and blankets had been slipped from their beds to prevent escape, and the stained glass windows were bolted from the outside. Even if they could climb outside, they would find a vertical drop of over sixty feet to a walkway below, and then a thousand feet below that.

The women had been silent for hours, since the Baron had introduced them to each other—as Trance's two lovers…Lauren, the banker, and Gretel, the spy. Animosity hung in the air like smoke, and they had kept their distance throughout the day, until they'd been forced to huddle together to stay warm.

"So you are the famous Lauren," said Gretel.

"Jack has talked about me?"

"Very little." Gretel smiled, but her eyes were like liquid steel, gray and cold.

"I'm sure," said Lauren under her breath. "Do you love him?"

"I…" *Watch yourself.* "Yes."

"von Hoffenburg said you're a spy."

Gretel sneered. "He lies."

"He said that you're using Jack to get to the formula."

"I know nothing about a formula."

"He said that your father was Koppleman," continued Lauren. "I've read about him. He was a good man, a dedicated man."

"He's dead."

"You work for Israel?"

"You could never understand."

"Try me," said Lauren gently.

Gretel began to chew on a fingernail, and absentmindedly pulled on wispy strands of her hair.

"I lived the life of a sheltered heiress, until terrorists killed my parents. I was fifteen."

"I'm sorry. It must have been hard."

"I wasn't the only one losing parents." Gretel laughed derisively. "The Mossad had lots of us to choose from. They took care of us...introduced us to the cause. It was easy. We needed something to believe in. *I* needed something to believe in. That was twenty years ago."

"You've been working for Israeli intelligence ever since?"

"I work for the Mossad, yes. With money and contacts, I travel in circles few others can."

"Your relationship with Breitfuss was no accident?"

Gretel laughed but her eyes remained cold. "There is a man named Swartz. He and my dad were friends. He became my surrogate father." Gretel breathed deeply, closed her eyes. "Swartz is Mossad. He knew Jack's father. He knows Jack, too. Twenty years ago Swartz came to me and asked me to make a sacrifice for my country. I did so, without a moment's hesitation.

"I don't know how Swartz learned about Breitfuss. But one day he told me that the fate of Israel might someday rest in his hands. I was good in school, so they decided my cover would be that of a professional student. I was ordered to befriend Breitfuss. It wasn't hard. He is a dear man. I was told to wait. For ten years I waited."

"You were a mole for ten years? Just waiting for Jack? Your life was waiting for Jack Trance to come to Austria?" Lauren's jaw opened and closed as if she were trying to speak, but no words would come. This was far deeper than anyone could have guessed.

Gretel nodded. "I learned everything about him. I was trained to become his perfect woman. I studied the way he thinks...what he enjoys...the things he does. Then I became his other half...I think to the point where it actually *became* me."

"All this was done without knowing you would meet him?"

"Oh, I have been destined to meet him. If it weren't here in Austria, it would have been somewhere else...once the formula surfaced. It was my job, my mission."

"You trained to be his...his woman? But what if he was married?"

"He was...once...And—"

"Oh no. You killed her?"

"Not me. Not us."

"What kind of people are you?"

"We are dedicated people, Lauren. We will stop at nothing to ensure that we remain free. That is how we survive. If the Baron got the formula—" Gretel shook her head. "He can never get the formula. It just can't happen. If Israel gets it…we need resources, you know. It is very hard for us. We must spend so much for our security, our military…People are always out to destroy us."

"What about Jack? Haven't you betrayed him?"

"I love him."

"You love him?"

"I do…It was something I hadn't planned on."

Lauren stared at Gretel and clenched her fists. "But you stand ready to kill him."

"I…don't know."

Lauren shook her head. "I can't do this…I can't ruin his happiness by telling him this. No, that will be your burden. But don't you hurt him, Gretel. He's been through enough."

"You love him, don't you?" said Gretel.

"I love that man more than you could ever know, or ever could," said Lauren. Her eyes grew unfocused, then misted with tears as she thought of the past. "I had my chance when we were young, but I wasn't ready. I thought I wanted more, and I have regretted it ever since. I've never found another man like Jack…never found another who could make me feel the way he does. He makes me feel alive…secure…content. But he met Janice and I stood aside. Since then, we have only been friends. After Janice died, he wouldn't take the risk with me. We've never been lovers again. I have accepted the role I play in his life." Lauren blotted the tears with her sleeve and fell silent.

"No other men in your life?" asked Gretel.

Lauren looked at Gretel with a mixture of surprise and puzzlement on her face. She shook her head slowly and said, "I envy you, Gretel. I'll never have another man…But I will never stand between you…I know my role and I will play it. But if you ever hurt him, I will be first in line to slit your throat."

"Excuse me. I am hoping that a general delivery package has arrived," said a polite, red-haired man to the Austrian postal clerk. The man wore a pair of round, antique gold spectacles, which kept slipping to the end of his nose. He hunched slightly forward in a diminutive manner and walked with slow deliberate steps. His High German resonated with a slight lisp.

"Your name, sir?" said the postal worker with a bored, nasal tone. Trance handed him a passport with his picture, in the name of Arthur Applegate, American.

The postal worker checked the name and the face, then said, "I will check and see, Herr Applegate."

The clerk shuffled into the back of the office. In a few minutes he returned with a large, brown manila envelope.

"You are in luck, Herr Applegate."

Trance stared at the package, glad to see the Florida postmark stamped in the corner. He took it with an obsequious smile.

"Thank you," he said. "I will also need two more envelopes like this, and some stamps to mail them..."

Trance walked laconically past two lines of people waiting their turn to be helped. As he reached the door several men peeled off from one line and followed him down the street. The men walked past him as he stepped into a green Volvo parked along the curb. Once inside the car, Trance burned the passport. He had another just like it hidden in America, along with many more—for situations just like this.

"No hitch, Stick," he said to the driver as they pulled away. "Stop at the library, will you?"

"Sure, boss."

Stick stopped the car on Hofstallgasse, in front of the Universitatsbibliothek Salzburg.

"Going to be long?"

"Ten minutes at the most," said Trance. "They're following me, but I've got a plan."

Trance stepped out of the car and carried the manila envelope up the steps. Inside the library he found a copy machine. He gently made a single copy of the original formula, two pages at a time. He then studied each page, burning the images into his memory. When he had finished copying the book, including the final pages, Trance took the copies, folded them, and placed them into another manila folder. He addressed this folder with a black Sharpie to a Mr. Samuel Richards in Stamford, Connecticut. He licked stamps onto the corner of the package, sealed it shut, and left it in a hollowed book within the stacks—where one of his men would retrieve and mail it. He walked back out the door into the waiting Volvo carrying the other new envelope, filled with blank copy paper and posted with new stamps.

Stick Granger peeled into the street and drove along with the traffic. After several blocks Trance said, "Stop here, will you?" Stick pulled the car to the side of the road. Trance opened the door, took two steps and dropped the package addressed for America into a postal box. He then sat back in the car. "That's it. Let's go." As they drove away, Stick glanced in his rearview mirror and saw three cars converge on the postal box.

"I take it that's not the formula?" asked Stick.

"Yeah. It's just a diversion." Trance shrugged his shoulders. "Wasn't my idea."

"Been rolling dice again?"

"Yeah." The men drove west in silence.

After a good twenty minutes Trance asked, "When was the last time you went climbing, Stick?"

Granger scratched his head. "Haven't done anything serious in a few years. Why?"

"I need your help on the mountain tomorrow night."

"A little pleasure before business, huh?"

"Yeah."

"Can I ask you a question?" asked Stick.

"Sure."

"How come you're not sharing the whole plan with me and the boys?"

"The boys will be told on a need-to-know. That way each can concentrate on his, or her, own small part, not the whole...And you...I might even keep some things from you." Trance looked at Stick and carefully watched as his friend's face remained fixed on the road. "Not like you to ask such a question, Stick. What's up?"

For several moments silence echoed loudly.

Finally Stick said, "I'm scared, JT."

"Well, holy shit!" roared Trance. He began to laugh from deep in his belly. "After all these years..." He shook his head. "I'm happy for you, Stick. You must have something to look forward to...Never thought I'd see the day again, when you'd be worried about death."

"There is this woman. Didn't know how I felt about her 'till yesterday."

"Ah...Always seems to work that way, doesn't it?"

"I'm going to retire, JT. I'm getting too old for this. I'm thinkin' I might get married again. Maybe have a kid or two."

"You'll make a damn good father, Stick. What's her name?"

"Marlee...and she's pregnant."

"You ol' dog."

"Promise me, that if I die...that you will take care of her...and the kid. Will you?"

"Thinking of checking out, are you?"

"I've just got that feeling. That's all. Never had it before..."

"You'll be fine, Stick. Don't worry. You can't worry, you understand?"

"Promise me you'll look after them."

"I promise."

"Thanks. I'll let her know."

"Jesus, Stick, you're scaring me."

The light on the Baron's private line was blinking red. This was a phone that only he would answer, and there was no message machine. It took twenty seconds before Trance heard the hard, gravelly voice of the Baron.

"Ya."

"Herr, von Hoffenburg...Trance here." Trance could almost hear ice crack along the line.

The Baron took several calming breaths before speaking. "So, you have called."

"I believe we have a transaction to complete."

The Baron closed his eyes and smiled. "What is it you suggest?"

"A meeting, in a mutually acceptable place. A neutral place."

The Baron laughed. "Come, come, Herr Trance. You must know by now that I do not leave my castle."

"I have something you want."

"And I have something you want."

"Then we must meet half way," said Trance. His heart was pounding. He could never hope to lure the Baron out of his castle, nor did he want to. But he must get him to concede some of his advantage. Otherwise they had no chance at all.

"Do you not trust me, Herr Trance?"

"No."

"I am a man of honor. If you deliver your package intact you will leave unharmed."

"And what assurance can you offer?"

"My word, Herr Trance."

"Not good enough." Trance's heart continued to rattle his chest. He struggled to control his breathing so the Baron would not sense his fear.

"And what would you suggest?"

"I already suggested, a neutral site."

"Impossible."

"Then we must make your castle more neutral." *Let him sit on that one,* thought Trance. He listened to the silence. He could almost see the Baron turning the words over in his head. What would it take to make the castle a neutral site? *The Third Infantry,* thought Trance with a wry smile.

"And why would I allow an enemy into my own backyard?"

"Because I, too, am a man of honor," said Trance. "Besides, Baron, I didn't know that we were enemies."

The Baron smiled. "Both men of honor, and each will not trust the other. What is it you suggest?"

Trance wondered how far the Baron would bend to get the formula.

"First I must be sure that the women are unharmed."

"Herr Trance. Dismiss the obvious. What is it you want?"

"You will remove all of your soldiers from the castle grounds. They will be kept under guard by my men until our exchange has been completed."

"But—"

"Quiet!" interrupted Trance. "I have not completed my list of conditions. Next, two of my men will make a complete tour of your castle grounds and report to me that the area has been neutralized. I will then fly in by helicopter, with two support helos for protection. You will wait for me in your study, and the main doors to your castle will be left open for me to enter. No one is to approach me when I land. I will be allowed to walk to your chamber with two men as bodyguards, and the formula in my possession. You will be allowed two guards of your own." Trance waited for several moments, then said "That is all."

"I cannot agree to those conditions," said the Baron, his voice growing louder with each successive word.

"Then we have nothing more to discuss." Trance hung up the phone.

The night was cool. A soft breeze tugged at the two climbers as they advanced toward the Baron's mountain in an electric ATV. There were few lights in the valley below. The Baron's land covered more than four hundred square miles of raw wilderness. No outsider was allowed within the confines of his property, except for a small scattering of family members that were allowed to reside at the mountain's base. Rusted coils of barbed wire stretched for miles in each direction, and parallel electrified fences clicked incessantly as they guarded the land. The land was posted with clusters of orange and yellow signs warning trespassers that they would be shot on sight.

Trance and Stick had worked their way through the protective maze, and were now climbing rapidly up the first gentle slopes of the mountain. When the ATV began to groan under the steepness, the men stashed it and continued on foot.

Trance was sure-footed, even in the dark. He had to stop now and then to let his friend make up the distance between them.

"You climb like a goddamn monkey," said Stick after a particularly hard stretch. He was panting heavily while Trance sat calmly on a rock.

"It's genetic. Dad was the same way. I think our ancestors lived in the trees. Years ago my father climbed to the top of this thing—in the winter."

"Yeah, well, the ice probably helped."

"Maybe it did. Nevertheless…" Trance's words trailed off, and he stared out into the night.

"How does that make you feel, about your dad and all?"

"Sad. I miss him."

"Sorry you lost him. I know what it's like. My dad died a couple years back."

"You never told me."

Stick shrugged his shoulders. "What was there to tell? He died. Couldn't bring him back."

Trance heard Stick sniff back the sadness, but didn't look his way. Both men lost themselves in thought—thinking about days gone by and the women they loved, wondering if they had a future with them, or if they would soon join their fathers in the circle of life.

"Sort of nice up here," said Trance as he looked out over the valley.

"It's lonely," said Stick.

"Makes you think of all you've got."

"Yeah. Guess it's the contrast...It's so...lifeless here."

"What will you do when it's over?" asked Trance.

"Thought I might enjoy life. Grow some roses, make some wine...maybe do a little fishing...raise some kids...You ever think of having a family?"

Stick saw a shadow cross Trance's face. "Sorry," he said. "I shouldn't have asked that."

"Don't worry," said Trance. "Most of the time I'm okay."

"You've got Gretel now."

"Yeah," said Trance. He exhaled and began to climb.

Neither man spoke for an hour. The mountain walls grew too steep to free climb, so they broke out the gear and climbed on with ropes and pitons.

"Exactly what are we doing up here?" asked Stick as they took a short break. "Not like you to be so secretive, old friend."

"I trust you, Stick, but no one else," said Trance. "Couldn't let anyone on the ground know we were up here. Figured you and I could discuss it alone."

"So, what the hell are we doing on the side of a mountain in the dead of night?"

"Got a minute?"

"Just hanging around." Stick, smiled, pulled his hands off the rocks and hung from the rope that was attached to his harness.

"Inside this mountain is a city. The two entrances that I pointed out on the map are openings to a vast underground military complex. Besides the jets, choppers and missiles, there are over twenty thousand soldiers. The mountain has its own nuclear power source, and there is enough food and water stored inside to keep everyone fed for half a century.

"The place is an armory of men and weapons, and a sophisticated command center from which the Baron intends to oversee the implementation of

Armageddon."

"And I thought it might be something dangerous."

Trance smiled, then his expression grew serious. "For us to succeed, Stick, we're going to have to perform minor miracles." Trance chuckled. "Because, if all we have is planning and execution to rely on, we're dead meat."

"Lucky for us."

"We can't defeat this army outright. But we can win the first battle and cut off the head of the snake."

"Well, that's simple enough."

"Yeah, piece of cake."

"How do we do it?"

"Timing."

"Shoot."

"We've got to isolate von Hoffenburg and make him surrender. Otherwise we've got no chance. He'll kill us all. What we need is time. Time to get to him and time to make him buckle."

"And your plan is?"

"We've got to paralyze his forces long enough for us to get to him, unguarded. We're spending a hundred million on a diversion, so we can get inside undetected. Me from one tunnel, the men from another."

"So we're up here climbing. I see. It's all very clear now. Couldn't we just try fireworks?"

Trance laughed.

"His main firepower comes from inside the mountain. So, we're going to set explosives to keep the doors from opening when we attack. If the rest of my plan works, there'll be few up top to keep us from gaining a stronghold. Once we take the high ground we should have enough time and manpower to do the rest."

"Perhaps we should call in the 82nd Airborne," said Stick.

"I wish it were so simple. The U.S. can't invade a sovereign nation without cause. The President's hands are tied on this one."

"How long will we have?"

"A few minutes, perhaps more, if we are lucky," said Trance. He sighed.

"Lucky, like with a miracle?"

"One can hope."

Trance checked his gear and began to stretch his way back up the rock face. "You ready to move on?"

"I was born ready."

The men climbed for two more hours without speaking. They were on the treacherous north face of the mountain—a seemingly endless series of marginal handholds and steel-bending rock. At this altitude the stone had become crystalline, and so hard that it fought each centimeter of Trance's pitons. Their grips were thin wisps of rock ledges wide enough for fingertips, nothing more. The climbing was painfully slow, and both men's fingers throbbed with pain. Trance nursed a deep blood-filled blister on his left index finger, while Stick fought leg cramps that could threaten his life on a climb like this.

"Couldn't you have found an easier way up this thing?" asked Stick, once more placing his life in the hands of a rope clipped to his harness. Trance shook his head and pointed above them. Stick followed Trance's finger and saw nothing. He looked at Trance blankly, held out his hands and shrugged.

Trance looked up the mountain, grinned and said, "Always thought you were a little blind."

"Blind hell. I've got 20/16 vision, better than you, wise ass."

"There," said Trance, pointing again. "See the light?" Stick looked upwards and let his eyes walk along the wall. He could see nothing out of the ordinary. He looked back at Trance, who smiled sheepishly, then handed Stick a pair of infrared goggles. Stick fastened them to his head and looked back toward the face of the wall. He saw two thin filaments of green light running horizontally along the wall.

"Ah," he said. "A little device for thwarting Sunday climbers?"

"Yeah."

"Don't they know this is impossible to climb? It's been made that way. Must have taken them decades to chip it like this." Stick paused. "What do you suppose happens if someone inadvertently blocks that light?" asked Stick.

"Fried within seconds, I suppose."

"You go first," said Stick. Both men laughed.

"Don't worry, Granger, I've got more important things to do than die up here."

"I'd hate to have to climb down alone."

"Be prepared for anything."

The two men locked eyes. Silent words passed between them, speaking of the times they had prepared, but the unexpected had occurred. Of all the opportunities they had had to save each other. They knew those days couldn't last forever. Nothing could. Was this their time?

Trance inched his way up toward the two rings of light that circled the side of the mountain. At twenty-foot intervals, built into the stone, Trance saw relay units made of molded ceramics and metal alloys. They extended twelve inches and thirty inches out from the stone, making it virtually impossible for a man to sneak under them, between them, or outside of them. Thin beams of light passed from one relay to the other, uninterrupted by rock or vegetation. He knew that each of these outlets was wired to a central alarm system inside the mountain. If a beam of light were to be broken, interrupted for just a fraction of a second, the alarm would be triggered. Trance didn't know what would happen then, whether an automatic laser would scorch the earth, or a flock of helicopters would come flying out of nowhere, or snipers would emerge from inside. But he knew that if he interrupted a stream of light, it would begin a countdown to death.

Trance pushed his way upward along the wall until his head was just inches from the beam. He hammered three pitons below the light and fastened himself securely against them. He drew out two more spikes and hammered them just below the two lights, deep into the wall, and more than three feet apart. He reached into his backpack and removed an object. Below him Stick could not tell what it was. It was made of metal, thin, and it unfolded easily. Stick watched as Trance clipped the object to one of the pitons below the outer beam. Once it was securely fastened, Trance reached into his pack and withdrew another. He fastened this one to the other piton. Trance checked each one carefully from every angle. He reached into his pack and withdrew a round metal disk, with thin rods attached to its edge. What it was for, Stick couldn't guess. He watched as Trance extended one of the metal rods and set it against the wall below the light. He adjusted the length so that it was exactly level with the beam, taking precise measurements with a laser level. Then he adjusted the disk against the two objects that he had attached to each of the pitons below the light to get the angle correct. Stick now understood the plan. He couldn't take his eyes off Trance.

When Trance finished his measurements he relaxed against the ropes and looked down at Stick, who was now just below him and to his right.

Stick could see that Trance was sweating heavily. "Having fun?" he said.

"Yeah. We'll have to bring the girls here sometime. Great place for a picnic." Trance took a long, deep breath through his nose, then exhaled through his mouth. "If I don't get these mirrors perfectly centered, we can say our prayers. I thought of using a partially reflective mirror with a drop down. That way I could have set them in place while enough light still passed through them. I could have made sure the measurements were perfect, but I wasn't sure about the sensitivity of their system. Either way it was a risk."

"You're not going to kill us, are you, JT?" Stick was sure he could feel death lurking in the shadows around them.

"Ye of little faith," said Trance. "I got to practice this once in school."

"That's reassuring. How'd you do?"

"You don't want to know."

Trance took hold of one of the objects. There was a mirror on both sides. It was square, and attached to hinged rods that would allow it to be moved into nearly any position. For several seconds Trance played with the hinges, getting the mirror into the exact position he wanted. He pulled his head back to examine his handiwork. There was only one more move to make. He reached out and firmly drew the mirror upward until it split the beam of light. Trance relaxed heavily against the ropes once the mirror was in place.

"Success?" asked Stick.

"We'll know in a few seconds, won't we?"

"You mean you don't know? Oh, that's just great."

"Shut the hell up, Stick. Can't you see I'm busy?" Trance adjusted the other mirror. He knew if his measurements were off, even by the lightest amount, they were dead. He took a deep breath, exhaled and pressed the mirror into place. He took another breath and leaned back against the ropes.

"There," he said. "Go ahead and chatter."

"I'm not saying a peep until you've finished with the second set."

Trance repeated the process with the inner beam. When Trance was done, Stick could see that he had cleared a space for them to continue climbing up the mountain. The beams of light hit the mirrors from both sides. The mirrors reflected the beam, making the receiver think that the flow was unbroken. Between the mirrors was a lightless space of over three feet, plenty of room for both men to advance.

"Slick," said Stick. "Perhaps we'll live to ride another day, Tonto."

"The night's still young, cowboy. Let's go set the explosives and get the hell outahere."

CHAPTER 28

▼

The mountains were a smoky gray, and rising like ghosts out of the final vestiges of darkness. Soon the sun would begin to make its climb into the daylight sky. Trance and Stick had worked through the night, making their final preparations. Trance felt as if he had been slaving for months, constructing a great pattern of dominoes, carefully setting each one into its proper position. He knew that each small detail must fall into place or the entire pattern would be useless. Everything must follow split-second timing, with each part successful, each domino falling exactly as planned, or they would all be dead. If they died, half the world would also perish.

As Trance climbed back onto his ATV, he took one final look back at the foreboding mountain, with the castle sitting on top like a skullcap. He wondered if he would have the strength to see this through. Part of Trance wanted simply to fall into bed and let the world pass by. Perhaps if he went to sleep he would wake up, and it would have all been a bad dream. But this was no dream. This was his highest sense of reality, with thousands of years of man's evolution teetering in the balance, depending upon him. Depending upon him? What would his father have said? We are just all part of the great Cosmic Order...only minor players in the Great Game. Yet, if he failed, think of all that would be lost. The lives...the historic monuments, all the images that stood to remind man of where he came from and where he was going. The suffering, the nuclear aftermath—disease, pestilence and mutations. The cold and the darkness as the world entered a nuclear winter. Did it all depend on him? Was he in control of his actions? Or was someone... something...controlling him?

At breakfast Stick said, "The A-4 Skyhawk is armed to the teeth and ready."

"And the Superfortress?" said Trance.

"The B-29 had a few minor problems. It's ready now, and filled to the gills with deadly gifts ready to flutter from the sky."

"The Harrier?"

"Good to go."

"That's it then," said Trance. "Run down the rest of the list."

"The Cobras are set. Two are in covered rail cars awaiting final transport. The Bell is ready to take you to the castle. My gunship is prepped. Two of the cannon are in place. The rocket launchers are good to go. One other helo will roll in with the train tonight. Our men are resting comfortably. All gear has been checked and rechecked. The bomber is fueled and ready at that little LZ Breitfuss secured. The locals are on our side, part of the 'resistance' against the Baron. They've helped us get everything well covered, invisible from the air and protected on the ground. All systems have been checked and rechecked...I seriously do feel the need for speed, brother Jack."

Trance laughed. "Okay, you overgrown jet jockey."

"Can't we just launch a few Tomahawks against this guy and call it a day?" asked Stick. "Maybe we could roust the Second Cav—"

"No go," said Trance. "We'll have to do it the hard way, even if it is like using a popgun to take down an elephant."

"Yeah. A real David versus Goliath," said Stick, still in good humor.

An image flashed through Trance's head of the giant man protecting the Black Madonna—the one with the crater between his eyes. He shook off the thought. "Now, go over the list again."

"Sure, kid. What else?"

"Finish up and get some rest. Come see me at Sixteen Hundred. I'll get you current."

Trance hadn't slept for two days and he felt the urge to feel tired. But there was too much to do, so he sat down, crossed his legs and began to breathe deeply, in through his nose, and out through his mouth. He felt the blood rush into his hands, feeling the warmth...the calm.

Soon Trance found himself walking in the sand. It was December, Christmas Eve, somehow he could tell. The beach was rather cool and the wind was chopping at the waves. The winter sky was overcast, the air a whitish haze. Trance walked slowly, the sand heavy on his feet. He watched as sandpipers rushed forward toward the surf as the waves flowed outward, and then turned to run inward as the waves headed back to shore. He thought of how peaceful and uncomplicated their life must be—with only one thing to think about, and doing it time after time.

Have we made our lives far too complicated? he wondered. A figure emerged out of nowhere.

"So you have come again," said his father.

"I suppose I have," said Trance.

"And how goes the battle?"

"I...I don't know. I'm doing all I can." There was a melancholy sadness in Trance's voice, resignation rather than anticipation.

"Good." The elder Trance looked at his son and his eyes squinted in mirth.

"And what is that supposed to mean?"

"It is good that you are doing all you can. That is all you *can* do."

"Aren't you going to tell me something meaningful?"

"And what is there that I can tell you that you do not already know somewhere inside?"

Trance felt a pull against his stomach, and a familiar tightness in his throat. "And what should I know?"

His father smiled and touched his face. "You are a good boy, Jackie. I see why it was you and not someone else."

"What is that supposed to mean?"

"I must be going now, my son. We will meet again soon. The universe is a strange and wondrous place." His father faded from into a mist and Trance edged back to consciousness.

"We will meet again soon," Trance said out loud. What had his father meant? Does that mean I'm about to die? He looked at his watch and returned to his rented room.

Two hours later Trance was ready. He looked at his watch. Where had the time gone? There was nothing more he could do except wait and rest. He set the alarm on his watch and walked over to the small bed in the corner. The bed was old and it sagged in the center. But it was clean, and he was asleep in seconds.

At three thirty Trance heard the beeping of his watch. At first he stayed on the edge of consciousness, mingling into a dream he was having. He and Gretel were at a quarry in Vermont. They were lying comfortably in the summer sun, out on the rocks with thick towels underneath them. He was aware of a presence behind him, a shadow. Someone was standing there guarding over them. Then the beeping came from in front of them, far across the quarry, and the shadow ran off behind the noise. Trance was trying to see the shadow when the world came back into focus. His eyes were straining and there was a strangling tightness in his shoulders and throat.

Trance stood up, removed his clothes and lumbered into the narrow fiberglass shower stall. He turned on the water and let it run hot against his body. Steam floated around him and he breathed it deep into his lungs. He felt himself begin to relax. Absentmindedly his fingers traced the wounds along his shoulder and ribs. They were still brutally tender to the touch. He contrasted these to the other scars that decorated his body like tattoos. How many of them were there, he wondered. Scars, physical and emotional scars. Too many to count.

"Janice," he said out loud without thinking. He still felt the tightness in his throat. "Gretel," he whispered. Part of the tightness subsided. "Lauren." His body relaxed. The water was working wonders.

Trance spent twenty minutes under the pelting jets of the Moen Shower Massage. When he stepped out into the room, he felt better, almost normal. He reached into a small suitcase and pulled out a clean pair of jeans. He threw on a short-sleeved golf shirt and examined himself in the mirror. At least he *looked* refreshed and confident. He combed his hair with his fingers and looked to see if he needed a shave. It could wait, he decided. He sat down, put on a pair of white athletic socks and a pair of running shoes, and laced them up tightly. When he was fully dressed, he jumped up and down to excite his muscles and get a little adrenaline running through his arteries.

There was a knock on the door.

"Yeah," he said.

"It's me," said Stick.

Trance removed the flexible wire attached to the doorknob, threw back the deadbolts, and opened the door slowly. "Hey, buddy," he said.

Stick looked at the shotgun strapped to a chair and rigged to the door. "Glad I knocked. Of course, you'd think anyone able to get through the six guys you had guarding this place would find a way to get around that, too."

"A fancy alarm clock. That's all," said Trance with a wink. "Are we ready?" Trance sounded giddy. It was almost over, one way or another.

"I'm ready to kick some Middle-Aged ass," said Stick.

"Sit down," said Trance. He motioned Stick to a chair near the edge of the bed. Stick took a seat and set his Kalashnikov rifle against the bed. Trance stood beside the bed and fingered the rifle as he spoke.

"There are a couple changes in plan from what we discussed."

"Expected that," said Stick.

"There may be a spy among us."

"How do you know?"

"I don't. More of a hunch than anything. Might be one of the boys."

Stick's eyes brightened. "So you fed us the wrong information?"

"Just a smidgeon of disinformation."

"Let's hear it then. I'll be damned if I am going to operate this thing in the dark. Level with me or I'm walking." Stick paced the small room with his hands thrust deeply in his pockets.

Trance laughed out loud and then sobered quickly. He grabbed Stick by the shoulders and shook him, "What good is fear going to do you, Stick?"

"I'm sorry, Jack. I...I just want to live. For once in my life I want to live, that's all. Now...not knowing...I've always known what was going to happen. But this has been so much different. I'm scared."

"So am I, Stick. But we can't focus on fear." Trance let go of Stick's shoulders and began to pace the room with him. "Here's how it's going down. I'm not going to the castle in the chopper. You are. They'll be waiting for me, and they'll be expecting me to walk straight into the castle with the formula."

"I take it that I won't have it?" said Stick.

Trance shook his head. "Spike and Boomer will be lifted up three and a half hours before you fly in. The Baron expects them to be securing the grounds. They will be, but not as the Baron expects. We've got several people on the inside. They're loyal to the Madonna, and I'm going to trust them. They will be setting C-4, with detonators, in prearranged places. It will be shaped like boards and painted to blend in. Spike and Boomer will check and make any changes needed to ensure we have a nice little fireworks display."

"Won't they be watched?"

"Yes," said Trance. "But I've got detailed plans of that castle, better than the Baron himself. I know each and every place that's unwatched and unguarded. I know everywhere he could be hiding men, and where they will be coming from. Those two exits from the mountain caverns we visited last night, we seal them shut first."

Stick thought of the explosives that he and Trance had set into the face of the mountain wall. They would cause some serious damage. He thought of the cannons they had aimed at the castle from below. These might be effective in the diversion. Then again, they could be taken out in the first few minutes, if the Baron's counter battery capability was there.

"Most of the Baron's soldiers should be neutralized by the time he calls them to action," said Trance. "Except for the Major, of course."

"Wilson?" asked Stick. Trance nodded, but said nothing more. "How are *you* getting in?" continued Stick.

"From the inside," said Trance. "See this here..." Trance pulled open an aerial photo of the Baron's mountain and pointed. To Stick it just looked like the side of a big hill.

"Yeah? So what?"

"Another entrance. Five thousand vertical feet of stairs if you can believe it. More than three miles of tunnel—right into a dungeon beneath the Baron's study."

"Won't it be guarded?"

Trance shook his head. "He doesn't know it's there."

"So you come from inside..."

"While he worries about you on the outside...thinking it is me."

"Very good, JT."

Trance smiled. "Let's hope so. Here's what you are going to do...."

The sky was cloudless, and one could see forever over the mountains in the late afternoon air. The wind had begun to blow from the south and the weatherman was predicting a Föhn, the hot devil winds that blow up from the Mediterranean through the Italian Alps. In the wintertime the Föhn melts the snow and keeps away the tourists. In the summertime it makes living unbearable, a bit like the Santa Ana winds in California, but not so dry. Accident and suicide rates skyrocket. Hospital operations require more blood. The Föhn becomes a legal defense for crimes committed under its influence.

Trance's men were growing irritable. The Föhn must be starting, thought Trance. This was good; it would give them an edge. He looked out over the valley toward the towering castle. It was over two miles in the air, and as menacing as a rabid pit bull. With luck, he would soon be inside its walls. After that, he could only hope for the best.

Lauren and Gretel heard shouting outside their room as the Baron's troops began gathering in the castle courtyard. Their sole window rested high upon the wall, and they couldn't see outside, even while standing on their toes. Lauren searched around the room and motioned toward one of two ponderous oak chairs by the fireplace. "There," she said. She and Gretel dragged the chair to the window. Standing on the arms, the women could just see outside.

Lauren tried to open the window, but it was sealed shut. She jumped off the chair, went to the fireplace, picked up an old fire poker and brought it back to the window. Together, the two women pried at the window until it slid open with a loud crack. Looking down, they saw men milling about, smoking cigarettes and joking with one another. Each man carried a rifle and a sidearm. Most of them wore green camouflage uniforms and slung large, greenish-brown backpacks. A swarm of helicopters descended from the sky and landed in the yawning courtyard

"Where do you think they're going?" asked Lauren.

"Couldn't imagine," said Gretel in her perfect English.

"Looks like they're clearing the grounds."

"Except for thousands more that live in the bowels of the castle," said Gretel.

Lauren looked strangely at her rival. "Do you think they're clearing them out at Jack's request?"

"Probably, 'though I doubt Jack knows about the others."

"Don't underestimate him," said Lauren sharply.

"Oh, I've studied him too long to underestimate him."

"But?" asked Lauren. She waited as Gretel pondered her reply.

"There is too much he doesn't know, and much you don't know. This is more intricate than you think."

"I can imagine. Your people planned for ten years."

"Ten years?" said Gretel. She walked away from the window. "Try fifty. Try a thousand."

"Jesus. Why didn't you tell him?"

"It's not as easy as you think. It wasn't just my life that was planned. Jack's life was planned too, from the time he was born. Was it co-incidence that his father brought him to his first dojo at the age of three? He was a black belt by the age of six, and that was just the beginning. The Jujitsu...the wrestling...all the weapons...sending him to Japan...Annapolis...the CIA...Do you really think that Jack had a choice in what he did? There were too many people making decisions for him. His father prepared him his entire life, just for this confrontation with the Baron. The Baron also planned for this, even before Jack was born. I wanted to tell him." Gretel paused. "Really, I did. But...it's so complicated. An entire nation...all that my father worked for...died for..."

"I don't believe—"

Gretel cut off Lauren's words with a wave of her arm. "It wasn't supposed to happen this way!" *Even our men inside the castle don't know what's going on*, she continued to herself. Their well-orchestrated plan had violently veered off course.

"You say that you love Jack. You obviously love your country. If you had to choose between them, which would you choose?"

"I'd want to choose Jack. Really, I would. But...if it helps millions of our people... I'd give up my own life in a second."

"If they ordered you to kill him, would you do it?"

"They have," replied Gretel in a far off voice. "If there was a time when I could kill him and get the formula, those were my orders."

"My God."

"God has nothing to do with this." Gretel's eyes narrowed. Then she sighed. "Jack never said he had the formula. I didn't have to choose." She paused. "At first it would have been easy. But then I fell in love with him."

"And would you kill him now?"

"I don't know. But someone would. Someone will. The needs of a nation transcend those of any individual."

"Bitch."

"Yes. I don't like myself either. But you don't understand. You are not me; you're not Israel. You haven't been through what I've been through, what we've been through. You could never understand." Gretel sat on her bed and stared at the wall.

Gretel was crying when they heard the hum of a new helicopter approaching the castle. She joined Lauren by the window as it circled high above the schloss several times. It continued to circle as it drifted lower.

"You think that's him?" asked Lauren. Gretel leaned very close to Lauren's ear and whispered, "No. But we must not talk about it. He may want them to think he's in there." Lauren took a step back and stared at Gretel, as if for the first time.

"Remember. I've had military training. I've studied him," said Gretel. "I know him better than anyone."

"In more ways than one," muttered Lauren.

"They're getting out," said Gretel. The women shared the chair and peered out the window. Two men got out of the helicopter. Each man carried a small Czech scorpion VZ-61 machine pistol—light, powerful, and surprisingly accurate for its small shape. The Baron walked out to see them, taking no heed of their weapons, or the helicopter as it veered away.

The women stood back and looked at each other.

"The Baron has balls," said Lauren. "I'll say that for him."

Gretel snorted. "He's got a dozen marksmen positioned to take those men out at the first sign of movement. See how they keep the guns pointing away from the Baron? That's one of their agreements, I'm sure." Gretel spoke as a professional. "Must be an advance team to secure the area. That's why all the soldiers were cleared. They are neutralizing the grounds. At least Jack thinks so."

"How can we warn them?" asked Lauren. "Should we scream out?"

"Don't be stupid," said Gretel. She was thinking as a soldier, not as a lover. A cry from a tower window would interrupt the flow...Things *were* flowing, perhaps as they should. Gretel closed the window. "They'll come for us soon. Let's move this chair back into place. We'll see nothing more. They'll take us from here before Jack comes."

Trance maneuvered a custom, electric four-wheel Honda ATV up the low incline portion of the Baron's mountain. It moved rapidly and silently up the slope. He was dressed in snug, dark gray assault gear with a matching Kevlar vest. Mottled black, gray and green camouflage paint covered his face, and he was just a whisper in the dusk. Strapped beside him was a medium sized backpack, with his blue nylon gym bag nestled inside. When his four-wheeler began to balk against the mountain, Trance ditched it into a clump of bushes and continued on foot. He had a thousand vertical feet to climb before he reached the hidden entrance built into the mountain by the Black Madonna. He recalled how she had told him it had taken over three hundred years to dig through the stone by hand and make a tunnel that would lead him through the mountain in secrecy to the Baron's laboratory, directly below his study—the same dungeon his father had visited a lifetime ago. Three hundred years—all for this?

Trance wore a spelunker's hardhat, with two Petzl lights wrapped around its base. The helmet was equipped with a satellite telephone, a miniature radio scanner, earphones, and a microphone. He also carried a miniature hand powered flashlight on his belt and some glow sticks in his pack. The night was clear but deathly dark, and Trance was tempted to use a light before he was safely inside the tunnel. But he climbed in darkness and let his senses guide him onward.

The Black Madonna had placed and marked a number of natural landmarks along the way to denote the trail to the entrance—a large, horse shaped rock, a distinctive cluster of boulders, an altitude-dwarfed tree with a prominent "Y" in its trunk. Trance pulled a iPhone with a GPS monitor and a detailed digital map from his pack and checked his position. His GPS was in sync with the landmarks. He was on track. He glanced at his watch. There was plenty of time; all was on schedule.

Trance was climbing when the first helicopter landed. He adjusted his helmet-phone and monitored the occasional flow of words between his men as he climbed toward his destiny.

The tunnel entrance into the mountain was built beneath a pile of angry rock covering a natural ledge jutting out from a near vertical wall. It looked like the remains of a rockslide, perfect camouflage for what was inside.

Trance withdrew a folded shovel and a small pickaxe from his pack and began to clear away the rock. It took nearly an hour for him to remove the rubble, longer than he had planned. When he cleaned the ledge, all he could see was more stone. *It is well hidden* they had said, and they were right. He hefted his pickaxe and began to chop into the soft limestone covering the inner wall. It yielded quickly, and ten minutes later he was crawling through the space into the mountainside.

Inside, there was a chamber perhaps twenty feet to a side. Beyond him stretched a tunnel as far as he could see. Trance took a blanket and covered the entrance to the chamber. Then he withdrew a radio relay and set it on the outside edge of the chamber door. Satisfied, Trance began his journey inward. He walked forward through the tunnel for twenty-six minutes, until he came to another wide hollow. There he found a stack of weathered, wooden torches and several ten-liter cans of kerosene. Above him he saw an endlessly spiraling stairwell, stretching upward to a dark pinpoint in the distance. Every one hundred stairs there was a platform built into the mountain, and another set of torches.

"Jesus," said Trance. He thought of how many men it must have taken to build a tunnel like this, in secret and by hand—one mile up and then another two miles inside the mountain. It was an architectural masterpiece carved out of solid stone. How difficult it must have been to chip away at the rock, day after day, year after year. He could feel the souls of a thousand dead workers floating around him in the dark. At least they didn't have to build walls to keep dirt from filling in the chamber, he thought. Even more would have died. Small consolation.

"We checked it recently," the Black Madonna had told him. "The way is clear. But heed my warnings. There are traps to kill any man who enters without their knowledge. Do not get careless.

"And don't be alarmed by the bones you find along the way," she'd said. "The bats will not harm you if you stay out of their way. The rats…well…rats are rats."

Trance unbuckled the hip belt of his pack and felt the weight fall heavily against his shoulders. He set the pack against one wall of the shaft, reached into it and pulled out another radio relay and set it on the bottom stair.

"Delta to Beta. Come in, over," he said into his helmet transmitter.

"Beta, here."

"Status?"

"Green."

"Delta over and out." No problems, yet. But he still had four hundred stories to climb.

Trance glanced at his watch and grimaced. He was running later than planned. He began. The stairs were made of thick wooden planking. Most of them were solid, but occasionally one sagged and creaked underneath his feet. Trance pondered why the stairs were made of wood, then decided they must have been built for easy destruction. He walked rapidly up the first hundred steps and stopped at the first landing. He hoped that he would not have to retreat this way. But, just in case, he decided to light torches to keep it lit for a quick getaway.

Smooth, finger-worn wooden handles stuck out of a square metal tank with a sliced rubber top. Trance could smell the kerosene inside. The top ends of the torches were covered with some sort of fabric, and had obviously been prepared for his arrival. Trance lit the first torch and it erupted with a bright oily puff, then settled down to a steady flame. A thin curl of black smoke trailed upward from the end and it gave off a surprising amount of heat in the musty shaft. The heat was welcome, as the temperature hovered around fifty-two degrees Fahrenheit.

Trance set the torch into a metal ring that had been driven into the stone wall, then looked at a schematic of the tunnel. The third step up from this platform was a killer. The planking was weight sensitive, and any weight over thirty kilos would cause a waterfall of rock to rain down. As Trance's foot passed above the step, he felt a strange urge to test it. Would it really work? he wondered. He fought off the whim and moved on.

Trance began taking the steps two at a time. He stopped at each platform to light two new torches. The first he would place by the platform. He would leave the other half way to the next one. It was on the fifth level that Trance noticed the first dead body. He saw the outline of a man's skull in a rounded space carved in the stone. The skull rested on a pile of bones, dust, and bits of rock. Underneath it all was a small bench built into the rock as a resting place. The bones were picked clean, white and smooth, but barely visible through the rubble. The skull was tipped to one side and there was no mistaking that its eerie smile was human.

"Hmmm," said Trance to no one. Not a nice place to die. He wondered if this person had been trapped within the tunnel, without food, and had just sat there to die—or if it had been the arrows. He pulled a Japanese bo cane from his pack and dug into the bones. Several short wooden arrows lay in their midst. Trance shivered and moved on.

Between this level and the next there were two deadly spots. The twelfth step would give way to any weight greater than ten kilos, triggering a spray of poisoned arrows. Trance shined his light against the wall when he reached the trap and counted twelve holes in the rock, each with a metal-tipped point visible from two inches within the wall. He jumped gingerly over steps twelve and thirteen and held his breath until several seconds had passed.

Trance wondered how many decades...how many centuries these traps had been in place. He climbed steadily to the next danger point, a thousand feet in the air. Stepping on the forty-first step would cause three giant scythes to swing out from the wall. It was weight loaded and would sever any intruder at the knees, waist and chest. While standing on step thirty-nine Trance reached up and felt the open ridges in the wall where the scythes were hidden. He hoped that he had counted correctly. Just in case, he decided to skip two extra steps. He braced himself on the stairs and jumped. He led with his left leg, landing firmly on the step. But the step gave way. Trance pitched backwards as his foot fell to the step below. He began to lose his balance. He waved both arms in circles to remain erect—not moving forward or backwards, suspended between life and death. But the weight of the pack was too great and Trance began to tip back down the stairs.

CHAPTER 29

▼

"Dis place is gonna laht up lahk da Fourth o' Julah," said Spike Johnson as he and Boomer Caldwell finished inspecting the final set of explosives.

"I just hope to hell I'm out of the way when this place blows," replied Boomer.

"Dat Trance is sompin' else," said Spike.

"I've worked with Granger, but not Trance," said Boomer.

"Sheeit," continued Spike. "I known em fuh yeahs..." Spike was a tall black man from Hells Kitchen in New York City. He had a broad face with clear, brown, intelligent eyes. "Ah r'member walkin' off dat plane in Columbia. Whew, mama, musta been a hundrd an' ten in da shade, an' da air, she was so thick youse cud swim. We was s'pposed to take out dis drug lord who was holdin' the govment hostage down dere. Ah gits assahned to dis crazy shit. Him an' Stick, Ah tell you, crazy-assed dogs, an tough! Whah I r'member one tahm when we was sneakin' behand da lines an' we was caught dead in ahr tracks. When we attacked dis drug lord dere musta been thirty guys pinnin' us down. Sheeit, they was ever'where. Dere was dis one machine gun nest... Dat sucker, Trance. gave da most blood curdlin' yell Ah's ever heard and he done launched hisself raht into it. I mean launched hisself. He was flingin' dese disks he carries and shoutin' some kinda shit. An'ways—he lands in dis nest and stahts sprayin' fiah all ovah da place. Damned if dose suckahs din't turn an' run. Never saw nufin' lahk it. He's one tough motha, and youse lucky ta work wif him."

"I just hope he isn't some asshole who will get us killed," said Boomer.

Spike grinned and held his hands to the side. He began to speak, but now in cultured English with a slight British accent. "I entered the Navy as part of a plea bargain with the local authorities—a last chance before I spent the rest of my life in prison. I had the good fortune to test out with an IQ of 160. Trance plucked me out of basic, showed me the error of my ways and then nearly got me killed half a dozen times.

"When I left the service Trance offered to help me out, in any way he could. I thought he was joking, so I asked him for a million dollars to help me buy a used auto dealership. He wrote me a check on the spot. First thing I did was to buy new clothes and get speech lessons. Then I bought that dealership. Now I own sixty-five new-car stores along the East Coast, thanks to him. Got a house in the Hamptons, a great wife, and kids destined someday for Harvard…" Spike smiled again, then lapsed back into his city speak. "You stick wif me, boa. I don't get shots by nobody. And dat Trance. God watches over dat mothaf…"

"The first one hits New Orleans," said the Chosen One.

"Why New Orleans?" asked the Russian.

"Because it's so vulnerable. We've got three cruise missiles sitting in one of our jackup rigs in the Gulf. I've placed another on an old posted inland drilling barge, just outside Lake Charles. They were easily hidden, since they're on rigs we own and control. We'll launch them and moments later…poof. We have others in place near every major city, but we're hoping we won't have to use them.

"It will be far more unsettling for bombs to be launched from within, with no chance to stop them…easier to set the contagion. New Orleans is vital to America's oil interests, and a place loved by everyone. After Katrina, the U.S. government poured billions into its redevelopment. To see it go again will be hugely demoralizing…No American president can sit by and watch New Orleans, Lake Charles, and Houston fall in a row, and do nothing about it. That would be like cutting out the heart of America's oil industry. That's something he can't ignore. We'll launch some missiles from Russia to give him a bogey-man. Our assets in China will do the same. If need be, we will hit New York and Los Angeles. The President will be forced to respond."

"Murmansk is the first Russian target. From a trawler just offshore," said the Russian.

"Wonderful."

"Isn't it," said the Russian, with little enthusiasm. He liked Murmansk, in the summertime. The Chosen One had wanted St. Petersburg, The Russian's own birthplace, but he had convinced his brother that Murmansk, a port city, like New Orleans, was the better choice—just in case he got to rule the remains.

The President stood alone, as the last of his advisors passed out through the door to the Oval Office. He peered out the windows toward the rose garden and followed the progress of one man and one woman as they moved from bush to bush, pruning here and there, and nipping off occasional leaves and buds.

They have absolutely no clue, thought the President. *Here I am waiting on an overseas call from Senator Hopewell. All NATO forces are in full readiness for war. I've been on the phone with the Russian president, and the damned asshole keeps insisting that the United States back off. Back off from what? I'm only responding defensively to his aggression. Back off hell! I've spent hours trying to convince the Europeans that we're not behind the global mobilization. Only the British Prime Minister believes me. All the others are Socialists anyway...It would serve them right...If they don't want to shoulder their part of the world's burdens...but the Chinese... Nobody can reason with the goddamn Chinese. We're on the frigging brink of a world war and gardeners are trimming the roses.*

The phone rang. It was the Secretary of State, Sam Ableson, calling from Brussels.

"I can't get them to listen to a goddamn thing," he said. "They say we're acting unilaterally, again, and that we better stand down or else."

"Or else what?" said the President.

"They just said 'or else'."

The President laughed and shook his head. "Typical."

The President closed his eyes and thought about roses. He said, "My talks with the Russians broke down, again. Now it appears that some nation's got a highly placed mole in our State Department. I just found out that our most sensitive, strategic military information has been purged from Intelligence computers. This information pinpoints the most vulnerable spots in our defense system. With this knowledge someone with brass balls and no conscience could sabotage the U.S. defenses, exposing major gaps that, if struck, could bring about the inconceivable. They could bring us to our knees.

"Intelligence tells me that Jacob Miller has turned. Hopewell uncovered some shady link between Miller and Trance, illegal oil trading, I think. I have him combing the European Continent to capture them. Both men are nowhere to be found." The President slumped and closed his eyes. "Tell me, Sam, how in the hell did this all happen?"

Another line rang. "Hold on, Sam." The President punched the intercom. "Yes?"

"Mr. President. It's Senator Hopewell."

The President pressed the line button. "Senator."

"Hello, Mr. President."

"What's your progress?"

"None to speak of, Sir."

"Damn it, Winner! What's going on over there?"

"We traced Miller to Switzerland, to the estate of a woman they call the Black Madonna. There was a bit of a confrontation. Her place was like a fortress and heavily defended. We had to use force. I'm afraid that there isn't much left of her home. You wouldn't believe what we found beneath it, Sir."

"Try me."

"From the outside, her house was modest, a small stone hut. But that was like the tip of an iceberg. Underneath the home was a city. She had a War Room that looked like a NASA control center—massive computer mainframes, dozens of desks with monitors. Unfortunately, much of it was destroyed in the raid. I am certain that Miller gave her information—"

"Was this Madonna plotting against us?"

"Either that or she was an elaborate front for some rogue nation. We can't find her."

"What about Trance?"

"We talked. I'm almost sure he's turned, too," said Hopewell. There was sadness in his voice. Trance had always been like a son to him.

"You met with him? And you didn't take him into custody?"

Hopewell couldn't help but laugh. "It's not like we didn't try. You know Trance. You can't just walk up to the man with an army and say, 'Turn yourself in or we'll shoot.' We did the best we could. But he outmaneuvered us...again."

"I want him," said the President. "And I want Miller. I don't care if you deliver them to me in pieces. You hear me?"

"Yes, Sir. I've got a meeting tonight that may lead me to them," said Hopewell.

The President grunted and asked, "Where?"

"Baron Gustav von Hoffenburg," said Hopewell.

"von Hoffenburg...von Hoffenburg..." said the President. "Didn't Miller mention that name? von Hoffenburg...big international financier, correct? Austrian. I remember...Miller rambled on about von Hoffenburg and Hitler. Some kind of bullshit nonsense."

"von Hoffenburg is into everything, Mr. President. He called me and said he could help. Just how, *I* don't know. But it's worth a try."

"So, you'll meet with him?" repeated the President. "Knowing nothing about him?"

"Oh, we've got information. I've got a file two feet thick on the man." He paused. "He's definitely shady, but nothing else seems to be working. The Baron promised me information on Trance, said he may be able to deliver him to us, for a price, of course."

"Make sure you're well protected."

"He says I must come alone."

"That's risky, Winner. We can't afford to have you kidnapped. You trust him?"

"Heavens no, Mr. President. Who *can* you trust these days? But if we're going to stop this whole damn thing from blowing into World War III, I've got to do all I can. So, if I've got to risk my life to meet with a Baron on his own terms, so be it."

The President sighed. "You've got a free hand, Hopewell. Just get the job done."

"Yes, Mr. President."

"And Winner..."

"Yes?"

"Good luck."

"Thanks. We'll need it."

There was a tentative knock on the door to the room where Lauren and Gretel were being held. A skeleton key turned the creaky lock and a young man, no more than eighteen, came into the room. He had innocent eyes and couldn't have shaved more than once a week. He was the kind of boy that older women loved to cuddle between their breasts.

"You are to come with me," he said softly. He turned and began to walk down a long, dimly lit hallway. They followed him through a seemingly endless series of stairways and hallways until they were ushered into a large, wood-paneled chamber. The room stretched thirty feet into the air. The walls were lined with shelves supporting thousands of leather-bound books. The Baron stood by the far wall warming his hands against a vigorous fire. When the door opened he commanded his three Dobermans to go with the young lad, then turned to the women.

"Ahhh, come in, ladies. So nice to see you again. I trust that your stay with us has been comfortable?"

"Bloody cold if you ask me," said Lauren. The Baron nodded and smiled. He appeared to be in tremendous spirits.

"Yes...yes...even in the summertime it can be cool in the mountains—"

"You have electricity," said Lauren. She glanced at the sophisticated communications console built next to the Baron's desk. "And you've got all the other modern conveniences. Why no central heating?"

"Costs too much."

Lauren glanced at Gretel, then laughed. "You have billions upon billions but you won't heat your house? Instead, you stand and warm your hands against a fire."

A voice came from behind Lauren and Gretel. "He's bored. Warming his hands gives him something to do all day." Breitfuss was being pushed into the room by two surly looking guards. His face was bruised and swollen, and there was a dark gap where he had lost his two front teeth. He smiled, but looked twenty years older. He felt older too; but walked into the room with a forced, jaunty gait. *I'll be damned if I'll let them break me.*

"Hello, Liebchen," he said to Gretel. "Have they been civil to you?"

"Yes, Uncle Fred. We have been treated well."

"And you must be Lauren?" he continued, bowing deeply at the waist. "Jack's father spoke of you often."

Out of the corner of her eye Lauren could see Gretel's eyes narrow. Inwardly, she smiled. "Pleased to meet you, Herr Breitfuss." She replied in hesitant, but passable German.

"Enough!" cried the Baron. "It is time for a toast." He uncorked a bottle of Dom Perignon, while his captives stared. None of them moved.

"You will all soon go free," he continued. "Herr Trance will deliver my formula and you will be allowed to leave." He looked to Breitfuss. "Your family as well."

"Do you expect us to believe that?" said Breitfuss. His eyes had lost the fleeting friendliness they had shone toward Lauren, and they glinted sharply, like a Marine saber. Gretel shivered at the intensity in his face.

"I am a man of honor," said the Baron, with a flippant gesture of his hands.

"I spit on your honor," cried Breitfuss. "All the people that you have brutally murdered over the years—"

The Baron grabbed a cane that was leaning against his desk and held it aloft with a clenched right fist. His lower jaw jutted forward, his bottom teeth pressed against his upper lip. His breathing was irregular and the cane began to flutter in his hand.

"Go ahead," said Breitfuss. "Show us how honorable you are." He took a step forward and offered his cheek.

Slowly the Baron lowered his hand. "If you wish to be ungrateful, that is your right." He rested the cane against the desk and began warming his hands in the fire. After rubbing his fingers together for several moments, he threw two more logs on the flame and turned to face his guests. "Let us be civil to each other. Trance shall be arriving shortly, as will several other important guests. If you do not wish to celebrate, I will not force you."

"Do you have schnapps?" asked Breitfuss. He had made his point. There was no sense in turning down a good drink. One never knew which one might be his last.

"Of course," said the Baron. He opened an expansive teak cabinet, which revealed a well stocked bar including several rare brands of schnapps and kirsch.

"Might as well relax," said Breitfuss. He poured himself half a glass and took a long, hard draught.

CHAPTER 30

▼

The weight of Trance's pack sucked him downward like an ocean riptide. He was falling backwards, and there was no way to fight it. There were no handrails to grab, only air. The wall to his right was smooth. No help there. He peeked behind himself at the stairs. The stairs were barely three feet wide. As they circled upward along the shaft they left a large black hole of empty space in the middle, stretching hundreds of feet down to a bottom of solid rock. Trance envisioned landing on his back, three steps below. A millisecond later the great blades would rip out from the wall and shred him into pieces.

"Shit," he said. Trance took another quick glance behind him and to his left to gauge the curve of the stairs. Perhaps he could jump out over the empty space, then catch them as they curved to his left. He dropped his torch, bent his knees and launched himself into the air. He kicked his feet high above his head and felt himself fly like a gymnast in a full back layout. His feet hit the stairs and his knees buckled. He slapped against the wall, fell over onto his back and began bouncing down the stairs. The back of his head thumped into the wood and nearly jarred him senseless. He reached his hands behind him and caught the stairs enough to flip onto his stomach. He reached out with his arms and used his chest to stop his fall, thudding to a stop with his feet just above the twelfth deadly stair and the poisoned arrows. He lay there motionless and took deep, measured breaths despite the pain in his ribs. He assessed the damage before he tried to move, going over his body piece by piece until he was sure nothing was broken. Only then did he stand up. He looked downward to the platform below him. He counted the steps and walked down, avoiding step twelve, and sat next to the pile of bones.

"Move over, buddy." Trance removed his pack and sat heavily. "Why didn't you warn me about that stair?" Trance concentrated upon his breathing and let himself fall into meditation. He had little time to spare. But unless he had the right emotional balance he would be useless. Soon he found himself walking along his beach. This time his father didn't join him. Trance could sense a warm, bright light shining above him. But each time he looked up to see it, it remained just out of sight. He walked alone in the void.

As Trance emerged from his relaxed state, he felt as if someone were watching from below. He sat with his eyes closed, held his breath and listened. He heard nothing. But the feeling wouldn't leave him. He shined a light down along the stairwell, looking for something out of the ordinary. He glimpsed a couple of rats on the stairs, their eyes gleaming red in the dark. But there was nothing. He thought briefly of walking back down a hundred flights to the bottom, but looked at his watch. He didn't have the time. He wondered what he would have done if he had felt up to it.

Trance took three minutes and used them to compartmentalize his pain. Each breath felt like fire in his chest. He took hold of the flame, doused it with water, and mentally locked it behind a thick metal door. He then removed the pain in his back, his knees, shoulders and finally his face. Then he envisioned his body healthy and whole.

Trance rose slowly on his stiffened legs and started climbing two steps at a time, increasing his pace as he reached each of the three remaining killer stairs. He jumped two steps beyond each one. This time the steps held.

The stairs came endlessly. Trance ached to stop. His legs felt heavy and hot, and his breathing sounded like a wheezy old locomotive. He envisioned the blood flowing strongly through his legs, and the oxygen filling his lungs to a bright red. Soon he felt more rested and relaxed.

When Trance reached the top of the stairway he stopped to listen for noise. He thought he heard a quiet shuffling below, but he couldn't be sure. He did hear the scratching of rats in the dark recesses of the cavern. What did they live on? he wondered. He shuddered at the thought.

Trance reached into his pack, removed another transmitter and attached it to an iron ring that was hammered into the wall. He looked beyond the ring, down a long tunnel. He switched channels on his receiver until he heard the outside chatter in his earpiece. At least this part was working well. He began walking down the tunnel.

The passageway was over six feet wide and nearly eight feet high, immense considering the circumstances under which it must have been built. *If the South African mine workers only had it so good*, thought Trance. This tunnel to gold was a joy ride in comparison to working the African mines. He remembered the time he had worked undercover in the mines of South Africa. He would never forget the pain he felt in the three-foot-high tombs, breathing heavy rock dust, enduring endless muscle cramps, and sweating non-stop for a few dollars a day.

This tunnel was lined with a wooden frame. Spaced evenly against the wall were thick rough-hewn posts, which ran into broad wooden rafters spanning the ceiling. The floor was flat limestone with little debris. Trance wondered if it had been swept for his arrival.

"I could use a maid this good," he mumbled.

There was an odd, eerie feeling to the passage. The air was thick and moist. It had a musty, earthy smell that clung to the inside of Trance's nasal cavity. He could taste the staleness of the air, and when he swallowed, it felt like he was swallowing a sponge. There was no light at all, no seepage from any outside grayness into the hall, and without artificial light, it would have been totally black. As Trance walked forward, he spaced torches close enough together to give him vision. Two miles later the end of the tunnel began to flicker into view, Trance looked back the way he had come. There wasn't the slightest curve to the walls, an incredible architectural feat, completely unknown to man. The torches stretched endlessly onward like the lights on a runway. The hall danced in the light and smoke, giving it an eerie life of its own. Trance shivered as he took the tunnel into full view, thinking how insignificant he was in relation to the forces of the world.

As Trance approached the end, the ceiling rose in height until it stretched over twenty feet high, stopping in a vast underground cavern. Trance saw the purpose for the added space. There was a metal track in the shape of a crescent cutting across the floor. At the base of the far wall he could see steel rollers on the ground. To the right was a giant, wooden wheel with a complicated set of pulleys and ropes stretching both above and below the floor in long grooves. This was the hidden entrance to the Baron's laboratory. Trance had just one more thing to do.

He walked to the ten-foot wheel and began to turn it clockwise.

"With a fulcrum strong enough, and a lever long enough, a single man could move the world," he whispered.

The wheel resisted at first, fighting against years of sleeping in place. Then, with a sudden jolt, it began to respond willingly, rotating lightly under his touch. A piece of the wall began to move. The stone was over four feet thick, and Trance could only guess at its weight. It must have weighed tons. Trance found another wall behind it. This one was composed of large bricks without mortar. Trance removed them quickly, creating a doorway to yet another sheet of stone. According to his map and instructions, this wall was only two feet of soft limestone.

When all of the bricks were removed, Trance went to the right side of the wall and fingered several thick ropes that appeared to be made of raw silk. The ropes extended up to the ceiling, to another set of pulleys. Attached to the end of the ropes, below the pulleys, hung a twenty-foot battering ram. It was made of hand-cut wood, and charred to steel-hardness by fire.

Trance adjusted the ropes with another pulley mechanism, until the ram hung at chest height, resting against the wall that separated him from the Baron's chambers. He took hold of a rope attached to the back end of the ram and threaded it through a set of round, foot-wide gears, set horizontally into the wall at eye height. Beside the gears was a red metal lever. Trance drew back on the lever. The rope was drawn through the gears and it pulled the battering ram up and away from the wall. Beside the lever was a wound spring, which coiled more tightly as the rope passed through the gears. Attached to it, behind the spring was a metal shaft with a flat top. Trance pulled on the lever, released it, then pulled again until the battering ram had slid more than fifteen feet away from the wall. When it began to groan under the pressure Trance slapped down on the red metal shaft, which released the spring. The gears spread apart and the battering ram swung forward with medieval power. The ram swung swiftly through the wall like a needle piercing thin cotton fabric. Trance lowered the ram's height and repeated the process. He adjusted the ram's level several times until he walked easily into the Baron's laboratory.

He peered into the darkened room, using no light at all. The flickering torches behind him gave life to the chamber. There were many distinctive shapes in the dungeon and each of them seemed to skitter as he watched. Rats. Trance's nerves were on edge, and every moving shadow was a living enemy in his mind. He was schooled to respond instantly to movement, and he had to work against this training to dull his senses and not jump at every shadowed sound. He took several tentative steps into the room and flipped on a small penlight. The rats scattered, and all other movement seemed to fade. He began to relax. He set another communications relay inside the chamber, then continued farther inside.

The laboratory was the size of several high school gymnasiums. Trance's watchful eyes followed the light along the wall, as he walked slowly and quietly on the balls of his feet. The stone floor still crackled under his steps. The air smelled heavily of sulfur. A group of chemical drums sat half-opened in a corner. A massive wooden workbench stretched the length of the wall. It was loaded with all sorts of beakers, scales, and measuring devices, as well as a curious assortment of heavy metal cauldrons and smaller, unusually shaped stone pots. A walk-in oven was built into the far wall. It lay open and in disrepair. All of the items showed signs of non-use. Many were covered with a thick layer of sooty ash and lay in a jumbled pile in the center of the bench.

Trance's eyes stopped when he saw a group of chains set into the wall with thick metal spikes. They were ponderously large and heavily rusted, except for the handclasps, which appeared freshly oiled. Trance grabbed hold of one of the chains and brought the end to his nose. He could smell the oil, and he was sure that the chains had been recently used. *What kind of madman is he?*

Farther on, Trance found a tall, dusty pile of ash sitting in a corner of the chamber. He brushed away some of the soot with the toe of his shoe. Underneath it was a sheath of weathered canvas. He reached down to lift the canvas, and as he bent over he could feel his heart beat in anticipation. This wasn't only the Baron's alchemical chamber—but also a room where the Baron had tortured men for a thousand years. The hairs prickled along his neck.

"Holy shit," he whispered. "There must be tons of this stuff..." Gold. The Baron's private Fort Knox.

CHAPTER 31

▼
____

It was well after ten o'clock and darkness had cloaked the mountains for the night. Trance's men were still securing the castle for his arrival.

"Alpha callin' Beta. Come in Beta," said Spike.

"Beta here," replied Stick Granger.

"So fah all seems cleah, Suh."

"Very good, Alpha," said Stick. "The cargo will be arriving on schedule."

Trance listened to his men inside castle grounds and smiled. This innocuous conversation told him that the explosives had been set. The Black Madonna's men and women had left the C-4 as instructed. His own men had checked it, and set it to inflict optimal damage. The Baron wouldn't know what hit him. He hoped.

Stick was waiting with the Baron's evacuated soldiers. The men were confined to a neutral site, a place chosen by Trance and approved by the Baron. They were housed in a rambling country inn and its adjacent farmhouses in Gmunden, a small town north of Bad Ischl—less than one hundred kilometers from the Baron's fortress. They were on the north side of the Traunsee. The men were milling about on a large veranda on the inn's south side, overlooking the picturesque lake, taking in the magnificent crests of the Erlakogel mountain range. The range made the sensuous form of a sleeping woman as it stretched into the horizon. They were drinking Stiegl beer, munching on an assortment of Austrian foods, and bragging about what they would do with a woman as well shaped as the woman of the ridge.

Stick was standing in a private room staring at the vista, sipping a beer and waiting. He turned to his adjutant and said, "Bring me Wilson."

A few minutes later the Baron's officer arrived. He was muttering to himself and wearing a deep scowl across his face. He did not like having his men held captive, in spite of the Baron's orders and subsequent reassurances. Now some second-rate asshole had called him to his room to chat.

Wilson remembered his last meeting with the Baron and told himself to calm down. "Look at it this way—" he'd been told. "If I meet with Trance, you might still keep your life. I won't need your protection. I'll have plenty of men below me. Now go."

Life-saving or not, Wilson was infuriated at being forced to leave his post. He had a sworn duty to protect the Baron—no matter how much of a shit he was.

When he walked into Stick's room, Wilson was ready for a confrontation. He looked up, startled, and said, "Stick? Stick Granger?"

"Hello, Colonel," said Stick. A sly smile spread across his lips.

"Well, I'll be damned." Wilson held out his hand. "So you hooked up with that incurably idealistic fool, Trance, again. What windmills are you two chasing this time?" He shook his head and chuckled. "Some people never learn..."

"Got to make a living, Colonel. Tell me, how in the hell did you end up working for that piece of crap, von Hoffenburg?"

"Got sick and tired of being poor, Stick. Poor, and under the thumbs of all those lard asses and pencil pushers in Washington…Bad combination, Stick, politicians and the military. von Hoffenburg may be a self-styled dictator, but he's no worse than any others that infest the world. He also pays well. A mil' a year, plus benefits."

"Hold it, Colonel—"

"It's Major now," interrupted Wilson, smiling at the irony of a demotion.

"Let me get this straight. You've been working with the Baron for how long now?"

"Five years...Closer to six, I guess."

"And what do you think about his attempt to control the world?"

Wilson laughed. "von Hoffenburg? Control the world? The guy may have some screws loose, but control the world? Hell, the guy can't control his own mind. All he talks about is some book and some formula. He thinks Trance has it." He sobered. "You know I've been ordered to bring Trance in?"

"Sort of like trying to catch a greased pig, ain't it?" said Stick.

"I'll say."

"So, what's it like running his army?"

"Army? Hell, I only control the Baron's palace guard. He's got half a dozen others like me, and gads of his own children running his little empire."

"There are a lot more troops underneath the castle, I suppose?" said Stick.

Wilson remained silent. So did Stick.

Wilson shifted uncomfortably. "The Baron's a little wacky, Stick. But I've never heard of any plan to rule the world. A man'd have to be off his rocker to attempt something like that. Anyway, what's Trance got to do with all this?"

Each man desperately wanted to know the truth, yet neither wanted to be the first to speak it. Both men urgently wanted to get to the castle as soon as they could.

CHAPTER 32

▼

There was little time for Trance to collect his thoughts. He had planned an hour's rest before all hell broke loose—some time to collect his thoughts and visualize every minute facet of his plan—but he had lost that luxury along the way. Where else had he miscalculated? How many other events would deviate from his plan? Would he be able to react to the unexpected? He was spent. His body was beaten, bruised and broken. His brain vibrated like a loosened car tire, and he fought to stay focused, alert and responsive.

"Now all I need is heartburn and hemorrhoids," he whispered. It could be worse, he thought. It could be snowing.

"All in all...a nice night to save the world."

Trance started up the stairs toward the Baron's study. When he heard muffled voices through the library wall he stopped. Now all he could do was wait.

It began as a soft drone in the distance. One by one each person in the room stopped talking, and soon all ears pitched toward the windows.

"Er kommt—He comes," said the Baron. He began ringing his hands and paced the room with the excitement of a man receiving a huge lottery prize.

Lauren and Gretel looked at each other and then to the floor. Breitfuss edged his way toward the glass sliders by the balcony. No one noticed the heavy doors leading from the central castle to the Baron's chamber as they opened silently. No one watched as two men snuck into the room, then shut the door behind them. Only after one of the men slid a heavy bolt across the doors did all eyes turn to the two men standing side by side. They looked almost like father and son. Each was dressed in a dark blue suit, custom-made on Savile Row. Each wore a freshly starched white shirt, French cuffs and gold cufflinks. The younger man's cufflinks were in the form of a bald eagle flying with the world in its talons. Both men were tall, powerfully built, and smiling.

"Hello Baron," said the man standing to the left. He gave a small bow. He looked at Lauren and Gretel and bowed again. "Ladies," he said, flashing the smile that had endeared him to voters throughout the United States. The man turned toward Breitfuss, "Herr Breitfuss," he said bowing again.

"So it *is* you," said Breitfuss.

"I'm sorry?" the man said. Hopewell looked toward Breitfuss with a blank expression. Then he turned to Lauren. "Lauren, honey, I've come to bring you home." Lauren had met Trance's uncle on many occasions, and was well acquainted with the Senator from her home state. She smiled and nodded toward him. "I'm glad to see you, Senator."

"I have been sent here by the President to mediate a compromise between Baron von Hoffenburg and Jack. Events have gotten entirely out of hand. Christ, this almost escalated into an international disaster." Hopewell turned and gestured to the man standing beside him. "This here is Vladimir Verushkin, of Russia. He and I, along with many others, have been working for the past week to resolve the misunderstanding. The Baron has agreed to allow the formula to be shared by a coalition of nations. You do know about the formula?"

"And why would he do such a thing?" asked Breitfuss as he angled his head toward von Hoffenburg.

The Senator smiled. "Call it a compromise, Herr Breitfuss. The Baron had his formula for a long, long time. Naturally, he wanted to get it back. Unfortunately, he got rather carried away. He has now agreed to share it with the world." Hopewell spread his hands and shrugged. "Of course, it was that, or we would tear this castle and his life to shreds."

"I don't believe you," said Breitfuss, in the accented English he had learned while playing football for the Fighting Irish of Notre Dame

"And I don't blame you. You've been through a difficult time," replied the Senator. He spread out his hands and said, "We've all been through hell."

A Sikorsky helicopter sailed over the lip of the castle wall and descended toward the castle landing pads. Hopewell ushered the ladies to the balcony. "Wave to Jack," he said.

The Baron held his breath as the helicopter sank the last few feet toward the earth. As it hovered just above the ground he spoke into a small handset, "Prepare to advance."

Stick Granger counted the seconds on his watch. At precisely ten thirty he said, "Preparing for touchdown."

He waited in the air until he heard, "Alpha go."

"Gamma go."

"Omega go."

"Epsilon go."

And finally, "Delta go."

"This is it, baby," said Stick. He brought the chopper lightly to the ground. Then he switched off his microphone and spoke to the man beside him, who was preparing to slide into the pilot's cockpit. "You ready?"

"Let's do it."

The lights were off in the compound as Trance had demanded. When Stick emerged from the helicopter he was shrouded by darkness. Stick walked slowly toward Spike and Boomer, who were standing at the open entrance to the castle. The seconds ticked off in each man's head. Five…four...three...two… As Stick took his final step toward the castle doors, the earth began to rumble. The noise grew deafening, as a series of explosions rocked the castle. The west wing of the fortress blew apart and erupted into flames. Giant shafts of fire spurted into the air like solar flares and the castle grounds looked like a volcano ready to erupt.

The explosives Trance had set into the side of the mountain detonated with a ferocious roar. The Baron's chamber shuddered, as the outside doors to the bowels of his fortress were sealed shut.

"You arrogant shit." shouted the Baron from the balcony. He shoved the women back inside, then screamed down to the ground, "You're a dead man, Trance!"

Three cannon shells were lofted from the railroad tracks below. They came whistling into the central hall of the fortress. The Baron watched in horror, mesmerized as pieces of his castle crumbled before him. He spoke again into his handset. "Advance! Advance!"

While the Baron raged, the Russian and the Senator stood passively on the edge of the balcony. Light from the outside fires danced on their faces. The Russian turned slowly, followed by Hopewell, and they walked back inside the study. The Russian stopped beside the Baron's desk and pushed a small white button. Thick steel panels slid out of the walls, surrounded the door and windows, and entombed the study.

"As you see, father, Trance cannot be trusted." The Russian spoke in a calm, quiet voice. "But we knew that—"

"He has my formula!"

"I am afraid you may never see your formula again," continued the Russian. Hopewell walked to the Baron's desk and sat in his chair.

"Advance!" yelled the Baron. He stared at his handheld transmitter as if it were some foreign object.

"They are jamming your signal," said the Russian. "We must wait until reinforcements arrive."

As the Russian spoke, three helicopters came roaring over the roof.

"They come," said the Baron. "You've no chance now, Trance."

Verushkin looked through a peephole in the shield and saw Trance's forces flowing into the courtyard from somewhere *inside* the castle walls. He uttered a stream of obscenities, until another volley of cannon fire landed close to them and drowned out his words.

"More of Trance's men," he said calmly. "They have found some hidden entrance into the castle." Nonchalantly, he lit a cigarette. "Our own men will arrive soon. But by then it may already be too late—"

"Too late for what?" said Trance, as he strode into the room from behind a moving wall.

"You!" screamed the Baron. He grabbed his cane from against his desk and rushed toward Trance, with the cane raised high. As the cane came down like a guillotine, Trance grabbed and twisted it out of the Baron's hand.

Then Trance turned toward the Russian. "I wouldn't do that if I were you."

Verushkin was reaching under his coat for a gun. Trance pressed his Colt against the Russian's temple.

"Take it out slowly," he said. "By the fingertips."

The Russian drew the gun out of his pocket. Trance took it and set it upon the desk. He laid his own beside it, while keeping his eyes trained on all three men.

"Over there." Trance gestured for Verushkin to move to the far wall. He bound his hands and sat him down. "Sorry for the indignity," he said.

Trance turned his gaze toward Hopewell.

"Thank God you're here," said the senator. He began to walk toward his nephew, but stopped abruptly as Trance shook his head and glared at him.

"Cut the crap, Hopewell."

"All I know is that—"

"I want answers," said Trance. He looked from Hopewell to the Baron.

"Your mother was my daughter," said the Baron in a clear, steady voice. "I sent her to seduce your father and marry him. You are *my* grandson."

The Baron pointed to a thick binder resting on his desk. It was held together with foot-long Chicago screws. "It's in there, the whole family tree. It was I who placed her near your father—to keep me close to the formula."

"No," said Trance. His voice was barely a whisper. "This can't be true—" But he knew it was. This explained why his mother had drawn away from him, and from his father.

"That's not true," said Hopewell. "The man is mad. Can't you see that? He'll do anything to get that formula. You do realize that he was trying to start a world war?"

"And you aren't?" said Trance. There was another explosion deep below the Baron's chamber. It was followed by a barrage of automatic fire aimed from somewhere across the courtyard. Trance heard the screaming of a Lockheed AC-130 Spectre rake across the grounds. Then another.

"They come! They come!" said the Baron.

Trance reached into his shirt and withdrew a thin, age-worn book. The formula. "This was better off hidden," he said.

"It can be yours," said the Baron. "Join us. The world can be yours, too. You can be the Chosen One."

"The world belongs to no one, and no one shall be chosen above all others." Trance tossed the formula onto the desk, between the guns and the three-ring binder. Then he began to walk in a small circle with his hands clasped behind his back.

"I need answers," he continued. Out of the corner of his eye he saw Hopewell glance at his watch.

"What time is it, Senator?"

"Ten fifty," said Hopewell, still sitting behind the Baron's desk.

Trance continued to pace. He had yet to look at the women. They sat with their eyes fixed on his movements. When he did look toward them there were tears in his eyes.

"I am so sorry this happened," he said. "You two all right?"

Both women muttered that they were okay. Trance winked at Breitfuss, who was sitting behind the girls, then walked slowly toward them all. What should he do next? Seeing the two of them together, he realized he loved them both. Lauren had always been his friend, his closest buddy. She had been there when he needed her, always with the full force of her being, never demanding, never asking. She was there when he wanted to share a joke, or rue the latest trials of the Red Sox. She was... *Was she his soul mate?* Then there was Gretel. She fit his life like a glove, almost perfectly. *Too perfectly?* he wondered.

Gretel was closest to him and she embraced him first. He hugged her and closed his eyes. How did this get so complicated? When Trance opened his eyes he saw Hopewell standing behind the Baron's desk, with the gun in his hands. Trance sighed. Hopewell had taken the bait.

"The party's over, Trance," he said. "This is your last hurrah." Hopewell sneered. "You know, I never did like you. Always filled with self-righteousness, as if you were better than us all." Hopewell began to walk toward him. "And now I will finally get the chance to kill you. And to think...after my entire family died in that *tragic* boating accident last year, I named you as my sole heir." Hopewell laughed. "You gave away your parents billions. But you're not going to get the chance to give away mine—"

"So it is you," said Trance softly. He slowly shook his head. "But you can't kill me, Winner." As Trance spoke, he slipped a knife from a pocket in his sleeve into the palm of his hand. It had a long, thin blade with a round finger-loop ring on the end.

The machine gun fire outside grew perceptively louder. Rocket propelled grenades shredded the night.

"You've already lost, Trance." Hopewell looked at his watch. "In fifteen minutes New Orleans will be nothing but a memory."

The blood drained from Trance's face. Hopewell had been his mentor. He had loved the senator like his own father.

"Why? You of all people, Winner. Why? You love our country. What about the country?"

"The only thing worth having, Jack, is power. Without it a man is nothing."

Trance slipped the knife into throwing position. *Don't make me do this, uncle—* But before Trance could act, a spitting sound came from behind Hopewell. The Senator's eyes grew wide and a mixture of spit and blood began to drool from his mouth. Hopewell turned in slow motion to face the shooter.

"Miller," he gasped.

Jacob Miller had followed Trance through the tunnels. He now stood in the dungeon doorway with a pistol resting at his side.

Hopewell began to slump forward. With one last effort he lifted his arm enough to aim and fire. His shot caught Miller in the chest and flung him backward onto the stairs behind the opened wall.

Hopewell thudded to the floor.

Trance reached down to his uncle and checked his pulse. "He's dead."

Trance walked over to Miller. Miller was breathing, but with a labored hiss. Trance knelt beside him.

"I...I knew it was him," whispered Miller. "I...should have told you...I...the Madonna—"

"It's all right," said Trance. He cradled Miller in his arms. "You'll be okay."

"I'm sorry about Janice," said Miller. "I didn't know they were terrorists. Hopewell asked me...I regretted it the minute it happened....God I'm sorry...Ja—"

"Lie down," interrupted Trance. "You *will* be all right."

Trance stood up and turned towards Gretel. She reached for Hopewell's gun, raised it and pointed it at Trance's face.

"I must have the formula, Jack," she said. "Please give it to me."

"Is this Cinderella's ugly sister?" said Trance.

"I'm sorry, Jack," she said. Tears were forming in her eyes. "I'm sorry. I didn't know that I would love you."

Trance reached to the Baron's desk and fingered the formula with his left hand. He thought about the knife resting against his right palm. He could flick it into Gretel's forehead before she moved a muscle. He could end her life in an instant. But he couldn't. He pinched the formula loosely by the corner and took a step toward Gretel.

"Toss it here," she said.

"Gretel?"

"Jack, don't say anything. Just do what I say."

Trance tossed the formula to Gretel's feet. He caught Lauren's eyes, as she stood behind Gretel. Tears glistened her face. Her lips were trembling and her eyes seemed to offer comfort. Breitfuss sat behind her, next to the fire, with a calm expression on his face. He had decided that his life was in the hands of some other power. This was nothing he could control, so he had decided to let go and let it happen as it would.

Gretel grasped the formula with her free hand and took several steps backwards toward Breitfuss, with the gun still trained on Trance. Trance followed her.

"Stop. I'll shoot," she said.

"I can't stop, Gretel. You must know that. You will have to shoot me." Trance continued walking—his eyes fixed upon hers. Gretel held her breath, pursed her lips and fought to squeeze the trigger.

There was a spit from behind Trance. Gretel's chest seemed to cave and her blouse splotched with blood. She grimaced, staggered briefly, and wilted to the floor. Trance stood motionless. For a moment he was too shocked to move. He drifted around, and saw Miller leaning on one arm, his silenced gun hanging limp at his side.

"Oh, you stupid shit," said Trance. He knelt and pressed his lips against Gretel's cheek. He felt for her pulse. It was beating weakly. She looked at him and smiled. There was anguish in her eyes.

"The...ugly...sister...I...didn't...I...love you." Her eyes closed. After one weak sob her breathing ceased.

Trance pressed his fingers against her neck. He laid her flat on the floor and lifted his fist to thump her on the chest; CPR was his only hope. Then he saw the blood. Miller had shot her through the heart and there *was* no saving her.

"Oh God...Oh God." Trance reached around her dead body. "Gretel...Gretel...Oh Gretel...How could this happen? How could they do this to us?" His tears plunked against her chest, entwined with her blood and trickled to the floor.

The Baron stood motionless behind Trance, with Miller only a few feet away. Miller was wheezing, now only half conscious. In front of him the Russian sat passively, still bound on the floor.

Outside the Baron's chamber the din of fighting continued. Helicopters whupped in the distance, mingling with the swearing and screaming of the soldiers below. There was a loud explosion, and the sound of a plane screaming as it fell from the sky. The sounds of war. Death soup.

Trance pried the formula from Gretel's death-tightened fingers and walked toward the fire.

"The world doesn't need this," he said.

"No!" cried the Baron. With almost supernatural speed the Baron pounced on Miller and wrenched the gun from his hands. Trance turned to face him, stopping one step from the fireplace. He looked on calmly as the Baron squeezed the trigger of the gun. As the shot rang out, Trance swerved to his left. The bullet passed inches from his face. He turned his back to the Baron and tossed the formula into the fire. With the same motion he whipped the knife from under his shirt, turned, and launched it. The blade sunk to the hilt between the Baron's eyes. His eyes crossed, stretching to see the handle protruding from his forehead. He tried to speak. His lips opened and closed like a fish. But there were no words. He reached under his robe and ripped off a gold chain. On the end were two glass amulets filled with a bluish liquid. The Baron tried to break one apart but failed. He took one step backward and fell to the floor. Time had passed the Baron by, and nothing could save him now.

Trance just stood there. He wanted to crawl into a ball and sleep. But he focused on the Russian, who sat smiling, his hands clasped behind his back.

"You're too late," said Verushkin. "Even you can't stop them now. Within minutes your leaders, and mine, will decide that mutual destruction is a better option than self-annihilation. Too bad we don't have the formula. The Elixir was supposed to protect us from the radiation." He motioned with his head toward the two amulets lying beside the Baron. "Not even those could save my father today."

"You're all mad," said Trance. He lifted the Baron's Elixir necklace off the floor and tossed it into the fire. When it hit the flames, it exploded into a heavenly glow, like a mini big bang. Then everything became quiet.

The Russian laughed. "Herr Trance, I've heard the admonitions before, the arguments of innocence. But power is a strange thing. Your former Secretary of State, Henry Kissinger, once called it the 'ultimate aphrodisiac'. I suspect even you would not refuse the chance, if you thought it through. I could not…although I must admit that parts of me tried to fight it, early on."

"And now you have nothing," said Trance. "Can you still sit back and let it happen? Do you want your contribution to the world to be its total destruction?"

"There is nothing I can do," said the Russian. His voice carried a melancholy sadness. Even his sweet St. Petersburg would soon be a memory.

"The hell there isn't," said Trance. He pulled the Russian to his feet and cut the plastic tie binding his hands. "You're at least going to try."

"And if I refuse?" asked the Russian.

Trance grabbed his Colt and shoved it into the Russian's mouth. "Choose," he said. The Russian nodded.

Trance walked to the phone, put it on speaker and dialed the President's private number. Exactly where it was routed he would never know. But soon the President answered.

"Mr. President. This is Trance."

"What the—"

"Stop, Sir. Senator Hopewell is dead. He was part of a plot to start a world war."

"It's already started, Trance. We just took out a missile off the coast of New Orleans. Twenty megatons…hundreds dead, thousands injured—lucky we got it in time. It was a clean bomb, though, neutron…Who the hell else has neutron bombs? Even we're not supposed to have them. Murmansk is in flames. They were not so fortunate—" Trance could hear men arguing in the background.

"We can still stop it. It's not what you think. Hold where you are, Mr. President. I'm going to get the Russian President on the line—"

"Trance, I'm in a meeting. I can't just—"

"Hold it, asshole! This is your only chance."

Trance put the President on hold. He punched another button on the Baron's phone and thrust it into Verushkin's hand.

"Dial."

Verushkin stared at Trance, then whispered, "My brother betrayed me. That shouldn't have been a clean bomb in New Orleans. It was supposed to be like the one I launched on my own people. We each had to choose who to kill first…I have ruined part of my homeland for twenty generations. What were we thinking?"

"It will soon be the world if you don't help."

A moment later Verushkin had the irate Russian leader screaming into the phone. The Baron's son interrupted him.

"New York *and* Moscow will be gone in exactly six minutes unless you do what I say…"

The Russian outlined the Baron's plans, and what must be done to stop them. The Russian President gave him the six minutes to work it out. Verushkin called the Baron's central command. "This is Vladimir Verushkin. The Baron is dead. Operation Armageddon is canceled. Abort all missions." He repeated the words in three other languages.

Verushkin walked to the Baron's computer and sent an encrypted message via the web and satellite.

The Russian sighed. He had stopped the Baron's missiles from being launched. The dozens of warheads already sitting in America would not be detonated. He just hoped that Trance could do the same.

Trance got the President back on the line. The President said, "I just spoke to the Russian President. He has agreed to stand down if we do. The Chinese are in the loop, too."

Trance nodded and closed his eyes. "Very good, Sir. I need you to keep the locals away from the Baron's castle until I'm done. Our own forces, too."

"I just can't—"

"Do it. Believe me, Mr. President. It is better this way."

"All right." The President paused, then said, "And Trance—"

"Yes, Mr. President?"

"I'm going to forget that you called me an asshole."

"Thank you, Sir. Just needed to get your attention."

"Good job, I think." He paused. "Keep me informed."

"Will do."

Trance turned to Verushkin. "I would thank you, but..." His voice trailed off. There was no thanking a man that had nearly brought about the destruction of the world.

"You know what they will do to me, don't you?" asked the Russian.

"It won't be enough," said Trance. But something nagged inside him. Perhaps this man, too, had been swept into a world that he could not control. He fingered his pistol. He pulled out the clip and flipped out all bullets but one, chambered it and handed it to the Russian.

"Choose your honor," he said.

The Russian took the gun and held it loosely. He pointed it at Trance and smiled. Trance didn't flinch.

"You are a strange man, Herr Trance. You know that I can undo all you have just done to stop the war." The Russian sighed. "But, I won't." He saluted Trance, turned the pistol to his head and fired.

Trance's shoulders slumped. It was over.

"Looks like you did it," said Breitfuss.

"Yeah," muttered Trance. He ran his fingers through his hair, then pulled at it in frustration. He exhaled completely, a final tired gesture, and sat on the floor next to Gretel's body. He looked slowly around the room, from Verushkin to Hopewell, and to the Baron who was lying with his face in a small pool of blood. Finally he looked at Miller. Miller was unconscious, but still breathing. *Should I put him out of his misery?* wondered Trance. *Oh, how I'd love to. He's killed my wife, my future wife and my mentor.*

Trance bit his lower lip and fought off the nausea. He wrapped his head with his hands.

"It was all so pointless..." He closed his eyes and began to rock. Tears seeped from under his lids and mixed with the blood on his hands.

Outside the Baron's study the fighting had nearly stopped. Trance was oblivious to that world. What did he have left? What did it matter now what happened? Except for Lauren. He raised his head and saw her standing before him.

"Hey, big guy. It's good to see you." She sat down beside him, reached out, and took his head in her arms.

"I'm so sorry," she said. Her lips still quivered and her hands were shaking. Trance leaned against her and she cradled his head against her chest.

"It's all right," she said. "It's all right."

Trance steadied himself and looked into Lauren's eyes. "Had enough spy shit?" Each of them managed a smile.

"Yeah," she said. "How 'bout you?"

"Yeah."

They rose together and walked to Breitfuss.

"Nice mug," said Breitfuss as he looked at Trance's bruised and bloody face. He smiled, showing his two broken teeth.

"You're not so pretty yourself," said Trance.

"What happens now?"

"We'll round up the Baron's army and shut it down," said Trance. "We'll retrieve all the nukes, and any other WMDs. I think I'll let fate do the rest." He ambled to the Baron's desk and pressed the white button to open the shields. Then he limped to the door and pushed it open. There was a man standing before it.

"Hello, Jack."

"Hello, Swartz," said Trance to the Israeli commander. "Thanks for your help." The hallway was filled with soldiers, all of them pointing their weapons at Trance's chest. "Now, please get out of my way."

Swartz didn't move. "Where's Rebecca?" he said.

"Was that her name? Rebecca?"

Swartz nodded.

"Dead."

"Miller?"

Trance shrugged. "Don't really care."

"Give me the formula, Jack."

"I burned it," whispered Trance. "They were both your agents, weren't they?"

"Rebecca helped with the cause."

"And Miller?"

"He knew the Madonna, but he wasn't ours. He was on your side, all the way."

"And you? Do you know the Madonna?" said Trance.

"Yes."

"Did you follow my men through the tunnel they took into the castle?"

"Yes."

"While Miller followed me?"

"We think the Madonna told him."

Trance nodded. That made sense. Miller's father had been there with *his* father at the beginning. He walked to the Baron's desk and lifted the heavy binder. He motioned with it toward Swartz. "This is the Baron's family tree. Did you know I was in here?"

"Of course."

"Your men knew, too? Is that why they hated me?"

Swartz nodded.

Trance shook his head. He stared for a long time at Swartz and then said, "Well, I didn't know." He placed the book in Swartz's hands. "I want you to take this and do the right thing. Leave my immediate family out, if you will. Leave Gretel…Rebecca…out too. Now get out of my way." Trance pushed past Swartz and headed for the door.

"I can't let you live, Jack. Not after what you've done, what you know." Swartz raised his pistol.

Trance looked into Swartz's solemn eyes and walked back toward the gun. He continued until it was pressed tightly against his stomach. He stood there for several seconds, the gun resting against his hardened flesh, and then turned and began shuffling down the hall past the soldiers. Swartz watched him go.

Breitfuss rose to follow Trance. "Miller killed Hopewell, and Hopewell shot back," he said.

"And Rebecca?"

"You mean Gretel? Miller shot her, too."

"I don't understand," said Swartz.

"No. I don't suppose you would," said Breitfuss. "I suppose none of us will ever understand. Miller thought she was going to take it. But she was going to throw the formula into the fire. She chose Trance above your cause."

"She wouldn't do that. Her mission was to—"

"I said what I saw," interrupted Breitfuss. He turned to leave.

Lauren crouched down beside Miller and looked toward the Israeli general.

"Mr. Swartz, do you have a medic with your team? Jacob Miller is still alive here and he needs attention."

The castle grounds were leveled. Twenty feet from the Baron's study the hallway opened to the sky. The rest of the structure was rubble. In the courtyard Trance could see twenty, perhaps twenty-five of his men being held at gunpoint by an Israeli guard detachment. Their guns were stacked in a pile beside the remnants of the wall. The rest were likely dead.

"Where's Stick?" said Trance to one of his men.

"He's dead, sir."

"I said 'where is he'?" repeated Trance.

The man pointed to a pile of broken rock. Dozens of bodies were strewn among the castle remains, looking like dead fish washed up on a beach. "Under there is an opening to the caverns below. The men kept coming through it, wave after wave. There were too many to take prisoner...So we mowed them down as they tried to escape. There was a fire below, and smoke kept billowing out. The men couldn't see, with all the smoke in their eyes, and we picked them off like cherries." The man threw up on his shoes.

Trance patted him on the shoulder. "I know it's hard, but it's war, son. You helped save millions today. Where's Stick?"

"When they stopped coming, Stick and that major went in."

"The Baron's major? Wilson?"

"Yeah. They went down to look around, wearing masks. Never came out. The explosions came, and you see what's left."

"You mean to tell me that Stick Granger is under there?" said Trance.

"What's left of him, I suppose."

"We leave no men behind. Start digging soldier!" screamed Trance. He glared at the Israeli guards. "My men are going to dig."

The Israeli commandos didn't move. They had Trance covered. One word from Swartz and they could slice him in two. Trance began to pull at the stones, just as Swartz emerged from what was left of the hallway. Swartz cradled the remains of the formula—just a small charred corner. He and Trance locked eyes. Then Trance returned to his digging.

Swartz bent down to help him. "Let's go, men," he said.

They all began to dig.

The jagged stone and metal debris gave way to what was left of a stairway leading below the castle. Smoke swirled out of the opening. It had an acrid electrical smell, from the burning of the computers, melted weapons and charred bodies. Swartz thrust a gas mask into Trance's hands and together they descended the stairs.

Trance knew that many men loyal to the Black Madonna had infiltrated the Baron's army. He knew that while Spike and Boomer were wiring explosives above ground, the Madonna's soldiers had been busy doing the same underground.

Trance and Swartz walked through the smoke until they found another stairway leading deeper into the mountain. They passed through several doors and stopped at one that looked like the entrance to a vault.

"This opens to a tunnel that runs under the fallout shield," said Trance as he removed the mask from his face. "Beneath the shield there is another command center...food for thousands...and a nuclear power system."

There was a set of ten buttons on the outside of the door. Trance punched in a series of numbers, supplied to him by the Madonna, and the door swung open. He and Swartz walked through a narrow hall that ended with another thick door. There was a camera above the door looking down on them and following them as they moved. Trance looked up and waved. Several moments later the door opened.

"Hello, Jack," said Wilson.

"Hello, Colonel. The Baron's dead."

"Figured."

"Where's Stick?"

There was a loud voice from deep inside the shelter. "Over here you son-of-a-bitch. You know you almost got me killed?"

Trance chuckled softly. "Good to see you, too."

The grin dripped off Stick's face. "Are you all right, JT?"

"Yeah," said Trance. "It was Hopewell."

"I'm not surprised."

"Gretel's dead."

"Oh, man. I'm so sorry Jack."

"Yeah."

"And Lauren? Breitfuss?"

"They're fine," said Trance softly. "Considering."

"I've got seven hundred men in here, and twenty thousand further below," said Wilson. "What do you want me to do with them?"

"Move them out," said Trance. "Tell them all to go home. We'll start lifting in twenty minutes."

"And me?" asked Wilson. Trance looked at Stick. Stick nodded.

"You're free to go, Colonel. Choose a better employer next time." Trance turned to Stick. "We've got a ton of weapons we don't need. See if you can cut a deal with Swartz, here." Trance nodded toward the Israeli. "Call in the transports. Start giving the money to the men...and their widows. Tell them I will thank each one of them personally when I can. Then meet me in the Baron's chamber in an hour." Trance began to walk out of the room, then stopped and turned toward Swartz. "I know you are disappointed at not getting the formula. But it had to be destroyed."

"I know," said Swartz.

Trance looked at him, with a question creasing across his brow.

Swartz said, "Like you, I do as I am ordered. But I can think for myself."

The two men regarded each other, then shook hands.

"Thanks again for your help," said Trance.

"Don't mention it."

"I won't." Trance paused. "You know that binder I gave you? It should lead you to billions. Perhaps that might take away some of the sting."

Swartz managed a thin smile. "Perhaps."

Later, when Stick walked into the Baron's study, Trance was nowhere in sight. The bodies had been removed and the blood was already cleaned from the floor. Everything was in neat order, a stark contrast to the chaos of the rest of the castle.

"Trance!" shouted Stick.

Trance came up the stairs from the dungeon.

"You don't need to yell," he said.

"Where the hell were you?"

Trance angled his head. "Follow me." He led Stick down the long flights of stairs.

"My dogs are tired. Isn't there an elevator?"

"A freight elevator," said Trance. "We'll be using it soon." They continued down until they reached the cavernous opening.

"Ah, the secret laboratory," said Stick. He walked beyond the work table to where Lauren was standing beside tall rows of stacked gold bars.

"Hey, Stick," she said.

"Hello, sweetheart. It's been a long time." Stick gave Lauren a hug and kissed her on the cheek. "So great to have you here," he whispered. Stick's eyes shifted to the piles of gold and he let out a soft whistle.

"Is that what I think it is?"

Lauren and Trance nodded.

"Jesus. Must be fifty tons of that stuff. What are you going to do with it?"

"Haven't decided, Stick. What do you think?"

"If it were me, I'd call it the `spoils o' war'."

"After you sell off the gear, I'm going to repay myself what I spent personally. I'm giving two million dollars to the families of each of our men and women who died or were seriously injured. I'll set up an educational trust for all of their children, and their children's' children. I'll also pay the medical care for any injured. Then I'll replenish the freedom fund with what's left." Trance paused, "I think I'll work with Swartz to start a foundation in Gretel's name." He paused, then said coyly, "But I thought that I'd give a quarter of it to you first."

Stick pursed his lips and thought for several moments. Then he shook his head.

"Nah. It would make life far too complicated. Just add my share to the fund." Stick's face brightened. "I won't need much on my little island."

"I'll do that." Trance bit his lip. "I am going to buy you a new plane, though. That patched up piece of shit you fly is a menace to the airways."

"No, JT."

Trance smiled and Lauren touched him gently on the shoulder.

Stick smiled. This was an argument he couldn't win. "Well. if you must. What next?"

"We've shut down the reactor. We're setting explosives in the catacombs. The B-29 is fueled and ready with some MOABS. They're setting charges below. When we're through, there will be no sign this castle ever existed."

"The authorities will allow this?"

Trance shrugged. "Don't care. This place is a global tinderbox. The less that survives, the better off we'll all be."

"And Swartz?"

"We've come to an understanding."

"He thinks the formula is lost forever?"

"Yeah. The Creator says that I am its keeper."

"And our Japanese Samurai?"

Trance closed his eyes. "I don't know, Stick. He wants so desperately to fly something into the mountain. To him it's a matter of honor. He's an old man who is ready to die. Nothing will ensure his place in heaven more than dying in battle."

"But the battle is over."

"Is it? He is Japanese. I cannot make you understand the importance of symbolism to his culture. He stood ready and willing to sacrifice himself for our cause. What difference does a few minutes make? And who can say that his sacrifice is not still needed? Is the battle *really* over? His death will be an honorable one."

"You'll let him die?"

"Am I my brother's keeper?"

"Yeah."

Trance chuckled. "It's out of my hands. Everything is in the hands of the Creator."

Stick began to walk away, muttering, "I'll never understand this Creator crap… I'll get some men to load this stuff."

"Good," said Trance. He took Lauren's hand and walked toward the stairs.

A loud, booming voice roared behind them. "Wait!"

Trance turned and saw a giant man stepping around the battering ram, and emerging from the opening to the tunnel Trance had used to enter the castle. Even in the shadows Trance could see the distinct crater between his eyes. Four men followed behind him. They had two thick wooden poles slung horizontally between their shoulders. Upon the poles sat a royal chair carrying the Black Madonna. She looked tired and weak, except for her eyes, which were bright with fire. The two men walked toward Trance and stopped when the Madonna was beside him.

"Hello," said Trance.

"Hello," said the Madonna.

"I'm sorry about your father."

"He had to die."

"Yes."

"Thank you. Now I can let go."

"You don't need—"

She held up her hand. "I didn't say I would. But now there is something I must tell you."

Not again, thought Trance. He waited for the Madonna to speak.

"The rumors you've heard are only partially correct, but you should know the truth." She paused. "I was born in the year 2466. My mother was half black, as you must have guessed. She was a tenured professor of theology at what we now know as Harvard University. You've met my father. They were quite happily married once."

"You're from the future?"

The Madonna nodded. "And the past."

"Are there more of you? From the future?"

The Madonna shook her head. "No, I don't think so. You'll know why in a moment."

The Madonna paused to collect her thoughts. "My father's name was Joseph Kelly. I'm Mary, as was my mother. My father was a world-renowned physicist, and pioneered several radical departures in scientific theory. His specialty was in a field spawned by today's quantum physics. His passion was time travel. He spent every waking hour trying to perfect it.

"My father proved that time is not always linear, something only theorized today. He showed that time can be shaped, like a river, a river that meanders across the countryside—sometimes even doubling back on itself. He also proved that our universe coexists with others in a multiverse. But that's not relevant here.

"In this century, many of the world's accomplished scientists argue the theory of time travel. Many well-respected men believe it is possible. In later centuries, we learned it was possible on a *macro* level. The debate became how *far* we could travel.

"Points in time can be transversed in more than one way. One method involves high-speed travel. With this we change time in microseconds. My father found a different way to blast through time—without moving an inch."

The Madonna reached beside her and grasped a water bottle that held a bluish liquid. She put the bottle to her lips and drank deeply. In seconds, she seemed measurably younger. She put the water bottle down gently and continued.

"My father began constructing time portholes when I was a girl. At first he could only travel back to the construction time of each porthole, like everyone else. Then my father had a vision. A vision from God. It showed him how to harness antimatter, the unseen twin forces to everything we see. It led him to discover the Elixir. Yes, somewhere along the time-matter, space-time continuum he found what tens of thousands before him could not—the Philosopher's Stone, the Elixir of Life. The Elixir suspends, even reverses time within the body. It helps us travel through time. It also brings metals to the elemental state of perfection—gold."

The Madonna paused. She peered into Trance's eyes with a concentrated stare. She closed her eyes, debating inwardly about how much to tell. "Are you familiar with the Higgs boson?"

"The God particle?"

"All elementary particles weigh nothing until they interact with the Higgs boson. Without it, we are nothing. Like God, you see. My father's vision showed him something similar, and a way to harness the Universe's most essential forces and bend them to his will. He found The Philosopher's Stone." The Madonna held up a vial of her shimmering blue liquid. "My father kept this secret from the masses, even from me. But he started selling the Elixir to the chosen ones, the ones who had the resources and didn't want to be half machine. He used this money to quietly further his research." The Madonna paused. "Then the asteroid came."

"The asteroid?"

"The end of life as we know it."

Was this God's wrath? Or was it a simple freak chance of nature? wondered Trance. *Were man and science acting too much like God?* "An asteroid big enough to—"

"Oh, yes. In my time, man no longer exists. Unless you change that." She paused to allow the enormity of her statement to sink in. "Quite simply, man ran out of time. When the asteroid was discovered, my father compiled a consortium of scientists to build a machine that would skip over a nearby portal, much like a skipping stone. The goal was to land somewhere farther back in time, far enough back to warn mankind before it was too late. I was a member of that team." She laughed. "You see, my father's first goal was a noble one. He wanted to save mankind, not rule it."

Trance's eyes narrowed. *Is man getting a do-over, a second chance to get it right?*

The Madonna smiled. "We were within months of perfecting the process when it was over. We simply ran out of time. Just days before final impact my father and I launched ourselves into the past, not knowing *when* we would land. My mother refused to come with us, choosing to accept what she said was God's will. My father and I thought it was God's will for us to warn mankind, and help prepare an expedition to the asteroid. Given time we could change its course, the course of man, or change the path of the asteroid before it could destroy the earth." The Madonna paused and took a drink of her blue Elixir. "Unfortunately we emerged in a time so technologically vacant that we had to wait hundreds of years before we could act."

"Maybe that was God's doing, said Trance."

The Madonna shrugged her bony shoulders and smiled. "That will become the great debate in the next century—how much man should play God. But that is a discussion for another day, Jack Trance.

"When we landed, we had enough Elixir to live a very long time—but not long enough. Father had to find a way to make it without modern machines and massive energy sources. It took him hundreds of years, but he succeeded. Right here. He kept his secret in one place only—a notebook he carried with him at all times.

"Father got bored and grew drunk with power. He lost all sight of our mission. There was nothing I could do to stop him. He started making gold and building armies. Over the centuries his megalomania grew, until it consumed him. He lost sight of his purpose, his role in the world. Saving mankind took a back seat to ruling mankind.

"When *your* father obtained the formula, *my* father was financing his son, Adolph. They probably would have won World War II, were it not for your father."

The Madonna laughed. "The Baron had forgotten how to make the Elixir. It was like part of his mind had been erased...by time. And when your father took the formula my father stopped making gold for the Nazi's and hoarded what Elixir was left. His supply grew low and he began to age. So did I. We conserved what little we had left. This was his last stand." The Madonna sighed, "Now it is time for you to fulfill your role."

"How do we know our true role?" said Trance.

The Madonna smiled. "I know yours." She motioned for Trance to come closer. She lifted a gold chain from her neck and placed it over Trance's head. At the end of the chain were two glass vials, filled with bluish liquid.

"You must keep these amulets close to you at all times. You will need them." She peered deeply into Trance's eyes, as if seeing into his soul and measuring the extent of his belief, commitment and abilities. "I brought history books with me from my time, Jack Trance. During the past day these books have changed. You see, like it or not, you, your sons, and their daughters will do great things."

"I have no family and I will not accept this burden."

"You cannot refuse it," said the Madonna quietly. "What must be, will be. This is your destiny. This is what God wants. Someday you will understand."

"How do you know what God wants?"

"Have faith, Jack. I know."

The Madonna brushed Trance away and motioned Lauren to step forward. She drew Lauren to her closely and whispered, "Be patient, dear. He'll come around. You two will be very happy, with a large family. I have seen it." She patted Lauren on the cheek, and then motioned with a flick of her wrist for her men to take her back into the mountain tunnel.

"Goodbye, Jack Trance. Godspeed and good luck."

"Wait!" called Trance as she began to leave the room. "Are you…Just how far back in time did you go?"

The Madonna's eyes twinkled. "Far enough."

"Did you have a child? Are you—"

The Black Madonna smiled and pressed her hand against Trance's mouth. Her touch was electric and warmth surged through his veins.

"Does it really matter?" she said. She turned away. "Goodbye, Jack Trance. I will send you what you'll need to know. We will meet again." Then she was gone.

EPILOGUE

As Trance and Lauren walked through the front door of the Dolder Grand Hotel, Carl Sauerbrunn came hobbling toward them from behind the desk.

"Jack!" he cried. "I thought you were dead."

"Me? Just took a little vacation, that's all. You don't look so good."

"Nor do you, my friend." Carl laughed, then leaned toward Trance's ear and whispered, "I didn't tell them, you know."

"I know." Trance motioned toward Lauren. "I'd like to introduce you to my closest friend. Lauren Haverford, this is Carl Sauerbrunn. Carl...Lauren."

Lauren stepped forward and grinned as Carl planted a noisy kiss on each cheek.

"How lovely, you are," he said.

"You look far more handsome than Jack described you," said Lauren with a broad smile. Then she kissed Carl in the same manner.

"And you, my dear, are one very gracious lady." Carl gave a full bow and kissed Lauren once more on the hand.

"Got any rooms?" asked Trance.

"But, of course. You will have the best room in the hotel." He paused. "We have no royalty visiting at the moment. You and this beauty will enjoy the view." Then he said with a conspiratorial whisper, "I will charge you the normal room rate."

Trance laughed. They went through this every time

"Can you join us for a cocktail?" asked Lauren.

"I am off the desk in thirty minutes. May I join you then?"

"Come to the room, will you?" said Trance. "I won't be needing any clothes this time, but bring a couple bottles of champagne."

"With pleasure!"

When Trance and Lauren reached their room Trance made a phone call, to a private number in the United States. It rang only twice, although it was well after midnight in Washington.

"What," came a voice.

"Mr. President...This is Trance."

"Ah...Trance."

"Are things getting back to normal?"

"Slowly. Two million dead worldwide. Few were Americans, thank God. It will take the world years to recover fully. But things are under control—thanks to you."

"I don't want to take much of your time, Mr. President, but I need a favor."

"What is it now?"

"Lauren Haverford, the executive vice president of Global Credit Bank is going to be spending the next month or two with me. We are going to do a little traveling, clear our heads. Would you call the bank chairman and explain that she is working on some vital government business related to the incident?"

The President chuckled. Trance was always bending the rules. "Sure, Trance. Anything else?"

"Have a good night sleep, Mr. President."

"You, too… Oh, I almost forgot. Do you want some kind of medal for this?"

"Nah. I've got my share. There are a few others who deserve them, though. Some are here in Europe. Others are in the U.S. Would it be okay if I emailed you a list?"

"Please do."

"Thanks."

"Thanks to you."

Trance hung up the phone and held out his hands. "And you were worried?"

"You are something, Jack Trance...You know I love you."

Trance's eyes clouded. He couldn't escape the truth. When he loved women, they died. As much as he might want to, he could never freely love again.

"It is all right to hurt, Jackie. You can hurt all you want. I will be anything you want me to be...anything you need me to be. I'll be here...I'll always be here."

Trance brightened. "And you, Lauren Haverford, are a treasure like no other. Let's just try to have fun. Can we do that?"

"I'm good at having fun, Jackie."

Carl joined them later, carrying two bottles of Benedictine Dom Perignon in one hand and two bottles of Taittinger the other.

"Couldn't make the choice between them," he said, smiling. "I trust these will be satisfactory?"

"Excellent," said Trance. His face sobered and he said, "Carl—"

"Yes?"

"Thank you for all you did."

"It was nothing—"

Trance interrupted. "If I were to give you a gift in thanks, you wouldn't refuse it would you?"

The way Trance had put it, how could he refuse? Carl tried to think of a way to politely say 'no', and said, "There is no need for you—"

"I know that there is no need. But I have a small gift of thanks. Will you accept it or not?"

Carl lowered his head and said, "I will be happy to receive your gift."

Trance handed him a Hallmark card. Inside the card was a check for five million Euros.

"Don't cash this until tomorrow. Wouldn't want it to bounce."

"I cannot accept this."

"But you already have. You earned it with your friendship and your loyalty. On behalf of myself, and my government, we say thanks. Besides, you give me discounts on the rooms." A thin smile crossed Trance's lips. He said, "Oh, and one more thing. The U.S. President would like to offer you the United States Medal of Freedom, our highest civilian honor."

"Me? A medal?"

"Ain't life grand?" Trance squeezed Lauren's hand and raised a toast.

"To friendship and loyalty."

The phone rang on Franz Koenig's desk the moment he walked into his office at the Nicolas Klug & Co Bank.

"Hello," he said in his efficient banker's voice.

"This is account JTT211650jldl004," said Trance.

Blood drained from the banker's face and sweat began sprouting on his paste-white forehead.

"How are you, Herr Koenig?"

"Ah...fine...sir. I thought you were—"

"I wanted to thank you for the efficient manner in which you handled my affairs," interrupted Trance.

"I was only following bank policy," said Koenig. How much trouble was he in?

"You acted perfectly."

"I did?"

"You did what you had to do, what I needed you to do."

"Yes, of course."

"I would like to make a new deposit, a rather large deposit, in gold. Could that possibly be arranged?"

"Why, of course."

"Have you bought that new Mercedes you have been hoping for?"

"Ah, no. I have children now. We are saving for their education in the United States."

"Good. You should be driving a new car. Perhaps I'll buy you one."

"I could never accept—"

"I have already cleared it with Nicolas," interrupted Trance. Nicolas Klug VI was the second ranking family member at the bank, and he made all of the important day-to-day decisions. "And I have also cleared my gifts with the Swiss banking authorities."

"You have?" *Could this be a trick?*

"Call Nicolas yourself. We just spoke. I believe he is in his office."

"Hold, please." Koenig's hands were shaking as he dialed his CEO's extension. They continued to shake long after he was told that Trance did, indeed, have permission to give him gifts. He returned to the phone.

"This is highly irregular."

"I'm an irregular guy, and I prize loyalty. We expect to be by at eleven. Please arrange for the back entrance to be attended for us," said Trance.

"I will be there myself."

"Good...good. Will you be able to join us for lunch? It will take a little time to unload our deposit. I would like a rough count before I leave. It must be split between a number of accounts."

"But, of course."

Later that morning Trance backed an unmarked eighteen-wheeler truck to the back entrance of the bank. He stepped out of the truck to greet Koenig and embraced him with a small hug. Then he took several moments to study the man's face. Koenig's eyes were still bruised and nearly swollen shut. There was a deep split on his bottom lip, sewn with black, blood-soaked stitches.

"I'm sorry you had to go through this," Trance said softly.

"It comes with the job."

"I bet."

Koenig shrugged, then smiled.

When Trance was satisfied with the security measures for his deposit he led Koenig to the front of the bank, where Lauren sat in the back seat of a Rolls Royce Silver Shadow. A uniformed chauffer sat at the wheel.

When Koenig walked through the doors of the bank he gave a muffled shriek and ran to the car.

"Not this?" he asked quietly, recovering his composure.

"Your driver's name is Claus." Trance nodded toward the chauffer.

"A chauffer?"

"He's been paid for five years. There's also a little gift for you and your family in the trunk. Your wife does like diamonds, doesn't she?"

Koenig stood dumbfounded, fighting the urge to jump up and down like a child at Christmas. He had risked it all—and won. *Perhaps there is a God,* he thought.

Trance, Koenig, and Lauren had a leisurely lunch. When they returned, a short, pug-nosed man with thin gold glasses approached Koenig with a small piece of paper. Koenig glanced at it and beamed.

"You have approximately six hundred and thirty million U.S. dollars. I will not know the exact amount until the gold has been assayed," said Koenig.

"That's close enough for today." Trance handed him a piece of paper with a list of numbers and letters. "Put the appropriate amount into each of these accounts. The rest should go into this account." Trance handed him another piece of paper. "Is that clear?"

"Very clear, sir."

"I think we can use our first names now, Franz. Please call me Jack."

"Yes...Jack." The men locked eyes and shook hands.

"Thanks again. Have a good day." Trance and Lauren walked out of the bank. As they left, Koenig rushed to a phone to call his wife.

As they reached the sidewalk Lauren said, "Which way?"

"Not sure."

"You know the Red Sox look like they are going to win the division," said Lauren.

"Don't start."

"They'll go all the way again. I feel it."

Trance reached into his old blue gym bag and withdrew a tattered blue Red Sox baseball cap with a faded red letter *B* stitched across the front. "You are a true romantic..." he said, smiling. "...and a patron of lost causes."

"Yes, I am," said Lauren. A sly grin spread across her face. *But, you're not a lost cause. I have it on very good authority.* "Not all of my causes are lost, Jack Trance. Someday you'll see. Let's go home."

EPILOGUE TWO

Bleachers: Fenway Park, Boston

Trance edged his way along the aisle, carefully avoiding a row of outstretched knees while balancing a tray holding four hot dogs and a pair of Diet Cokes in his left hand. He held Lauren Haverford's hand with his right.

"Excuse me and good evening, sisters," Trance said to a pair of nuns, as he slid beside them to take his seat.

"Isn't this great?" said one of the aging nuns.

"It sure is," said Trance.

A few minutes later the crowd stood for the National Anthem. Trance placed the tray on the ground, wrapped his left arm around Lauren and placed his right hand over his heart. Both of them sang the words, and neither fought back the tears that misted in their eyes. When the song finished Trance looked solemnly at Lauren, kissed her cheek and held her for a long moment.

"I'm so glad we're here," she said.

They took their seats and began to eat their food.

"Newlyweds?" a nun asked of Lauren.

Lauren laughed, nearly choking on a bite of her hot dog. "Just friends," she said.

"Uh, huh," said the nun, smiling. The woman huddled with the other nun, exchanging words and quick glances toward Lauren. Both nuns nodded, then turned their attention back to the game.

During the seventh inning stretch, Lauren turned to Trance and said, "You know, your uncle left you his estate. You're going to have to do something with it. It must be thirty billion or more, after taxes. That's just his U.S. holdings. Then there is the Baron's money. Who knows how much that will be?"

"The Baron left everything to my uncle, the Chosen One, not me."

"And your uncle left everything to you."

Trance closed his eyes. He didn't need this, didn't want this. "Sweetheart, I don't want to think about it. Not now."

"It's a lot of money, Jack."

"I do not want the responsibility of mankind on my shoulders."

"It's already there, Jack. The Madonna says you have to keep the money. But that doesn't mean you can't use it to have some fun."

Trance looked at Lauren. "What are you talking about?"

"It's enough money to buy something big. Really big. Billions big."

Trance frowned, then turned his attention to a long fly ball that sent the crowd into a frenzy. He watched as a ball arched high into the air, sailing two seats beside him into the outstretched glove of one of the nuns.

"Awesome catch!" he said.

The nun smiled, then looked toward Lauren. "She is."

Trance turned back toward Lauren, a questioning look on his face. "Is there some sort of conspiracy going on here?"

Lauren shook her head. "Obviously. Why are we out *here*?"

"Because we like baseball."

"Your uncle had twenty box seats…You have twenty box seats. We could be sitting on the first base line, but you gave them to those veterans. You also have that indoor suite, which is now crawling with kids from Big Brother and Big Sister. We are out here for a reason. That's the only conspiracy."

"You like the bleachers."

"Yeah. Someday I even hope to sit in the Ted Williams seat. But something's up. What is it?"

Trance shook his head. "I like being normal. I just want to be normal."

Lauren smiled knowingly. As much as he might want it, there were things about Trance that could never be normal.

Lauren said, "You will never be normal, Jack Trance. You have to face that." Her eyes brightened and she smiled—a big, bright mischievous smile. "If you could own anything, anything, what would it be?"

"What do you mean?"

"You know. What would you want? Think of something big."

Trance looked at Lauren for a long while, then laughed. "You're trying to manipulate me. You are. I can see it."

Lauren smiled. "Who, me? Try to manipulate *you?* Into having fun? Why on earth would I do that?"

"I *know* what you are doing."

"And what is that?"

"You want me to buy a baseball team."

Lauren grinned. "*I* never said that. You said that."

"Yeah, but I know what you're thinking."

"*Do* you?"

Trance smiled and shook his head. "No. Not really."

"I just want you to be happy, Jack. That's all I'll ever want."

"I'm not buying a team…I'm not buying *the* team."

"All right."

"I'm not."

"Uh, huh." Lauren kissed Trance on the cheek. "I love you, Jack Trance. But you've *got* to pay better attention to the game."

Author's Note: I hope that you have enjoyed the first installment in the Jack Trance series of books. This story is continued with *The Varicose Vigilantes,* also available from Shaksper Books. It is continued in *The Presidential Pretender* and *The Varicose Vigilantes II - Hedge Money.*

You can order these books through your favorite bookstore, online at major retailers, by mail and through my websites, www.lumbert.com and www.jaylumbert.com. Please feel free to contact me directly. You can do this easily through my websites. My direct email is jay@lumbert.com. Because of security and spam filters, it would be helpful if you add a book title to the Subject heading of your email.

Also on my websites, please feel free to sign my guestbook, post comments, join my mailing list and subscribe to my blogs. I like to hear from readers. I welcome both praise and criticism. Also, if you find mistakes or typos in any of my books, please let me know. I want them to be as good as they can be.

Life is what you make it... Enjoy!

**Please note that Jay Lumbert's books are available
through local bookstores everywhere.
They can be purchased at all major online bookstores, such as
Amazon.com, BarnesandNoble.com and Borders.com.**

You can send an email to Jay Lumbert through his websites.
www.lumbert.com   www.jaylumbert.com
If you have difficulty going through his websites, Jay's direct email
addresses is
jay@lumbert.com
Because of security and spam filters, it would be helpful if you added the
title to one of his books to the Subject heading of your email.